BAREFOOT AND DUMPED!

DEDICATION

To my book bitches without you I wouldn't be writing xx

To my editor in chief, thank you for all that you do and it goes way beyond editing and being a sounding board.
Love ya guts!

To my family, thank you for allowing me to write and forgetting to cook for you sometimes. Love you always xx

*****

Barefoot and Dumped!

Cover designed by Chelle Pimblott

This book is a work of fiction. Names, characters, places, and incidents either are products of the author's imagination or are used fictitiously. Any resemblance to actual persons, living or dead, events, or locales is entirely coincidental.

Chelle Pimblott
http://facebook.com/chelle.pimblott

First Printing: May 2020

Barefoot and Dumped!

CONTENTS

Chapter One

LEXI

I'm not sure what just happened but I think Stephen freaking Phoenix just dumped me! Barefoot on the beach, at my parents 30th wedding anniversary! Of all the places he could have chosen to tell me he's leaving me, he chose in front of my family on the beach!

"What do you mean, you're done?" I ask him.

"Exactly that Lexi. You know I didn't want to come today. You made me come and in doing so, you forced my hand. If you'd just let me go and do what I wanted to, we could have had this conversation in private like I'd planned." The jerk says. Frustration as clear as the blue ocean behind me in his voice.

Hang on did he say? "Like you'd *planned*?" I ask him, completely taken aback. "You'd *planned* on breaking up with me? This weekend? The weekend I'm celebrating my parents being married for thirty years?"

"Yes Lexi." He rolls his eyes at me, like I'm some stupid child who can't comprehend what's happening. To be honest, I'm struggling. I didn't see this coming, he's completely blindsided me *and* he chose to do it in front of my family and friends! Who the hell does that?

"Don't talk to me like I'm an idiot *Stephen*. You and I both know I'm not." I spit back at him, barely controlling my anger.

"And that right there is part of the problem *Lexi*." He points his finger at me, "We both know how smart you are, because you're constantly reminding me, and I'm done." He says irately.

I give up. "Fine." Is my only response to him, I'm not going to cause any more of a scene for my parents. "Don't be at my apartment when I get home tonight." I snap. "Actually, you can hand over the key now, please." I say, holding out my hand and wiggling my fingers. "I'll pack up whatever you've left behind and let you know when to come and get it."

"It doesn't have to end like this Lexi, we can still be friends." He says, as he hands over my spare key.

As if I want to be friends with anyone who could do this to a person. "I can always pack up your shit and leave it out the front ready for you if you like?" I ask him with a sweet smile.

"You don't have to be a bitch about it, Lexi." Stephen whines. How did I never notice that whiny voice before?

"I said I *could* do it. Instead I offered to let you pick it up, but that can change at any given moment if you piss me off."

"You can be such a bitch Lexi. You're never going to find a guy that will be as good to you as I have been, you know that, right?" He says.

I hold my hand up stopping him from saying anything else. "Don't even go there, Stephen. I'm not the one breaking up with his girlfriend of just over a year at her parents wedding anniversary party." I close my eyes and shake my head. When I open them again he's still standing there, waiting. For what, I'm really not sure. "Go Stephen. You don't want to be here, so leave. NOW!" I'm furious, but I know he'll misunderstand my angry tears as me being upset about him breaking up with me. When in reality, if he knew me at all, he'd know that I cry when I'm mad. Don't get me wrong, I cry when I'm upset too, but angry tears are really freaking annoying because people misinterpret them all the time.

"Guess I'll see you around then Lexi." Stephen says as his parting words.

From behind me I hear, "Not if we see you first cocksucker. Now get the hell out of here before I find a security guard to escort you out."

"Goodbye Lacey. I won't miss having you in my relationship. They say every guy dreams of a threesome, but not like this." Stephen says as he turns and walks away.

"I can't believe he used my name. After all the time I've known him, I didn't think he even knew I *had* a name." I can't help the laugh that escapes me. "You know, he was never good enough for you anyway lovely. You're better off without the douchebag."

"That may be true, but I wasn't expecting him to break up with me Lacey! Specially not here, today of all freaking days." My best friend pulls me in for a tight hug.

"Ohh Lexi honey, Lacey is right. He wasn't the right man for you." I hear my mum, Julia say from behind me and I cringe. I was really hoping that neither of my parents had to witness Stephen and his little tantrum. When my mum reaches us, she looks at Lacey and says, "Although I do wish she would use some less colourful language to get her point across, it doesn't make Lacey's opinion wrong."

I laugh at my mum's permanent dislike of Lacey's vocabulary, it's the one thing they've argued about since forever. As my mum wraps me up in her arms I laugh because I can see Lacey rolling her eyes.

"They're both right Lexi." My sister, Catherine says as she wraps her arms around me from behind. "He *was* a douche!"

"Catherine!" Mum admonishes my sister, then says to Lacey behind her, "And don't think I didn't see you roll your eyes Lacey Edwards!"

"*How* the *hell* does she do *that?*" Lacey mouths at me, while my mum's back is turned to her.

"I'm a mother of two daughters, and I've adopted a few extras over the years too. *That's* how I know, Lacey." Mum says, without even looking at Lacey, causing the rest of us to laugh, while Lacey looks shocked and a bit awestruck.

Lacey should know better than to try and get anything past Julia Stratton, she's known her for almost as long as I have. Since we met when were five years old, Lacey's spent more time at my house than I think she has at her own.

"You should know Julia better than that Laceybug, she's got eyes everywhere." My dad says as he walks past Lacey and reaches out for me. "As for you, that douche was never good enough for my Lexibear and he knew it too. *That's* why he broke up with you, he knew that eventually you'd come to your senses and see him for the idiot he was, baby girl." Then he pulls Lacey into the circle and gives us all the biggest, warmest group hug that I've ever experienced, and he's given a few of them in his time.

When we break away from each other, I say to my parents, "I'm really sorry that he made that scene here, tonight. I didn't know he was going to do that and I'm sorry if we've ruined your party." I sniff because now that I'm apologising to my parents, my emotions about what happened are catching up with me. That and the fact that they're being so supportive, and they're supposed to be enjoying their night, not comforting me.

"Oh no Lexi, that dweeb did this, not you." Mum says at the same time Dad says, "This wasn't an embarrassment for *us* Lexi, and it wasn't your fault either."

"Lexi." Catherine grabs me by the shoulders making me look her in the eye. "Lex you know that twatwaffle did this, right? *He* made a choice and *he* made a scene. Now *we* get to enjoy the rest of the night and party without him being the fun police." I nod my head and smile in reply, knowing that my voice won't work because it's too clogged with emotion. How did I miss my baby sister, who is five years younger than me, growing up into a strong woman? She's definitely not a little kid anymore, sometimes I forget that.

Lacey throws her arm around my shoulder and pulls me into her side. "Fuck him Lexi. On to bigger and better things. If you know what I mean." She says with a wiggle of her eyebrows.

My parents laugh and my dad shakes his head. "Ohhh Lacey, never change." He says chuckling. "Please never ever change who you are! Come on, let's enjoy the rest of the party. He can't take that away from us, in fact we can enjoy it more now because he's *not* here." He says and walks away, with one arm slung around my mum's shoulders.

I watch them walk away. I'm so glad that they're still together and in love. I see my mum shake her head and hear her mumble something to my dad, but I can't make out what she says. My dad laughs though, and I *do* hear him, "At a guess, my dearest, that's *why* our daughter finds her so endearing and as a matter of fact, so do I. It's refreshing that someone so young can be so comfortable in her own skin."

I hear the hint of laughter in her voice when she replies, "You certainly know where you stand with Lacey, that's for sure."

"You know, one day my dear, sweet mother is going get really annoyed at you and your potty mouth." I say to Lacey without looking at her. I'm enjoying watching my parents and their affection for each other.

"Meh! Let her, I'm not her daughter she doesn't scare me." This drags my attention away from my parents, and to Lacey. I raise my eyebrow in question at her. "OK, so you're mum is sweet, but scary as hell and she can put me in my place, sure, but she's still not my mum." She pokes her tongue at me and continues, "You know you're an adult now, making your own way in the world and not asking her for anything, she shouldn't scare you so much anymore either."

The fact is my mother doesn't scare me. I want her love and respect more than anything, but I do have a healthy respect for her and that means biting my tongue around her. "It's called a healthy respect for your elders missy, and you'd do well to remember that." I scold Lacey. All I get in response is an eyeroll. "One day the wind will change, and you'll stay like that you know." She looks at me with a straight face for half a second, and then we're both laughing, loudly.

This is what I need. There's a reason she's been my BFF since primary school, the girl has always had my back. "You know what? I think we need a drink and to get our dancing shoes on. Come on Cat, let's go get a drink." I loop an arm through my sisters, the other through Lacey's and then lead them to the marquee with all the food and drinks.

"You know we can't drink too much Lexi, it *is* still our parents anniversary party." Catherine whisper yells in my ear to be heard over the music.

I lean into her ear and whisper yell back, "Yeah, I know Cat, but I just need to relax for a while. You know the gossips are going to town now right? They're all wondering why he waited until tonight to show his true douchebag qualities!"

Cat moves to reply but Lacey pops up between us and yells, "Can you two cut it out, I'm trying to listen to the gossip of the night. Apparently, this crazy chick just got dumped by her good for nothing boyfriend. Shit is just getting interesting tonight Lexi."

There's about ten seconds of silence where I'm not sure what any of our responses are going to be and then, all three of us are laughing hysterically at the absurdity of it all.

"It's OK Lex, I won't let you get too drunk. Your mum would kill me." Lacey says quietly in my ear and I know she's serious. She wouldn't upset either of my parents if she could help it.

"I'm pretty sure she'll understand. I just got dumped at her party and I think I deserve a strong drink or two." When I look around and notice a few people staring at me until I look at them, then suddenly they're looking anywhere but at me! "But you're right. I've had enough attention tonight to last me a lifetime."

So, instead of causing a bigger scene, we dance and laugh while having a few drinks.

We stay at the party until most of the guests have left. We're standing at a table laughing together after saying good night to a family friend, when my parents make their way over to us.

"Why don't you girls get out of here?" Mum asks.

I start to protest, but my dad speaks before I can. "No Lexi. Don't argue with us, this is our night, remember? You've had a rough night sweetie and we want you to go and have some fun. You girls don't need to hang around here until the last guest has left, we'll be fine without you."

"But what about the cleaning up?" Cat asks.

"Nothing to clean up sweetie. That's the joys of getting these things catered." Mum answers with a giggle. "We don't have to set up or clean up a damn thing. It's fantastic!"

"Honest?" I ask, looking to see any cracks in their armour that tells me they might be lying.

"Honestly Lexi." My Dad says. "The night is still young for you girls. Go out and have some fun without us oldies around." He says with a chuckle.

Before I know it, there's hugs and reassurances all round and we're being pushed into the backseat of a taxi and being told to go and have some 'real' fun.

Sitting in the back seat, squished between my sister and my best friend, I have to laugh at my parents behaviour. If I didn't know better I would think they're the ones who have another party to get to and they don't want *us* to know about it.

That's not as funny as it sounds really. Maybe they *do* have other plans themselves tonight.

Chapter Two

GABE

I don't know why I let Brent talk me into coming out tonight. He called at the beginning of the week, and I declined the invitation, but he kept calling and annoying me. When I stopped answering his calls, he started sending me text messages. While they're easier to ignore, they're also more annoying because he can send one after the other and I can't hang up on him. He sent so many I came close to blocking his number for a while, but I realised that would just cause the idiot to show up and tell me I was going out.

So, here I stand at the high top table we managed to grab when we first walked into his favourite bar, and not wanting to be here, but being here to shut him up. I know he means well, but I don't want to 'pick up and get over shit', as he not so gently suggested. Subtlety isn't his strong suit, but I know he's got my back if anything happens. We've been there for each other since we were teenage boys with raging hormones and doing stupid shit together.

While I'm not interested in finding someone tonight, Brent is, so I stand back and watch as he chats to a beautiful woman he hopes will go home with him tonight. Her friends, there were two of them, have gone off to the dance floor leaving their friend behind when they realise I wasn't interested in anything more than conversation. I'm here to make Brent feel better about getting me out of the house, not pick up a random woman. It's never been my scene, but I really don't have the desire for it these days.

"Mate, are you OK?" I feel his hand land on my shoulder and feel his hot breath in my ear. It's kind of creepy how close he is to me right now, and I move away from him slightly before I turn to look at him. I sure as hell don't want to accidently lock lips with my mate. Ever.

"I'm fine." I say, a smile on my face that I hope doesn't say, 'I'd rather be anywhere but here' but says 'I'm doing OK thank you very much', because if he reads the first part on my face, then I'm just in for more of his hassling about getting back out there.

"You right if I take Sophie here and go dance?" He's not asking my permission this much I know, because he knows he doesn't need it. What he's doing is making himself look like he cares about leaving his lonely friend behind.

"Feel free." I say to him, then look I towards Sophie and say, "Look out for this one Sophie, he's got two left feet." She laughs, and Brent scowls, making it absolutely worth being here tonight. "I'll keep the table warm." I say, slapping him on the shoulder, pushing him and Sophie towards the dancefloor. I watch them do their groove thing for a few minutes, but then my mind and my eyes wander around the room.

As my gaze reaches the entrance, I notice the three women that have just walked in. They're smiling and laughing, drawing my attention from the rest of the room, I watch them make their way through the crowd directly to the bar.

They're dressed to kill, in what can only be described as modestly sexy. Causing my imagination to suddenly kick into overdrive wondering what I might discover under that soft blue material of the dress on the brunette. Or how her silky, wavy hair might feel running through my fingers.

They order some drinks, after declining a few offers from men at the bar, and laugh at something the bartender says. Their laughter is dulled by the already thumping music, but it catches the attention of almost every male in the bar. Those who aren't occupied with someone in their arms and even some that are, look their way.

"Why don't you go over and say hello before some other guy gets there before you?" Brent says from behind me. I didn't even see him leave the dance floor. Then again, I wasn't really watching for him either.

"Where did Sophie go?" I ask him, turning around to face him, completely ignoring his question.

"To the ladies room." He says. "Don't change the subject dude. Why don't you go up and talk to her?" He slaps me on my shoulder and tries to push me towards the bar. We both know it won't work, I outweigh him by a fair margin, but it's cute that he still tries every now and then. "Why don't you get us another drink? I'll wait here."

Barefoot and Dumped!

I make my way over to the bar, because he won't let this go until I do it and because I could do with another beer. I hear his loud laughter behind me. "See, I knew you wanted to." He yells over the music and noise. I flip him the bird without looking back and keep on walking.

When I reach the bar, I don't stand next to the ladies like Brent suggested. Instead, I leave a few people between us, but I can still watch them. When I realise how creepy I sound, I chuckle quietly and turn my attention to the bartender. I have no intention of getting involved with anyone, I've never been a one night stand kind of guy to be honest, and I don't plan on changing that any time soon. I don't have anything against anyone who makes that choice, it just isn't mine.

"What the hell was that man? You didn't even make eye contact. You didn't have a chance of getting them to talk to you!" Brent yells in my ear, surprised that I didn't make a move. I shrug my shoulder in answer.

"I don't want to talk to them Brent." I say, even though that's not 100% true. I would love to talk to the vision in the blue dress, with brown hair falling around her shoulders, that seems to shine under all the lights. My thoughts return to what that hair might feel like in my hands and block out Brent's lecture about how I need to move on, until he jabs me in the ribs.

"Are you listening to me Gabe? I'm telling you the best way to get over a girl is to get *under* another girl. I keep telling you, you need to pick someone up and let loose a little man." I shake my head because I know what's coming.

"Is that so is it Brent?" Sophie asks, her arms crossed over her chest, her left hip popped out to the side and her foot tapping away.

"You could have told me she was there man." Brent grinds out between clenched teeth, before turning to Sophie with a charming smile. "Sophie. Baby. I didn't mean for me, you misunderstood what I said. Gabriel here had a bit of a nasty break up and he's been sitting at home miserable. I was just trying to push him to get back out there and enjoy life."

"Enjoy life by getting under a different woman to get the last one out of his system?" Sophie asks, but not stopping to give Brent the chance to answer. "Is that what you're doing with me? Well, is it Brent? Am I just another hook up that you're getting under you?"

"Geezus." Brent mutters, running his hand over his face. For his sake I'm hoping I'm the only one that heard him. Unfortunately for him I'm not and Sophie turns around, storming off in the opposite direction. "Sophie. Sophie darlin' wait." She doesn't stop walking, she does however lift her arm up behind her without looking back and flips him off. I laugh loudly until he spins around and glares at me. "This is all your fault you know. I wouldn't have said anything if you weren't so hellbent on being a miserable bastard and staying at home not getting on with your life. I wouldn't have felt the need to help you out."

I can't let him finish. "Brent, I didn't ask for your help man. I told you I didn't want to come out tonight and it's not for the reason you think. I just didn't feel like being social. I've told you so many times before, I'm not on the hunt for someone else to help me get over my supposed heartbreak. I just wanted to come out and have a beer with my friend and I knew that it would make you happy." I sigh. Brent doesn't say anything, he just turns around to walk out the front door, following behind Sophie trying to catch her, leaving me alone at the table with two beers to drink. Letting out another weary sigh, I take a couple of large swigs from one of the beers and watch the dancefloor without seeing people. They're just shapes and movements out there.

"Ummm excuse me." I feel a soft tap on my shoulder and turn around to find the ladies from the bar standing behind me. "Would you mind if we share your table? We saw your friend leave and thought maybe you wouldn't mind. If you have others joining you or your friend is coming back, then we can find another table."

There are no other tables, and we both know it. I don't answer her straight away and she takes that to mean that I don't want to share, but nothing could be further from the truth. She looks at her friends and they turn to walk away, not wanting to wait in the awkward silence. I reach out and gently put my hand on her arm to stop her from leaving and finally speak. "That's fine. My table is your table." Then cringe at my lame joke, but it elicits a laugh from the ladies.

"Hi, I'm Lacey and these my friends Lexi and Cat." I take the hand she's offering and shake it.

"I'm Gabe, nice to meet you." I say. I turn to her friend Lexi, and see she's offering her hand for me to shake as well. Our eyes lock as I take her hand in mine and feel a zap in the tips of my fingers. The smile on Lexi's lips falters for a few seconds and I'm hoping it's because she felt it too. She pulls her hand from mine like it's diseased and while I wouldn't mind holding her hand a little longer, I let it drop to my side.

Lexi coughs and says, "It's nice to meet you Gabe, thanks for letting us crash your table, we appreciate it."

"No problem at all, as you can see it wasn't exactly full to overflowing." I say, with a grin.

Lacey laughs and asks, "Yeah, what happened there? That chick looked pretty pissed off with your friend."

"Yeah she wasn't happy with him at all." I laugh. "He was giving me some advice and it wasn't the most, shall we say, gentlemanly and she overheard him. Sophie took offence and walked out."

"So she heard him telling you to get back on the horse and she took it to mean that's what he was doing with her?" Lacey asks me. I smile and nod, while tapping the side of my nose, letting her know she's right on the money.

"So you're nursing a broken heart then?" Lexi asks quietly, drawing my attention back to her.

"No, I'm not. If you ask Brent I am, but no. We've been over for a long time, I just don't particularly feel the need to have sex with everyone and anyone that I can." I answer truthfully.

"That's very mature of you." Lacey says and I look back her way when I answer.

"Not really. I just don't want to do the dance anymore. I want a real connection with someone, not a one night stand." I stop and take a second to think. "I don't like the fake people you meet, or large groups of people either really."

"So, why are you here tonight then, Gabe?" Lacey asks, a smile spreading across her face, telling me she already suspects the answer.

"I came out tonight to shut Brent up and look where that got me." I say with a smile. "A table in a busy bar that I'm now sharing with three beautiful ladies. I think it was well worth me leaving my apartment for a few hours."

Lacey rolls her eyes at me like I've just given her some cheesy pick up line. "Do you mind watching our drinks while we dance Gabe?"

"No. Feel free to go out on the dancefloor and shake your booty. I promise not to tamper with them or let any other douchebags near them." Lacey grabs Lexi and Cat's hands and pulls them towards the dance floor. Lexi's brown eyes catch and hold mine for a few seconds and then they're gone, and I'm left watching them move to the music. If only Brent was here to see this turn of events.

I'm not complaining about the view either. These ladies can dance, but my eyes keep getting drawn back to Lexi. I'm not the only one watching them either, and I'm ready to jump in if I need to handle any creep that bothers them, but I don't need to. They manage to handle any unwanted attention all on their own and with more grace than any other group of women I've seen.

It's really quite impressive.

Chapter Three

LEXI

"Oh my god! Can you see the delectable drink of water over there? He's watching you like you're an oasis in the desert." Lacey says in a voice that is too loud, even for a bar where the music is pumping so loudly that I can feel it in my eyeballs.

"You're got such a way with words Lacey." I laugh. "We just got here Lacey and I'm not looking for a hook up tonight. I just want to have some drinks and let my hair down. I don't want to think about any male, no matter how Adonis like he seems to you. If you're attracted to him then go for your life." I say, hoping that she doesn't make a move on him because that would mean I can't later when I'm ready to date again.

"Maybe I will do just that my friend." I look up to see my best friend wearing a smirk she's trying to hide behind her drink. "That's what I thought Lexi. You'd appreciate me trying my luck with him as much as you'd enjoy getting a nail pulled out."

"You're a bitch." I say laughing at her way too accurate assessment. I can't go after a guy so soon after breaking up with Stephen, can I? I shake the thought from my head, because no, I can't.

"Oh don't look now but he's coming this way." Lacey says and I lean on the bar, not looking his way because I don't want him to think he has a chance. Not tonight anyway. "Crap, he's just ordering some more drinks, and he didn't even try to stand anywhere close to us."

He didn't need to come over. We've received enough male attention since we walked in for Lacey to be distracted within seconds. Don't get me wrong, I love my girl, but her attention never focuses on one guy for very long. Specially if there's another one waiting in the wings to give her just as much, if not more attention. Even Cat didn't take long to find someone to talk to. I'm the only one of us saying thanks, but no thanks, even though I'm single now and Cat has a fiancé at home.

I hate standing at the bar and Lacey knows it. It gives off the wrong impression and without fail manages to attract all the weirdos that happen to be in the bar. Tonight appears to be no exception.

Although, I can't help watching the 'cool drink of water', as Lacey called him, and his friend, who seems to have put his foot in it with his lady friend who has her hands on her hips. I laugh as she turns and stomps out the door and he throws his hands up in the air. The guy I've been watching throws his head back and I can *just* make out his laughter from here.

Without looking behind me, I nudge Lacey and she leans over to rest her chin on my shoulder. "Can you see an empty table?" I ask her, not looking at her.

"I think I can see a table that we can ask about sharing." She says, walking away with her drink in her hand. I excuse myself through the crowd to follow her, Cat is hot on my heels.

She reaches her hand up and taps the guy on the shoulder and when he turns around, he takes my breath away. "Excuse me, would you mind if we share your table? We saw your friend leave and thought maybe you wouldn't mind. If you have other people joining you or your friend is coming back, then we can find another table."

We all know there isn't a chance in hell that we'll find another table even close to being free, but when he takes a few heartbeats to answer, we turn to walk away.

"That's fine. My table is your table." I watch as he cringes slightly from his very bad joke, but I can't hold back my laugh. It's that bad, it's good and Lacey is laughing as well.

"I'm Lacey and these are my friends Lexi and Cat." Lacey says recovering her breath before I do and offers him her hand to shake.

"I'm Gabe, nice to meet you." He says. When he turns to me I offer my hand to shake as well, when our eyes lock and he takes my hand in his, I feel sparks and my smile falters a little. I pull my hand from his like he's just shot me with a bolt of lightning.

Feeling stupid, I cough to cover the awkwardness and say, "It's nice to meet you Gabe, thanks for letting us crash your table."

"No problem at all, as you can see it wasn't exactly full to overflowing." He says, with a grin.

Lacey laughs and asks him what happened between his friend and his girl, but I'm not listening. I'm not interested in why they left. I'm happy they did, because it gave us the opportunity to come over and meet him. Gabe and Lacey are talking away, so I take a seat on one of the stools at the table and slowly sip my drink. I listen to them talk. OK, so really I'm using it as an excuse to watch Gabe talk, Lacey isn't that interesting. The next thing I know Lacey is taking our drinks from our hands and dragging us out onto the dancefloor.

"Are you sure it's safe to leave our drinks with a guy we don't know?"

Lacey shrugs her shoulders, "Who knows, but I'm willing to take a chance." That's Lacey in a nutshell. I keep glancing over to watch Gabe, but not to check him out, to make sure he's not doing anything to our drinks and every time I look in his direction, he's watching me. It *should* make me nervous. It *should* be creepy but every time our eyes connect I feel a buzz roll through every part of my body.

"I need a drink." I say, leaning over to yell in Lacey's ear. She nods in reply and follows me back to the table, Cat is right behind her.

"It hasn't been touched. I swear." Gabe says, smiling at me and making my insides feel weird. "I saw you watching me while you were dancing, and figured you were watching to see if I slipped anything into your drinks." He replies, with a glint in his eyes and a smirk on his face.

"You can't be too careful these days. You never know what kind of creeps are around, you know?" I don't mean to sound so snarky, but I can't help myself.

"Oh my god Lexi!" Lacey says, slapping my shoulder. "I'm so sorry about my friend Gabe, she just broke up with her douchebag of a boyfriend. Not that that excuses her bad attitude. She should be overjoyed that the dirtbag is gone, but it might go some way to explaining why she has trust issues." Lacey says, shooting me a look so dirty it could kill.

"Whatever." I mumble. "I'm going to get another drink."

"Let me." Gabe says. "I swear I'm not planning any funky business," His hands up in the air like he's surrendering. "There's just a bit of a crowd up there and I know the bartender so there's a small chance I might get served slightly quicker." I hesitate for a second and then nod. "So, what can I get you ladies?"

Lacey answers for all of us and Gabe leaves the table to walk to the bar.

"What the hell is your problem with Gabe?" Lacey asks me, the frustration in her tone clear as day.

"Nothing Lacey. You should just be more careful when you're out. You can't trust everyone you meet to be as honest as you are hun." I say, trying to make her understand that she's putting herself in danger if she thinks everyone is kind and not planning to roofie her drinks.

"I know that Lex, I'm not a naïve idiot." She says rolling her eyes at me, but I can hear the hurt in her voice as well. "I also know that we just met Gabe, but I'm not getting any sleazy vibes off him and I trust my sleaze vibes without question, I've met a few, so trust me? Please?" The begging in her voice is clear.

"He does appear to be a very genuine guy Lexi. If my opinion counts for anything." Cat says, and then adds with a grin, "He's also absolutely gorgeous and might I add, generous."

This time, it's my turn to roll my eyes. "He might be a very gorgeous man, but that doesn't make him trustworthy Cat, and it would do well for you to remember that!"

"Yes mum." Cat replies, with a salute and a giggle.

"Look, he wasn't one of the guys that came onto us as soon as we walked in the door. In fact, he didn't even try to talk to us when he came to the bar, and in my mind, that makes him alright with me. You were bit of a bitch to him just now for no real reason and that's not like you."

Cat giggles loudly again and slaps her hand on the table, bringing our attention to her. "That's because Lexi Lou here thinks he's hot and would loveeeeee to see and feel what's under that charcoal grey button up shirt of his. I mean, he fills it out quite nicely and I wouldn't mind seeing what was under there myself, if I'm being honest."

"Geezus Cat, I think we need to cut you off! I think you had more drinks at the party than I thought?" I say, watching as my sister sits at the table giggling to herself.

"Whatever Lexi, Cat is a big girl she can look after herself." Lacey rolls her eyes at me. "Just promise me you're going to be nice to Gabe until he doesn't deserve it. He hasn't done anything wrong."

"Have I really been that awful?" I ask quietly.

"Yes." She says simply and without hesitation.

"Well, tell me how you really feel Lacey!" I say with a small smile. I can always count on her to be honest with me, sometimes brutally.

"I thought that was what I just did!?" She looks at me with fake confusion on her face and I crack up. "That's better. Now can we have a good time for the rest of the night, please?" I nod my reply and she seems happy with that.

"We should start a Gabe appreciation group." Cat says, giggling again. I've never seen my sister in such a giggly state before and I don't know whether to be happy or worried.

"Why thank you Cat, but I hardly think that's going to be necessary." Gabe's deep voice rumbles beside my sister, his amusement written all over his face, as is his embarrassment as it colours his cheeks, making him even more attractive if at all possible. He places the drinks tray on the table.

"I'm free." I mumble. Then I look at Lacey and scream, "I'm freeeeee!" While swinging my arms out wide, and in the process almost knock the drink that Gabe's passing me out of his hand. "Oh my god! I'm so sorry Gabe."

"That's OK, no damage was done." He smiles at me and I forget to breathe for a second. "You're in a better mood than when I left to get drinks. What happened?" He asks me.

"I'm sorry for being bad-tempered earlier." He goes to speak, probably to deny that I was being a bitch, *but* I hold up my hand to stop him. "No, I snapped at you, but I've promised my best friend that I will relax and enjoy my newfound freedom. So that's what I intend to do." I tell him with a smile, while looking at the drinks on the table and noticing there's two for everyone. "Are you trying to get us drunk Mr Gabe?"

"I'm Mr Gabe now am I, huh?" He chuckles. "No on the getting you ladies drunk. I just thought it would be easier to get two rounds while I was at the bar, instead of waiting for them the next time you want them."

"You're a smart man Gabe." I say and take a large gulp of my vodka and smiling, I reach for my bag to get out some cash, but Gabe stops me by resting his hand on mine, shaking his head no, and those tingles that I felt earlier when he touched me are back again. I wonder if he feels them too?

"It's OK Lexi, we can fix it up later." He says quietly. So quietly I almost don't hear him. Maybe he's not so unaffected after all.

I know that the next few weeks of dealing with the fallout of Stephen deciding to break up with me is not going to be fun. So, I decide right there and then that if Lacey wants me to relax tonight and have some fun, that's what I'm going to do.

Chapter Four

GABE

I watch Lacey as she walks to the bar with a slight stumble in her step, and I hope this is their last round. I stopped drinking beer a few rounds ago but the girls seem to be hellbent on having a heavy night and getting drunk. I'm watching Lexi because I don't want any of the guys that have been hovering around the girls all night trying to take advantage of her. The guys have mostly kept their distance because the girls are with me. I feel strangely protective towards the three of them even though we only met tonight. While I'm sure they can hold their own for at least a little while with any one of the jerks sniffing around them, tonight they don't have to worry about it at all. They can relax and just have a good time.

"I got us one last round Lexibear and then I guess we should get going home hey?" Lacey says as she reaches our table. She stumbles just before she can sit her butt on the stool, so I grab the drinks off her and then help her steady herself enough to sit.

Lexi laughs and says, "Why the hell do I have to go home? I've got no-one there waiting for me, ready to tell me how drunk I am and what a whore that makes me or asking how many men did I dirty dance with. Cause you know, a girl can't go out with her bestie and just have fun." She shakes her head and almost falls off her stool she's that enthusiastic about it. "All men are arseholes."

"Hear, hear!" Lacey and Cat cheer . "I think we should stick to women from now on."

Ignoring Lacey, Lexi turns to me, her eyes are wide, and she says, "Oh I'm sorry Gabe, I didn't mean you of course. You're a real sweetheart. A true gentleman for looking after us tonight and we thank you. Don't we girls?"

"Yes we do!" Lacey answers, swaying in her seat.

"Sure do." Cat agrees with a nod.

"OK ladies, I think it's time we called it a night, what do you say?" I ask them, hoping like hell this time they'll say they're ready to leave. I've been trying to convince them it's time to go for the last couple of drinks now.

"Yes! I say it's a night Gabe. Come on my darlings, let's go home." Lacey says and loops her arm through Lexi's, then Cat's and starts to move away from the table. "Let's order an Uber."

"There's no need for that, I'll take you ladies home."

"See. That's a gentleman right there." Cat says and the other two ladies laugh at her. "And he's really hot too!" She adds in a loud whisper.

"He can hear you *Cat*, he's not fucking deaf. Although, I could be now with how loud you just whisper yelled in my ear." I chuckle quietly behind them, steering them towards my car. The lights flash as I click the button to open the locks and reach passed the girls to open the back door for them. I help Lacey up, then Cat and Lexi, I close the doors behind them.

I walk around to the driver's side and as my butt hits the seat I hear Lacey's loud whisper from the back seat, "Wow! This car is huge, do you think what they say about a man's car is true?"

"What do *they* say about the size of a man's car Lacey?" I ask, I swear I hear Lexi mumble, 'god no make her shut the fuck up,' but I can't be sure.

"Well, now Gabe let me tell you. It could be one of two things really. The first is that he's compensating for lacking a decent sized penis. Or the second thing is, the size of his car directly relates to the size of his penis, and if I had to guess that would make you very well endowed indeedy Mr, hey I don't know your full name."

"Romanetti. Gabriel Romanetti , but I prefer to be called Gabe if you don't mind." I say, as I pull out of the carpark and start to drive.

"Gabe Romanetti. That sounds very well to do Greek to me." Lacey says in a haughty voice, with a flip of her hair and then she collapses into the back of the seat, in a fit of giggles.

Barefoot and Dumped!

"We're neither well to do or Greek, Miss Lacey. We *are* however Italian, and we don't do too bad for ourselves, if you want the truth."

"So no mansions or condos?" Lacey asks, sighing and looking for all the world like she's going to relax into my car seat and sleep the night away there.

"I need an address to go to please ladies. Just one will do." I say trying to grab their attention. Lexi and Cat have gone awfully quiet.

"Can you take me home first please Mr Romanetti? I can feel sleep creeping up on me now and I want to be in my bed."

Lacey gives me her address and we're there in less than five minutes. I get out of the car and walk around to open the door and help Lacey out. "My, my aren't you the gentleman just like Lexi said?" I ignore her remark and help her to her front door. "Thanks Gabe, but I'm good from here."

"Are you sure Lacey?"

"Trust me, my house is locked up like Fort Knox, I'm safer here than anywhere else in town." She says it with a smile, but I can see sadness behind it. I can also see she doesn't want to explain, so I don't ask any questions. She reaches up and pats my cheek, "I'm ok Gabe, don't you worry about me."

"Good night Lacey."

"Good night Gabe. Thank you so much for looking after us and driving us home. You're a good man." She sighs as the door opens and she walks over the threshold. When I don't hear her scream or make any other sound that might mean she's in trouble, I head back to the car and climb into the driver's seat. When I look into the backseat to ask Lexi and Cat for their address, I see that they've both got their eyes shut tightly and while I don't want to wake them, I know I'm going to have to.

A light tap on my window makes me jump slightly until I look out, standing there barefoot and in a robe is Lacey. I open the window to ask what she's doing out here in next to nothing but before I can, she speaks. "You're going to need their address. Here I wrote it down for you, and Lexi's mobile number. Just in case you might want it." She says with a wink and before I can say thank you, she's gone again, and I hear her door close. I watch as a few lights turn on and then off again before I take off for Lexi's house.

Lacey was right, her house was closer to the bar, but Lexi's isn't that far away either and I can't help but wonder if she did it on purpose.

I pull up Lexi's driveway and turn off the car. I'm not letting her walk inside without me making sure she's OK. I jump out of the car and open her door. She's curled into as much of a ball as she can be in the backseat of a car, and she's snoring softly. I'd almost call it a purr. "Lexi, we're home you need to wake up." She lets out a slightly louder snore and grumbles something unintelligible, trying to curl up a little more.

"You won't wake her up." Cat says sleepily. "Not only is she normally a really deep sleeper, but when she's been drinking, it's like trying to wake the dead. With the amount of alcohol she put away tonight, you've got no hope buddy." She informs me as she slides out of my car groggily and not focusing on anything except getting to the front door.

I shake my head laughing. I guess there's no way she's getting out of my car on her own. I reach over and undo her seatbelt. Without that support she suddenly flops down to lie on the seat. Damn it. I pull her out and tuck her into my body, grateful that she somehow managed to sling the strap of her bag over her shoulder and across her body. It means I don't have to worry about carrying it or where the hell it is. I kick the car door closed, lock the doors and pocket my keys, and walk us to the front door. That's when I realise I have to juggle Lexi around a little to find her keys. Thankfully, her handbag is small, and it only takes me a few seconds to find them. Even better, there's only a few keys on the fob, therefore I don't have too many to go through before I find the right one.

"Thanks for your help Cat." I grumble.

"You're very welcome handsome." She replies, her eyes shut as she leans against the brick wall waiting for me to let her inside.

I finally manage to let us in, and after Cat walks in, I push the door shut with my foot. I'm looking around trying to get my bearings, glad that they thought ahead and left one lonely lamp on before leaving for the night. I take a step and Lexi moves in my arms, causing me to hold her closer to me because I don't want to drop her. She wraps her arms around my neck and snuggles in tight to my chest.

"I call dibs on Gabe, Lacey. You too Cat. Even though I know it's not fair, I don't care." She whispers, then sighs and relaxes a little more in my arms.

Cat laughs, patting her sister on the shoulder she says, "It's OK Lexibear, we were already well aware that you called dibs on Gabe. He's yours and you know we wouldn't dare take that away from you, not after *Stephen* and his small dick." She takes a loud breath and kisses Lexi on the forehead. "Night big sis, I really hope you can remember all of this in the morning."

"Night Kittycat. I love you." Lexi mumbles into my chest. The nicknames these girls have for each other is very endearing. You can tell how much love there is between them.

"That's her room just there. Second door on the left." Cat informs me with a jab of her finger in the right direction. Then stumbles off to what I can only assume is her own room up the hall.

"Thanks again for your help Cat." I grumble louder than I think while Cat yells back, 'you're still welcome handsome,' as I hear a door close loudly.

Guess I'm on my own now.

I know she's mostly asleep and not to mention drunk off her arse, but I liked hearing her say my name, on her lips it almost sounds erotic. Even if I do feel a little guilty about hearing what she said, because I have no doubt her words weren't meant for my ears.

I bring my mind back to the here and now, because it can't happen. Not tonight and probably not ever, if I'm being honest. I doubt we'll see each other again after tonight. I find what I think is Lexi's bedroom. I mean, there's a king size bed and a few clothes flung around the room. So, after opening doors to both a bathroom and a laundry, finding a bedroom is a godsend. Not that Lexi is heavy, because she seriously isn't, but I need to get out of here before temptation becomes too much.

The covers are still pulled back from when I'm guessing she got out of it this morning. So, I sit her down on the edge, peel her arms from around my neck and gently lay her down. She sighs and snuggles into her pillow, curling up on her side. I go to pull the covers over her, but they get caught on her shoes, so I bend down, take them off her feet and place them on the floor beside her bed. I pull the covers over her and she snuggles in and gets comfortable, letting out a sigh of satisfaction.

What I wouldn't give to have her make that sound because I was giving her pleasure.

Shaking my head and telling myself to move and not stand there watching her like a creep, I walk into her bathroom and open the medicine cabinet looking for some painkillers. She's going need those and a drink of water when she wakes up. Luckily there's a glass on the sink, so I fill it with water and take it, with the container of painkillers into her room, placing them on her bedside table. That's when I notice a notepad and pen sitting there and decide to leave her a note.

Do yourself a favour and take two Advil and drink the glass of water when you first wake up. You're going to need them. Gabe I write my number under my name.

With one last look at Lexi, I turn and walk out of her room and the house, locking up behind me as I go. I get in my car and drive home. Once inside, I head straight for the kitchen and pour myself a glass of water, then head to my bedroom.

It's been a longer night than I expected and I'm suddenly exhausted. I strip off my clothes and fall into the comfort of my bed. I fall asleep quickly, which is a miracle in itself, but I dream about long brown wavy hair with gold streaks and mesmerising eyes the colour of molten chocolate with gold flecks.

What I wouldn't give to have her curves in my hands and my tongue on her skin.

I wake up Sunday morning hot, bothered, and wondering if she'll call me when she sees the note I left her with my number on it. Then I run my hands over my face, annoyed with my own self-importance, because I doubt she's even going to remember anything she did last night, and I'm sure I wasn't a huge highlight that she'll remember.

Chapter Five

LEXI

Waking up Sunday morning is horrendous! I don't remember getting home, closing my curtains or getting into bed. I feel like death warmed up and my mouth is dry as the Australian Outback. At least drunk me was nice enough to leave a glass of water and some painkillers next to the bed. I've never done it before, but hey, there's always a first time for everything I guess.

I lean up on my elbow, open the bottle and grab 2 tablets. Grabbing the glass, I swallow them down, along with most of the water. I sit up fully, leaning against the headboard of my bed with a couple of pillows behind me, my eyes still closed. Once my head stops spinning, I open my eyes and survey my room trying to remember how I got here last night. That's never a good thing after a night out.

I fling my right arm over my eyes and reach over for my phone, that I'm hoping I put on my bedside table, but I only find the half glass of water. My head hurts too much to move it too far, so I just lean on my elbow and bring the glass to my lips and drink the rest of the water and then laugh. I'm relieved that drunk me didn't pour vodka into the glass instead of water last night and knowing drunk me, it wasn't out of the question. I lie myself back down onto the bed, my eyes squeezed closed.

The house is quiet. Eerily quiet and lying here in its silence is really creeping me out.

I jump when there's a muffled noise out in the living room, then I call myself a few choice names when I realise it's just my phone. I don't have the energy to go out there and see who wants me so early in the morning. It's probably one of my parents wondering how I am after everything that happened yesterday.

There's silence for almost a minute and then my phone starts ringing again. I groan, loudly because I don't care who it is, I don't want to get up and answer it. The only problem is, I know it's only going to shut up when I get up and go answer the freaking thing.

It stops for another minute and I hope that's it, whoever it is has given up thinking I'll answer. Then, it's ringing again, much to my disgust.

"Answer your god damn phone Lex, before I get up and smash the damned thing!" Cat yells out from her room. Days like today, I wish I didn't share a house with my sister. It was supposed to be temporary, but it feels pretty permanent after almost 2 years.

When it's quiet again, I return her croaky yell with my own. "Shut up Cat, I'm getting up alright?" All I hear in answer is a heavy moan from her end of the hall. Making me wonder if Joshua came over after we got home last night? Meh, I can't be bothered asking her, she can do whatever the hell she pleases.

My phone startles me when it starts ringing again as I reach for it. My nerves must be completely frazzled if just the sound of my ringing phone can make me jump this morning. Not just once either. When I look at the screen to see who wants to talk to me so badly, I almost throw the phone against the wall.

"What the hell do you want Stephen?" I say as a greeting when I finally answer.

"Well, hello to you too Alexis." He answers, full of cheer.

"Why are you blowing my phone up so early in the morning? What could possibly be so important that you have bombard me with call after call on a Sunday morning?" I demand.

"First of all, it's not Sunday morning, it's early afternoon. Secondly, you said you'd have my things packed up for me to pick up. I know I didn't leave much there, so it won't take you long and I want to come and get them today." He demands.

"I haven't even looked for your stuff Stephen." I start, but the guy I once thought was so sweet and loving, before yesterday anyway, interrupts me.

"What do you mean you haven't started yet? You're always up before nine in the morning no matter what day it is. It's one of the many things that really started to annoy me about you." He admits, or should I say he whines. "I want my stuff back today Alexis."

Barefoot and Dumped!

I pull the phone away from my ear to check the time, only to find he's right. It's almost two in the afternoon! I never sleep until the afternoon, but I also have no idea what time we got home last night, so maybe I slept for the same amount of time as I usually do, it just meant that I slept until afternoon. In the distance I can hear my name being called and I remember I was actually talking to the douchebag on the phone.

"I'll call you when I have your stuff ready to be picked up." I tell him.

"No. No Alexis, I want my stuff today." He demands

"Goodbye Stephen." I say as I hang up.

"Was that the ever charming small dick *Stephen*?" Cat asks in a husky voice.

"Yes, it was." I reply, annoyance evident in my voice. "What a lovely way to wake up on the Sunday morning after he dumped me, hearing his delightful voice. Actually not morning, afternoon as it turns out."

"It's a bit too early in the morning for that kind of sarcasm don't you think Lexi?"

"Not at all Cat, considering it's early afternoon."

"It is?" She sounds surprised.

"Yes Cat, I just told you that about two minutes ago." I can't help but wonder about my little sister. Some days she's as smart as you can get, and other days she's well, this.

"You did?" I just stand there, looking at her dumbfounded. "Come on Lex, you know I'm not a morning person. Seriously." With a huff, she stomps off to the kitchen. With any luck, she's making some coffee for the both of us.

"Hey Cat," I say as I follow her into the kitchen. "How did we get home last night, and how much did Lacey and I manage to drink?"

My sister spins so fast to look at me, she spills her hot coffee over her hand, but she doesn't seem to notice. "You don't remember how we got home?" She sounds surprised and that rattles me more than I care to admit.

If Cat doesn't know how we got home, and I can't remember, that leaves asking Lacey and that means she's going to give me a hell of a time for getting that drunk. Not that she cares, oh no, my best friend loves it when I get knock out drunk. Why you might ask? Simply because it's exceptionally rare. I don't like feeling like I'm not in control of my body or mind, and what's happening around me. On the other hand, Lacey loves to watch me let loose and not care what the world thinks. She makes me feel like a stick in the mud sometimes, just because I'm not all 'whatever happens' like her. You know how they say opposites attract? Well, I can attest to the fact that that's not just in romantic relationships, believe me.

"Are you even listening to me Lex?"

"I'm sorry Cat, I kind of spaced out there for a minute."

"Were you thinking about that hot guy we met last night?" We met a hot guy last night? I wish I could remember him. "Gary? Greg? Geoff? I don't know, his name may not even start with G for all I know. I wasn't interested in his name, just ogling him."

My mind is struggling to remember his name and face. The only thing I'm sure of is that the names Cat just mentioned, aren't right but I just can't quite find the right name. "Does Joshua know you're checking out other guys just weeks before you guys move in together?" I'm feeling irritated that she's talking about this guy I can't remember in such a pervy way, but I don't know why.

"Of course he does. Well not specifically, but I'm moving in with him, I'm not blind and neither is he for that matter. Looking, but not touching is perfectly fine." Cat answers me with a roll of her eyes and turning her back to me to make another coffee. Hopefully not her second one, but my first.

I'm going to miss her when she moves out. Mainly because she cooks, cleans and makes a mean coffee first thing in the mornings, but also because I've kind of gotten used to her being here, in my space. Stephen didn't appreciate that either.

God he was such an idiot and so annoyed with everything. Now that I've had time, yes I know it's only a few hours, away from him I can see him so much clearer. How did I stay with him for so long? The question gives me the shivers and I feel them move through my body.

"Are you OK Lex? You kind of did this weird little dance just now." Cat tips her head to the side and raises one eyebrow in question.

"Yeah I'm fine. I was thinking, wondering really, why I stayed with Stephen for so long. How did I not know he was such a douchebag? And well, the thought sent a few shivers through my body."

Barefoot and Dumped!

"We all make mistakes sometimes. Even you big sister." Cat says as she walks by me patting my shoulder. "I'm going to go have a shower, your coffee is sitting on the bench."

"Thank you." She's almost at the bathroom when I say, "Hey Cat, I'm going to miss you when you move out."

"Yeah, yeah I know because I cook and clean and generally look after you." She says with a laugh as she closes the door and I hear the shower turn on.

She's wrong. I *am* going to miss her for all those things, but I'm also just going to miss having her around. With that less than cheery thought for this morning, sorry afternoon, I grab my coffee and sit down at the table, staring at my phone. I'm contemplating telling Stephen that he can come by early evening and get his crap just to get it over and done with when my phone starts singing at me and I know it's Lacey.

Lacey: *OMG! I just woke up and I feel like death!! My mouth is as dry as a desert, my head feels like it's got a punk band playing in it and my eyes don't really want to open.*

Lacey: *What the ever loving hell did we do last night and how much did we drink?*

Lacey: *Ohhh SHIT! Are you home? Safe? By yourself? I mean with Cat but shit, you know what I mean*

I can't help but laugh as the three messages come in quick succession of each other. Somehow, I think she's been awake for a little longer than she wants me to believe and she's feeling a little less seedy than she's making herself out to be as well.

Me: *What? You mean you don't know how I got home either? And there's this strange guy in my bed. I don't know his name and I don't want to wake him up!*

I laugh as I hit send. My laughter stops dead in its tracks with her reply.

Lacey: *I'm on my way. You didn't leave with a guy! Don't go back in your room and is Cat there with you? I'll call the police for assistance on my way. DO NOT MOVE!!*

I start to panic. She's going to kill me when she gets here and there's no guy here especially after she calls the police and tells them there's a strange guy in her friend's house. Shit! What have I done?

I pick up my phone in a shaking hand and try to dial Lacey's phone to talk to her. To stop her from driving here and calling the cops. I tap her name in my contacts list, my finger is hovering above the call button as my front door explodes open and there stands Lacey, ready for a fight.

"Is he still in your bed?" She screams like a mad woman. I can't speak, I'm so stunned by her behaviour I can't even find the words to answer her. If there was a guy here and he was sleeping, he wouldn't be now. "Well, where is he Lexi?" She demands, stomping towards my room like a woman on a mission.

"Where's who?" I ask her, dumbfounded for a second. My brain isn't firing on all its cylinders just yet. I haven't been awake for long enough and I haven't even had my first coffee of the day.

She doesn't say another word, just stomps herself into my room, banging the door open. All I can hope is that there isn't a hole in the wall that I'm going to have to fix.

"Ummm there's no guy in here Lexi, sweetie." She says almost quietly. Then she hears the shower running. "Is that him? Did he get in the shower before I could get here?"

"Nooooo!" I yell, as a bloodcurdling scream comes roaring out of the bathroom.

"What the hell do you think you're doing Lacey? Give me some god damn privacy would you. You can't just barge in on a person in the shower chick." Cat yells at Lacey.

"Sorry Cat, I thought you were the guy." Lacey says in a weird voice.

"What guy? There's no guys here." Cat thunders at her. "Stephen broke up with Lexi yesterday remember and Joshua is interstate for the next few days."

"Right yup. OK. I'm so sorry Catherine."

"Thank you. Now can you get out of here so I can finish my shower in peace and without the freaking audience."

"Yes. Sure. Of course, my apologies again Cat." Lacey mumbles, the wind having been completely knocked out of her sails.

"Thanks. That would be mighty grand of you." I hear my sister yell as the bathroom door slams shut again.

"Alexis." Oh crap, she full named me. She *never* and I mean never, ever, uses my full name unless she's really freaking mad. "Alexis, best friend of mine. Are you telling me there *is* no guy here? In your bed or otherwise?" Shit, if looks could kill, I would well and truly be six foot under while my parents said their last goodbyes to their oldest daughter.

"No. I mean, what I mean to say is that, well. I'm sorry Lacey bestest friend on planet earth." I smile at her, knowing that I could pull the sad puppy dog eyes on her, but they probably won't work and they're my last hope. "Honestly? No, no there isn't a guy here. It was a joke, apparently not a funny one, but a joke all the same."

In the minute of silence between us I feel so many different emotions, I feel a little insane. Guilt, humour, more guilt, anger, guilt, humour and then I circle back to anger again. Anger because she can't take a joke, she pulls this kind of stupid crap on me all the freaking time. Then I hit laughter again, because the look on Lacey's face is hysterical.

The silence is broken by our uncontrollable laughter and the effort of trying to drag in a few breaths along with the laughter.

"What the hell is wrong with you two?" Cat asks, I hadn't noticed her walk into the lounge room but there she is, looking at us like we've lost the damn plot. Who knows, maybe we really have this time. We both go silent when she speaks but when she asks, "Was it really *that* funny to have your best friend walk into the bathroom to see me naked and wet, was it? Well was it?" She looks and sounds angry.

"It was just a simple misunderstanding Cat. We're sorry." I tell her.

'It'll be a simple misunderstanding when I walk in on one of you two and start laughing hysterically too." She scowls at us both and storms off to her room. Which sends the two of us back into another uncontrollable fit of laughter.

"Oh Lexi, just so you know," Lacey starts as she grabs a tissue to wipe the tears from her eyes and blow her nose, "I knew there wasn't a guy here and I was already on my way over. I bought breakfast and coffees." She says, waving her hand towards a brown paper bag and a tray with three drinks in it, sitting on the little table at the door. When the hell did she put that there?

Hang on. "What? How did you know there wasn't a guy here?" I ask her, trying not to feel at least a little insulted that she thinks I couldn't have picked up last night. I didn't want to, but that's not the point.

"Because that's not your style my friend." She answers with a knowing smile, there's something she's still not telling me. "Not to mention, I got the feeling that Gabe isn't *that* kind of guy either."

"Gabe? Guy? What guy called Gabe and how the hell do you know what he's like?" I ask without taking a breath and making the words all roll into one.

"You don't remember Gabe huh?" I shake my head no. "Damn that is a *real* shame because he was one exceptional example of a man and he had the hots for you and boy oh boy, did you have them for him. You called dibs on him and everything." She laughs and I don't know whether to cry or do a little happy dance.

"How do you know what kind of guy this Gabe is and how come you can remember everything, and I can't?" I ask, this time it's my turn to scowl at Lacey.

"Well, for one, I had some very lovely conversations with the charming Gabe last night. Two, I didn't drink as much as you did last night, little miss 'how's the hangover today'?" She looks way too happy for my liking, I know she's up to something. Hey, hang on.

"What do you mean you had less to drink than me? You were with me shot to shot and glass to glass. We had the same amount of drinks."

"Well, it may have looked that way to you and I guess to some extent that is technically true. I drank water in between every drink and my mixed drinks weren't quite as strong as yours. Not when I went to the bar anyway."

"You got me trashed on *purpose*?" I ask, astonished.

"Well, I didn't think you would get blind drunk and not remember anything, but yes, I got you drunk my friend because you needed to relax last night. You needed to stop thinking and just let life happen for a few hours."

"Geezus, with friends like you, who the hell needs enemies?" I mumble, but I know she hears me by the grin on her face and the sparkle in her eyes.

"You love me Lexi, you know you do. What would you do without me?" She asks, that grin of hers spreading even further across her face.

"Hand over the breakfast you brought over and tell me all about this Gabe guy."

Barefoot and Dumped!

"You really don't remember him at all?" She asks, surprised, as she hands over a triple chocolate muffin and a still hot mocha.

"No, I don't remember anyone by that name." I say even as a picture of the most amazing eyes I've ever seen flash through my mind. Hazel eyes, but they've got gold and green flecks in them depending on the persons mood.

"He didn't leave you his number, or a note even?"

"Nope." I say with a pop of the 'p'. "Nothing. No number, no note, no name. Nothing."

"Check your phone. Maybe he entered his number in there so that you wouldn't lose it."

I pick up my phone and scroll through all my contacts to 'G'. "Nope, no new Gabe entries into my contacts list. Guess he's just a memory now, well not even that because I can't remember a damn thing."

"That's a damn shame. He was a really nice guy. I honestly thought he'd leave you his name and number, perhaps even a note. I'm feeling a little disappointed right now, I had more faith in Gabe than that."

"Well, he didn't, so I guess that's that."

"Yeah, I guess so." Lacey says quietly, she looks honestly disappointed.

"Is there a muffin in there for me too?"

"Of course there is Catherine. There always will be, well until you move in with Joshua, then the deals off." Lacey hands Cat her apple cinnamon muffin and caramel latte with an apologetic smile. "Peace offering for the shower incident of two thousand and nineteen?"

"I guess I can accept your apology." Cat says with a straight face, but she only holds it for a few seconds before we're all crying with laughter again.

 Chapter Six

GABE

I wish I'd asked Lexi for her phone number, rather than taking it off Lacey. I know that Lexi wasn't in any shape to give it to me and Lacey was looking out for her friend but still, I wasn't comfortable having it without her knowledge. I wanted to send her a message on the Sunday afternoon to see how she was feeling, because I knew she'd have an aching head. What stopped me was not wanting to look like a creepy stalker, and I didn't know how impressed Lexi would be with her best friend for giving out her number to a guy they just met. We only spent a few hours together, drinking at a bar.

Instead of thinking about Lexi all day, I take myself for a run along the beach. I zone out and the only things on my mind are the pounding of my feet on the pavement, the music pumping loudly in my ears and the traffic around me. When I reach the beach, I take a deep breath of salt air, relaxing into my run once my feet hit the hard sand, I'm in the zone.

Nothing feels better than deeply breathing in the salt air, listening to my favourite tunes and feeling the sand thumping under my feet. Except maybe sex. OK, so no maybes about it, sex with the right person is amazing. Even with the *wrong* person it can be incredible, just because you know it's wrong.

I run until I hit what is my five kilometre marker, jogging on the spot and taking in the view for a few seconds. My eyes drift over to the stores across the road, and I contemplate stopping for breakfast and a coffee before I run back home. Who am I kidding? I know I'd be walking home if I get something to eat. As I decide to get breakfast, my eyes catch on three women entering a café, laughing at something one of them said. For a split second they look familiar. I think maybe my luck has changed and it's Lexi with her two friends from last night. I shake my head to clear it, it can't be them.

I didn't realise that I'd stopped moving while looking at the women to see if Lexi was one of them. Instead of crossing the road to see if I'm right or wrong, I turn on my heels and run back towards home. The music and the ocean breeze aren't as comforting on the way back as they were when I started out this morning. My mind is running over last night and how attracted I was to Lexi. I haven't felt that pull towards someone in a long, *long* time and it has taken me by surprise.

The honk of a car horn right next to me as I step onto the road scares the crap out of me, because like a distracted idiot, I didn't look before I moved forward. So I wave my hand in apology and see the driver shake his head, throwing his hands up in the air in annoyance. I can't say I blame him, I would feel the same way, but I keep on running to the other side of the road towards my apartment building. As I reach for the door, my phone rings in my ear, and because I'm hoping that its Lexi, I don't look at the screen before answering.

"Good morning, Gabe speaking." My voice is coming out in long pants as I catch my breath after my run, but it's full of happiness, until I hear who is on the other end.

"Well, aren't you chipper this morning? I guess you got luckier than I did last night." Brent half grunts, half laughs in my ear.

"I'm guessing Sophie didn't fall for any of your bullshit last night then?" I ask, a hint of amusement in my voice. It's about time he found someone who is going to kick his arse.

"Not exactly. No." He sighs. "She let me take her to one of those late night café's to let me explain what I meant, but no, she wasn't very forgiving. Not forgiving enough to let me go back to her place anyway."

"Good." I chuckle. "I think you've met your match in Sophie."

"I think you might be right man, and I have to admit, I'm liking it. A lot." He sounds happy and lost in thought.

"I bet you are. I'm happy for you man. You need a good woman who won't let you get away with your usual crap."

"It's time to grow up my man." There's a pause between us and he coughs and says, "Well, anyway. Did you want to come over for beer, pizza and action packed movie watching?" He asks, and before I can answer he continues, "Dumb and dumber are going out somewhere. Stevie broke up with the girl he was going out with, so he wants to go out on the town and get over her. If you know what I mean?"

I do know what he means. Stevie's going out to do exactly what Brent told me to do the other night. Brent might be a player, but he was always upfront with the ladies he took home and he wasn't a douche about it. Stevie on the other hand, I'm pretty sure he was cheating on his ex for almost their entire relationship. *That's* what I call being a sleaze and a douchebag.

Kyle, Brent's brother and his best mate Stevie were morons, who have very little respect for women, other people or themselves to be honest. Before Kyle met Stevie, he was a reserved kind of kid, who I had a healthy respect for. He worked hard and he respected other people's feelings. I'm glad he found a buddy to bring him out of his shell, I just wish he wasn't learning all his sleazy ways. To be fair, Kyle looks uncomfortable whenever Stevie's talking, so maybe he doesn't agree with his choices after all, but still, he chooses to hang out with him. Brent knows I won't go over to his place to chill out if they're there if I can help it. Which is why he mentioned them heading out for the night.

"Yeah sure." I reply. "I'll bring the beer."

"Awesome!" I know better than to think he's already got beer. If he has it, those other two idiots drink it and don't replace it.

"See you tonight."

I put my phone back in my pocket and nod to Sam at the front desk as I head to the stairs instead of the elevator. "I don't know how you manage to take the stairs after you been on your *little* jog." Sam laughs.

"One day you'll be beside me Sam." I hear his laughter following me up the stairs. Sam is in his late sixties, maybe early seventies and he's been at the front desk for as long as I've lived here. Yes it is *that* kind of apartment building. You need to pass by Sam or one of the other security guys to get into an apartment, and all mail goes through them first as well. You might think that's a little excessive for a guy like me, it's not like I'm a movie or a rock star but I have my reasons for needing the extra security. It's the same reason behind me not wanting to get involved with anyone for the last year or so, much to Brent's amazement.

I make my way up the five flights of stairs, to my front door. As I unlock the deadbolt to let myself in, my neighbour Jessie pops her head out of her door. "Morning Gabe, you back from your morning run already?"

"Morning Jessie. Yeah, I headed out a bit earlier today. I've got a few things on my mind." I reply, making sure I've got a smile on my face.

"Is everything OK?" The concern in her voice cuts me, because I understand why she's so nervous and why she checks it's me coming and going every morning and afternoon. Or whenever else I happen to come and go.

"Everything is absolutely great Jessie. Just trying to work a few things out in my mind for work and I find running clears things right up. Well, most of the time." Again, I make sure I have a genuine and hopefully comforting smile on my face.

"OK. Good." She nods her head, her eyes darting around the small landing on our floor. Each floor only has four apartments and we know everyone on our floor. I hate that Jessie still feels nervous almost a year after her ex and mine stopped causing any grief around here.

"Have a good day Jessie." I say as my door opens.

"You too Gabe." I hear before her door closes softly again. Her ex didn't like loud noises and she still can't slam the door.

I walk inside my apartment and close the door, quietly so as not to startle Jessie. The walls aren't paper thin in this building, but I don't want to make the woman jump, she's jumpy enough as it is.

My run in with Jessie has made me think about my ex. The same one that Brent keeps trying to help me 'get over'. Little does he know that I've been over her for more than a years now, if not before we ever even broke up. She's the reason I now live in an apartment building where you can't get past the front desk without the OK from a tenant. If a visitor tries to get passed all that by saying they're here for another tenant, they'll never get away with it. All the tenants here enjoy their privacy and security for different reasons, and no-one would ever break that unspoken code.

Barefoot and Dumped!

My ex tried it, and almost got away with it, until Sam's shift started, and he realised who she was. God love him, Sam told her the next time he saw her on the property he would be calling the police. Unfortunately for her, she called his bluff and returned later that day, assuming wrongly that his shift would be over. Sam's shift never seems to be over and he called the police. She got arrested for trespassing, causing a menace and stalking. So far, Sam's actions have worked, and I haven't seen or heard from her in just over a year. It's been great and that's why Sam is one of my favourite people. He did it all without me even knowing that she was causing anyone any stress until the whole thing was over, and the police were questioning me about her behaviour. Before that, the police hadn't really wanted to know about my problems with her. I'm a big guy, bulky and tall to boot, so of course I can handle a woman. I just wonder if I was a different kind of guy and handled her in a physical way where would I be now. The police would have been on her side then, and yet it was me that had suffered for almost a year previously.

She didn't appreciate me breaking things off with her, to put it mildly, and she went nuts. We hadn't even been together for a year and somehow she'd managed to move into my house and every aspect of my life. I woke up one day wondering what the hell happened and when I asked her if she wanted to spend her life with me, because I knew I didn't want to spend my life with *her*, she'd snorted and said, 'you're my first husband. My stepping-stone to something better. Men like a woman better when she's already married or been married, they think they're getting someone else's toy or someone else has already trained her. So no, I won't be here forever, not if I can help it you idiot. I thought you understood that?'

It took me just 24 hours to put my house and everything in it up for sale and telling her she wouldn't be moving with me and that I wanted her to move out. It wasn't part of her long term plan, so she lost it. She destroyed almost everything in my house, and I had to sell it for way less than it was worth, but I just wanted out by then.

When she disappeared for a few weeks I thought I was clear and free, but no. The last couple of weeks in the house I was alone, only I never *felt* alone, and weird things kept happening. So, right before settlement I moved in with Brent for a couple of weeks. I had to wait for the apartment to be emptied and cleaned out from the previous owners.

When I called the police about her wrecking and vandalising my property they didn't take me too seriously.

Long story short, this is why I now live in a pretty secure apartment building. I've got a whack job ex and I need it to feel safe. She took a lot from me in the months before the police finally arrested her, and I'll never forgive her for that.

I shake my head, I don't want to think about her anymore. I don't even use her name when I reference her anymore. She's just the 'ex'.

Instead of dwelling on the past and letting it get me down, I sit down at my laptop and get some work done. Before I know it, it's time to go grab some beer and head over to Brent's for pizza.

I walk in the front door after knocking once to let him know I'm there. It's what we do. Well, he doesn't get the opportunity at my apartment, but you know what I mean. When I walk in his brother and Stevie are sitting in the couch with Brent, who looks over their heads and winces. Fuck! I really don't want to spend my evening with them.

"Hey Gabe." The terrible two chime together, fuelling my annoyance further.

"Boys." I say with a nod in their general direction. I see Stevie flinch at the greeting, this is why I do it, I know it annoys the absolute shit out of him. He doesn't like to be below anyone, even when he's younger.

I walk into the kitchen to put the beer in the fridge and I know without looking, Brent is right behind me.

"Gabe, I'm sorry. They said they were going out for the night, but then Stevie's ex wouldn't let him go and pick up his stuff, so now he wants to hang out here."

"And drink *my* beer." It's not a question, it's a damned fact. That little shit never pays for anything. I don't know how he ever got a girl to go out with him in the first place.

"No. Well yes, but they did go out and get some of their own." He stumbles over his answer.

Barefoot and Dumped!

"Yeah I know, I saw the six cans in the fridge Brent." I sigh, it's his brother and they all live here so he can't exactly kick them out, but I'm not really in the mood for them. "Fine. Whatever."

Brent sighs in relief, and I can't help feeling a little guilty. He shouldn't feel that wound up about his brother and his mate hanging out at home. "Do you want to order the pizza now?" He asks with a clap of his hands.

"The sooner the better man, I'm starving." Even though I took a quick break for lunch in between working, I'm really hungry now and want some food.

"Why are we ordering dinner so early grandpa?" Stevie asks, a smirk on his face, until he looks at me, then it falters. Yeah that's right you little fucker, you're not the alpha in this group. I am.

"You got a problem *Stevie*? You can always head out for the evening." That shuts up him and his smart mouth for the rest of the night. I almost heard Brent sigh with relief, and I know I'm being a prick, but the guy just rubs me the wrong way. He has no respect for anyone, and I am more than happy to put him back in his place whenever I can.

We spend the evening watching explosive action movies, drinking beer and eating pizza. It's actually really enjoyable. I do catch Kyle telling Stevie to shut up a few times, after Stevie's looked at his phone in anger. Guess the ex is giving him a hard time about getting his crap back. Good on her I say.

It's about time one of these women show him whose boss. I like her without ever having met her. Which makes me grin. "What are you grinning at man?" Brent asks me.

"Nothing man, I'm just enjoying hanging out."

"Are you sure about that? Cause you kind of look like you've got a funny secret that you're not going to share." He's not wrong.

Instead of answering him, I thump him on the shoulder, taking great joy out of the wince he tries to hide and say, "Thanks for inviting me over man, I really needed this."

"So, you didn't get lucky last night either huh?"

I laugh, loudly. "Not in the way you think, no. I did meet someone though and I can't wait to see her again."

"Aww how sweet." Stevie pipes up from across the room, laughing. His laughter is cut short when I glare at him.

"Yeah, she is sweet, and you should be so lucky to find yourself a woman just like her."

"Yeah I don't want sweet, been there, done that. I'll pass." He mumbles, but I choose to ignore him. I don't care what he thinks but now my thoughts have travelled back to Lexi and I hope I see her again soon.

Chapter Seven

LEXI

Since my parent's party, everything has been quiet on the Stephen front. He came and picked up his crap after I called to tell him I'd packed it up. I'd actually had it packed up on Sunday after he called, I just didn't want to give him the satisfaction of knowing that, so I called him a few days later. Bitchy? Maybe but I don't care. There wasn't that much here anyway, it took maybe thirty minutes to collect and put in a box.

He brought me a small box of my stuff that was somehow at his place. It really was a small box of nothing very important to me, and that was when the realisation of what our relationship had really meant hit me. Neither one of us had really *been 'in'* it for a while. If we were at all. We were convenient and I'm not stupid, I knew he was cheating on me. I just didn't care enough to say anything to him and that tells me everything I need to know.

I'm not angry that he broke up with me. I'm pissed that he decided that my parent's anniversary party was the best place to do it. He could have easily chosen to do it prior to leaving or after we got home, but no, he chose to break up with me at a time that would humiliate me the most. That's just the kind of jerk he is.

I'm not too surprised with the very small box of unimportant things he brought for me. I'm pretty sure it was so that he could say, 'Here's your crap too', and had nothing to do with him wanting that stuff gone. He probably never even noticed it beforehand. I rarely stayed over at his house because he shared it with two other guys, and it wasn't a place I ever really wanted to spend a lot of time at. It was a real guys pad and I never felt comfortable there and he never cared enough to make me feel comfortable either. So, we agreed without talking about it to mostly stay at my house.

My mum called me a couple of days after the party to see how I am, and when I say I'm good, I mean it. I'm freaking great. The best thing that could have happened to me was Stephen leaving me.

The next night my dad called me to check in with me as well. The only difference between the two calls, besides day and parent, was that he offered to find the idiot and beat the shit out of him. I laughed so hard, causing my dad to laugh loudly along with me. "That's what I'm here for." He said, "To make my baby girl laugh and feel better."

"I don't feel bad Dad but thank you for the laugh." I said before we ended the call saying I love you. My parents are awesome, but I'm a daddy's girl through and through. I know that no matter what, my dad has my back.

After I hung up from my dad that day, I knew that what I had said was right. I didn't feel any sadness or remorse over Stephen breaking up with me. The relationship wasn't much to write home about and we both knew it. We were just kind of floating along because it was easier. I'm glad he was the one to bite the bullet, because I would have done it soon myself anyway.

All week Lacey and Cat give me grief about this guy, Gabe that we met the weekend of the party. Apparently I called dibs on the guy and he was OK with it. The girls were more than OK with it because I needed someone like him to get over the dweeb that was my ex. I'm quoting Lacey there. I needed a real man, so I was told, and Gabe was her choice for me.

I remember going into the bar and walking over to a guy at a table on his own after watching his buddy's date stomp out of the bar in a very bad mood and his buddy chasing after her.

In my mind I see a flash of hazel eyes with flecks of grey and green through them, staring into mine, but I don't remember the man himself. I mean, I don't even remember getting home, into the house or my bed that night. I do remember feeling grateful for the drink of water and painkillers sitting on the bedside table though.

Barefoot and Dumped!

Late in the week, I'm checking messages on my phone as I walk to get a coffee from my favourite café. I'm barely paying attention, but I have to pause at the door to let a lady leave so that I can enter. Only when I walk in what I think is an open doorway, I find a hard wall of muscle instead. The impact of our bodies knocks my phone out of my hand and with the quickest reflexes I've ever seen, an arm reaches out and catches it before it can hit the ground and smash into pieces.

"Oh my god! Thank you so much for catching my phone and I'm so sorry about walking into you. I should have been watching where I was going, but I had a one track mind heading into buy the best lemon slice in the world."

My hand is still resting on the solid wall of his chest and I feel the rumble of his laughter work its way through his body before it finally reaches his vocal chords. Then it's the most amazing sound I've ever heard. I can't hear the traffic or anything else. "No worries. Things happen, there was no harm done at all."

There's something familiar about him, his face is registering as someone I know but I know without a doubt, if I knew him from anywhere I'd remember him.

"Thank you." I say, my voice barely a husky whisper.

"You're welcome Lexi." He says, handing me my phone.

"Excuse me, but can I get past please? I need to get to work." Asks the guy behind Mr Hazel eyes, who has been patiently waiting for us to move out of the way.

"Yes, of course," I say as we both move out of the doorway to let the guy through. That's when it registers that this guy knew my name.

"I was hoping we could exchange phone numbers this time ..." I don't let the guy finish. What the hell is he talking about and how does he know my name?

"This time? How do you know my name?" He opens his mouth to speak but I hold up my hand to stop him. "No actually, please don't say another word. I'm going to walk away now and forget this ever happened and hopefully we can live the rest of our lives happily knowing that I didn't let the creepy guy kill me." I don't let him say anything, I just take off in the opposite direction to where I'm supposed to be heading. I didn't do it on purpose, I just wanted to get away from the guy I don't know, but who seems to know me. I mean he knew my name and asked for my number. Who the hell does that?

I hear him call my name from behind me, but I don't look back, he's freaking me the hell out and I pick up my pace. I'm not quite jogging, because well heels, but I am definitely power walking at this stage, until I find myself ducking very quickly into an arts supplies store. I make a quick circle of the shelves so that I don't look like a crazy person to the lady behind the counter and then smile at her on my way out.

"Did you need some help to find what you were looking for?" She asks as I reach for the door and I panic.

"No. Thank you, I'm fine." I reply quickly, knowing I look and sound as sketchy as hell. No pun intended. Without another thought I shoot out the door and look up and down the street to see if the guy has gone. When I can't see him anywhere I head back the way I came, but I don't go into the bakery like I had intended before I ran into 'the guy', instead I walk, at quite an impressive pace, to work. I can't wait to meet up with Lacey for lunch later and tell her about my stalker. She's going to want to call in ASIO or the FBI or the CIA. I can't think of any other acronyms for any more government organisations. I'm pretty sure the American agencies don't have any authority in Australia, but that won't stop Lacey from trying.

I get in to work and say hello to a few people as I walk to my desk, but I feel weird. Wired and strange. That guy felt familiar, but I couldn't put my finger on where I knew him from. For all I know he's some creepy mate of Stephen's and that's how he knows my name. Or I've met him through work somehow. There's something in the back of my mind that I can't quite recall that's telling me neither of those things are right and even though I ran away from him, I wasn't truly *scared* of him.

When I reach my desk, I put my bag away and pull a few things out to get settled for the morning and then decide I need a coffee. I get back to my desk feeling calmer and with a hot coffee on my desk, I settle in and bury myself into my job to forget about the guy I can't place. I work until the reminder I set on my phone scares the crap out of me while reminding me I've got a lunch date with one of the hottest ladies I know, and she'll be mad if I'm late.

Barefoot and Dumped!

When I get to the restaurant, Lacey is already seated and searching the menu for something to eat. She'll get what she always does, but she still likes to examine the menu like it has something new she might be interested in. We've finished eating and I'm nibbling on a bowl of hot chips we got to share when I start telling her about my encounter with 'the guy' earlier today.

She stops eating, fork paused halfway to her mouth and I swear she's frozen and silent for a full minute before asking me to describe what the guy looks like to her.

"He was tall, gorgeous, dark brown hair, broad shoulders." I take a second to think before continuing, Lacey still hasn't moved. "He was big, but not huge, you know?" She nods. "He looks strong. Like he could lift the both of us up without breaking a sweat. And his eyes. Oh my god, I've never seen any like them. They were hazel, but with flecks of grey and green. Do you want to know the strange thing though Lacey?"

"Sure, tell me the strange thing about him Lexi." She says, finally steering the fork into her mouth so she can chew on the food.

"I felt this strange pull towards him. Like I'd already met him before and I knew him, but I can't remember him at all. There's just something niggling in the back of my mind that I know him, and I would be safe with him."

"MmmHmm. Yeah I understand. Sure." She drinks a mouthful of her coffee and I know she's using the moment to think about what she wants to say. I can see the cogs turning round in her brain, it's all over her face. I've known her for way too long for her to hide something like that. "I don't know how to break it to you Lexi, but you *do* know him. At least you've met him once before anyway."

"What do you mean, 'I've met him before? Where the hell have I met him before Lace, cause I would like to think I'd remember a man that looked like that." If Lacey knows who this guy is just by my description, and she says I've met him before, then I believe her.

"Remember the night of your parents' party? We went out to the bar afterwards and had a good time?"

"You mean we went to a bar and you decided to get me drunk off my arse." I clarify.

"Let's not worry about those details." She says with a smirk and the wave of her hand. "But yes, that night. The one you seem to have blanked from your memory?" I nod, allowing her to keep explaining. "That's the night we met Gabe. He looked after our drunken arses, kept the creepers at bay and then drove us home at the end of the night."

That niggling at the back of my brain is starting to remember that night, and Gabe.

"I got him to take me home first, but I gave him your address and phone number so that he could call you later. He was as taken with you, as you were with him that night."

"I was taken with him, was I?" I ask, rolling my eyes at her old fashioned expression.

"Yes smartarse. Don't you recall calling dibs on Gabe? Cat told me that you called first dibs on the guy while he was standing right there."

"I didn't, did I?" I ask, dropping my face into my hands when she grins and nods her head.

"You sure did Lexi and according to Cat he didn't seem too unhappy about the declaration either, but it's OK, I never had any plans on making a play for him because I could see the sparks between the two of you from the start, and well Cat has Joshua."

I let her words sink in. One thing strikes me though and I have to ask, "So, if you gave him my phone number, why hasn't he called me yet?"

"I don't know." She answers with a shrug. "Maybe he lost the paper I wrote it on. It happens you know."

"But you said he drove us home, so he would know where I live, right? He could come by and check in."

"Yeah and come off like a complete creeper. You bumped into him accidentally today and you thought he was a creepy stalker. How would you have felt if he'd shown up on your doorstep saying he knew you, but you couldn't remember him? I'm sure that would have gone down exceptionally well, and you would have invited him in for a coffee, cookies and a chat." The bitch is rolling her eyes at me again, god damn it!

"Well, what am I going to do now? I don't know anything about him, I don't even know what his job is, or his last name."

"Romanetti." She offers up.

"What's a Romanetti?" I asked, completely confused.

"It's his last name. Gabriel Romanetti, but I'm sorry, I can't help you out with where he works. We didn't have that conversation."

"How do you know all this?"

"Because I talked to the guy *and* I wasn't as drunk as some that night."

I don't bite on the statement of how drunk I was, she was the one buying me the drinks. "My question still stands. What do I do now?"

"Well, you've run into him once, I guess you can only hope that fate steps in and you'll run into him again." She pauses for a minute and then says, "*Or* you can look him up. I mean there can't be too many Gabe Romanetti's in the area."

"So, I can be a stalker, or I can dare to hope that I see him again? Is that what you're saying oh wise one?" I ask sarcastically.

"Pretty much, yes." She says with another smirk and shrug of her shoulders.

"Great. You're so bloody helpful." I sigh, hoping that the universe will take the choice out of my hands sooner rather than later.

"I'm here to help." A grin spreading across her face she's so pleased with herself.

Without a doubt she helps. Helps giving me a damned headache.

Chapter Eight

<u>GABE</u>

I couldn't believe my luck when I ran into Lexi at the café this morning, her reaction to seeing me wasn't what I'd expected though. The second I realised she didn't remember me, I took a step back, my reaction didn't help though, because it was too late. She was already flipping out and wondering how the hell I knew her name. I understand why she ran, I'm a big guy so I imagine it's scary to think of the possibilities that I'd be stalking her, it's not like she'd have much of a chance to get away from me if I decided to hold her. Which is why I stepped back and gave her some distance, I have no plans of holding her against her will. If she's into that kind of thing, I'm not against it, absolutely not but never against her wishes.

As I backed away from her, she took off like a bat out of hell and I was left standing in front of the café. I didn't know whether to laugh or run the other way myself. In the end I *did* go in the opposite direction as Lexi because my car was that way and headed to work. My head was a mess of thoughts but what else could I do? I certainly wasn't going to use the number that Lacey gave me to call her now. Then she really would think I was a weirdo.

I guess I had to resign myself to whatever I thought was between us, not happening. That kind of makes me feel like I've lost something that could have been great. *Really* great. The pulse that ran through my entire body when her hand came up to rest on my chest to balance herself when we bumped into each other, is something I've never felt with anyone else, but it happens every time we touch. There's this zap or pulse kind of effect that runs through every nerve in my body, lighting me on fire from the inside out.

When I get into work, I drop the box of cakes I bought on the table in the break room and head to my office. I lower myself into my chair and there's a light knock on the door frame. Without waiting for a reply Rosa walks in looking at the papers in her hand and not me. "Here are the papers I need you to sign this morning, Gabriel. If you can get them to me by lunch time that would be perfect." I sigh loudly, but she doesn't comment. "That way I can get them copied and sent out."

"Thanks Rosa." I reply, my voice flatter and less interested in business than usual, finally making her look at me.

"Is everything OK Gabriel?" Before I can answer, there's a commotion in the office outside my door and then Brent strolls into my office.

"Good morning Mr Romanetti! How are you this fine morning?" He asks, loud enough for the entire office to hear him. He's in a mood that can only be described as over the top excited. We don't work together, just in the same building. I work in the family business and there's no hope in hell that my father would *ever* let Brent work here. That's not to say that he's not a hard worker *or* brilliant at what he does, but they would end up killing each other. Then I'd have to choose a side and there's no way that could end well.

"Good morning Brent. What's got you so happy this early in the morning?" I ask, not commenting on him calling me Mr Romanetti, he knows I hate it. That's my father, not me.

"Oh you know. The start of a new week, a new day. The sun is shining and I'm just happy." He answers my question with a goofy grin on his face. If I didn't know better I'd say he got laid.

"Did Sophie forgive you?" I ask him, imagining there's no way she's given in that easily. At least I hope she hasn't.

"As a matter of fact, no. That being said she *did* agree to go to dinner with me tomorrow night though, so maybe we're on track." He says, a thoughtful scowl changing his face for a second. "The real reason I'm happy as a pig in mud, is because the project I've been working on succeeded."

"That's a perfect analogy for you, you belong in the mud pit with pigs. I can't believe women fall for your bullshit in this day and age Woods." Rosa mumbles under her breath, but I hear her and chuckle. I don't disagree with her, Brent can be a jerk around women, but I've never seen him chase one before. Ever. I've never seen him care about whether they'll go out with him a first time, certainly never about having another chance.

"Rosa." I admonish her, but I'm grinning at the same time, so she knows I'm not actually angry at her, just that she needs to watch what she says at work.

"Sorry boss." She says quietly. If Brent hears either of us, he doesn't say anything, he's too busy rattling off details of his new contract. "I'll get back to work if there's nothing else you need from me?"

"I'm good, thanks Rosa. I'll get these back to you by lunch." I say, waving the papers she handed me in the air. I'm rewarded with a smile and a nod before she heads back out the door. Brent doesn't even seem to notice that Rosa left. Then again he didn't seem to notice she was in my office to start with, which is unusual because they always spar about something. His attitude, her attitude, so on and so on.

"... which means I can't wait to start this new project and get it all off the ground and up and running. I'm so happy they chose us, well me, to head up the campaign." He hasn't stopped talking since the minute he walked in the door, I'm not sure he would even notice if I wasn't in the room.

"Good I'm glad. You worked hard to get that account and I hope it works out how you want it to. The job and with Sophie." I say and he kind of startles at my voice as if he truly forgot I was in here. In my office. I can't help laughing at the look on his face.

"Yes. Yes, I hope I can work both things to my advantage." He says nodding.

"I don't think Sophie is going to bend to your will quite as easily Brent, but I still wish you luck. She seems like a very nice person."

"She is. She really is man." He says sheepishly and, I think he's blushing. Holy crap I've never seen Brent Woods blush in his life, and I didn't think I ever would in this lifetime. Before I can comment though, he coughs loudly and starts backing out of my office. "Yes well, I can't be in here talking to you all day I have work to do." Then he's gone. Closing the door behind him, making me grateful for his need to escape quickly.

My office is quiet and I'm alone with my thoughts. Thoughts that immediately wander back to a beautiful brown eyed girl with shiny long brown hair, with streaks of caramel. Geezus, listen to me get all poetic but the truth is, she brings something out in me that no woman ever has. I bring myself out of my thoughts of Lexi, by telling myself that they're just not productive. She bolted today like I was going to murder her if given half the chance. I don't think even Brent could come back from something like that.

I eat lunch at my desk, even though Rosa hates it when I do it, she's still the one who orders and then brings me food to eat. Every time I get the same lecture. "It's not healthy to sit at your desk all day, Gabriel. You should get out into the fresh air and get yourself something to eat."

She's a couple of years younger than I am, and yet I still feel like a child who has been reprimanded. It feels like she's been here longer than I have and that's saying something, because she worked for my dad before he retired and now she's working for me. Either way, I smile and thank her for bringing me lunch, then promise to get outside later for that fresh air. She sends me a look that says she doesn't believe me, takes the papers that I signed for her, and then she's gone again, back to her own work.

The next time I look up from my computer Brent is back in my office. "Don't you have your own office to be in Brent instead of mine? On a completely different floor too. Why are you up here again?" I ask, with more frustration in my voice than I intended there to be.

"I'm up here because all the normal people have clocked off at this hour and are going out to have drinks." He replies with a low chuckle. He's not offended in the least by my short temper and clipped tone. "Thought we could go grab a couple of beers and dinner, but hey, if you'd rather be a grumpy bastard sitting all alone here in your office and turning into dear old dad, be my guest."

He lets out a loud hoot of laughter when I growl like an old grizzly bear. There's nothing I hate more than being compared to how my old man used to be. "Let me just finish what I was doing and then we can go." I say, not really giving him an option. He can stay and wait for me for a few minutes, or he can leave, that's up to him. He doesn't say a word, just drops himself down into one of the chairs that faces my desk and starts doing something on his phone.

Barefoot and Dumped!

I'm almost finished writing up the last line of my report when he looks up and asks. "How much longer man? I'm hungry."

I knew he wouldn't be able to sit there for too long. He's like a toddler who has to keep moving and if you make him be still for too long, he goes a little insane.

"Come on. Let's get out of here before you do something you shouldn't and get us both in trouble somehow."

"Only if you're done. I don't want to be the reason the old man doesn't get his much needed emails and reports in the morning." I know he's joking, but he doesn't know just how close to home he's hitting.

"I was actually finishing off an email to Rosa smart arse." He shrugs his shoulders. He knows one way or the other I was finishing something so that my Dad got the reports he still asks me to send him, even in retirement. "Come on, you're right about one thing, it's time for some good food and beer. Lead the way." I wave my hand, directing him to lead the way out of my office and to the elevators. I've had enough of this place for the day.

~~~~~

We go to a bar close to the office, where we find a table and order food, along with a beer. I could go for something stronger after this morning's run in with Lexi, but it can wait until I get home.

"Hey, are you listening to me?" Brent asks me.

"I'm sorry, what did you say?" I look over at Brent, taking my eyes from the window we're sitting next to, to talk to him.

"You didn't hear one word I just said, did you?" He asks, amused.

"Sorry."

"Where were you just now? It's not like you to zone out on me, on anyone actually, even when they're boring and talking crap." That makes me smile, because he's right. I pride myself on being able to listen and hear when people talk. It's one of the good things my father has taught me about business. "So, what's her name?" That question is asked with a smirk.

"What makes you think it's about a woman?" I ask, curious.
~~~~~

"Mostly because you don't get that glassy eyed, faraway look over a business proposal, acquisition or project. Ever." He takes a breath, "It's not about your Dad or sister either. I've seen you angry and frustrated many times but never lost in thought."

"Awww Brent, I didn't know you cared." I say, laughing and hoping against hope to get him off the scent. It's not my lucky day though. "You know I do miss my Mum most days." My Mum died a few years back and there isn't really a day when I don't miss her. My Dad was always at work, he never spent a lot of time with my sister and I when we were kids, and Mum always picked up the slack. When she died, he changed a lot. He reduced his hours at work and was much more available to us. I just wish it hadn't taken losing my Mum to make him see what he'd been missing, mainly because we were older by then and didn't need him so much. She'd already done all the hard work and I was already working my way up in the business. Then, when he finally retired and handed the reigns over to me, he started to relax even more, but he still insists on me going to his house on Saturday mornings to discuss the business.

I could really do with some of my Mum's words of wisdom right now and I don't think my Dad's advice will cut it.

"What do you need her advice about?" Brent asks, taking a drink of his beer, making me wonder if I spoke out loud rather than just thinking my wish. "No, you didn't say it out loud, but you miss your Mum the most when you're looking for advice. Specifically when you're having trouble with a lady."

"When the hell did you become so observant?" He's been my friend for years, decades actually, and I've never known him to notice anything about anyone. "Sophie's bringing out your softer side, man." It's not a bad thing, and I'm definitely not complaining. It's just weird.

"You're right, she is. You can't be blasé and unfeeling around that woman. She calls me out on it every single time." A huge smile has spread across his face and he shrugs a shoulder. "I'm not going to fight it anymore. When you find the right one, you know."

Well, Brent just proves that love can change a person. "I, for one, am glad you've found the right one for you Brent. It's about time!"

"Thank you." His grin gets bigger, so much so that I think his face might just be on the verge of splitting in two. "But don't think for a second that you've managed to distract me from the original question my man." He raises an eyebrow at me and repeats his earlier question. "So, who is she?"

"No-one." Is all I say.

"That's not true." He keeps staring at me over his beer, sitting there, waiting. I have a short reprieve when the waiter brings over our burgers and chips. We thank the waiter and he walks away, Brent continues. "Come on man, just tell me, you know I'm not going to give up until you do."

He's right and I know it. There's no point holding out on him because he's like a dog with a bone, he'll just keep coming at me. Today, tomorrow or next week. "Fine."

"I knew it! I knew it wasn't work." He almost looks giddy, which is just bizarre for a grown man. That's when it hits me that he was fishing for information, he had no damned clue that I was interested in someone and I fell for it. I throw a chip at him, and clock him right between the eyes. "That's not nice man, but thanks for the chip." He grins, eating the it.

"Do you remember the ladies from the bar the other night?"

"You mean the ones that walked into the bar that every guy in the place was talking to and you wanted nothing to do with?"

"That's them."

"I tried to forget them honestly. They got me in trouble with Sophie to start with." He frowns. "But that resulted in the *best* make up sex I've ever had in living memory." And there he is, the jerk resurfaces for a minute and I shake my head. "What about them?"

"Well, after you left to talk to Sophie, they came over and asked to share the table with me."

"You dog, why didn't you tell me this sooner? See, I knew you'd go home with Red." He says, without giving me a chance to speak.

"Actually, no I didn't. We shared the table and a few drinks. I looked after them so that the creeps didn't circle them and then I took them all home."

"YOU TOOK THEM ALL HOME!!" Brent yells, grabbing the attention of half the diners in the damned bar. "You dog!"

"NO!" I yell back at him, although I'm not even close to his level of loud. "Keep your fucking voice down you idiot."

"Oh sorry, you don't want everyone knowing you're a lucky bastard?"

"I don't want anyone getting the wrong idea. I didn't take, *take* them home Brent. Red, I mean Lacey, was going to call an Uber but they were all pretty drunk and I didn't want them to getting into any trouble, so I offered to take them home. I dropped Lacey at her place and then Lexi and Cat at their house."

"Well aren't you the gentleman?" I don't know whether he's being sarcastic or genuine, sometimes he's just too damned hard to read. "So, did you get Red's, sorry Lacey's number?"

"No I didn't but she did give me Lexi's details." I mumble.

"Is that the tallish blonde one?"

"No, that's Cat. Her and Lexi are sisters."

"Of course. I should have known you would choose the brunette." He nods his head like he's thinking it through. "Yeah, she was definitely more your type. Not as fiery as Red, and not as tall or blonde as her sister. Yeah I see it now." He nods his head again like he's just figured out a puzzle, as he bites into his burger.

"What does that mean, *my type*?" I ask, a little annoyed with his assumptions, but interested in how he came to that conclusion.

"Well, she's nothing like." He pauses, not knowing whether to say her name, or not and choosing not to. "She who shall not be named. She's nothing like what your father would expect and hell, she's bloody adorable, in a take no bullshit kind of way."

"Anyway, I carried her inside the house because she fell asleep in the truck on the drive, and Cat, her sister, told me that there was no hope in hell I was going to wake her. So, instead of trying, I put her to bed. I left *my* details in a note on her bedside table, along with a glass of water and some painkillers."

"Awww aren't you sweet?" He chuckles. "So, what's the problem? Haven't you heard from her?"

"No I haven't and that would be OK, except." I hesitate, not sure if I want to tell him about our encounter this morning.

"Except. What?" He pushes me to keep going, so I do.

"We accidently bumped into each other outside Berry's café this morning."

"OK. So what's the problem? Did you speak to her, and ask her why she hasn't called?"

"Well, no." I say, hesitating again, but he raises his eyebrow at me again, questioning me and telling me to keep going all at the same time. "She didn't remember me, and when I called her by name she thought I was a creepy stalker and ran away. Literally, took off in the opposite direction as fast as she could before I could explain a thing."

For a couple of minutes, Brent just sits there, mouth open and burger halfway to his mouth. Then suddenly, he lets out a loud and long roar of laughter. Arsehole, this isn't funny.

"Are you kidding me? She didn't remember you? She forgot *you,* after you looked after her and everything?" He takes a deep breath trying to control himself, but it's a losing battle.

"Apparently. Now you know what I was thinking about as I stared out the window. I was thinking about the first woman I've even remotely been attracted to, or even wanted to get to know since, *she who shall not be named,* and I screwed it up."

"Man that sucks. I'm sorry." He sobers pretty quickly after I mention my ex. He was there for the whole shitshow and he knows that I struggle now to find a woman who I can trust. Which is one of the reasons he pushed me to go out for drinks that night. You can't meet someone else if you never get out of the house, was his reasoning. "What are you going to do?"

"What can I do?" I ask shrugging my shoulders. "There's nothing I *can* do, man, she thinks I'm a creepy stalker. If I call her now, even though Lacey gave me her number, I'll look like an even bigger creeper and I think I'll pass. I know how it feels to be stalked and creeped out every day, I wouldn't wish it on my worst enemy. I sure won't be the cause of Lexi feeling nervous every day."

He doesn't say anything. There's nothing he can say, it's true. I can't be the cause of anyone else's distress, but certainly not Lexi's. So, while it kills me to know I've missed my chance, I have to let her and the connection I was sure we had, go.

We move on to other, less depressing subjects while we finish eating and grab another beer. Then Brent heads out to meet up with Sophie. He gave me a guilty look when he mentioned Sophie, but I'm happy for him and he has nothing to feel bad about.

Sometimes, shit happens and there's nothing you can do about it.

Chapter Nine

LEXI

When I get home from dinner that night, I strip out of my work clothes and lie down in bed, with just my undies and a loose t-shirt on. I can't help thinking about what Lacey said about Gabe. Gabriel Romanetti. It's a strong name, for a very strong looking guy. Just that one quick touch of him when I ran into him this morning, told me everything I need to know about his body.

It's rock hard and very, very tempting. My hands were dying to linger a little longer.

His eyes were just, mesmerising. I've never seen eyes that colour before. Green and brown, with flecks of gold through them. And his lips. Oh My God! His lips! They were just begging for me to kiss them. I would have answered their call too, if he hadn't said my name so casually and like we knew each other. Of course, I find out from Lacey tonight that we've already met, so that means he had every reason to believe that we knew each other and it's also OK that he knew my name.

I roll over onto my side and bury my face in my hands. I'll probably never see the man again, but I'm still embarrassed as hell. He must think I'm an absolute lunatic or a complete freak. So even if we *do* ever run into one another again, he'll probably pretend not to know me this time. Not that I was pretending, oh damn it.

I'm exhausted, it's been a long and stressful day, so I pull the covers up to my chin, snuggle in to get comfy and warm, then I'm out like a light.

~~~~~
~~~~~

"Lexi, baby, open your eyes." I know that voice, just the sound of it makes my nipples hard and my clit pulse, but I can't place it. "Come on baby, look at me."

"I'm trying." I say, my voice husky with sleep.

The front of his body is flush with my back, and I feel the laughter in his body more than I hear the low chuckle vibrate out of him. "How about you just lay there and relax then? Let me do all the work for you." I can feel his smile on the back of my neck, as he kisses me there and on my shoulder.

The hand he had resting on my hip, slides onto my stomach, then reaches up to knead my breast.

"Mmmmm." I moan, not able to put together words, it feels so damned good.

He presses kisses down my back and his hand follows him down the front of my body until his hand rests on the inside of my thighs, gently pushing them apart. Do I allow him to easily part my legs, gaining access to my pussy? Damned straight I do, but his hand skims the inside of my thigh down to my knee and back up again.

"More." I beg quietly.

"You want more of me baby?" I nod yes to answer his question. "More of my fingers?"

"Yes." I say on a breath.

Without hesitation, his finger presses on my clit and my whole body shudders. I feel him shift behind me but I'm not taking enough to notice to realise what he's doing until he's doing it. He's kissing across my lower back, and pressing on my clit, then I feel a finger slide into my pussy and let out a long, low groan.

"Does that feel good baby?" He asks, his deep voice pulsing up my spine.

"Yes. Oh god yes. Don't stop. Please. Don't. Stop." I say each word between the breaths panting out of my body, desperately trying to gain some control.

Barefoot and Dumped!

"I'm not stopping until I make you come Lexi." He whispers into my hair and I feel it in every nerve ending in my body. When he slides a second finger into my pussy and begins to press harder on my clit, I know I'm done.

My hips move back and forth, slamming back into his hard body behind me. I reach for my boobs and squeeze them tightly, tweaking each nipple slightly and that's it.

"That's right Lexi. Let go baby. Come for me."

I come so hard I see stars and it takes me a minute to come back to earth. I look over my shoulder and see his hazel eyes sparkling with satisfaction. He rolls over onto his back, staring at the ceiling with a smile on his face. I roll over to lay on his chest and hold him but instead of the hard wall of a chest that I know he has, I feel a soft almost pillowy sensation. I open my eyes and a frustrated growl escapes my lips.

There is no guy in my bed, just the pillow I'm holding onto for dear life and the blankets that are now barely covering me. I throw myself back onto my pillow, bringing the spare one down with me and covering my face, screaming loudly into it to muffle the sound so I don't wake up Cat. The disappointment I'm now feeling waking up alone is ridiculous.

I haven't had a good sex dream in a *very* long time and *that* was one hell of a hot dream, made even hotter because I know exactly who he was. I'll probably never get the chance to repeat the performance for real, not only because we'll no doubt never meet again, but also because the last time we did, I made an idiot of myself.

I throw the pillow off my face and it lands with a quiet, but solid thump next to me on the bed. My body and clit are still aching with need. I lean up on one elbow to check the time on my phone. It's 6am, too early to be up if I'm being honest, but early enough that Cat won't be up yet.

I shouldn't. I can't. Can I?

Screw it! Normally I don't do it unless I'm alone in the house, or know without a doubt I'll have the privacy, but this morning after that hot dream I need relief more than I need to know I have the house to myself.

I open the drawer next to my bed and pull out my favourite dildo, all dark pink and veiny. I slide quietly out of bed and tiptoe to the door, cracking it open hoping it won't creak. I listen for movement in Cat's room but there isn't any, so I pad quietly to the bathroom and close the door behind me. I rest my back on the closed door and breathe a sigh of relief. I guess I could have stayed in my room and gotten myself off, but I figured I could kill two birds with one stone. I mean I have to shower anyway, right?

I take a half step from the door, then reach behind me to lock it. That's better. It's like an insurance policy against being interrupted. Placing the dildo on the shelf inside the shower stall, I reach over and turn on the hot water to get it warmed up, then I'm stripped out of my t-shirt and undies in record time. I step into the shower, closing the door behind me, the steam from the hot water fogging up the glass almost immediately, providing me with even more privacy.

I thank the shower gods for the forethought of putting one of those inbuilt steps into the tiles on the wall. You know the ones that you're supposed to use to help you shave your legs? Yeah, well it's also helpful for when a girl wants to masturbate. Placing one foot up there, and firmly planting the other on the floor, I reach over and grab the dildo. Pressing it against my pussy lips with one hand, I brace my other hand on the wall. As the dildo presses further and further into my pussy I let out a loud, long moan. It feels so damned good, but I have to remind myself to be quiet. I really don't want to wake Cat up and have to explain what I'm doing in here. Or why. I close my eyes as I drag it in and out of my pussy. For a fake cock, it feels amazing and it doesn't take long to bring myself right up to the edge and then I'm coming right there in my shower, eyes closed and imaging a certain dark brown haired, hazel eyed man smiling back at me as I do.

That was just what I needed after that dream. I mean nothing, *nothing* ever compares to a red hot blooded man in your bed, or your shower for that matter, but when you can't have that, the bonus is you can fake it. I let the dildo fall to the base of the shower and bring my foot back down to the floor, bracing both hands on the wall to catch my breath.

"Are you going to be in there much longer? I need to leave early today." Cat asks, banging on the bathroom door loudly. "Hey, why is the door locked?"

Barefoot and Dumped!

I can hear the door handle jiggling as she tries to get in. Thank god I had the forethought to lock that sucker as I came in.

"I'll be out in a minute." I yell out. "And the door's locked because sometimes I like to shower or use the toilet in private without you wandering in whenever you like, to do whatever you like." There's been more than one occasion where she's used the toilet while I've been in the shower. It's not that I'm a prude, or that I mind that much, but sometimes a girl has company, and well I guess those are the times you lock the door. Trust Cat to have to go into work early today of all days.

"Lucky we have an endless supply of hot water with the amount you've used already this morning." She yells back, but I can hear her walking away from the door.

Now all I have to do is get out of the bathroom without my little sister catching me carrying around my dildo. Like I said, I'm not a prude, nor am I ashamed of what I just did, or who I imagined doing it with. I just don't want to have that conversation today, if ever, and I don't want to listen to the 'I told you so' or the endless teasing about flicking my bean to thoughts of Mr Gabriel Romanetti .

After quickly washing my hair, my body, and my dildo, I step out of the shower to dry myself off. As I'm wrapping a towel around my body and another around my hair there's another knock on the door.

"Ummmm Lexi, are you going to be out soon? Cause I really need to pee sis." I can hear the desperation in her voice and can't stop myself from laughing at her.

"I'm coming now." Then I chuckle at my own private joke. I wrap the dildo in my t-shirt with my undies and hold them all under one arm as I open the door to step out of the bathroom. The sight of Cat standing on the opposite wall, dancing from one foot to the other, obviously in desperate need to use the bathroom, I stand in the doorway and say, "Hang on a second, I think I forgot something."

I barely get the last word out, before I'm pushed aside, and the door is slammed in my face.

"You can be such a bitch sometimes Lexi, you know that?"

"So, when are you moving in with Joshua?" I laugh.

"Sooner rather than later." I hear her grumble. "Why didn't you get a place with two bathrooms?"

"Well, because I never planned on having a roommate Cat." As I walk away, I can hear her mumbling something from inside the bathroom, but I don't care what it is. The truth is, I don't mind having her around. Although, I am kind of looking forward to her moving in with Joshua and getting my space to myself again. I can have an office again and not have to work at the kitchen table. That being said, I will miss her once she does finally leave.

I unwrap the dildo from my clothes and put it back in the drawer beside my bed, just as Cat bounds into my room and jumps on my bed.

"Don't you have to get ready for work? Early I recall you saying not five minutes ago." I ask, not really annoyed with her being in here.

"I do but I really needed to ask you something important first." She says, a hint of a smile touching her lips.

"Oh yeah, what's that?" I ask, not sure what to expect. With my sister, it could be anything.

"So, do you have a name for your dildo or vibrator?" She asks, with a straight face and then starts laughing hysterically. She can't possibly know what I was doing in the shower. Can she?

"What the hell Cat?" I hit her with a pillow. "Get out of here and get ready for work before you're late."

She's up and off my bed and standing in the doorway of my room, when she turns slightly sideways to look at me and says, "Is your favourite one named Gabe or Gabriel these days?"

Before I can respond, she's gone and I can hear her laughing in the bathroom, even as I hear her lock the door behind her.

It's definitely a day for locking that door, because if she hadn't, I would have been there dumping cold water over her when she least expected it.

Cheeky bitch! She's been spending way too much time with Lacey and she's been a bad influence on my little sister. I've changed my mind, it

Barefoot and Dumped!

will be a good thing if Cat moves out, sooner rather than later, and I think we might have a chat about that over dinner tonight.

Chapter Ten

GABE

Knowing that I'd blown my chance with Lexi really annoyed me. I know that she felt the connection that night at the bar just like I did, I could see it in her eyes because they lit up any time we accidentally touched one another, and she twitched a little, like she'd been zapped.

After her reaction to bumping into me at the café though, I had to come to terms with the fact we were done. Done before we'd even gotten a real chance to start. I am so annoyed with myself for screwing it all up, but I know I have to move on.

Brent has been trying to get me to go out with him a few times over the last month, but the only time I went, Sophie bought a friend along. She was nice but she wasn't Lexi. Brent just couldn't understand why I couldn't move on from a woman I barely knew but the truth is, I felt that woman in my soul and I've never felt that way before about anyone. Not even she who shall not be named. We've been out for a few beers after work since that ill-fated 'not a blind date I swear'. Tonight we've come back to the bar where I met Lexi and a part of me is hoping that Lacey will somehow talk Lexi into returning to the scene of the crime and we could have another accidental meeting, only this time Lexi would remember who I am.

"I take it your princess hasn't shown up again?" Brent asks me with a sad smile on his face.

"I'm sorry, I didn't know I was being so obvious." I don't want him to think that's the only reason I came out for a beer with him tonight.

"I don't know if you are or not, but I can tell that's what you're hoping for." He says with a shrug of his shoulders.

"I didn't come out with you hoping I'd see her." I say, but I can see the scepticism written all over his face. "Honestly dude, I didn't."

"I know you didn't. I really do Gabe, mainly because the first few times I suggested coming here in particular you said no and chose somewhere else. That doesn't mean you're not hoping she'll show up though."

"You're right. I'm looking around the room to see who is here and every time the door opens I look up, hoping to see her face, but I guess I just have to live with the fact that it's over. Let's face it though man, it never really began." I laugh, trying to make light of the whole situation. I feel like an idiot hoping that one day she'll just magically show up. "I'm sorry, I'll stop."

"Nah man, I'm just yanking your chain. I think it's adorable that you're still hoping to run into her even though she called you a stalker and basically told you to fuck off."

"She didn't tell me to fuck off, she just ran off because she was scared of the stalker guy who knew her name and she didn't know him."

"So, figuratively told you to fuck off then, right?" He says, barely holding back his laughter now.

"Yeah, yeah it's really funny. Thanks for your support man." I say, trying to sound angry but not succeeding because I can't help laughing as well. He's right. He's absolutely right. She ran and flipped me the bird as she went. "It's time to move on, obviously."

"I wouldn't be so quick to make that decision man. You never know what might happen." He's got this crazy look in his eyes and a flicker of something I'm not quick enough to catch. "I'll be back in a minute, just going to the men's room." He stands up immediately, while hooking his thumb towards the bathrooms.

"Yeah sure." I say, not understanding why he's making such a huge production of it. "I'm sure I'll survive for a few minutes without you." Then he's gone. I'm sure it's the fastest I've ever seen the man move.

There's a light tap on my shoulder, so light I have to wonder if I felt it at all, so I don't look around until I feel another, harder tap. "Excuse me, Gabe isn't it?" My whole body freezes, I recognise that voice, I'm sure I do, but I don't want to look like an idiot if I say her name and it's not *her*.

Slowly, I turn my head to see who I'm talking to, and I can't hide my shock when I see Lacey standing next to me and I almost feel relief, mixing with my disappointment, that it's not Lexi.

"No need to look so disappointed handsome. Lexi's here, she just went to the ladies room to freshen up before she meets me at the bar. I saw you over here and thought I'd come say hi."

"Hi Lacey, how are you?" I ask her, her gigantic smile freaking me the hell out.

"Oh I'm much better now, thanks for asking." What the hell does that mean? I don't get to ask her though because there's another voice speaking behind her, and the minute I hear it, my entire body is at attention.

"Lacey, what are you doing? I thought we were meeting at the bar, not a table?" She hasn't looked up from rummaging around in her handbag, to see that her best friend is talking to me.

"I needed to speak to someone first." Lacey says, mischief making her eyes sparkle and shine. "Now, it's my turn to go to the ladies room. If you'll excuse me." Then, she's gone, and I'm left staring into a pair of shocked brown eyes, but I don't speak. This time, it has to be her. Lexi has to make the move this time, I'm not going there again and being called a stalker in a reasonably full bar. One that I come to so often, it's almost my second home.

"Hi." She says in what can only be described as a squeak.

"Hi."

"How are you?"

"I'm great, thanks." I don't know what else to say to her, I'm so surprised that she's standing in front of me that I can't think straight.

"That's great." She says, and then stands there, saying nothing.

"Ummm how have you been?" I ask, to break the awkwardness.

"Good. Yes good thanks for asking." She answers me with a couple of nods of her head.

Beside me I hear Brent quietly chuckling. I don't even know when he got back from the men's room. "I'm just going to go and get us a drink. Can I get you anything Lexi?"

"No thank you." She answers without looking at him, her eyes never leaving mine.

"Look, Gabe I'm sorry." She starts.

"Lexi, I'm really sorry." We speak at the same time and then stop together. I hold my hand up to stop us both and then say. "You first, Lexi."

"Thanks." She says with a small smile, then takes a deep breath before continuing. "I'm really sorry about freaking out on you the last time we ran into each other. I behaved like a lunatic and I wouldn't be surprised if you thought I was too strange to even contemplate ever seeing me again." She looks down at her feet, obviously embarrassed, but she has no reason to be.

"No, you were right to call me out. Once I realised you didn't remember me, I knew how weird it would feel to you that I knew you and your name. I'm sorry for making you feel uncomfortable." I say, honestly.

"You're being very kind, but I was a weirdo." She says, shaking her head but only glancing at me for a second before looking away again.

I reach out and place my finger gently on her chin, even though I know it's a risk touching her like this, to raise her head so that I can look in her eyes. Hopefully she'll hear and understand what I'm about to say. "You're not a weirdo. You weren't being strange or acting like a lunatic. You didn't remember that we'd met, and I was pretty forward. I'm sorry, Lexi. I didn't realise you were that drunk that you wouldn't remember that night."

"I wasn't." I raise my eyebrow in a silent question, and she laughs before she speaks again. "You're right. I *was* that drunk, I just didn't *plan* on getting *that* drunk. It was just a really shitty day and I decided to let loose. While I don't want to blame someone else for my behaviour, Lacey led the way that night, and kept buying me drinks." She laughs.

"I guess we can blame Lacey for being your booze pusher then?" I say, with a smirk, causing Lexi to laugh a little harder. I realise we've been standing next to the table, rather than sitting at it when someone comes over and tries to sit in one of the chairs. I make a move to speak and half sit on one of the chairs, "I'm sorry, this is our table. We were just saying hello to one another before we sat down." The young lady looks between us, sighs and walks away. I'm pretty sure I heard her muttering, *'I knew it was too good to be true,'* to herself.

I lean over and say in Lexi's ear, so only she can hear me, "Now *that's* weird and kind of crazy." And I'm rewarded with another round of beautiful laughter. "Do you want to sit down, before someone else tries to steal the table?"

"Yes." She says her voice raspy still from her laughter, and hopefully happiness at being with me this time. "I'd like that."

I wait for her take her seat before I sit back down. "Can I get you a drink? Or something to eat?" Before she can answer a waiter stops at our table and places beer for me, a glass of wine for Lexi and a plate of snacks we can nibble on. "Ahh we didn't order these, sorry ." I say as the waiter goes to walk away.

"No you didn't," He says with a smile. "Your friends at the bar asked for them to be sent over." Lexi and I look over to the bar only to find Lacey and Brent standing together, smiling and waving at us.

"Shit, I forgot I was here with Brent." I say, thinking I said that in my head, but it's obvious I didn't when the waiter and Lexi start to laugh at me.

"I would forget my mate if I was sitting with a beautiful lady as well, so don't stress yourself about it man. They don't seem to be too bummed about it either." Lexi blushes at his comment, but he's right, I got the chance to sit with her and I forgot all about Brent!

"Thank you." I say to the waiter, he nods and makes his way back to the bar. "Well, I guess our friends have decided to leave us then?" I ask, because I don't want her to freak out again and go running.

"I think you might be right." She laughs. "I can't say I'm too upset with their thinking though." She says, with a cheeky smile.

"Are you sure? Because I like this place and I don't want to feel like I can't come back because a gorgeous lady accuses me of stalking her." I'm smiling, so that she knows I'm just teasing her, but I'm also testing the waters, because if she really doesn't want to be here, I won't make her stay.

"Oh god!" She groans and buries her face in her hands. "I can't believe I did that to you!"

"Hey. Lexi." I say, reaching over to uncover her face so that I can look in her eyes when I say, "Lexi, it doesn't matter. Honestly. I was just teasing you."

"Oh Gabe, I'm so sorry. I didn't even think of the repercussions of my yelling at you about being a stalker. I could have caused you a lot of trouble."

"Well, I'm sure you could have but you didn't. We weren't inside the café and no-one heard you tell me to stop stalking you, at least I don't think anyone did. I haven't had the police on my doorstep, so I think we can assume I'm pretty safe." I laugh.

"That doesn't help at all you know." I've still got her hands in mine from when I pulled them away from her face, and she wiggles one of them free only to hit me on the upper arm.

"Ouch! Geez woman, now who's getting all abusive?" I've got a serious look on my face, but I can't hold in my laughter for long, as she looks around the room to see if anyone noticed.

"Shut up you, that didn't even hurt you. You didn't feel a thing, it wouldn't have even stung that bulging bicep of yours." She says, laughing as well, but not moving her hand away from said bicep I notice. I'm not complaining, not even a little bit. She can touch me anywhere she damn well wants to.

"Are you trying to tell me I'm an insensitive bastard now? I see the compliments just keep on rolling on in don't they?" I mime a wow her way and she laughs. I swear, if we can make this thing between us work by some miracle, I will do everything in my power to hear her laugh every single day. It's the most musical and magical sound I've ever heard, and it brings a smile to my face that I can't hide. Truth be told I don't want to hide it.

"You're such an idiot." She says, laughter weakening the insult considerably.

Barefoot and Dumped!

"I'll take that as a compliment Miss Stratton." I say, my voice low, hoping I can get her to relax with me.

Before she can answer me, I hear her phone chime. "Sorry, just let me check who it is." She says, and I pull mine out to check it quickly, as well.

"That was just Lacey checking and making sure I was safe." She smiles at me and continues, "Cause you're my stalker and all." Her grin gets wider.

"Very funny." I say shooting her a look that says I'm unimpressed, but then I laugh. "Your best friend might think she's being funny by calling me a stalker, but she's the one who wrote all your details out for me Alexis Stratton. So if I'm a stalker, Lacey is my enabler."

Lexi laughs, "Of course she did! I'm just glad she didn't actually give all those details to an actual creepy stalker." She blushes slightly, and I can't help but wonder if I can get that blush to cover her entire body one day. Or night. Coyly she says, "I think Lacey mentioned your last name, but for the life of me I can't remember."

I don't know if that's the truth or not, but I'm happy to give her every detail she needs to feel comfortable with me. "Romanetti. Gabriel Romanetti, at your service." I say reaching my hand out offering to shake hers. Instead when I hold her hand in mine, I bring it to my lips and kiss every knuckle, taking my time because she doesn't pull away from me.

"Nice to meet you Gabriel Romanetti." She says, her smile radiating absolute pleasure. How things have changed from the last time we bumped into each other. I don't know what changed, but I don't care to find out either.

"If Lacey gave you all my details, does that mean you have my phone number as well?" She asks, taking a sip of her own drink.

"Yes." I answer, telling her the truth, because I'm not going to lie to this woman.

"So, why didn't you call me? You know after the night we met or even after the day at the café? We could have cleared everything up earlier." Is she wishing that I had, and we'd gotten here before now?

"I didn't think you would answer me or would have been very receptive about getting a phone call off me after the café incident. I would have just proven that I *was* a creepy stalker." Lexi nods her head, confirming my thought. "The night we first met, I took Lacey home, then you and Cat back to your house. When I left you that night, after tucking you in and leaving a glass of water and the painkillers for you in the morning, I also left you a note with all of *my* details on it. I figured I would leave the ball in your court and when you didn't call, I just assumed you weren't interested." I end with a shrug.

Chapter Eleven

LEXI

A note? "I never saw a note on my bedside table. The glass of water and the painkillers, they were there, and I have to say, I was very appreciative of them that morning. I didn't think drunk me would have thought of doing that, I never have before." I laugh, because I was more likely to have poured vodka into that glass and think it was hysterically funny.

"Well, that explains why you never called me and goes some way to also explaining why you didn't remember who I was a few weeks ago." Gabe says, generously.

"You mean beside me getting stinking drunk that night?" His eyes twinkle with amusement and if that's not enough to know he's trying not to laugh, he's got this gorgeous smirk lifting the corner of his mouth. Damn but the guy has the *most* kissable looking lips I've seen in a *very* long time. I feel this overwhelming need to explain to him *why* I was drinking so heavily that night. "I'm not a lush OK? I don't normally drink that heavily, especially when I'm out. I don't like not being in control of my body and my actions. I also like remembering what I've done and who I've met."

"I would have really enjoyed you remembering who you'd met that night too. It could have saved me from an embarrassing encounter with you a few days later." He says with a serious look on his face, but I can hear the laughter in his voice.

"God, I'm so sorry about that morning. It hasn't stopped you from getting the best coffee in town has it? I couldn't live with myself if it did."

"No, I still go there for my caffeine fix, so no problems at all." He says with a smile. "So, what happened that made you want to be out of control the night we met?" He asks quietly.

"I broke up with my boyfriend." That's the simple explanation isn't it? "Actually, *he* broke up with *me*, and Lacey decided a few drinks were in order. I'll be honest, I readily agreed. What I didn't realise at the time, and probably should have, was that she was only drinking half of the drinks that I was. I think Catherine was almost keeping up with me."

"He's an idiot." Gabe says, the tone in his voice allowing no room for an argument, and I smile at his compliment.

"Thank you, but you barely know me."

"That doesn't make him any less of an idiot Alexis." I look down at my hand resting on the table, I don't know what to say to this man I barely know, but who is firmly defending me. "Were you together for a long time?"

"I guess so. We were together for just over a year, but honestly I realised after he broke up with me that I hadn't really been invested in the relationship. I wasn't upset that he left me only that he chose to do it at my parents' thirtieth wedding anniversary." I shake my head, still not quite believing that's where he chose to walk away from our relationship. "Of all the places he *could* have chosen to have that conversation, he chose there. He could have done it before we went, or even waited until after, but no, he decided the actual party where my parents', relatives and all their friends were celebrating love, to tell me we were over." I drop my face into my hands and shake my head some more. I truly am stunned that's where he chose to break up with me.

"He chose the place where he figured you'd make less of a scene, and that makes *him* an arsehole Lexi." The anger in his voice makes me look up and I'm met with the most amazing eyes I've ever seen. Something in the back of my mind wiggles free and I remember looking into them before, and not the day I embarrassed myself in front of the café either. "Are you OK?" Gabe asks me, reaching over to hold my hand, and I don't pull away from his touch.

"Yes, I'm fine, thanks for asking." I take a breath and say. "Trust me, I know exactly what he is, but I also understand that I had a part to play in all this." I hold my hand up to stop him from speaking, I'm going to take a guess that he was about to defend me, again. "No, not on his choice of timing, obviously, but I knew our relationship wasn't good, and I was just biding my time before I was going to break up with him. Neither of us had really been in very deep with each other and the small boxes of possessions we exchanged a few weekends ago are evidence of that."

"I think you're amazing for taking half the blame, considering how he broke up with you. He sounds like a grade A jerk to me. You may not have been all in, but neither was he." Gabe says. How can a man, or any person for that matter, be that understanding?

"Thank you but I honestly can't let him take all the blame." I say, with a shrug on my shoulders. "He was a grade A jerk though, on that you're 100% right." I say, laughing and Gabe joins in with his own laughter.

"His loss and hopefully my gain." Gabe says once our laughter has died down, and I can see the hope shining in his eyes.

"You never know you're luck, Mr Romanetti." I reply cheekily and his face lights up even more.

"You have no idea how lucky I am Lexi." He says with a sexy smirk and a wink. How the hell can I find all these cheesy things that this man does, charming and sexy? If any other man used them to try to pick myself or a friend up, I would be laughing hysterically at their behaviour, and walking away. Fast!

A small voice in the back of my head answers me with, *because you like this man. You like him very much and you want to find everything he does adorably charming.*

The annoying bitch might just be right, but I still don't want to rush into anything so soon after Stephen. I know I wasn't in love with him, but I still think a healthy break between relationships is a good idea.

Although, Gabriel Romanetti might have the ability to change my mind on the subject.

"Are you OK Lexi?" He asks me, again.

"Yes." I smile at him.

"Lexi, I'm heading out now." I hear Lacey's voice, and I feel guilty that I came here with her but didn't spend any time with her. Neither Gabe nor I look her way. "Did you need a lift home?"

"No. I can take her home. If that's what you want Lexi?" Gabe answers my best friend.

Lacey chuckles and I finally break my eye lock with Gabe to look at her. "I think I'm OK with a lift home. If that's OK with you Lacey? I'm really sorry we didn't get to hang out tonight."

"Oh, it's perfectly fine Lexi, don't you worry about me at all." She smiles at me, and then turns her attention to Gabe. "Your friend Brent isn't so bad, he kept me company."

"I hope he behaved himself?" Gabe asks, which causes Lacey to laugh again.

"Of course he did!" Lacey says. "Now, you take care of my girl here Mr Romanetti or you'll have me to answer to. You got me?"

Gabe answers her with a lopsided grin. "Of course, I completely understand." He turns to me with the same smile and says, "I won't do anything Lexi doesn't want me to. Promise."

"I'm good with that." Lacey exclaims, leaning over to give me a kiss on the cheek, while whispering, "Go for it. Don't do anything I wouldn't do."

I let out a sharp laugh and tell her, "I love you."

"I know you do." She replies and then she turns and leaves. I watch her as she walks away and wonder how the hell I managed to get a best friend like her.

"She's a real firecracker that friend of yours." Gabe barks out a laugh. "I really like her."

"She's more like a sister, but yeah, she's pretty unique." I say with a smile.

"Everyone needs someone who will have their back no matter what. You're lucky you found someone like that." He says.

"Isn't that what Brent is to you?" I ask, curious about their friendship.

"He has been recently, yes, but it hasn't always been that way, unfortunately." I feel like there's a story there, but I don't want to push him to tell it. If he'd wanted to, he had the perfect opportunity to.

"Well, you have that with him now, so that has to be a good thing." I say.

"You're right." He says, just as his phone dings with a message. "Speak of the devil." He says with a smile. "Do you mind?" He asks, pointing at the phone.

"Go ahead." I say, nodding.

He takes a minute to read the message and then lets out a small laugh, and when I lift an eyebrow in question he says, "He messaged to let me know that he got Sophie to come and pick him up." He shakes his head, "I completely forgot that we came over together in my truck and he needed a lift home." He says, still laughing.

"Well, we've been awesome friends tonight, haven't we?" I say, joining in with his laughter.

"They could have sat down with us, but they chose not to. They're the ones that sent over snacks, we didn't order it or exclude them." Gabe says, serious all of a sudden, so I reach over and place my hand over his.

"I know. They made their own choice, I'm just saying, we were a little preoccupied that's all."

"I know. I guess I just get a little defensive when someone says I haven't been looking out for a friend. It's something my ex used to accuse me of constantly. Looking out for friends and not her, or she'd accuse me of the complete opposite. That I was spending too much time *with* her and my friends all hated her for it. I could never win, so I just got defensive." He answers with a shrug of his shoulder.

"Wow. I'm sorry she was like that, she sounds like a real piece of work." I say, holding tighter onto his hand to show my support. "I think it's healthy to keep your friends when you're in a relationship. Everyone needs a break some days, and in a perfect world all your favourite people get along, but that doesn't always happen, and you just have to deal with it."

"I couldn't agree more." He says, moving his hand to be palm up, making our hands palm to palm. We're not holding hands in the traditional sense, but I still feel that connection with him. We sit like that, staring into each other's eyes for what feels like forever, until the waiter coughs and asks if we want another drink, or something else to eat. We both answer no thanks, without looking at him and he moves away again.

"Do you want me to take you home now Lexi?" Gabe asks, breaking the spell we've been under. I nod a yes, because it takes me a few seconds to find my voice.

"That would be great, thank you Gabe." He smiles and goes to stand up. Our hands are still resting together on the table and I grip onto his to stop him from getting up just yet. "But I want to make it clear that I'm not ready to jump into *anything* just yet."

"I want to make it clear that I'm OK with that. I was offering to take you home, nothing else." He must see the disappointment on my face because he continues with, "Until *you* invite me in and tell me that you want more, because I *do* want to get to know you better Lexi."

"I want to get to know you better too Gabe." I say, smiling at him while I reach for my bag.

I stand up from the table, and I'm right beside him because we haven't let go of each other's hands and he turns me to face him. "Let me just say though, in the spirit of being clear with one another, I want more with you." I go to speak, but he presses a finger lightly to my lips to stop me. "I'm willing to wait Lexi until you're ready, I'm not saying this to pressure you into anything, I just want to put all my cards out on the metaphorical table. I like you. A lot. I feel this pull to you that I've never felt before, and I need you to know that."

"I feel it too Gabe." I say, my voice barely loud enough for him to hear me over the noise of the bar, but I know he heard me because his mouth breaks into a wide smile. "I'm just not ready to jump into something new this fast. I know I said I wasn't really invested in my relationship with Stephen, but we *were* together for a long time and I think it deserves some respect just for that."

"I agree, and I can wait Lexi, just not forever." He kisses me on the forehead and leads me out of the bar and to his truck. The drive to my house is quiet. Not uncomfortable or filled with tension, just quiet. Like we're both just thinking about what happened tonight and what was said.

I feel like I just friend-zoned the sexiest, most charming man I've ever met. The man that *could*, without a doubt in my mind, be the *one*, and I feel like an idiot for doing it, but I know I need the space to think.

Gabe pulls his truck into my driveway before I realise that we're even close to my house. I look over to him, sitting there with both hands on the steering wheel, looking all handsome and sexy and I start to reassess my rules.

"Can I take you out for dinner sometime soon, Lexi?" He asks, hope filling his eyes as he looks at me.

"Yes." I smile in return. "Very soon."

He nods and looks at his hands resting on the steering wheel, before holding his hand out towards me, and asking, "Can I have your phone please?" I don't ask why, I just hand it over. "Well, I have your number, but you don't have mine. Fairs only fair Lexi." He winks as he scrolls through to my contacts and adds his number. "Although, I did leave you my number, so maybe I should leave you to look for the note and to message me first instead." He raises an eyebrow at me, as if trying to decide.

I reach over and grab my phone out of his hand, I watched him, I know he entered his number in there and I'm not taking any chances that he'll delete it now. "Thank you for putting your number in my phone. I don't know where that note is, it's probably lost into the abyss that is my sisters cleaning habit. I may never find it."

"You're welcome." He makes a move to get out of the truck and I panic thinking he wants to come in. Before I can make a move to get out of his car, he's got my door open and is helping me out. "Just walking you to your door Lexi, don't look so worried."

"Thank you Gabe. You're such a gentleman."

"Well, you can see it that way if you like. I'm just taking advantage of getting to spend a few more minutes with you. You know, as friends." He says, with a cheeky smirk. Damn that smirking thing he does is so damned sexy.

"Well, thank you anyway, whatever your motives." I say with a smile of my own as we stand at my front door, neither one of us really ready to say goodnight just yet. That is until I hear a cough coming from inside my house and I laugh.

"Thank you for tonight Gabe. I really enjoyed it and thank you for walking me to my door."

"You're welcome. Thank you for joining me, it was definitely my pleasure." He says, then leans in to kiss me on the forehead for the second time tonight, and I sigh. There's something about a kiss on the forehead that makes a girl feel treasured. "I'll call you to set up a day for dinner." He says, then turns on his heel and walks back to his truck. He gets in and starts it up but doesn't leave. That's when I realise he's waiting for me to go inside. Oh geez this man just melts my heart, and my underwear honestly.

I wave and turn around to put the key in the lock, only for the door to be whipped open by my sister, who drags me inside and locks the door behind us.

"You have to tell me *everything!*" Cat exclaims, dragging me to the couch.

"There's nothing to tell Cat. We ran into each other at the bar. We had a few drinks, snacks and we talked. Nothing else to tell." I say, shrugging my shoulders and trying to be nonchalant about it all, but inside there are excited butterflies fluttering around like crazy.

"Sure Lexi, that's why you've got this dreamy look on your face." She says, crossing her arms over her chest like the petulant child she can still be sometimes.

"That's all that happened Cat, I promise." I bring her in for a hug and she melts into me instantly. "We agreed to go out for dinner sometime soon but didn't set a date."

"So you have a date with Gabe?" She asks, excited.

"No. We're going to dinner as friends, nothing more. Yet." I clarify.

"Yet." She says with a smile.

"Goodnight Catherine, I'm going to bed. See you in the morning." Walking to my bedroom I can't help but smile. She's right, it might not be a date yet, but I have a feeling it will be soon. I want a date with Gabriel Romanetti, I just don't want to rush into something new right now.

"Night sis. Love you."

"Love you too. Sleep well."

"Sweet dreams." She says and then cracks up laughing. I hope I have some very sweet and sexy dreams tonight.

Chapter Twelve

GABE

Running into Lexi and Lacey at the bar tonight was awesome. More because Lexi actually remembered me *and* wanted to talk to me. I hardly noticed that both Brent and Lacey had left us alone. I only had eyes for Lexi, but when Lacey asked her if she needed a ride home, I held my breath waiting for her answer. I was hoping against hope that she would decide to stay with me at the bar just a little bit longer, but I also wanted her to trust me enough to take her home too.

When she accepted the offer of my hand when we stood up, I thought I'd won at least part of the battle but then she said she wanted to make it clear she wasn't ready to jump into anything just yet. It took me a minute to gather my own thoughts. I knew I had to let her know that I would wait for her to be ready, but that I wouldn't wait for ever. I can and *do* respect *her* boundaries, I have to have some of my own as well.

I like this woman. I mean I *really* like this woman, and I can see a future with us together, but I still have to have some pride. Just as I expect Lexi to have some pride as well.

I can see the panic all over her face when I get out of my truck to walk her to her door, after I just secured the promise of taking her out to dinner, and soon. Honestly, I just want to spend as many minutes as I can with her, and I want to make sure she gets to her door safely. Yes, I know I can watch her from the car, but my mother didn't raise a jerk and she'd kill me if she knew I didn't walk a lady to her door. Date or not.

I heard Cat cough inside and chuckled to myself. Did she think she was being stealthy, or was she trying to see if we were *both* going to be going inside? I kissed Lexi on the forehead for the second time that night, and I wished for more, but I didn't want to push her. I wanted her to want me as much as I wanted her. Hopefully that happens sooner rather than later, but her admission that she feels the connection between us reassures me.

Before I know it, I'm driving into my garage and parking the truck. I've driven home on autopilot thinking about Lexi and our accidental drinks tonight. Letting myself into the house, I'm drawn from my thoughts by my phone ringing, and I can't help hoping that its Lexi on the other end, which is why I don't look at the screen before answering.

"Hello." Even I can hear the hopeful tone in my voice.

"Hoping for someone other than me to be calling tonight then were you champ?"

"I have to be honest Brent, I wasn't hoping to hear your voice, that's for sure." I grumble into the phone. "What can I do for you?" I ask him, knowing that my irritation is obvious.

"I was just checking in to see how it went tonight?" He says, trying to sound innocent, but most things Brent does are far from innocent.

"What do you mean?" I ask, suspicious of his question.

"Geeeez Gabe stop being so suspicious, I seriously want to know how you went with your mystery girl. She seems really nice and her friend Lacey, is a real firecracker."

"I hope you were nice to Lacey?" I ask him.

"Of course I was. Damn Gabe, what do you think I am? I know I've been a bit of a player in the past, but that's exactly what it is, in the past. I've got Sophie now and there's no way in hell I'm going to do anything to stuff that up. She's it for me man, and I was hoping that your date with Lexi went well. Lacey and I had a few drinks, and something to eat together to leave you two kids alone, and this is the thanks I get?"

"It wasn't a date." I say.

"OK. We kept our distance so you two lovebirds could enjoy your no-date, date. Next time I'll sit there and interrupt your non-date, date, arsehole." He huffs in my ear, and now I feel like the arsehole he's accused me of being.

"You're right. I'm sorry. I guess I'm just a little on edge." I explain and apologise at the same time. "I *was* hoping you were Lexi, because we had a great time tonight. So, thank you for keeping your distance, I really appreciate the effort."

"You're welcome." He replies and I can hear the smirk in his voice I know him too well. "Now, I'm going to assume you didn't get lucky seeing as you're home so early, but did you get another date, or non-date out of Lexi?"

"I'm not going to sleep with her on what wasn't even a date Brent. Geezus, but yes, we're going out for dinner again soon. It's not exactly a date though. We're going out as friends, and before you put your five cents worth in, her ex did a real number on her and she wants to take things slow. I mean, she only broke up with him a few weeks ago Brent, she needs some time and I'm willing to give it to her."

"OK, as long as you're both on the same page then I guess you've got it sorted." He's quiet for a few seconds and I know he has something else to say so I keep quiet. "I'm glad you got another chance with her man, she seems like a nice girl. One who is good enough for you."

I wasn't expecting *that*! "Thanks man, I appreciate that. Now get lost so I can have a shower before I go to bed."

"So you can dream about a certain brunette, hmmmm?" He laughs.

"Fuck off Brent." That just makes him laugh harder. He knows he's hit the nail right on the head, and he thinks he's hilarious, so I hang up before he can say anything else.

I take off my suit jacket and tie, then hang them over the back of the chair in my room, I start unbuttoning my shirt when my phone chimes with a message. I pick it up and chuckle.

Brent: *dude that was rude just hanging up on me like that!*

Gabe: *I didn't want to give you a chance to say anything else. Goodnight.*

I chuck my phone on my pillow and continue taking my shirt off, then I sit down on the edge of the bed and start on my shoes, but when my phone starts ringing again, I consider not answering it. I look at the screen to see if it's Brent again, because I'm not talking to him again tonight, but it could be about business or my Dad. Which would mean business, but it's neither of them.

My heart starts pounding my chest as I answer the phone, "Hi." Is all I say. My voice is rough and husky.

"I found the note." Lexi says quietly. "Thank you for looking after us. Looking after me."

"It was my absolute pleasure Lexi." I say, and I can't help the grin that spreads across my face. She looked for my note and then she called me. Which means she was thinking about me too. I put the phone on speaker so I can finish taking off my shoes and socks, and without thinking, I drop my pants to the floor, the belt making a loud clattering sound as it hits the wooden floors.

"Wh-what are you doing?" She stutters out, and that's when I realise I've been stripping off while she's on the other end of the phone. Now I need to make a choice, do I lie and make something up, or do I tell her the truth? "Are you-are you getting changed?" She stutters again. I think I like making Miss Stratton a little nervous.

"I was just about to get in the shower when you called." I say, picking up the phone to take her off speaker, and bring it to my ear.

"Are you." She coughs and then starts again in a husky whisper. "Are you, naked, Gabe?" I hear a door close somewhere behind her and wonder if she's in her bedroom now too.

"Would you like that Lexi?" I ask, my voice not much better than hers.

"Holy shit, this isn't how I thought this phone call would go."

"But are you glad it's going this way, or is this against your rules?" I ask wanting to push her to see what I can and can't get away with here.

"My rules don't cover you being naked on the phone, Gabe."

"I'm not, yet, but I can be in a few short seconds sweetheart, if that's what you want."

"Yes." Just one word. Breathed in my ear, and I can imagine her hot breath on me.

"Yes what, sweetheart?" I ask, wanting, needing her to admit she wants this.

"God yes! That's what I want Gabe." She says in a rush, like if she doesn't say it all at once, she's going to back out of saying it at all. Or maybe she's just really eager to get me naked, and that gives me chills.

"What do you want sweetheart?" I need her to spell this one out for me.

"Are you really going to make me say it out loud?" She groans.

"Mmhmm. I am yes. You drew the line in the sand earlier tonight Lexi, and I *really* need you to tell me what you want. What you need from me." I'm not going to beg her, but I need to hear it.

"I want you naked Gabe." She says, and this time her voice is louder, more sure but still husky with need, and it sends a shiver down my spine.

"You got it sweetheart." I put my phone on speaker again and toss it on the bed. Within seconds, my boxer briefs join my pants on the floor. "Now, where do you want me?"

"You were going to have a shower before I rang, right?"

"That's right."

"Were you just going to have a quick shower and then go to bed?"

"I don't know how long it was going to be, but I was considering having a cold shower because this gorgeous brunette I know had me all worked up, and I needed something to cool me down." I reply, then I decide to push her a little bit further. "But I would probably have ended up touching myself anyway, I hate cold showers."

"What would you have thought of, you know, while you were touching yourself?"

"You. I would have been thinking about you."

"And if you get in that steamy shower now, would you be thinking about me?"

"God yes!" I close my eyes, seeing what she looked like tonight and wishing she was here with me.

"Are you touching yourself now?"

"No, not yet."

"Yet? Mmmhmm. Can I listen to you?" She asks, her voice rough with need.

"You want to listen to me have a shower and masturbate Lexi?"

"God yes. Please Gabriel?" I don't let anyone call me Gabriel, but coming from Lexi's lips, I can't resist.

"You don't want to see me, just listen?" I ask, picking up my phone and walking to the bathroom. I turn on my shower and let the water heat up. It's about to get really steamy in here.

"I just want to hear you. If you don't mind?" One baby step at a time I guess, and I don't mind at all.

"Whatever you want sweetheart."

Lucky for me, when I rebuilt this bathroom, I made the shower big enough for two people, complete with two shower heads, which means I can have my phone close enough that we can hear each other, but it won't get wet.

"It's really steamy in here Lexi, what do you want me to do?" I ask, not knowing how receptive she'll be to giving me directions on what she wants from this.

"What were you thinking about when you were getting ready to get in the shower before I called? Tell me what you were going to think about to get yourself off, Gabriel."

There she goes again, using my full name. "Say it again."

"What part?"

"My name. My full name, sweetheart." I say on a groan, my hand is already soaped up and around my cock.

"Gabriel." She says it with a question in her voice, and it still makes my cock harder than it already was.

"Yes." I hiss out between my teeth.

"OK Gabriel, tell me everything you were going to use to get yourself off tonight." She says, without hesitation in her voice at all this time, and it gets my blood hot.

"As I undressed I was thinking about how gorgeous you looked tonight. How I wanted to strip you out of that silky shirt and that tight skirt you were wearing and drink you in. I knew you'd be wearing some blood boiling, sexy lace underwear under all those clothes, and I would have taken seconds, no minutes, to drink you all in. Heels and all. Did you have lacy underwear on tonight Lexi?" My breathing is laboured.

"Yes, I had lace and silk underwear on today, Gabriel." She breathes into my ear.

"Fuck." I hiss out. "What colour were they Lexi?"

"What colour do you want them to be?" She asks, but that's not the game I want to play tonight.

"Tell me Lexi. Tell me what colour underwear you had on tonight. Tell me now."

"Blue. Sky blue." Lexi says on a moan.

"Are you in only your underwear now Lexi?"

"God yes, I'm too hot to have clothes on." She pants out.

"Me too sweetheart, me too." I soap up my hand again and continue rubbing up and down my cock, I use my other hand to play with my balls. "Oh god. I can see you Lexi. Lying on your bed, legs spread, and your hand down your underwear. Is that what you're doing Lexi? Is it?"

"Ohhh god yes. Gabriel. Oh. My." Her voice is barely a whisper.

I can hear her breathing heavily into the phone and my mind goes crazy. I can see her, picture that beauty spread out on her bed, legs spread, her fingers pumping in and out of her pussy. Her finger pressing on her clit, sending bolts of pleasure through her body. That image does me in and my hand pumps my cock faster. I brace my other hand on the wall of the shower, holding myself up because I can feel my knees starting to buckle, as I feel the familiar tingle starting at the base of my spine. "Come for me sweetheart, I need to hear you come before I do, and I need to hear it now."

"Ohhh Gabe. Gabriel. I'm going to come. Oh. My." Lexi's panting and I think she may have lost the ability to speak. I know I'm pretty close to that point myself. "Gabriel!" She screams out, her voice raspy and raw.

"Alexis." I croak out, my own voice not much better than hers, coming into my hand and all over the shower floor. "Holy shit! That was ..." I can't finish my sentence, but Lexi does it for me.

"Hot. That was fucking hot Gabe." She says, her breathing returning back to normal much faster than mine.

"Don't hang up." I say, more urgently that I really wanted to sound. "Let me clean up and then we can spoon. Metaphorically so to speak."

"Yes." She answers me, quietly. Damn I really hope she doesn't regret what we just did, because that was the hottest thing I've ever done. Not wanting to waste any time, or give her a reason to disappear on me, I wash off quickly and turn off the shower. I grab a towel, rub it over my body quickly and then wrap it around my waist.

"Are you still there?" I ask, I can see that she hasn't hung up, but I don't know if she's still listening.

"Yes, I'm here Gabe." She says, softly.

"That was the hottest thing I've ever done Lexi, and I mean ever. I've never had someone listen to me come like that."

"I've never had phone sex before Gabe. It was hot and I'm glad you're the one who popped my cherry, so to speak." We both laugh at her joke and the tension melts away.

We spend almost another hour on the phone just talking. About everything and about nothing, until I hear her yawn and know it's time to hang up the phone.

"I'll call you tomorrow and we can set a date for our dinner, what do you say Lexi?"

"I think we can call it a date now, don't you Gabe?"

"We can call it whatever you want Lexi, as long you agree to come out with me." I smile into the phone, happy that she wants to call dinner a date now.

"Well, I'm calling it a date." She says followed by another yawn. "I'm also calling it a night before I fall asleep on you and embarrass myself by snoring." She says with a laugh.

"I'm sure it's the cutest snore I've ever heard Lexi." She snorts and I don't think she realised she did it and I laugh quietly. "I'll call you tomorrow to pencil in our date. Goodnight sweetheart, sleep well."

"Night Gabriel. Sleep well." She says, so quietly I almost miss it, and then the phone is dead.

Well that's not how I saw tonight ending up, but I can't say I'm disappointed. Not at all. I got a date with Alexis Stratton and I'm holding her to it.

Chapter Thirteen

LEXI

Never in my wildest dreams did I think I would be having phone sex with Gabriel Romanetti tonight, but when the opportunity came up, pun intended, I wasn't going to say no. I'm not crazy!

I was already in my bedroom when I called him, because I found the note he left for me weeks ago under my bed, and I wanted to call him straight away to let him know. If I'd thought for one second that I'd catch him naked, or even half naked, I might have reconsidered making that call. Ahhh shit who am I kidding? I would have called faster!

When he offers to get naked for me, I almost swallow my damned tongue. Would any woman refuse that offer? I don't fucking think so. When he offers to let me listen in while he touches himself in the shower, yeah definitely not going to knock that one back. I know I said I wanted to take this thing slow with him, but it's not like we're touching or anything like that. Right?

Then he starts demanding I tell him what I want. What I want him to do to himself. What I want to hear him do to himself and holy hell! Telling him to jerk himself off while thinking about me, lying on my bed in only my underwear, was as hot as hell.

It was *so* easy to lay back on my bed and imagine him stroking his cock to an orgasm. Did he come in his hand? Or did he come all over the floor and walls of the shower? I know I could have asked him, but I like imagining what he may or may not have done. I was glad I was lying down when my own orgasm hit me, because I don't think my legs would have held me up. I've never had phone sex before and let me just say I didn't know what I'd been missing out on.

We talked afterwards for I don't know how long, I didn't count because I had better things to do. Like get to know Gabriel Romanetti, but after a while I couldn't keep my eyes open, and I knew I was struggling to answer him.

After my latest yawning interrupts Gabe speaking, he says, "I'll call you tomorrow and we can set a date for our dinner, what do you say Lexi?"

"I think we can call it a date now, don't you Gabe?" I reply quietly, not really sure what his response will be.

"We can call it whatever you want Lexi, as long as you agree to come out with me." I can hear his happiness through the phone.

"Well, I'm calling it a date." I say followed by another yawn. "I'm also calling it a night before I fall asleep on you and embarrass myself by snoring." I say laughing.

"I'm sure it's the cutest snore I've ever heard Lexi." I laugh quietly. "I'll call you tomorrow to pencil in our date. Goodnight sweetheart, sleep well." He says.

"Night Gabriel. Sleep well." At least I hope that I said it out loud enough for him to hear me, and then I hang up the phone. I can barely keep my eyes open, so holding my phone up is near impossible. My hand falls down onto the pillow next to me and knowing that my phone is safe I leave it where it lands and fall into a wonderful sleep, filled with dreams of a sexy man stroking his cock until he comes.

I wake up the next morning from the best sleep I've had in years, with a smile on my face and Catherine sitting on the edge of my bed, smiling and waiting for me to wake up. A normal person would jump and be freaked out finding someone just sitting on their bed staring at them, but I'm used to seeing my sister the second I wake up. It started happening when we were very young, and she's never stopped doing it.

"When did you say you were moving out again?" I ask, but there's no anger in my voice. "Surely Joshua would prefer you sitting in *his* bed rather than mine?"

"*Joshua* is fine with wherever I am Lexi." Cat smiles at me and then asks, with a smirk across her face, "How was your phone sex with Mr Romanetti last night? It sounded like he knows what he's doing. I hope it translates into great sex when you're in the same room sis."

She heard me? I thought she was asleep when I went to bed last night. Not to mention I had my bedroom door shut. That, I realise, is how she knows I was up to something private, because my bedroom door is always open. She had to open my door to come in here and annoy me.

"So, you're leaving soon. Right? Do I need to have a serious talk with Joshua?" I ask, only half joking. I really cannot wait to have my house back. The privacy of being home alone is something I will *never* take for granted again. Ever!

"No you don't need to talk to Joshua and don't think I don't know that you didn't answer my question." Cat smiles at me in a knowing fashion that I just don't appreciate. "I'll let you get away with it, but I still want to know how your dinner date went."

"It wasn't a dinner date Cat. How many times do I have to tell you that? Lacey and I went to the bar for some drinks and they were there. Gabe and his buddy Brent. I didn't know they were there and neither did Lacey." I shake my head, but the first seeds of doubt are moving in. *Did* Lacey somehow *know* that the guys were going to be there last night? Did she set this all up? No, she couldn't have because she had no way of knowing. She didn't know either of them well enough, or at all, to be able to set that up. "We bumped into Gabe and his friend, and I took the opportunity to apologise for being a neurotic idiot the last time we quite literally bumped into each other, then we sat together and talked and had some snacks."

"Where were Lacey and his friend? Brent was it?" Cat asks me.

"They were at the bar. Talking and having a couple of drinks themselves." I look at Cat's face and I know that look. She's telling me that she *knows* I think I didn't *have* a date, but I *did* really end up having a date, as she raises her eyebrow in question at me. I *know* that it turned into a date, but it wasn't an intentional date.

"And who bought you home last night Lexi?" Her eyebrow is still raised, and there's a smirk on her lips as well now. I could really do with having my house back right about now. Then I wouldn't be getting the third degree this morning.

"You already know that Gabe did, because Lacey left to go home and we weren't finished our drinks yet, so we decided to stay a little while longer. At Lacey's suggestion." Ohhh now *that* one she planned, sneaky bitch.

"And if I hadn't had a coughing fit at the wrong time, would he have kissed you goodnight? Would you have let him?"

"I don't know." But of course I know the answer. Hell yes I would have let that man kiss me. I would have let him do a hell of a lot more than *that* to me last night, and in a way he did. I can feel my cheeks heat as I think about what we got up to last night.

"You *do* so know, and the answer is a hell yes and we both know it! Why can't you just admit that you like this guy? This man?" She asks me. "Because he is *all* man honey and we both know it!"

"I don't know Cat." I say quietly, even though I *do* know what's holding me back. "Isn't it too soon Cat?" I ask my sister quietly, because I'm kind of scared of her answer. If she agrees that it's too soon after jerkface to move on, then I'll know I have to put the brakes on, and I have to be honest, as much as I told Gabe last night that I want to be friends first and take it slow, I'm not sure I can with him. I'm completely and inexplicably drawn to him. He's smart, he's sexy, he's charming but not in a sleazy way, and he's kind.

"What do you mean too soon?" She asks me, looking totally baffled by my mumbled question. Then her eyebrows raise, and her eyes widen as she understands my meaning. "You mean after dickface?" I nod my answer. "Now you listen to me Alexis, and you listen good cause I'm only going to say this once, OK?" I nod my head again and indicate for her to continue. "You. Did. Nothing. Wrong. You weren't happy with that idiot for a while and he wasn't happy with you, ever! Yes, before you ask me and I know you're surprised by that little revelation, but he wasn't Lexi and you know how I could tell? He never said anything nice to you or about you. He never complimented you in any way, shape, sense or form. He. Was. An. Arsehole. And he was an 'A' grade one at that. So, in answer to your question, no I don't think it's too soon to move on. You weren't invested in that relationship, so there's nothing for you to mourn or get over. Simple."

She's right. He was rarely kind to me and often his compliments were thinly disguised insults. Things like, my dress was pretty, but it would have looked better in a different colour. Or those shoes were really nice, but

I should have gotten smaller heels, because I was likely to break a leg with those ones. Nothing was ever said without a little dig in there as well. "You're right. He was nasty and I don't know why I stayed with him as long as I did, except that it was just convenient, and I didn't want look like a loser being single."

"You're not a loser single or as part of an amazing couple Lexi. You're beautiful, smart and amazing and dickface could never see that. Or maybe he did, and he was jealous and tried to bring you down at every opportunity he had? Who knows, but you know what? Who the hell cares? He did you a favour breaking up with you. Granted he could have done it almost anywhere else, but hey, he did it."

"You're right." I say, then realise I just agreed how amazing I am and correct myself. "I mean that he's a jerk and I'm better off without him, not all that other stuff."

"Believe all that other stuff as well sister of mine." She says with a smile, then smacks my shoulder and says, "Now, go have a shower. I'm going to make us some breakfast, then we can talk some more about last night." She winks, and before I can answer her and tell her there *is* nothing else to talk about, she's gone.

I decide that having a shower is a good idea and hop in there and quickly get the job done. Getting in my shower, reminds me of what Gabe did in *his* shower last night and a smile spreads across my face. It's so big I swear I look like a crazy woman and I thank every deity I can that I remembered to lock the door this morning.

After drying myself I walk into my bedroom with my towel wrapped around me, because you know, not alone in my own house. Yet. I can hear my phone ringing, but its muffled and I have to search for it. I finally find it half under the pillow, and half under the covers. Just before I pick it up, it stops ringing, so I look at the phone log to see who it was and whether I want to call them back right or not.

It was Gabe. I throw on some clothes, because I really don't want a repeat of last night, well not with my sister definitely within earshot anyway. Then I call him back.

"Good morning Alexis." He says as an answer when he picks up the phone. His voice is deep, voice that is still husky from sleep. He's barely awake and he's calling me?

"Good morning Gabriel. Sorry, I just got out of the shower."

"The shower? Really? Are we starting today like we ended last night sweetheart?" His voice gets even deeper and rougher at the thought.

"Ummm no. As much as I might like to start the day off with a bang, my sister is very much awake and no doubt trying to listen to every word right now." I strain my ears to listen, but all I can hear is banging around in my kitchen. "How are you this morning?"

"I'm very good, thank you for asking. How are you this very fine morning Lexi?" Damn, the way he says my name in his husky voice, sends thrills down my spine. How can just his voice do that to me?

"I'm quite damned good myself this morning Gabe. Thanks for asking." He bursts out laughing. "What?" I ask, laughing quietly myself.

"I was just thinking, after what we did last night, and I know there wasn't any actual touching, but it was still damned hot, we've turned into very polite friends."

"Is that what you want? To be polite friends?" I know I shouldn't ask. I know what he wants. Well, I think I know what he wants, and I already told him I want to go slow, so I shouldn't push him like this. It's simply not fair, but the question was out before I could stop myself.

"No Lexi, that is as far from what I want as you can get, but I am going to respect your wishes. Until you tell me otherwise anyway." Was I stupid for putting the brakes on with him last night? I didn't think so then but maybe I was just afraid of all the feelings and the electricity bouncing around us. I know he feels it too. No, I wasn't stupid, I'm allowed to do this at a pace that I'm comfortable with, but if this date goes as well as I think it will, all bets are off. He takes my silence as my answer and continues talking. "I want to see you today, please? I have to go see my father this morning, otherwise I'd be bringing you breakfast. I don't know how long he'll want to talk. Honestly, I could be there for hours, or I could be there for half an hour at most. Can I see you this afternoon? If you don't have any other plans that is, and you can be bothered to wait for me to be done."

"I don't have anything planned that I can think of right now." I say, but before I can say anything else, he cuts in.

"This isn't our first official date either. I want to make that perfectly clear. I want to see you. Let's just call it hanging out together and setting up that date."

"So, it's *not* a date?" I ask, and even I can hear the obvious disappointment in my voice.

"It can be a date if you want it to be Lexi, absolutely." He says, his voice has gone even lower. It sounds full of need to my ears. Maybe I'm just a horny bitch after last night. "But I still get to take you *out* on our first real date. You know, where I get to take you out for a nice meal, in a nice restaurant. I want to show you off to anyone who wants to look, because I know they'll all wish they were me, but they don't get you, I do."

"I'm not just a piece of arm candy you know Gabriel." I say, the heat of anger lacing my voice. How dare he think that I'm just something to show off, and here I thought he was one of the nice guys.

"That's not what I meant Lexi, and I'm sorry it sounded that way. I meant that I get to show people just how special you are, and how much of a lucky bastard I am to have you on my arm."

"I'm not a trophy Gabe and I won't be treated like one." I huff out, still a little annoyed.

"I know and I'm sorry, again. It wasn't my intention for you to take it that way." He sighs, and I can imagine him rubbing his hand over his face in frustration. "I just feel like the luckiest bastard on the planet that you said yes to anything, but specially a date."

"Yes." I say.

"Yes, what?" He asks, confused.

"Yes you can call me when you're done with whatever your father wants, and I'll tell you whether I'm available or not. I don't have anything planned, but who knows what might come up." I say, trying to sound like I'm not going to be sitting around waiting for him to call me. He needs to know I have a life too, and I'm not going to just drop what I'm doing because he calls. Been there, done that, not ever doing it again.

"OK." He says, taking a breath and I think he sighs with relief at my answer. "I'll call you when I'm done and if you're busy, hopefully it's something I can join you in. I'll call you as soon as I can."

"OK Gabe. Talk to you later."

"Talk later sweetheart." I hang up the phone after we say goodbye and sit on the edge of my bed for a minute. That didn't go like I hoped it would, but it is what it is.

I get up and walk out to the kitchen to find Lacey sitting at the table, coffee in hand and Cat dishing up scrambled eggs, bacon and some toast.

"Good morning Lacey, I didn't know you were joining us for breakfast." I say, the sarcasm hopefully dripping off my tongue.

"No I didn't tell you I was coming over, but I wanted to hear about last night, so I thought I'd just show up. Luckily for me Cat here was cooking up a hot breakfast."

"Yes, lucky you." I mumble.

"I think last night ended very well for all concerned." My sister tells my best friend with a smirk. "Well, not so much for me to be honest. I don't really want to hear my sister screaming out a man's name as she comes, but hey, it is what it is I guess."

"Move out then." I say, with a smile I don't mean.

"You mean to tell me you bought him home last night and did the horizontal tango?" Lacey screeches, jumping up to grab my shoulders and shaking them quite violently.

"No I did not bring Gabe home, and do anything mambo or tango with him. Horizontally or vertically. Geeeez Lacey." Cat raises her eyebrow at me in question again and Lacey chokes on her shocked laughter. "Let's just say that last night didn't end up like I thought it would but, I *can say* I'm not disappointed in the slightest in what *did* happen and leave it at that shall we?" I'm not disappointed at all. I've got a date with Gabriel Romanetti and I can't wait.

Chapter Fourteen

GABE

I wish I could put this meeting with my father off, but since my mother passed away, I can't bring myself to cancel on him too often. So, when Vincent Romanetti asks me for a meeting I don't say no. Business doesn't always come first with Vince, but if I show any signs of not being totally interested this morning, he will pick up on it, and I'm not sure if I'm ready to share Lexi with my dad just yet. I'm not sure there's that much to share to be honest. It's days like today though that I really wish my sister had decided to join me in the family business, because then maybe I could have gotten her to come today instead of me. Who am I kidding, I would have come anyway just to see my dad.

I pull into the winding driveway of my parent's estate, and yes, that's exactly what it is. The house is a sprawling white brick double storey grand design, and by house I mean mansion. There's more than enough rooms for our family and friends to stay in and the staff have their own quarters too.

I pull my truck, that my mum hated and called 'my rebellion', into the garage that is bigger than most people's homes. If I leave it out in the driveway, even though it can't be seen from the road at all, Maria the house manager will have a fit. She seems to think my well maintained truck will leak oil all over the pristine driveway and cause her staff more work. So, into the garage we go.

"Good morning Gabriel. Can I take your jacket?"

"Good morning Edward. Thank you, but don't go hiding it, I'm hoping to make this a quick trip." Edward has been my family's butler for as long as I can remember, yes we have a butler, a housekeeper and a cook OK? Maria thinks she's the house manager but really it's Edward, he just doesn't have the need for the title.

"Of course Gabriel, I'll keep it on hand for a quick exit." He replies with a grin. He knows that I love my father, so something or someone must be making me want to get out earlier than usual.

"Gabriel, stop harassing Edward and come say hello." My dad bellows, and I catch Edward rolling his eyes.

"You're never harassing me Gabriel, it's always a pleasure to see you." He says loud enough that my dad hears him, all while still smiling at me. My dad laughs loudly when Edward walks off without so much as a backwards glance at him.

"Thank you Edward." I return his smile as he walks away, then I walk towards my dad.

"Good morning Dad." I say, giving him a hug. We step back from the embrace and he shakes my hand vigorously like he hasn't seen me in months rather than a few days and he's very happy to finally see me. I have no doubt he's happy to see me, but this is just my dad, happy to greet everyone like he's greeting his oldest friend.

"Good morning Gabriel, how are you son?" He asks, and not because it's the polite thing to do, but because he is truly interested.

"I'm great dad." I answer him with a smile "How have you been?" I ask him, knowing that we only spoke on the phone yesterday to confirm me coming over this morning. Like we do every week.

"Yes I'm well thank you Gabriel." My dad answers using my full name. He very rarely calls me Gabe, even though I've asked him to a million times since I was a teenager, but that's what my parents agreed to call me and so that's what he calls me. I've heard him slip in a Gabe much more often since my mum died, and I think it's because she never called us anything but our full names. He was Vincent, not Vince or Vinnie as some of his friends call him. I was always Gabriel and my sister Susanna. Names were never cut short, which is why I have everyone else call me Gabe.

From behind my dad I hear the house manager, Maria say, "Did you need anything from me Vincent? Do you want drinks or something to eat before you start?"

Barefoot and Dumped!

My dad turns to face her, and says, "Thank you Maria, but I'm all set for now." She gives him a swift nod and then turns to me.

"Good morning Gabriel, how are you?"

"Good morning Maria, I'm good, how are you today?"

"I'm very well thank you." Maria has managed the house for years. While my mum was alive they did it together and rarely had a disagreement. Since my mum's been gone, Maria has tried to step into her shoes in more ways than one, but my dad politely misunderstands her intentions every time. Why Maria stays and why my dad continues to employ her I have no idea, but they work well together the rest of the time.

She turns from me back to dad and says, "Well, if you two don't need anything from me Vincent, I'll leave you and Gabriel to talk business."

"We'll be in my study." They smile at each other, "Come into my office and let's talk." He says to me and we walk into his study. "Shut the door behind you." He says, but I'm already doing just that. God forbid that anyone might hear what we're talking about. Which is nothing really. Anyone would think we're trading in state secrets, not the running of the family business.

"Anyone would think we're trading state secrets, you're so concerned about privacy." I laugh. It's an old joke, but we both still laugh at it.

He stops laughing and gets a serious look on his face that means he's thinking about the past. "You know, your mum hated it when we disappeared in here on the weekends to talk about business, so I always closed the door, that way she at least couldn't hear the business talk. I'm not sure if she appreciated that or not, but it's become a habit that I can't seem to let go." He explains unnecessarily.

"I know Dad." We're both quiet for a few minutes, lost in our own thoughts. My mind wanders past my parents and straight to a certain brunette I can't wait to see later today.

"Did you hear a word I just said Gabriel? Are you OK son?" He has both concern and frustration in his voice.

"Sorry Dad, I blanked for a minute there, it won't happen again." I smile at him. It won't, I want to finish up here as early as I can so I can go meet up with Lexi.

"I take it you and Brent were out late again last night then?" He asks, a chuckle in his voice now. "He's a bad influence that one, but I know he's also been a great friend to you over the years, Gabriel. Although I'm not sure he has your best interests in mind when he takes you out on the town so often." I'm not going to correct him because he's right on both accounts. Brent is both a bad influence and a great friend, and he won't mind either of us saying so.

"He's just trying to get me to relax more often Dad." I smile, I can't wait to tell him that Brent's been tamed. " I doubt there will be too many more late nights anyway, he's got himself a girlfriend and she does not let him get away with any of his Brent like behaviour. It's amazing to watch. I really like her."

My dad lets out a loud laugh, "Ohh I can't wait to meet her then and see her in action." Then he sobers and asks me the inevitable question. "And what about you? Any new ladies on the horizon for you?"

"Don't say it Dad, she's history." I sigh. "There is someone that I'm getting to know, but it's early days yet, so don't get too excited, OK?" I almost beg him.

"OK Gabe, but I'll keep my fingers crossed that this young lady can bring some happiness back into your life. You need it son." He says and suddenly the air in the room seems too heavy.

"Thanks old man, but I'm here now, so let's get on with business." That way I can go see where this thing with the sexiest woman I know can lead to.

Getting down to business is exactly what we do for the next two hours. Two fucking hours, going through all the happenings within the business in the last week. These meetings are something we have every week, come rain or shine. I get that technically he's still running the business, even if he does rarely spend any time *in* the business, his name is still attached to it. I also understand that he's earned that right after working his arse off to make it a success, but that doesn't mean he needs to have a toe in every damned pie still. He's supposed to be letting *me* make the decisions, I knew it was too good to be true when he announced his 'semi-retirement'. I want him to enjoy his retirement and relax, not worry about every little detail of the business. Then again, I'm sure he'd planned on spending this time with his wife and now she's no longer here. The minute I think *that* I feel like an arse for being annoyed about his involvement in the company still.

He sighs and takes a large gulp of his coffee. I don't want to rush him, but for the first time in a while, I have a reason to get out of here.

"Is that everything?" I ask, apparently a little too eager.

"Am I keeping you from something Gabriel?" He asks me, even though I can see by the twinkle in his eyes that he thinks he knows the answer.

"Not at all Dad. I was checking to see if there was anything else you wanted to discuss today." I say, a smile plastered to my face.

"Go get her son." The shock must register on my face because he lets out a hearty laugh. "I may be an old man son, but I know when a fella has a lady he wants to go see. I can see it on your face." He looks down into his mug of coffee and his smile slips a little, and I don't know what to say to him to make him smile again. "If she makes you feel like that Gabe, if you can't wait to see her again, go after her and don't let her go. I did that with your mother once. Did you know that?" I shake my head no, not wanting to speak and break the spell. I haven't heard this story before, and I want to. "The worst decision I ever made let me tell you." He says with soft contempt for his own stupidity.

"You won her back though, obviously. Otherwise Susanna and I wouldn't be here." I say with my own soft chuckle, trying to lighten the mood a little.

"This is very true son, but there was a time there that I didn't think I could ever win her back." He shakes his head again in dismay. "We went out on a few dates and things were going well. Too well for me apparently and I decided she was too much of a distraction from my work. I'd just started at the company and I knew it was just the step up I needed to get to where I am today. I didn't want to let a woman, or love get in the way and I told her as much." He takes a sip of his coffee and smiles slightly. "Ohhhhh you should have seen Rosanna. She told me that I was a selfish so and so and if that was how I felt I could get stuffed, she didn't want to be with me any way and another fella had asked her out. She'd said no because of me, but she wasn't going to say no anymore. That was that. I walked away." He takes another sip of his coffee and I can almost see the memories playing across his face. "That is until I saw her with one of the 'other fellas' at the local café one day and I just saw red. I went storming over to their table and asked her what the hell she thought she was doing. I had no right son, no right at all to ask her. We hadn't seen each other in two weeks. Your mother looked me square in the eyes and said, 'how dare you come storming in here and ask me what I'm doing. You gave up any rights you had to ask that question when you told me I was a distraction and no good for you. Barry here doesn't think I'm bad for him, do you Barry?' Oh son, let me tell you, I've never been so angry in all my life. There was no way Barry Winklestein was getting my damned woman, even if she wasn't technically mine anymore. So you know what I did?" He looks at me, a sparkle of mischief in his eyes for the first time in years.

"What did you do Dad? It must have been brilliant because you obviously won her over to your way of thinking." I say laughing.

"I walked so close to her that our noses were almost touching, looked her squarely in the eyes and said, 'Rosanna Rees you won't see another man other than me, and do you want to know why?' She simply nodded at me. I like to think that I'd taken her breath away by being so close to her, but I think she was just so shocked that I had confronted her to start with that she didn't know how else to react."

"Did you tell her why she wasn't going to see any other men?" I had a feeling I knew where this was going, but I wanted to hear my dad finish his story. It bought a little life back into him.

"I did. I told her that no other man could ever love her like I did, and that one day I would make her my wife and we'd have a family together." This time he laughs obnoxiously loud and I love seeing him like this. "Then, without warning, I pulled her to me and kissed the hell out of her. Poor Barry, he never saw it coming, or maybe he did, I don't really care honestly. From that day forward, your mother was mine. I was never as stupid to think I could live without her again." He sucks in a jagged breath as he realises that he has to live life without his wife now. When he turns in his chair to look at me, I see the tears shining in his eyes. "What I'm trying to say son is, if you like this woman as much as I think you do, don't let the past hinder your future. She's not the same woman as the last one, and she has given you your spark back. A spark I haven't seen in too long. So, go for it. Don't let her get away if she's the one you see yourself spending the rest of your life with, because let's be honest Gabe, even while you were with the crazy one, you knew she wasn't forever. I could see it in your eyes, and you look so much happier now."

"I've only known her a few weeks Dad. I have no idea what the hell is happening between us, but I'd like for it to be something that's for sure." I can't help the smile from spreading across my face. Just thinking about Lexi and seeing her again makes me a happy man.

"Then I look forward to meeting her, because any woman who can make my favourite son smile like that, is a winner in my book." He says, waving a hand in the general direction of my face.

Before I can say anything else, there's a light knock on the door, and Maria walks in without waiting for an invitation. My dad looks her way waiting for her to speak.

'Haven't you two been in here long enough?" She teases. "Vincent Romanetti haven't you kept Gabriel long enough? Let the boy go and have some fun, it is the weekend after all." She smiles at me and I'm certain these two have plans that they don't want me around for and I don't want to know about them. At all. Susanna and I have long suspected that they have a relationship that isn't strictly employee/employer but neither of us want to ask. Honestly, I'd rather live in denial. I'm happy if my dad's happy.

"OK, I'll leave you two to your plans. Enjoy the rest of your weekend." I say, standing up from my chair at my father's desk.

"Your father is having a few guests for dinner Gabriel and I'm helping him get it organised. It is my job after all." Out of the corner of my eye, I see my dad laugh at her protests, and Maria jabs him with her elbow. Yup, there's definitely something going on there, but as long as they're both happy, it's none of my business.

"I never said anything different Maria." I walk over to her and kiss her on the cheek. The surprise on her face was worth the effort to plant a kiss on her.

"What on earth was that for Gabriel?" She asks, her shock evident in her voice and I can't help chuckling at her reaction, especially as she rests her hand where my lips just were.

"Just for being you Maria, isn't that enough?" I reach over and pull her into a hug and say quietly in her ear, "And for looking after my Dad. Thank you."

When I pull back she's blushing and sputtering.

"Yes. Well on that note I best get back to the kitchen and make sure everything is going to plan."

"Knowing how well you organise things Maria, I'm sure there's been nothing left to chance." My dad smiles warmly at her, and she blushes. *That* would be my queue to leave them to whatever they've got planned for the evening.

"OK, well I'm going to head out, enjoy your night." I say, giving my dad a hug and then I give Maria another quick one too.

"Gabriel." My dad calls out just as I reach for the door to the garage, and I turn to look at him. "Don't forget what I said son. If she's worth it, let her know how you feel."

"Thanks Dad, I think I will. See you soon." As I open the door Edward hands me my jacket. My dad and I haven't always gotten along, but since my mums passing, we've made a real effort to try. Our relationship is all the better for it too and for that I'm exceptionally grateful.

"Here you are Gabe. Enjoy the rest of your weekend. It appears that you have managed to get out of here rather quickly today." He says with a smile.

"Yes I did. I have a previous appointment to get to and Dad was more than happy to let me go today." I can't help but wonder how much he knows about Dad and Maria, or my own reasons for wanting to get out of here today. It always amazed me when I was a kid just how much Edward knew about what we were up to, even when we thought we were being sneaky.

After a quick goodbye, I get in my truck, open the garage door and back out to drive back down the winding driveway to the gate. As the gate slowly opens, slower than I ever remember it opening previously, I tell my phone to call Lexi. She answers and her voice fills the cabin of my truck and my whole body relaxes.

"Hello Gabe. I didn't think you'd be calling this soon." She says, and I can't tell whether she's pleased or not by the tone of her voice.

"I finished up pretty quickly with my Dad. I'm just driving out the gate and thought I'd call to see what you were up to, and ask if I could maybe join you in, ohhh about ten minutes." I say. I'm trying not to sound too desperate or like I'm begging to spend time with her, but I *really* just want to see her again, and soon.

"I wasn't expecting to see you until our dinner date tonight."

"I didn't realise our date was for tonight Lexi, but I'm not complaining." I say, happy with the prospect of our first real date happening this evening. "That being said though sweetheart, I'd really love to spend some time with you this afternoon. If you're not too busy that is." Please don't be busy, I think to myself.

"Well, I'm actually out shopping." She says, like I won't want to join her.

"OK. Where are you?"

"At the shopping centre near my house." She pauses for a second and then says, "You don't have to come here though, I'm shopping for a dress to wear tonight."

"For our date?" I ask.

"Yes. For our date." She confirms.

"I'll be there soon." I say with a smile.

"Won't that defeat the purpose of you seeing me *in* that dress for the first time tonight when you pick me up?"

"For our first date? I'm more than happy to have some input into what you wear tonight sweetheart. I'll see you soon."

I'm already on the highway before I hang up without giving her another chance to tell me not to join her. It doesn't even occur to me for a second not to go. I want to spend time with her today, and I don't care what we do, just as long as we do it together.

Chapter Fifteen

LEXI

It surprised me when Gabe called. I wasn't expecting him to get in touch so early in the day and I sure as hell wasn't expecting him to want to come shopping with me. I must have looked like a deer in headlights, because Lacey walked me over to a chair in the middle of the centre and made me sit down, and I guess I was shocked because I let her lead me.

"Are you OK Lexi?" Lacey asks me once we're both seated.

"He's going to come here and meet me." I'm staring at my hands resting in my lap and, suddenly I look up to her face and say, "He *wants* to come shopping with me. Who does that?"

"Who does what sweetie? What are you talking about?" When I don't answer her within seconds, she says, "Ummm Lexi, sweetie, you're scaring me now. Who's coming here to meet us?"

"Gabe." I say, taking a shaky breath. "Gabe's coming here. To meet me. Did he not understand that I was shopping?" I ask her and I can hear the panic in my voice. No guy *likes* shopping, right? In fact, all I had to do was mention going shopping, of any kind, and Stephen couldn't leave fast enough. It was the perfect escape, for both of us, in the end of our relationship.

"Sweetie. I heard your end of the conversation and you made it abundantly clear what you were doing." She takes a breath as she takes both of my hands in hers. "Did you ever consider that he just wants to spend some time with you, and he doesn't really care what that means you guys do? He's just happy to be around you."

"No. I honestly hadn't considered that." Is that why he's coming here?

"I'm going to get you a cold drink, I'll be back in a minute." Lacey says, I nod my head and she places my hands back in my lap and I just sit there not moving. Before I know it, Lacey is back with a cold bottle of water and is shoving it in my face.

"Come on Sweetie, have a drink, it'll make you feel better. I promise."

"Oh shut up Lacey." I say, hitting her on the arm and she laughs. "If you don't stop calling me *Sweetie* I'll kill you. *Sweetie!*" Where the hell did that one come from?

"Well, at least I know you're back on earth with me now." She laughs hysterically.

"Is everything OK here?" I feel him before he even speaks. The hairs on my arms stand to attention like their searching out his touch, as he speaks he comes right up behind me and I can feel his body heat on my back. I don't know if I blush because of the heat or because he's standing right there.

"Good afternoon Mr Romanetti, it's nice to see you again." Lacey says, a large smile spread across her face and her hand offered for him to shake.

"Call me Gabe, Lacey." She starts laughing as he takes her hand to gently shake it. "No, really Lacey, just call me Gabe. There's nothing else for you to call me. Please." He's almost begging her, and I watch him as he closes his eyes for a split second.

"But I like saying your last name." She says, smiling broadly.

"Then I'll introduce you to my Dad, but even he'll tell you to call him Vincent."

"I look forward to that, *Gabe*." She grins and he winces. I can't help the giggle that escapes me as I watch them. "Well then, I'm going to get going, and let you two kids have your fun afternoon without me."

"What? No!" I almost screech while jumping to my feet. I know I sound desperate, but she was supposed to help me pick out a dress to wear on my date. My date with the man who is now resting his hand on my lower back. "You're supposed to be helping me pick something out, *Sweetie!*" I ground out, with an emphasis on our new nickname.

Lacey leans over to give me a hug, and whispers in my ear, "You don't need my help now Lex, and I have somewhere to be." She pulls out of our hug and says, "You two kids have fun now, I have an appointment to get to, so I'm going to shoot off. Call me later Lexi." She says with a wink, and her hand making the shape of a phone at her ear. "Enjoy your afternoon, Gabe." She smiles at him and waves, then turns her back to us and walks away, leaving me standing there, dumbfounded and with Gabe's giant hand resting on my lower back.

"Are you OK Lexi?" Gabe asks, leaning down slightly to speak quietly in my ear.

I smile up at him, hoping that I don't look like an absolute freak. "Yes, everything is perfectly fine, Gabe. Why do you ask?"

"Because you seem almost nervous that I'm here. I'm sorry if I ran Lacey off on your girls shopping trip, but I won't apologise for wanting to spend time with you." He takes a step back and the wounded look on his face almost kills me. "But if you don't want me here, I can leave and you can call Lacey, then you can continue with your shopping."

"No!" I reach out and take his hand in mine. "No, Gabe, I don't want you to leave."

"Then what's the problem? Don't say nothing Lexi, because I can see the panic on your face." He says, quietly.

"It's not that I don't want you here, I'm actually really happy to see you and sooner than I expected." I take a breath, I'm not sure how to explain it to him, so I go with blunt honesty and just hope he takes it as I mean it. "The truth is you surprised me by *wanting* to come shopping with me. I'm just not used to guys *wanting* to come shopping. None have ever wanted to before, they've all hated even the idea of shopping, even for food."

"Then they're idiots." He says, passionately. "Look, I'll be honest Lexi, it's not my favourite thing to do, not even close, but I'm an adult and I know we all need food and clothes. For another, any time that I get to spend with you isn't a chore. I enjoy your company and I wanted to spend more time with you, you were shopping and so I'm here now too. It's that simple, honey."

"Really?" I ask.

"Really." He says, resting his hands gently on my shoulders so he can look in my eyes.

"Yes, honestly." I say reaching up to take his hands in mine, holding them between us. "Lacey was helping me choose a dress for our date tonight." I can't look in his eyes, because I'm kind of hoping he doesn't think I'm going overboard and putting too much effort into our date.

"You were thinking about our date?"

"Yeah."

"Let's go find you a dress then, and if you don't want me to see it until tonight, you don't have to show me, but it won't make any difference to me if I see it now or later. You're still the most beautiful woman I know." He leans down and kisses me on the forehead. I don't care what any woman tells you, or what guys think about being an idiot when they show affection, but that move right there? That's the one that makes a woman feel precious to a man. He drops one hand and steps in beside me. "Let's go find you something to wear tonight. Do you have anything in mind?"

"Not really. Lacey told me I needed something new, fresh. Her exact words were, 'something that moron ex hasn't seen you in and that will knock Gabe over when he sees you in it', if you want the truth." I say, laughing.

"I always want the truth Lexi." He smiles at me. There's something new from a guy for me as well, and it's so frustrating that I believe that he's the abnormal one of the bunch.

"Now that's a novel idea too." I mumble.

"Hey Lexi, I don't know what your ex was like, but he sounds like a douchebag from what you've told me, but I'm not him. I want you to understand that. I'm not any of the other guys from your past, I'm just me. I can tell you that I appreciate honesty, kindness and someone who likes me for me. You have no idea how hard it is to meet genuine people who care about who you are. Or maybe you do understand considering how your ex has behaved."

"Open and honest?" I ask him, and he nods his head, yes. "I can do that Gabriel Romanetti ."

"You have no idea what you do to me when you say my name like that, Alexis." He groans in my ear, causing a shiver to run down my spine.

"I think I might. It's probably something like what happens when you say my full name." I reply, closing my eyes thinking that will dull my senses.

"What happens when I say your full name, Alexis Stratton?" He asks as he pulls my back tight into his front. I can feel what reaction he has to me calling him Gabriel, it's poking into my lower back, just above my butt crack, and I can't help the wiggle I do to feel him against me. His hands that *were* just resting on my hips are gripping me tightly to him.

"Don't you dare move yet Alexis." He grounds out between clenched teeth.

"What happens if I move Gabriel?" I ask as innocently as I can. "I really want to look in the shop just over there." I point, stifling my laughter as he growls like a wild animal in my ear.

"If you move, everyone here including that little girl just there, will see *exactly* what you do to me Alexis. Is that what you really want? To scare a young girl with my erection bulging in my pants?" I gulp in surprise, and shake my head no. "Then you better walk in front of me for a few minutes honey." His voice is strained like he's struggling to walk.

We walk passed a couple holding hands and the guy looks at Gabe, nods at him and smiles knowingly. Gabe nods back, and I swear it's like an unspoken bro code of some sort, because the other guy whispers at his girlfriend, and I look over my shoulder because I hear laughter. She's looking back our way, when she catches my eyes, she winks and gives me a thumbs up. I feel the laughter bubble up and I can't control it.

"I'm glad you find this funny Lexi." He says in a disgruntled voice, but when I look over my shoulder at him he's smiling too. "Let's go find you a dress to wear tonight and get out of here, honey."

We spend the next hour and a half searching for a dress and I'm amazed at Gabe's patience. I know when I've found the right dress, because his eyes close, and he curses quietly under his breath when I walk out of the changeroom. I do a twirl and wiggle my butt at him, then walk away to get back into my jeans and top. Just as my hand lands on the doorknob, I feel the heat of his body behind mine.

"Where are you going honey?" Oh my god, his voice is so freaking deep and sexy, I have to put my other hand up on the wall to steady myself.

"I'm going to change into my clothes so I can buy this dress Gabe." I answer him without looking back at him. I don't know what either one of us will do if I look at him right now, and I'd rather not be arrested or kicked out of the store. Especially before I pay for this dress.

"You're wearing this dress tonight? On our first official date?" I don't even know how to describe his voice. It's deep, but kind of a husky whisper, I've never heard anything like it before. I like it. A lot.

"Yep." I answer him, emphasising the pop of the 'p' on the end of the word. "Don't you like it?" I ask, opening the door and stepping inside the changeroom.

"You know damn well I like that dress Alexis." He hasn't moved since I stepped away from him.

"Good." I say with a smile and close the door. "Because I'm buying it to wear tonight, Gabriel."

"Fuck I'm a dead man." He mutters to himself, but I hear him through the door and laugh quietly. It's nice to know I affect him like he does me. Sure does make a girl feel good about her sex appeal.

I get out of the dress, put my own clothes back on and walk over to the register. Gabe is standing there waiting for me, so I smile at him and hand the dress over to the sales assistant. She smiles, wraps it up and packs it in the bag, then hands it to me. When I go to pass over my credit card she shakes her head. "Your husband already paid for the dress, and may I say you've both got great taste."

"My husband?" I ask, turning around to find Gabe standing there looking like the cat that got the cream.

"Yes." She says while giving my 'husband' the once over, in what I can only call a ballsy move. She thinks he's married, yet she's still checking him out right in front of me!

"Thank you." I say, grabbing Gabe's arm, turning him around and walking out of the store before the sales assistant can say or do anything else.

We're almost out of the shopping centre before I realise it, and Gabe is just walking along beside me as if he doesn't have a care in the world. I stop just outside the door, mainly because I realise I've got no way of getting home because I came with Lacey, but also because I'm mad.

"Why did you do that?" I ask, my hands on my hips.

"Do what?" He asks, and honestly he looks confused as to what is going on.

"Buy the dress. *Why did you buy me that dress Gabe?*" That last sentence comes out as one word.

"I bought it because you wanted it, and I wanted to see you in it. I have the money, so I paid for it for you." He explains like it's that simple.

"But I was buying it Gabe. I have money, I don't need your money, I have my own." What does he not understand about that? "I didn't ask or expect you to buy that dress or any other piece of clothing for me Gabe." I say infuriated that he thinks he has to buy me things. "Is this why you wanted to come shopping with me, to buy me things?" I'm really hoping his answer is no, but I'm really not sure what he's going to say. I knew he was too freaking perfect!

"I know you didn't ask or expect me to buy the dress Lexi. Believe me I know, I just wanted to. I really like that dress on you, and I paid before I even thought about it." He rubs his hand over his face in frustration. "I'm sorry if I upset you Lexi, it wasn't my intention."

My anger deflates with his apology and the look of regret on his face. "OK."

"OK?" He asks.

"Yeah, OK."

"So, did you come with Lacey? Do you need a lift home?" He asks, I can't believe he's being nice after I yelled at him. Stephen would have walked away and left me here to find my own way home, the arsehole.

"I came with Lacey." I say.

"OK, well I can give you a lift home. If you want one that is." He sounds so unsure of himself and I don't like it at all.

"If you wouldn't mind, I would really appreciate a lift home. Thank you." And now we're being so polite with each other, it's almost uncomfortable. I reach out and take his hand in mine, and see his shoulders relax a little.

"OK." He nods and starts walking without dropping my hand, so that I have to follow him. OK, so I don't *have* to follow him, I *could* let go of his hand and protest, but I don't want to, so I don't. I follow him without another word.

When we reach his truck, he opens the door for me and waits until I'm seated properly, then he closes the door and walks around the front of the car to get into the driver's seat. He pulls out of the carpark, driving towards my house and the only noise in the car is the music on the radio. The silence between us is just that, it's not awkward as such, just silent. I think we're just sitting there thinking about what just happened and what we want.

When he pulls into my driveway, neither of us move right away, but when I grab my handbag and shopping, he rests his hand on my arm stopping me, so I sit back in the seat and wait.

"Lexi. I'm sorry if I stepped out of line by paying for the dress. It's just that I really liked seeing you in it and I was looking forward to seeing you wear it for our date tonight. While I'm not excusing my impulse, I wanted to explain to you why I did it." He takes a deep breath and looks at me, so I nod for him to go on. "I'm used to women wanting me for what I can do for them, buy for them and what I have."

"That's not me." I say quietly.

"I know that, at least I was hoping that wasn't you but let's face it we're just getting to know each other still, but that's not why I bought that dress for you."

"Then why did you? If it wasn't a test to see how I would react, what was your reason?"

"I knew I could afford to buy, and I just wanted to. I didn't think about whether you could afford it or not. I just wanted to buy that dress for you. As a gift."

Barefoot and Dumped!

"OK. Thank you for explaining and thank you for the dress." He smiles and it makes him devastatingly handsome. "But I want you to know, that I don't expect you to buy me things. That being said, I'm not used to guys wanting to buy me things or doing things without there being a reason behind it. So, I'm sorry that I got mad at you. I guess we've both got some things to get used to if we're going to do this thing, huh?"

"If? I thought we *were* in this relationship. Early stages sure, but I'm all in Lexi, I want to try to make whatever it is that's happening between us, work."

"Me too Gabe." His hand tightens around mine. "It's going to take some time to get used to how people, mostly women, behave around you though."

"What the hell does that mean?" He asks, surprised.

"It means one of the reasons I was so annoyed in that shop was because of the way the shop assistant was checking you out. God, she called you my husband and she *still* ogled you right in front of me. I mean I understand why, but she could have at least *tried* to hide what she was doing. Do you know what I mean?" I look at Gabe when I finish speaking, waiting for him to answer my question, only to find him struggling to hold back his laughter. "What's so funny?"

"Nothing," He coughs, trying to clear his throat of laughter, but he's struggling. "Another woman looking at me doesn't matter, because I'm not looking back. I only want you, so even if another woman talks or flirts with me, she's not on *my* radar. That woman in the shop, she can feel free to look baby, but you're the only one who gets to touch. Take it as a compliment to your good taste." He says with a wink.

"Oh my god! You're so full of it!" I say, shaking my head.

"Ahh yes but it's a charming kind of full of it that you're attracted to." He says smirking. "So, do we still have a date tonight or did I blow it?"

"There was no blowing. Yet." It's my turn to smile at Gabe. "Yes, we still have a date tonight. Otherwise it would be a waste of a dress and money not to, but because I also want to go out on a date with you." I say, pressing my finger against his lips to stop him from protesting. "Which means, I have to go inside and get myself ready."

"You look beautiful to me already, you don't need anything except that dress to look great."

Blushing I respond, "Thank you handsome, but I really need to go get myself ready so that we can have our first date. Thank you for coming shopping with me today and thank you for the dress." I reach over and kiss his lips lightly. "I'll see you at six o'clock tonight." Then jump out of the truck.

Before I close the door Gabe says loudly, "See you at six honey."

I walk to my door, turn and wave at Gabe, then walk inside to start getting ready for our date.

Chapter Sixteen

GABE

I watch Lexi walk into her house, then I back out of the driveway and drive the few minutes to my place and for the entire trip my mind is filled with Lexi in that dress. I wanted to spend the rest of the afternoon with her, but there's only a couple of hours until our date and even though I told her the truth when I said she was already beautiful to me, I know she would have insisted she needed to 'get ready' for our date. So, dropped her home.

When I walk in my front door, I look around my apartment and wonder what Lexi will think of it when she comes here. Not that I'm assuming that's how tonight will end, but one day, if I play my cards right, she'll come here. The thought makes me nervous but happy. Until I look around my home. Don't get me wrong, I'm very proud of everything that I've worked hard for, but if I want to entertain even the *thought* of Lexi coming here tonight, or any other night, I need to clean.

My phone makes a noise letting me know I've got a message. Checking it, I see Brent's name on the screen, I know I shouldn't be disappointed to see the name of my mate, but when I see it's not Lexi, that's exactly what I feel. I miss being with her, even though we'll be seeing each other in a few short hours. I understand some people would see me as pathetic, but I can't help wanting to spend as much time with her as I can.

Brent: *Dude, beers tonight?*

I shouldn't have to think about whether I want to tell my friend the truth about what I'm doing tonight, but it still takes me a minute to decide to tell him that I'm actually going out with Lexi.

Gabe: *Can't sorry. Taking Lexi out tonight*

I wait for his text telling me I'm pussy whipped or something worse, because if there's something worse to be called for wanting to spend time with your woman, Brent knows it.

Is Lexi my woman? I want her to be my partner in everything, but I'm not sure how she feels about me. I do know that I'm ready to give her as much time as she needs to decide what she wants. I just hope she decides that she wants me.

My phone vibrates in my hand, bringing me out of my thoughts.

Brent: *Cool man. The four of us will have to do dinner soon, man*

I can't believe he didn't give me any grief about going out with Lexi tonight, Sophie has been really good for him. Don't get me wrong, he's not a bad guy, he's just somewhat relationship challenged but it would seem that he's found 'the one' and he's happier than I've ever seen him.

Gabe: *Let me talk to Lexi and we'll work it out*

Brent: *For sure. No rush though man, whenever she's ready*

I send him back, 'thanks' and stand there staring at my phone for another few minutes. It's not usually that easy to get out of going out with him. The night I met Lexi is proof of that, although I'm glad to have been coerced into that one. Looking around, I still have a few things left to do before I can have a shower and get myself ready, so I can see Lexi again.

I spend the next hour cleaning, washing and putting away dishes that should have been done days ago. When I'm happy with what I've done I head into the bathroom. Sighing, I give that a clean too, and then get in the shower.

Under the hot water and breathing in the steam, I finally relax. Tonight I get to take Lexi out for dinner and whatever else we choose to do, finally. Thinking about Lexi sets my body on fire. I've never wanted any other woman like I want Alexis Stratton and my body's reaction to just thinking about her proves it.

Barefoot and Dumped!

I close my eyes, thinking back to how she looked in that dress we bought for tonight and soaping up my body takes on a whole new meaning. I run my soaped up hands over my chest and stomach, trying without much luck, to not touch my cock. If I start that, I won't be able to stop, but then I think, maybe if things progress well tonight, getting myself off now will help later. Maybe I won't be so ready to bust a nut before either one of us is ready if I relieve some of the tension now.

I'm not even sure when I made the decision or if I was conscious of it, but my hand wraps around my cock, dragging up and down the length of it in a rhythm that's all about pleasure. If only I was inside Lexi and giving us both pleasure right now, but I use the image I've pictured in my mind so many times and give myself over to it. The hand that's still rubbing my chest and up and down my body, I use to steady myself by leaning against the shower wall. Without warning, my knees start to buckle, and I have to fight to keep myself upright, leaning harder against the wall. My release is quick and lands on the base of the shower, washing down the drain. I take a deep breath, clean myself up and turn off the shower. Then I rub a towel over my hair and body, finishing up by wrapping the towel around my waist.

Walking to my bedroom I think about what I want to wear tonight. I don't want to be under dressed, especially knowing what Lexi is going to be wearing but I don't want to dress up either. Not in a monkey suit anyway. I get enough use out of that horrible thing when I have to go to business events and things for my dad. Dress pants and a button shirt it is. I'm not going to wear a full on suit, I wear them almost every day to the office and I don't want to be reminded of work while I'm with Lexi.

Opening my cupboard, I decide on black pants and pair them with a deep sea green plain button up shirt. I know what shade of green it is because the sales guy told me and for some reason it's stuck in my head. It may have been the way he said it and the fact that he was trying to pick me up at the time, that made that particular shopping experience memorable. I chuckle to myself, and then wonder if it would make Lexi feel better or worse to know that I get hit on by men as well. The thing is, it's never worked, even before Lexi and I met, so she has nothing to worry about. Her ex must have been a real piece of work for her to be so paranoid about it though, so I think I'll keep that little story to myself, at least for now anyway.

I look at my watch as I fasten it to my wrist.

5.45pm. Time to go pick Lexi up for our date.

I walk out to the front door where I keep my boots, I shove my feet in them and lace them up. There are lot of things I conform to within the business world, but dress shoes are not one of them. My boots are worn in, but clean and well looked after, and as comfortable as shoes can get. Stretching to stand up, I pull open the hallway cupboard and find my leather jacket. I throw it over my arm, then find my keys and wallet where I left them on the small table near the front door and I'm ready to head out. Then I check my pocket for my phone and, I'm happy when I find it there because it means I don't have to go looking for it.

I don't want to be late, but I don't want to be super early either, I might be eager for this date to start but I don't want to appear weird. I figure a few minutes early isn't going to be a bad thing though. So, I lock up the apartment and head downstairs to my truck. Throwing my jacket on the passenger seat, I step up into the truck, closing the door behind me and start the car. Backing the truck out of my car space and driving out of the building's underground parking garage, I head off in the direction of Lexi's house, humming to myself in anticipation.

I haven't looked forward to a date this much in a *very* long time. In fact, I haven't looked forward to getting to know another person, not just a woman, in a very long time. That's a pretty sad admission but it's the truth. My ex burned me in more ways than one and I lost faith in human beings because they let me down. For all of Brent's issues and insensitivity sometimes, he's the one person who stood by me through the entire saga and didn't flinch in his loyalty to me. For that reason alone I will be forever grateful and it's also why I put up with his antics. He's a great guy, he just needed to grow up a little.

I pull into Lexi's driveway, park and turn off my truck. I take a few seconds to gather my thoughts and blow the old feelings out of my head. I don't want to walk into this date with Lexi thinking about my ex and all her issues. Or Brent for that matter. I love the guy, but I don't want to think about him right now.

I jump out of the truck, close the door and walk across the driveway to the front door. I notice out of the corner of my eye, the curtains in the front window move slightly, making me chuckle. I wonder who was spying on me from the window. Lexi, Catherine or Lacey? Raising my hand to knock, I hear loud whispering inside, but I can't make out any words because they're muffled through the door. I laugh again, maybe I'm not the only one who's excited about this date? I knock on the door and wait for one of them to answer.

"Coming." That's Cat.

"Just a minute." And that's Lexi. They speak at the same time, but I can tell the difference between the two sisters. One I'm falling for, the other one is her sister. Easy.

I don't get the chance to answer them before the door is flung open and Catherine is standing there with a huge smile on her face. I don't know her well enough to decipher whether it's a happy one or not, but she kind of looks constipated so I'm going to go with not entirely happy.

"Hi Cat, how are you?" I ask.

"You remember my name? We only met once." She asks surprised.

"Yes, but I've spent some time with Lexi since and she talks about Lacey and yourself quite a lot, so I feel like I know you a little bit." I smile, trying to soften the blow so I don't sound like I'm stalking all three of them.

"Oh." Is all she says, then takes a step back from the door, opening the entrance a little more in the process. "Come on in, Lexi won't be long. She just has to finish a couple of things."

"Thank you." I walk past her and into the house. It's everything I thought it would be after getting to know Lexi better the last few days. Although I can see Cat's contributions to the décor here and there, even some that I would say are Lacey's contributions, mostly all I see is Lexi. That's when a few photos on a shelf catch my attention. "Is this you and Lexi when you were little girls?" I ask Cat who is standing behind me.

She laughs quietly and answers, "Yes it is. She wasn't too impressed with getting her photo taken. She's not a huge fan of getting her photo taken even now, in case you haven't noticed." She laughs quietly again.

"Well, I can see that she wasn't impressed with that one being taken, that's for sure." I laugh, looking back at the photo and seeing Lexi's cute little face, scrunched up in distaste and her arms crossed over her body in frustration. "Did she stamp her foot too?" I ask Cat, because I see the younger version of the woman I'm hoping will be my girlfriend by nights end, totally throwing down that gauntlet to her parents.

Cat laughs hysterically, while nodding her head yes. "Oh my god, how could you know that?" she asks between gasping breaths.

"Lucky guess I suppose." I smirk at her. She studies my face for a few seconds before replying.

"Or you know my sister reasonably well already and can picture her doing it." Her statement hits home, because that was exactly what I was doing. "That's exactly what you were doing, isn't it?" I nod my head in answer, and Cat cracks up laughing again.

"What's so funny you two?" Lexi asks as she enters the room. She smiles at her laughing sister and then she looks at me. "Is everything OK Gabe?"

I haven't moved since I heard her voice and looked up to watch her walk into the room. If I thought she looked amazing in the dress at the store, it had *nothing* on the vision in front of me.

"Sorry to make you wait, but Cat came home and just had to help me get ready. Unfortunately, that took more time than me getting ready for myself because she likes to fuss."

Alexis is a vision in the dark purple dress, that has lace up the top and a silky skirt that goes to just above her knees. The top is cut in a way that makes it curve to her breasts in just the right way. Not flashing any flesh but it *is* showing every curve that men love. That I love. She's got on heels that match the colour of her dress and show off her amazing legs. What can I say except, she's even more of a vision than she was in the store.

I want to take hold of her at the base of her neck and draw her close to me so that I can kiss her plump, red stained lips but Cat coughs, loudly, reminding me that we have an audience. So, instead of reaching out for her, I say, "You look amazing Lexi. Absolutely gorgeous."

She blushes lightly and looks down slightly, embarrassed, but she shouldn't be because I only spoke the truth. "Thank you Gabe. You look pretty handsome yourself."

"Why thank you." I smile, hoping to relieve this awkwardness that seems to have settled in.

"Well, you kids have fun tonight. Off you go before you miss your reservation." Cat ushers us towards the door.

Resting my hand lightly on Lexi's lower back, I lead her towards the now open door. As we go to pass her, Cat leans over and kisses her sister on the cheek and whispers something in her ear that makes Lexi glance back at me and blush.

"Take care of my sister Gabriel, and don't do anything I wouldn't do." The first part she says with a stern look on her face. The second part with a massive grin and mischief all over her face.

"That doesn't leave much of anything to *not* do." Lexi mumbles so that only I can hear her.

"I promise to look after your sister Cat."

"I know you will Gabe."

When we hear the door close behind us, I step up beside my date and hold out my hand. She hesitates for half a second before placing her hand in mine and smiles up at me. If such a small gesture can bring her that much happiness, I can't wait to do all kinds of little things like that for her all night and every other night we're together.

Chapter Seventeen

LEXI

Somewhere between me getting out of the shower and doing my makeup, my sister got home and decided she needed to 'help' me get ready for my date. All this so called 'help' just makes me run out of time and when Gabe arrives to pick me up, I still have to put on my shoes and put a few things in my small handbag. You know, the essentials, lipstick, keys, purse, tissues and a condom. Or two. Oh come on, if you were going on a date with Gabe, you'd be carrying protection too. Trust me on this one.

Cat squeals out in the living room, so I run out there without my heels on to see what's going on and she's stealing a glance out the front window.

"What are you doing Catherine?" I ask in a weird stage whisper. I mean no-one except my sister is going to be able to hear me.

"I heard a car pull up in the driveway, so I thought I'd sneak a peek at your handsome date, and I found him sitting in his truck, engine off, and eyes closed. Looks like he's giving himself a pep talk." She finally looks at me instead of outside, looks me up and down and continues. "Guess you're not the only one that's a little overexcited and nervous about tonight. Mr Romanetti is too. You two are so damned cute I swear I could smoosh you both."

She reaches out to my cheeks and I hit her hands away. "Stop being ridiculous Cat. It's a date. One that I'm actually looking forward to, yes, but a first date none the less and they're nerve wracking little sister."

"I don't think you have anything to worry about big sister." She smiles, looking out the window and letting out an even louder squeal than before. "Oh, he's coming. He's walking towards the door."

"Well, he won't knock if he hears you squealing, so can you shut up please?" I beg in a loud whisper, hoping that Gabe can't hear us.

"He looks so handsome though Lexi. Geez you're one lucky lady, let me tell you!" She says in an excited whisper that almost can't be called a whisper. When Gabe knocks on the door, I jump a little because even though I was expecting it, obviously, it reverberates through the quiet house.

"Don't let him in until I'm back in my room Cat, or I swear I'll make you pay."

"Coming." Cat calls out at the same time as I say, "Just a minute," and take off towards my bedroom. I close the door quietly and take a few deep breaths.

What would he think if he could see me now, behaving like a silly schoolgirl? Cat's right about one thing though, I am nervously excited about this date. I want it to go well. I want him to like me and I want to like him too.

I can hear the mumble of voices out in the living room, and I don't want to leave the two of them alone together for too long. It has nothing to do with trusting my sister or Gabe, and everything to do with the embarrassing childhood stories my sister is likely to tell.

I slip my feet into the shoes that match my gorgeous deep, royal purple dress and take one last look in the mirror. Turning this way and that, checking every angle that I can. The dress is amazing with a deep v neck lace bodice, but not so deep that I'm showing my navel. It's sleeveless and moulds around every curve of my boobs perfectly. The girls look absolutely incredible in this dress, I don't have a small chest, but they're not huge either, and they're nicely on display tonight. The satin skirt flows from my waist to just above my knees, it silky and floaty and feels divine against my skin. Cat put light curls in my hair, and we pinned it back a little so that it's off my face but flows over my shoulders and down my back.

I *feel* beautiful.

Barefoot and Dumped!

Taking another deep breath, I open my door and walk back out into the living room to find Cat laughing over something Gabe said, and he's smiling at her with a twinkle in his eyes. He looks gorgeous. Edible in fact. I've seen him in casual jeans and t-shirts, I've also seen him in the suits he wears to work, and he looks gorgeous in all of them. Tonight though, in his dark dress pants, boots, and gorgeous green shirt with a leather jacket over the top, he's gorgeous. So gorgeous in fact that my underwear might self combust with the heat generated all over my body. I must have stared at him for too long because the next thing I know, Cat is pushing us out the door.

Leaning in under the pretence of kissing me on the cheek, the cheeky bitch whispers in my ear, "I hope you put a condom or two in that handbag of yours, cause I think you're going to be needing them sis." I look at her, shocked. Here I was thinking my little sister was quite an innocent, even though she's getting married soon.

The touch of Gabe's hand on my lower back as we make our way outside sends a tingle up my spine. When the door closes soundly behind us, we both stop walking and Gabe stands next to me and reaches out his hand for me to hold. It's such a simple but sweet gesture. I smile at him and without a word I place my hand in his and he leads me to his truck, opens the door and helps me into the car. When he's sure I'm settled into the seat, he closes the door and walks around to the driver's side and with the ease of a man who knows his truck well, swings himself in behind the steering wheel. He starts the truck but hesitates to back out of the driveway and I can't help but wonder if he's having second thoughts. I should have known better.

"You really do look amazing tonight Lexi." He says, with a smile that lights up my whole body. "Not that you don't look good enough to eat any other time, but tonight, you truly look incredible."

I can feel my heart pumping faster, feeling like it might fly out of my chest.

"You look pretty incredible yourself Gabe." I say, hopefully giving him the same appreciative smile that he gave me. "Not that you don't look totally delectable on any other given day, but tonight, you truly look amazing."

Without another word, he reverses the truck and heads towards our dinner destination. When we reach the highway, he rests his hand, palm up, on the seat between us and I take a second to think whether this is an invitation or not. Then he wiggles his fingers, and I look up to his face to see him quickly glance at me, then back to the road ahead, and he wiggles his fingers in invitation again. This time, I place my hand in his, palm to palm and I can feel the heat from his body spread through mine. I like how it feels. I smile over at him and his eyes are still concentrating on the road, but his smile is wide across his face. So, I sit back and relax, enjoying the ride to our destination.

We travel for almost half an hour before he turns off the highway. It's been a quiet drive. The only noise is the radio playing quietly in the background, but the silence isn't awkward. It's comfortable, almost relaxing. I like being in his easy presence. He doesn't talk for the sake of making noise and I can see that he's concentrating on getting us to wherever we're going in one piece, but I also know that if I decided to start a conversation with him, he would join in and it would be fun. I find myself not needing to fill the silence, because unlike in my previous relationship, we're comfortable enough within ourselves and each other to just enjoy the ride.

I find that I'm enjoying myself without the need for talking. Looking out the window watching the scenery pass by, I periodically look over to Gabe just to see him. Listening to the quiet music and enjoying the gentle touch of just our hands. I look over to find him looking at me, his eyes darting back and forth between myself and the road, a frown on his face.

"Is everything OK Lexi?"

"Yes, why wouldn't it be?"

"Well, it's just that you're so quiet and we're not talking."

"I'm enjoying the drive, and the company. Absolutely nothing wrong with me Gabe." I smile at him and start to look away again when a sudden thought hits me. "Is everything OK with you? Would you like to talk about something?"

"No, I'm happy to sit here like this if you are." I smile at him and nod. "I'm just not used to the quiet, the stillness I suppose."

"Why is that?"

"My ex."

"Who shall not be named." I say with a serious face and Gabe laughs.

"That's the one. She just always seemed to need to talk. It didn't matter if she had something to say or if she thought I would be interested in what she was saying, she just talked. I often wondered if she did it because the silence made her think too much and her feelings might catch up with her wrong doings. Especially once I found out about her poor behaviour."

"She didn't like the silence because she wasn't comfortable with herself and that made her uncomfortable around you. It wasn't your fault Gabe, she obviously has some pretty serious issues." I feel sorry for his ex, but their breakup has given me the opportunity to get to know this gorgeous and intelligent man. So while I can feel for her, I'm glad she screwed up and they broke up.

"You're too understanding Lexi. I feel like you're talking from experience though and that makes me want to hunt the guy down and let him know what happens to arseholes." The muscles in his jaw tightens, as does his hand that's on the steering wheel.

I take my hand from his, making him glance my way quickly before settling back on the road, when I rest my hand on his cheek and rub his tense jaw. "As sweet as it is that you want to defend me Gabe, it's totally unnecessary." I put my hand on his mouth to stop him from speaking and then place my hand back in his on the seat between us. "He doesn't matter anymore Gabe. He was nothing and while I can understand wanting to teach the jerk a lesson, he's not worth the time or effort. Trust me. Lacey gave him a mouthful that I doubt he'll forget too soon when he came to pick up the small amount of junk he left at my house."

That knowledge gets a laugh out of him and when I see his body relax, I know I said the right thing and the fact that I mean it, is a bonus.

"So, you're not pining over him or wishing he hadn't broken up with you then?"

"No. Not even for one second. Don't get me wrong I was mad, but now, I realise it was more than time to leave him behind."

"Good." He sends me a genuinely relieved smile. Was the man really worried that I was missing Stephen? When I'm with Gabe I barely even remember that idiot existed.

"No more talk about our ex's, they're in the past where they belong. This our first official date and they're not invited. This is our future and it has nothing to do with those two idiots." I send him a wink and a big smile. He squeezes my hand, weaving our fingers together and I squeeze lightly back.

"Is that what we have, a future together?" He asks, and I can see the hope in his eyes even in the dark cabin of his truck.

"I'm hoping for a future with you in it Gabe, if that's what you want as well?" I can hear the hope bleeding out of my own voice, and I hope it's not too much for him.

"We're here." He announces and I look out the windshield to see we have most certainly arrived at a beautiful restaurant that I've heard of but never been able to get in to because they're always booked out months in advance.

"How did you manage to get a reservation here?" I ask and then before he can even think of answering I say, "Or did you already have the reservation and I'm just the lucky girl who managed to get the invite?" I know I sound like a bitch, and it's quick turnabout from the conversation we were just having, but it's almost impossible to get in here, definitely with the short notice he had for our date.

"There was no other woman or date. No previous plan, I swear." He holds the hand that was on the steering wheel over his heart. "I know the manager, we're old friends from school and I called in a favour. I came for dinner opening night and only few times since when I've been invited for something. I've never bought a date here Lexi, ever."

"You didn't come here with the ex?" I can't help asking, call me a sadist but I need to know.

"No. We rarely went out. I now understand why but that doesn't matter, no ex's tonight, remember? They're the past and they don't belong here tonight, with us on our date."

"You're right. Let's go, I'm looking forward to eating here, I've heard amazing things about the food." I make a move to get out of the car, but he stops me, placing a hand lightly on my arm, so I turn to look at him.

"Wait! I'll come open your door, if that's ok?"

"Sure." I smile at him, I'm not going to refuse a little bit of gentlemanly behaviour, as long as it doesn't become possessive behaviour it will be welcomed. He moves quickly and before I know it he's standing in the open door, holding out his hand to help me out of his truck and my heart almost bursts out of my chest. Again! This man is one of a kind and for tonight at least, he's all mine.

He takes my hand, helping me to navigate getting out of his truck with high heels and when my feet hit solid ground he closes the door behind me and locks up. He hasn't let go of my hand as he's done all this, and the butterflies are starting flutter in my stomach.

"Ready?"

"Absolutely." I smile at him again. I'm ready for the date, to spend time with him, getting to know him and to the good food that is no doubt ahead of us. Without dropping my hand, he manoeuvres us around so we're side by side and walking towards the entrance to the restaurant. He opens the door, stepping back to allow me to walk in first because there's not enough space for us to enter together. It means he drops my hand and I feel the loss of his touch immediately. That is until I feel the heat of his palm resting on my lower back. That simple touch sends tingles running up my spine and I shiver a little.

He leans down, his lips close to my ear and says, "Are you cold honey?" The whisper of his warm breath sweeps over my ear, causing another heated shiver to run through my body and I close my eyes to enjoy the sensation.

"Not cold. Nope not cold at all." I mumble.

I didn't realise that we'd kept walking until I hear Gabe speak. Opening my eyes I realise we're standing at the reception desk of the restaurant and he's talking to a man he appears to know pretty well. So, I guess this is the friend of his who is the manager.

"Jeremy, this is Alexis. Alexis, this Jeremy, an old friend from school." Gabe makes the introductions and I just stand there smiling and nodding and answering a few questions, because I'm still in an overload from all the sensations he's woken up in my body.

The guys stand there for a few minutes joking with each other like old friends do. I hear Jeremy tell Gabe he's a lucky son of a bitch and then, he tells me to come find him when Gabe doesn't treat me properly. The whole time we were standing there, Gabe's hand was still lightly resting on my back. Then Jeremy made his offer of being my back up if Gabe stuffed up, and he wrapped his arm around my waist and pulled me in tight to his side. It's a possessive move that I would have pulled out of with anyone else, but with Gabe, I like being close to him. I've seen the women in here giving him second and third and some even fourth glances, so I can understand why he feels like he needs me close.

"I'll take you to your table. Are you OK with sitting outside on the deck? We've got some heaters set up out there but if you want to sit inside I can set that up too. It's just that, the table outside is a little more private and away from prying eyes. The view out there is amazing too, even in the dark."

Gabe looks to me, silently telling me it's my decision. Again, this man amazes me, Stephen would have made the decision without even consulting me. "I'm happy to sit outside if you are Gabe?"

"Outside it is then thanks Jeremy."

"Follow me." He says with a smile, while collecting two menus for us.

I feel the slightest pressure on my waist as Gabe squeezes me, then his hand returns to my lower back to guide me through the tables, following behind Jeremy. When we reach the table, Jeremy pulls out my chair for me but when he goes to help me push it back in the table, Gabe is there first and does it for me. I see a smirk spread across Jeremy's face, but he doesn't say anything, he just places the menu's down on the table in front of us, as Gabe sits in his own chair.

"Can I get you something to drink while you look over the menu?"

Gabe looks to me, waiting for me to answer. I think of ordering a wine, but I really feel like a cider. I look at Gabe and decide, what the hell, I'm going with what I want and if he doesn't like it, well then I guess we had a nice night.

"Do you have any ciders on tap?" I ask. I saw some taps when we walked past the bar on the way to our table, but I'm not sure if they're just beers or not. My question makes both men smile, but Jeremy answers me.

"Yes, we do actually. We have a local apple or pear cider on tap. The apple is sweeter than the pear, which is quite tart in comparison."

"Can I have an apple cider then please?"

"Absolutely. You've chosen well Alexis, I'm not much of a sweet tooth myself, but I prefer the apple over the pear." He smiles at me and I relax. "What about you Gabriel?"

"Are you going to be serving us all night?" Gabe asks, he sounds annoyed, but he's got a smile on his face as he speaks. Jeremy doesn't answer him, he just smiles politely back at his friend, obviously trying to be professional. "I'll have one of the local craft beers you have on tap tonight please. You choose, I don't care which one." With our drink orders done, Jeremy takes his leave, letting us know someone will be back with our drinks and to take our order shortly. Gabe thanks him and Jeremy leaves us alone.

I pick up the menu to start looking to decide what I want. I had no idea where we were going tonight, so I don't even know what I feel like eating, nor do I know what to expect from the menu here.

"Is everything OK Lexi?" Gabe asks me, his voice quieter than I've heard it before.

"Yes, everything is great Gabe." I smile at him hoping that he can see that I'm being sincere. I know we went quiet, but I didn't think it was an awkward silence at all. "Are you OK Gabe?" I ask, because now I'm worried that he doesn't feel comfortable and that's why he was asking me.

"All good, honey." His smile is easy and relaxed, so I relax too.

"You've been here before, tell me what would you recommend I try?"

"That depends on what you're looking for, tonight."

"Hmmm well I guess that depends on how dinner goes. Then I might think about dessert."

"What are you thinking might be for dessert honey?" Without realising it, we've moved closer together, leaning across the table with the need to touch each other.

"I'm not really sure, but I think chocolate and whipped cream *has* to be involved. Don't you?" Gabe lets out a low groan and with a movement that I barely see, he reaches around the table and pulls my chair around so that we're no longer sitting opposite one another, but next to each other.

"Sorry, but I needed you next to me, not across the table from me." He tells me, but then thinks for a second and says, "But if you want to go back over there, I won't stop you. I want you to be comfortable here, and any time you're with me."

"I like it where I am, I think I'll stay right here."

There's a happiness and a hunger in his eyes. If I'm being honest, I missed his touch, even though it always short circuits my brain for a few seconds.

There's a cough from behind me and the waiter Jeremy sent out to us places our drinks on the table. "Did you want me give you a few more minutes to make your choices?"

"No, I think we're ready." Gabe looks at me, silently asking me if that is correct and I nod slightly. "I'll have an eye fillet, medium rare with salad please. What would you like honey?"

"I think I'll have the same please." I tell the waiter, my eyes never leaving Gabe's. I want to see his reaction to me ordering a steak. The idiot always told me it wasn't ladylike, and I should order chicken. He never entertained me getting dessert either, because it would, 'go to my arse." Yeah, he was a charmer, can you see why I stayed with him for so long?

"We'll also have a chocolate fondant for dessert please." Gabe tells the waiter.

"Cream, ice cream or both?" The waiter doesn't look up from his notepad, but Gabe meets my eyes and doesn't look away when he answers.

"Whipped cream, please." I'm not sure if the waiter speaks again, I'm not even aware of the moment he left us.

What I *do* know is, Gabe made ordering dessert with whipped cream sound like a dirty, delightful and sensual occasion. I can feel the blush creeping up my body and my desire for the man beside me is in full force. He takes hold of my hand, and presses a gentle kiss into my palm, then looks back up to meet my eyes and says, "That future together, that you mentioned in the car when we pulled up outside? I just wanted to let you know, because I feel like I left you hanging a little bit back there, that I want that too. If you'll have me."

I think I fell in love with Gabriel Romanetti in that moment.

Chapter Eighteen

<u>GABE</u>

Sitting at the table with Lexi and yet feeling so far away from her just wasn't working for me. So, I fixed it and pulled her along with her chair, around the table to sit next to me. It wasn't until after I did it that I realised that I might have made her uncomfortable, but relief washed over me when she said she was more than happy to be sitting closer to me.

Ordering a meal has never felt sexually charged for me before but ordering that dessert and purposely asking for whipped cream on top, sent my arousal and need for the woman beside me into overdrive. All I had to do now, was survive our dinner and not scare her away with my intensity.

I see Alexis Stratton in my future. I *want* Alexis Stratton to *be* my future.

We sit close together, her hand resting in mine on the table between us, and we just talk. About everything and nothing. We just get to know each other, and I've never felt more comfortable or more myself with anyone else. Without even realising it we're caressing each other's hands, wrists and fingers while we talk, until we're interrupted by our dinner arriving. I can't say I've ever been disappointed to see a well-cooked steak arrive in front of me before, but tonight I am.

Lexi pulls her hand from mine to start eating and I miss her immediately. I know we have to eat. I wanted to bring her out on a proper date so that we could get to know each other and spend time together, but I miss the connection with her. Needing to touch her in some way still while eating, I move my leg, leaning my knee in to touch hers. She doesn't look up from her plate, but the smile on her face lets me know she knows what I'm doing.

It's beautiful here and I appreciate Jeremy making the effort to put us outside so that we can see the view, even in the dark. It's amazing, but honestly, I'm enjoying the vision beside me a whole lot more.

"It's gorgeous sitting out here Gabe, thank you for bringing me here." Her smile is so sweet and genuine, it warms my heart knowing that bringing her here has made her happy.

"You're more than welcome honey. The view is spectacular tonight." While Lexi thinks I'm talking about the view she's been looking at, my eyes haven't left her, and my joy is in watching her enjoy herself. "Did you enjoy your meal?"

She turns to face me before replying. "Yes! That's the best piece of meat I've had in a very long time." Now, I don't know if she catches that double meaning, but I sure do, and I can feel my cock growing behind the zipper of my pants. I'm grateful that dress pants allow more room 'to move' than the average pair of jeans, otherwise I could be in a most embarrassing situation right now.

Lexi excuses herself to go to the bathroom and I'm left alone at the table. Just after she disappears the waiter comes by to clean off the table.

"Was everything to your satisfaction this evening?" He asks.

"Yes, it was delicious thank you." He nods and quickly moves away, and the table is once again spotless. I take another drink of my almost finished beer and think about how lucky I am that Lexi gave me after she thought I was a crazy stalker.

"What are you thinking about because it looks like it's leaving a bad taste in your mouth and I know it can't be from dinner because that meal was delicious." Lexi says as she returns to our table. I don't say anything because I don't know what to say, I can't tell her the truth, can I? That would make me sound even stranger, surely? 'Thanks for giving me a second chance after you thought I was a stalker', not quite the conversation you want to have on your first date.

"Nothing really. I was just sitting here waiting for you." I smile, hoping that answer doesn't make me sound like a moron.

Barefoot and Dumped!

She looks down at her hands that are resting on the table, but I notice are nervously twisting the napkin around and around. So, I reach over to stop her, because she never needs to be nervous around me and she can tell me anything.

"Sorry." She smiles at me. "I was just expecting you to be on your phone when I got back. You know checking to see if anyone has messaged you or checking emails and such."

"Is that what he did to you?" She looks down at her hands and nods. I hate this unsure and nervous version of herself that she's showing me right now. I love the spitfire who has opinions, laughs at my stupid jokes, laughs at herself and calls me out on my bullshit. "Honestly? I didn't have enough time to think about getting my phone out. I invited you out tonight because I wanted to spend time with *you*, getting to know *you*, not my phone. I already know what my phone can do. Will I check my phone? Sure but later when we're back at the car or something, but look, it's on silent. Anyone who would or could contact me can wait." I pull my phone out of my pocket and show her the screen.

"You don't need to prove anything to me Gabe, I'm sorry I was being silly." She says quietly.

"No, you weren't. I understand." I reach across and take her hand in mine to reassure her. "I'm not going to say that I will never check my phone, or I won't answer it when we're together, but tonight, this is about us and the rest of the world can wait for a few hours."

Jeremy chooses that minute to bring out dessert, and the smug bastard has a smirk on his face that tells me he knows *exactly* why I ordered the chocolate fondant. He places the cake in-between the two of us on the table, along with a larger than normal bowl of whipped cream and two spoons.

"Thank you Jeremy." I say looking at him with a slight frown, making him chuckle.

"You're welcome. Is there anything else I can do for you?" He asks politely, but with a smirk.

"No, thank you Jeremy, we're good for now." With a low chuckle, he leaves us in peace.

"I never meant to say that you couldn't look at your phone Gabe. I know you run a business, not to mention you have family and friends that might need to contact you for whatever reason." She takes her hand from mine and buries her face in her hands for a few seconds and then looks at me through the gaps in her spread fingers. "Oh my god! Now I sound like I'd be a bitch of a girlfriend and limit your contact with family and friends."

I pull her hands from her face and hold them lightly in mine. "No, you don't. You sound like a woman trying to explain how she feels, and the explanation got a little, shall we say, weird and twisted." I laugh quietly. I put my finger under her chin bringing her eyes up to meet mine, because I want to see her eyes when she answers my next question. "Is that what you want?" She looks at me confused. "To be my girlfriend?" I see the second it registers with her what she's said, and her cheeks blush. "Because, I have to be honest, I would not be opposed to that at all honey."

"Really?" Her eyes light up at the idea and I can't help feeling like I could move mountains when she looks at me like that.

"Really." I kiss her lightly on the lips and sit back a little. I hand her a spoon and tap the side of the bowl of cream with mine. "Why don't you cut into this sucker and see if Jeremy's right about this being their most decadent dessert on the menu." A slow sweet smile spreads across her face.

"I love chocolate and I haven't met a chocolate cake I haven't enjoyed, but I've never had a fondant and I'm looking forward to it."

"I remembered you saying you loved chocolate and I know that to get this particular dessert right after dinner, I needed to order it when we ordered our mains. Timing is crucial to getting it right and I wanted it to be perfect." I explain.

"Thank you." Her smile is radiant still, and yet almost shy. I want to do these small things for her every day, just to see her smile like that.

Putting her spoon right dead centre of the cake, I watch as she slices through the cake layer to the gooey middle that oozes over her spoon and the plate. She mutters, 'oh my god', so I motion to her with my head to keep going, for her to have that first mouthful. Lexi scoops a mouthful off the plate and when it reaches her mouth and past her lips, her eyes close and a guttural, raspy moan escapes her. A dribble of molten chocolate rolls across her bottom lip and her tongue pushes out to swipe it away as quickly as it appeared, not giving me a chance to wipe it away for her. She takes her time, enjoying her mouthful and when she finally opens her eyes, it's to find me watching her mouth, her lips, her tongue, completely enthralled. I could sit here all night and watch her eat this dessert.

"That is the most delicious thing I have ever had in my mouth." She says, and my eyes jump up to meet hers, in them I find mischief and desire. I'm pretty sure that same desire is reflected in my own eyes.

"Really?" I ask, barely able to speak.

"Really. You want to change that?" She asks, not breaking our connection.

"I really want you to finish this dessert. It would be a waste for you not to." I see disappointment flash across her face and hurry to finish speaking. "You're going to need as much fuel as you can get for what I have planned for us tonight. That's if you want me to worship -" I don't get to finish before Lexi answers me, needing me as much as I need her apparently.

"Yes." She says, dipping her spoon into the cream and then scooping up some more of the best thing she's ever had in her mouth. When she offers the bite of deliciousness to me, I crumble. I'm half in love with this woman and the fact that she wants to feed me, fuck I may have just jumped over the ledge.

Looking deep into her eyes, I open my mouth and wrap my lips around her spoon. Her eyes dilate with lust and she moans as I slide my mouth off the spoon and lick the remnants of cream off my lips. When she mimics me by licking her own lips, my cock joins in the party, growing to uncomfortable proportions in my pants.

Not wanting to cut short this drawn out food version of foreplay, I drag my own spoon through the cream and then scoop up some chocolate as well. Then I copy exactly what she did to me and offer her the spoon. Her mouth opens and I run the cold metal across her bottom lip, making her fidget in her chair, but she still never loses our connection. I draw the spoon back slightly, teasing her, thinking she'll stick out her tongue and take a swipe at the sweetness but instead she does something I didn't predict and makes me harder than I've ever been before.

"Don't tease me Gabe. Put it in my mouth." She knows what she's doing and I'm not sure who moans the loudest, but either way, I'm damned sure it's a good idea that we're the only people out on the deck tonight, otherwise others might be feeling uncomfortable. Not me, well my pants are pretty tight, but right now all I want is Lexi. I wouldn't have seen anyone else if they were hitting me on the head with a hammer.

My mind drifts and then Lexi moves forward and takes the spoon in her mouth. She wraps her fingers around my wrist and twists my hand until the top of the spoon is now the bottom and she draws her head back, dragging her tongue across the upside down spoon, and flicking out her tongue to lick the last drop of cream off the tip of the spoon.

My heart stops beating. My brain, the jumbled mess that it is, manages to imagine her doing just that to the tip of my cock and suddenly, I don't care if we leave most of the dessert behind. I stand abruptly and Lexi's eyes are level with my crotch, where the outline of my *very* hard cock is showing as clear as the bright blue sky on a Summers day. Holy fuck! Staring at my cock, her tongue thrusts out of her mouth and licks her lips. When I growl, the quick movement of her face to look up at me, brings her lips closer to my cock and it jumps in anticipation, catching her eye again with the movement. I see her hand moving, and I know exactly what she's planning on doing, but I'm not letting her touch me like that here, in public, because I don't think I'll be able to stop once we start. I don't want to put on a show, I want her for myself. To take my time and map out every inch of her body. With my tongue, my hands and my lips.

"Don't." I barely manage the word, my voice is more of a growled grunt, than an actual word. She tries to pull her hand from my grip, so I tighten the hold I have on her wrist a little to stop her. Is she embarrassed or thinking she's gone too far, I need to explain why I stopped her. "If you touch me here, like that, I won't be able to stop. I need you so badly, but I want you where you're mine. No one else gets to see you, or us."

"OK." She rises to her feet, manoeuvring her wrist out of my grip, to place our hands palm to palm and twisting our fingers together. "Then take me home Gabriel."

I don't need to be told twice. We move through the busy restaurant, Lexi in front of me. Her back close to my front, hiding my reaction to the gorgeous woman leading me out. As we reach the exit, I speak loudly to Jeremy.

"Hey man, have you got what you need from me to pay for tonight?"

He looks up and notices how fast we're moving to get out of his restaurant and how tightly I'm holding Lexi to my front and he smiles, "Yeah man, I know where you live. Have a good night." Then he waves goodbye and gets back to his work. He's a great guy, I might even let him win the next game of poker we play together.

My thoughts distracted me for a second and it's only when the cold air hits me that I realise we're back outside and heading quickly towards my truck. A shiver runs down Lexi's body and I drop her hand to rub both hands up and down her arms. "Are you cold honey?"

"No. Quite the opposite. I'm hot Gabe." She says just as we reach my truck and I click the unlock button.

I push her back into the side of the car and place my hands on either side of her head. "Tell me to wait Lexi and I will, but I need to taste you right now." She doesn't speak, instead she reaches up to wrap her hands around my neck and pulls my lips down to hers.

"Kiss me." She whispers, her lips a breath away from mine. Never one to make a woman ask twice, I drop my head the rest of the way and plant my lips on hers. It's a slow, cautious kiss at first. Tentative, until the lust and passion takes over and when she opens her mouth in invitation, I take it. Our tongues tangle and our teeth clash. Her hands creep up into my hair and they tug, lightly on the ends causing me to moan long and loud in her mouth, but I leave my hands on the door behind her, not trusting them not to go too far.

After what feels like forever, I pull back from her lips, gasping for air. I rest my forehead on hers and listen to her heavy breathing. I'm glad I'm not the only one feeling out of fucking control here. "We need to go. Your place or mine?" I ask, not caring at this point where we go, just as long as I get this gorgeous woman in front of me, alone and naked.

"Mine. I'm not sure if it's any closer but we don't have to navigate doormen, stairs, elevators or nosy neighbours." She kisses my neck and my head lolls back, wanting more. More of her. More of her touch, everywhere, anywhere. Now.

"Your place it is." I agree with her reasoning.

I step back from the truck, bringing Lexi with me so that I can open the door. I pick her up by the waist, placing her inside the truck. She lets out a little squeak of surprise but when she turns to look at me, I can see the heat radiating off her. "Oh my lord Gabriel." I smile, because what else can I do?

She sits her gorgeous arse down and I close the door, making quick work of getting around to the other side so that I can get in and hit the road.

"What about Cat?" I ask, when I get us on the highway, and I'm cruising along as fast as I can.

"She's staying at Joshua's tonight. In fact, she's moving in there soon."

"So, we have the house to ourselves tonight?" I ask, just to make sure.

"Absolutely. Otherwise, I would have said to hell with it and gone to your place." Reaching over the centre console, who got rid of bench seats honestly? She takes my hand in hers and slowly draws circles in my palm. I look over at her for as long as I can without driving us off the road and smile. "I don't want any obstacles to get in the way tonight, least of all my little sister."

Good. This is good. Now I just have to concentrate and not wipe us out before we can get to Lexi's house and explore each other's bodies. All night long.

Chapter Nineteen

LEXI

The drive home from the restaurant was full of tension. Sexual tension that is.

That dessert was divine but the groan that left Gabe's mouth with that last mouthful was damned near sinful. OK it was sinful, simple as that. The man is sex on legs, and I can't wait to have my mouth and hands all over him.

What was I thinking, teasing him like that? Oh boy though, what results! I'm so wet I'm worried I might be leaving a mark not just on my new dress, but on Gabe's seat as well. Not that I think he'd mind too much by the heated looks he's giving me.

I know we're almost at my house, and I know I should let him concentrate on driving so that we can make it home in one piece, but I can't help wanting to touch him and make him want me.

I pick up our joined hands, bring them to my mouth and kiss the back of his lightly. Then I kiss each finger that same way, from thumb to little finger and move to make my way back again, but I stop at his middle finger and draw it in to my mouth. His hot gaze flicks to me and then back to the road again.

"What are you doing Lexi?" His voice is almost pure gravel now and it vibrates through my entire body, from head to toe.

"I'm just giving you a preview of what I plan to do when we get to my house." Then I curl my tongue around the tip of his finger, slowly but without hesitation. Then I nip on the tip and suction my lips around it. The groan that he produces is carnal, making my clit start to throb, but when I draw his finger into my mouth, suck it and then draw my mouth away again, I see him close his eyes for a second. "Should I stop? Is it too much Gabriel? I don't want to make you crash." I start to move away, knowing that he can't reach for me without taking the other hand off the steering wheel and losing control of the car.

"Don't you dare stop now honey. I promise not to crash, but please, don't stop." The begging in his voice makes me cave faster than I'd planned and before either of us know it, I'm sliding back over and bringing his hand back to my mouth. Without hesitating, I draw his finger into my mouth and start moving up and down like I plan to do to his cock later. Just the thought of doing it makes me moan and close my eyes. I'm pumping his finger in and out of my mouth, rolling my tongue all over, lost in my actions. Suddenly, he pulls his hand from mine and my eyes fly open, finding his molten eyes staring right at mine. "We're here and you need to stop before I embarrass myself in my truck."

Before I know what's happening, he's out of the truck and at my door, opening it for me so that I can jump out. Only before I get the chance to move, his hands are on my waist again and he's lifting me down until my feet feel solid ground under them. If I was the swooning kind, that's what I'd be doing right now but I'm not so instead I say, "I'm more than capable of getting myself in and out of your truck you know Gabe. You don't have to manhandle me like I'm a child you know."

"I know, but I need to be touching you and you're moving too slow for my liking."

"You're going to have to learn some patience then mister because -" But I don't get to finish.

"Is that what you were practising in the car just now by sucking my finger like it was your favourite lollipop or something? Are you calling that restraint now honey?" His grin is cocky and if I didn't know better, I'd say he's being a jerk right now and I should send him home. But I know better. At least I think I do.

"That was called the entrée before the main course." I turn and start walking towards the front door of my house, not waiting to see if he's keeping up. I'm nervous because as much as I want this man, I can't help but wonder if I'm moving too fast. Am I jumping from the idiot to Gabe too quickly?

Then Gabe is behind me, his hands on my hips as I find my key in my bag and go to unlock my door. Gabe runs his lips along my neck, and I stretch to give him better access but he's distracting me from the job at hand and I can't find the lock.

"Stop. I can't." I mumble.

"Finding it hard to concentrate honey? Here, let me help." His hand reaches over and instead of taking the key from me, he guides my hand to the lock and unlocks the door. His front is crushed against my back and I can feel every hard inch of him, and he is *hard*!

In a daze, I let him gently push me inside and I drop my handbag, along with my keys on the small table I keep beside the door. He closes and locks the door behind him. The click of the lock echoes through the house and we're just standing there, looking at each other in silence.

"Are you sure Alexis, because once I get a taste of you I don't think I'm going to be able to stop. I mean I *will* if you tell me to, I'm not a monster but I want you so much right now that I can hear my heart beating." I've never been with someone who has wanted me as much as I can see that Gabe does. He's clenching and relaxing his hands, like he's struggling not to reach out to touch me and there's desire burning in his eyes.

I don't speak. I take two steps back from the man that is driving me insane and I see his chest expand in the darkness of the room, because we haven't even taken the time to turn on any lights. I reach behind me to find the zip on my dress. I can see the shadows on his face, he thinks I don't want this, him, anymore but nothing could be further from the truth.

Before he can react, I drop my dress in a puddle at my feet, leaving me standing there in my heels and revealing the matching lacy purple underwear he didn't know that I bought. I hear his sharp intake of breath, but I don't move.

"Fuck Lexi!" He takes his jacket off and hangs it on a hook next to the door. I watch his every movement and I can't help thinking he's moving too fucking slow, so I take a step forward. "Stop!" I'm mid-step, wondering what I've done wrong. "I take it this means you want me too?" He asks with a smirk.

"Yes." My voice is a hoarse whisper, but I don't repeat myself. We're surrounded by the silence of my house. All I can hear is my heart beating and our heavy breathing. There is nothing else except the two of us. I know he heard me.

In two long strides, he's standing in front of me but we're still not touching, and I need to touch him. I could pretend otherwise but the burning desire I have to touch him and for him to touch me is something I've never felt before and I don't want to hide from it.

"You're beautiful honey."

"Touch me Gabe. Please." He does as I ask, but it's a gentle touch. His hand cradling my cheek, his thumb stroking along my jawline and bottom lip. Poking my tongue out, I catch his thumb as he swipes it across my lip, and he groans. I have to break eye contact with him when I draw his thumb into my mouth to suck long and hard on it, because it's too intense. I hear him mutter, 'fuck' under his breath and I bring my eyes back to his because I want to watch this man, who is normally so composed, lose a little bit of his control. In my heels, our hips line up perfectly, so I step into his body and rub against him, feeling the hardness of his cock behind the zipper of his pants. "I need to see you naked Gabe."

He takes his hand from my hip and starts to unbutton his shirt but only does a couple before reaching behind him for his collar and pulling the shirt up over his head, in a move only guys seem to be able to pull off and throwing it on the floor where it joins my dress. "Holy shit!" The man is *built*! I mean you could see he was fit even with his clothes on but holy cow! I've never been this close to a six pack, but his could almost be an eight pack and I'm in awe. At some point he undid the button of his dress pants and they're hanging off his hips and without thinking, my finger trails along the hair that's leading into his pants . I pull down the zip all the way while I'm there and his pants drop to the floor. Then suddenly there's a cold breeze on my heated skin and I'm trying to work out why. Just as suddenly as he left, I feel his heat wrapping around me again, and his fingers are twisting themselves in my hair, pulling me closer to him.

"I take it by that, 'holy shit', you approve of the time I spend in the gym?" He asks, standing there in his boxer briefs, his breath tickling my ear.

"I do." I say quietly. "But I can't help wondering how many chocolate cakes you're going to indulge in with me if you're dedicated to keeping this body so." I can't find the words, so as explanation I run my hands all over his body. I feel more than hear his chuckle vibrate through his body.

"Don't worry honey, I'll always join in with some sweetness with you. Always."

Then he pulls my lips to his and kisses the breath out of me.

Our bodies collide, chest to chest, hips to hips and I can't think about anything except the feeling of his lips on mine, his taste and the feel of his body under my hands. He's overloading my senses, there's nothing else in the world except the two of us right now.

"I need you Gabe." I mumble into the side of his neck. His hands shift quickly from my hair down my shoulders to the clasp of my bra and before I know it, it's hanging off my shoulders. "Not out here, in my room, just in case." His hands move down to hold my butt and he lifts me up into his body. Wrapping my legs around his waist, my heels drop to the floor with a loud thud. Then he walks us both to my bedroom, where he lays me gently down on the bed, lowering his body over mine and I love feeling his weight over me.

"Shit." I hear him curse and he starts to move away.

"Where are you going?" I ask, knowing I sound panicked, but I don't want him to leave.

"I'll be back in five seconds, I promise Lexi, I need to get a condom from my wallet."

I take hold of his arms to stop him from moving. We both know if he wanted to keep going, he could but he stops and looks at me. "I've got some in here. You don't have to go anywhere." His face darkens and I understand where his mind has gone. "I bought them new. For us. I even put a couple in my handbag before you picked me up tonight." I blush at my confession, but I don't care, I want him to know that I want this. That I want *him*.

"Where?" I stretch out my arm so that I can touch the handle on my bedside drawers, I try to move my body over a little so that I can reach easier, but the weight of Gabe's body is stopping me from moving too far. A long arm stretches across me and a hand passes mine, opens the drawer, reaches in and pulls out the box that I mangled to get open earlier tonight. "Last chance honey. If you don't want this now is the time to speak up."

I don't say a word, I draw his head down to mine so that I can kiss him and when he's busy kissing the life out of me, I slide my hands over his shoulders, down his back to grab his arse giving it a squeeze for good measure. He growls in the back of his throat and tries to move his lips away from mine, but I kiss him deeper and he sinks into it. His arms are holding him up off me, so he has no choice but to let me do what I want right now, unless he wants to crush me. I smile against his lips, kissing him some more, then I spread my legs wide and pull his hips down to meet mine, grinding my hot, wet pussy against his hot, hard cock.

"Fuck!" He grunts, and in one swift move, we're both in the middle of the bed, with my head on my pillows. He sits up on his knees, between my legs and says, "These are coming off now." And he drags my lacy underwear down my legs, tossing them to the side somewhere.

"Your turn. Boxers off, now." He doesn't hesitate, he's up on his feet at the end of the bed, then his boxers are tossed somewhere to the side too. I can't help staring.

"Like what you see?" He asks.

"Very much so. Now get back down here and fuck me." I don't know where that came from. I've never been one to talk dirty, or demand a guy do anything but something about Gabe brings out the wilder side of me. I think I like it and I'm pretty sure Gabe does too, because he drops to his knees on the bed and crawls up my body.

"As you demand Lexi." He starts to kiss down my neck, wrapping his lips around my nipple, I don't give him much time to enjoy them because I pull his head up and wave a condom in his face.

"Next time Gabe. This time, I need you now. Please?"

He doesn't hesitate. His movements are fast and not as smooth as they were a few seconds ago. I'm glad I'm not the only one feeling the pressure of the anticipation. He rolls the condom onto his cock and positions himself between my legs. His hands run over my breast, down my ribs and over my hip, then he touches my clit and my body jumps.

That little bundle of nerves is super sensitive right now and I'm about ready to explode, especially if he keeps rubbing his finger over it.

"Sensitive here? Good to know." He says, his voice a deep rumbling sound. Then his finger slips lower, easily sliding into my pussy. "Lexi, honey, you're so hot and wet. You're ready for me." He sounds surprised, but I don't know how he can be, I already told him what I need him to do. He pulls his finger out and drops to kiss my throat.

I sit up slightly, so that my hands can squeeze his butt cheeks, pulling him in closer to where I need him to be. Then the tip of his cock is there and slowly he's pushing into my body, too slowly. I push my hips up to meet his, causing both of us to moan loudly as his cock fills my pussy.

"You're perfect." He rests his head in the crook of my neck, leaving sucking kisses along my neck and shoulder. Then he starts moving in and out of my body, slowly at first and then his pace picks up. My hands grip on tight to his shoulders, helping to leverage my body so that I can push up into his thrust. The sounds of our panting and grunting, skin slapping together, fills the room.

"Oh Gabe, harder." He launches himself up, sitting back on his legs to get leverage. His fingers dig into my hips as he pulls them up to get the right angle and then he starts pounding into me. I grip on to my breasts, squeezing and pulling my nipples, bringing me to the brink of my orgasm. "Gabe." I breathe out. "Fuck! I'm going to." I can't finish my sentence because his finger presses on my clit and everything is just so ready and sensitive, that one simple touch sends me off. I squeeze my eyes closed, grip on tight to my breasts and scream out. It's almost a roar.

I come back to earth just as Gabe's movements become a little less controlled and then he throws his head back and lets out a deep growl. It's like nothing I've ever heard before. He sits up like that for a few seconds. I watch his chest rise and fall as he tries to catch his breath. He is the sexiest man I have ever known.

He pulls out of my body, leans down and kisses me softly on the lips. "Let me take care of this." He says and disappears into the bathroom to throw away the condom. I can't move, I just lie there watching him move around my room like he's always been there. Like he belongs.

He strides back into the room and my eyes don't stray from watching him move.

"Are you OK honey? I didn't hurt you, did I Lexi?" He asks, concern all over his handsome face. He didn't hurt me, but he sure does have the potential to. Way more than Stephen ever did. It's only been a few short weeks and for some of them I thought he was a stalker, but I think I'm already half in love with him. Which is more than I could have ever said about my ex.

"I'm fine. You gave me exactly what I asked for Gabe." His smile is amazing.

"Come here." He says, pulling me into his arms and pulling the blankets back, then up to cover us. "Get some sleep. You'll need it for round two." I shudder in anticipation.

"Are you staying the night?" I ask, snuggling my back into his front and hearing him groan quietly.

"Is that what you want?"

"Yes." Is my simple answer.

"Then my answer is hell yes. I'm not going anywhere until I have to honey." Wrapping a leg over mine and pulling me tight into his arms, he sighs. "Now, get some sleep, because I have a few plans for you later and you'll need your rest."

"Goodnight Gabriel." I whisper, a smile on my face.

"Good night Alexis." He whispers into my hair. "Sleep well honey."

Chapter Twenty

GABE

Lexi demanding I strip off and then telling me to fuck her, is the hottest thing I've ever seen or heard in my *life*. I never would have guessed that she got a little bossy in bed, but I'm certainly not complaining. In fact, I doubt there are too many guys that would complain, it's nice when you don't have to take the lead every time you're in bed with someone.

Inviting myself for a sleepover was a risk, but one I was more than happy to take. I wanted to stay with Lexi. I wanted to have her body again, to make her scream out in pleasure. I did just that at some point in the night and then we fell back to sleep, and I've never slept better than when I'm wrapped around Lexi. My sleep was deep and restful. It's been a long time since I can say that about my sleep.

Opening my eyes the following morning, I feel her gorgeous body wrapped around me and I'm glad I stayed. We're lying on our side and the sun is shining one long strip through the tiny gap in the curtain and it's highlighting the blonde in her hair. I smile, knowing that this is where I want to be, where I belong.

"What are you smiling at?" Her voice is soft, almost dreamlike.

"I'm happy." It's simple, and it's the absolute truth. I pull her in close to me, her head resting under my chin and I kiss her on the top of her head. I feel the light kiss that she plants on my chest and affection for this beautiful woman lights me up.

"I had a dream that you woke me with your tongue." She mumbles into my chest.

"That wasn't a dream honey, that actually happened a few hours ago and you enjoyed it very much." I smile against the top of her head and she hums.

"Does that mean that I gave you the, and I quote, 'best blow job of your life'? Cause I thought that was a sexy dream too, one I planned on making a reality this morning, but you know, if we've been there and done that, there's no point really." She says, trying to move away from me, but I've got a tight grip on her and I'm not letting her leave this bed just yet.

"Oh, you blew my fucking mind Lexi, but that doesn't mean we can't *both* get a repeat performance this morning." My voice is still deep from sleep and my need for Lexi sure isn't helping to clear it.

"Maybe I should give you another one, just to make sure I'm doing it right and it wasn't all a very sexy, very vivid dream?" She pulls back from my chest and plants her hands there instead and pushes me backwards. Well, she tried to and we both know the only way I'll be on my back is if I let her push me but I'm not going to resist her. I'm available for her to play with and touch however and whenever she wants to.

Just as things start getting interesting, I hear voices float in from the front door and I sigh, knowing this session is about to be cut short. That is until Lexi's head drops onto my stomach, an inch away from where I need her and my cock jumps trying to get closer to her. I groan, not because Cat is here, no this is her home, but because I wanted some more time alone with Lexi and that's not going to happen now.

I hear Cat's mumbled voice tell whoever she's with that her sister went out on a date last night and that by the state of the living room, it looks like it ended well.

"You mean with the guy from a few weeks ago?" A male voice asks, he's not trying to keep his voice low like Cat is, there's a pause and then he says, "I'd like to meet this guy and thank him for looking after my girl and her sister." Ahh so this must be Joshua, Cat's fiancé.

"Awww you're sweet Joshua, but Lacey was there too you know *and* by the looks of it, I think Lexi thanked him for all of us last night."

Barefoot and Dumped!

"I can't argue with you there, they had some fun here last night by the look of it. I'm glad we stayed at home." He chuckles and I can't help laughing myself, but I try to disguise it with a cough.

"This *is* my home Joshua." Cat says rather harshly.

"No Catherine, this is where you're living because you didn't want your sister rattling around this place alone. Our house is *home* sweetheart, so let's grab some more stuff and get out of here before the lovebirds wake up."

"You know they're awake and listening to everything we say, right?" I can't hold back my laughter any longer. I was starting to feel a little awkward because I thought we were going to be listening to an argument, but I think that's just the way they talk. "Good morning Lexi, Gabe. I hope we didn't wake you up?" Cat calls out.

"Or interrupt anything." Joshua calls out and I hear a solid thump and he grunts. "Fuck Cat you didn't have to hit me!"

"That's my sister you idiot, I don't want to know what or *if* we interrupted anything. Ever."

"Good morning Catherine, and no, you guys didn't wake us up or interrupt anything." I call out, hoping to make this situation a little less uncomfortable for everyone.

"Yes they did." Lexi mumbles into my stomach. "They *did* interrupt something! I was going to prove that my blow jobs were epic." How can any woman be pissed off that she can't give a guy a blow job? I can't help laughing at her pouting lips, and I kiss them to take away the sting of my amusement.

"Surely it should be *me* that's annoyed I don't get your magic mouth wrapped around my cock?" That obviously doesn't make Lexi happy because she's scowling up at me from my stomach, and I can see the temptation to do it anyway, all over her face. "Come on honey, let's get up and talk to your sister and her fiancé. We have the rest of the day to enjoy each other."

"Hmmph. Make us some coffee Cat." She yells out at the top of her voice, making me jump a little because I wasn't expecting it. "Sorry." She mumbles.

"Lexi, can you go get my clothes for me please? I left them all out in the living room." I'm not going out there in my boxers to retrieve my clothes, not in front of her sister and I don't even know Joshua. He might want to punch my lights out for walking around basically naked in front of his girl.

"Of course, just give me a second to put on my own clothes and then I'll get them." She says, a smile spreading across her face as she drags her eyes up and down my body, checking me out.

"If you keep looking at me like that honey, your sister and Joshua are going to get a show they'll never forget." Her eyes dart up to meet mine and a blush creeps up her throat and onto her cheeks. I can tell by the way her eyes darken she knows exactly what kind of show we'd give them.

She breaks eye contact with me and coughs quietly, "I'll be back in a second with your clothes."

When she opens the door to leave, she lets out a startle squeak. "Hell, Cat you gave me a heart attack!" She says her voice a high pitched squeal.

"I thought Gabe might like something to wear before he came out here, and I thought I'd save you a trip. You're welcome." She smiles at her sister and then looks passed her to find me. Her eyes widen in surprise and it's hard to decipher in this light whether it's a good kind of surprise or not.

"Thank you Cat, I appreciate it." I say, smiling genuinely at her as I reach out for my clothes that even though Lexi has a hold of, Cat hasn't let go of yet. "Can I have my clothes now please?"

"Oh yes, of course." Cat says and they both let go and I walk back to the bed to sit down and pull on my pants.

"Holy crap Lexi!" I hear Cat say, even though she thinks she's whispering.

"I know. Now go away and make us coffee. We'll be out in a few minutes." Lexi says and pushes the door closed in her sisters face.

I walk over to the door where Lexi is still standing, and ask, "Are you OK honey?"

"You're dressed."

"I am and so are you." I chuckle. "We can get naked again once Cat and Joshua leave, OK?"

"Promise?" She asks sweetly.

"Absolutely honey. Now let's get out there, the sooner we talk to them, the sooner they'll leave." I say, hoping it's the truth. I just want to spend more time with Lexi, clothed or naked, I don't really care honestly.

"We can only hope." Lexi mumbles. She's mumbling a lot this morning and I can't help laughing at her disgruntled attitude.

As we walk through the living room to the kitchen, I have to admit, Cat and Joshua were right, there are clothes and shoes everywhere. I didn't even notice that we'd spread them around the place last night, but I wasn't concerned about where the clothes landed, only that they were no longer covering up our bodies, stopping us from being as close as possible to one another.

"Look, sweetheart, I'm not saying you and Lexi can't handle yourselves, I'm just saying that Lacey can hold her own no matter where she is or who she's with, that's all. You're my fiancé and Lexi is your sister, I'm just saying that I'm glad you found a guy that looked out for you, rather than one that took advantage of you girls being on your own. That's all." Poor guy, he sounds beyond frustrated and I know how he feels. I'm glad I was there for the girls the first night we met too, even though I could imagine any of them kicking a guy in the balls if he stepped out of line, it's still nice to know I could watch out for them.

We walk into the kitchen just as Cat pulls him in for a hug and says, "I know sweetie, but you don't have to worry so much."

"It's not about whether you girls are capable of taking care of yourselves, it's more about the jerks that are out there that don't like taking no for an answer. We know what they're thinking and some of them are willing to just take whatever they want." I say, earning a high five from Joshua, and scowls from both of the Stratton sisters. "I know you girls know what guys can be like but most guys like that will get physical with a woman, no matter how big or small he is, he thinks he has the advantage."

"Exactly! Thanks Gabe." I shake the hand he's holding out for me. "That is your name right? I wouldn't want to get it wrong. Not that Lexi has guys coming in and out of here all the time or anything."

"Just shut up Joshua." Cat shakes her head, laughing at him.

"Stop talking Josh, please." Lexi pleads, her face in her hands.

"Sorry. I get a bit carried away sometimes." He says, and I laugh. "I'm Joshua, Catherine's fiancé." Again, he hold out his hand for me to shake.

"Gabe, Lexi's boyfriend." I say to introduce myself. Lexi looks at me so fast I'm surprised her head doesn't fall off and Cat's mouth is hanging open in surprise.

"You guys don't waste any time do you?" Joshua asks. "Good on you. I'm happy for you both, just make sure you treat our Alexis right or there will be trouble, you hear me? That ex of hers is a real bastard and I would love to get my hands on him for just a few minutes, but the girls won't let me. They keep telling me he's not worth the trouble."

"When you know, you know, right? Lexi is special and I promise to do everything in my power to make her *very* happy and if I ever see her ex around here, he'll want to hope I don't get my hands on him." Joshua nods and I get the feeling he approves of me. I hadn't realise how much I wanted him to, I've never cared too much before if people approve of me or not. I pull Lexi into my side, needing to touch her while we talk about her ex.

Silence fills the room, but funnily enough, it's not awkward, just quiet.

"Stephen won't do anything, he's too scared of my dad for a start, and he knows he would lose his job if he got caught harassing any of us. His father would leave him to pay whatever price he had to. Daddy used to help him out of any trouble he got into, but he really screwed up a year or so ago and he told him he wouldn't be helping him out again."

Cat nods in agreement, so does Joshua as he says, "He's had so many second chances, I'm not surprised his dad has washed his hands of him. Him and his mate Kyle need to grow up."

"Kyle is a good kid, he just lets Stephen tell him what to do and even though that's a stupid way to live your life, he's never the instigator or ideas guy."

There's something about those names that are familiar. There's something about them nagging in the back of my mind trying to come forward, but I push it aside. I just want to spend time with Lexi and get to know her family and friends. Nothing else matters to me right now.

Chapter Twenty-one

LEXI

I've never been so disappointed to see my sister. Don't get me wrong, I love Cat and Joshua to pieces, but I really wish that they'd stayed away this morning, instead of ruining my morning with Gabe.

I'm not sure what happened last night. I've never and I mean never had sex where everything just felt so damned right. Stephen isn't the first guy I've been with, but he certainly wasn't the best one in bed. The more I think about him, and honestly I'm trying to *not* compare Gabe with him, but the differences are staggering, and I can't help wondering why the hell I stayed with him for so long. Was it really just because it was easier to be in a relationship with someone than not? Should I slow this thing with Gabe down? I mean we haven't known each other that long and last night was really our first date and we slept together.

"Are you OK honey?" Gabe asks, leaning in to speak into my hair quietly so that no one else can hear him.

I look up to answer him and his eyes show so much concern that I can't brush him off with a simple answer of yes. "I'm just thinking, that's all."

"About us or last night?" Before I can answer him my sister does it for me.

"Oh don't worry she's over thinking about everything. Being with you, your date, being *with* you last night." She shrugs when I give her a dirty look, trying to convey through that one look that I want her to shut the hell up. "What? It's true and you know it Lexi. It's why you stayed with Stephen for so long."

She says it so matter of factly that I can't help asking. "What's that supposed to mean?"

"Come on Lexi, you know what that means. He wasn't good for you or *to* you. I know he wasn't good in bed and seeing you this morning with Gabe only proves that point."

"Catherine, that's enough." Joshua says, but this isn't something new to him and he only wants her to stop because he doesn't want to be a part of the conversation.

"No. Joshua, it's not." She says to him before looking back to me. "It's the truth Lexi. He was a jerk and not just to you, but to all of us. You stayed with him because it was easy and convenient, but if I wasn't living here, I wouldn't have seen you because he pulled you away from everyone."

I want to disagree with her, but the more she says, the more I realise it's the truth. "You're right Cat, but I wasn't really thinking about him. I was thinking that I didn't want to make those same mistakes with Gabe. I don't want things to move so fast that I lose myself again." I take a deep breath and look up at Gabe. I feel like a monster having this conversation with him in the room, especially after the night we just had.

"I'm not him Lexi. I know you told me to slow down, so maybe this is all my fault. I pushed and I shouldn't have. The fact that you love and respect your sister and Lacey so much is admirable, and I would never try to take that away from you." He looks down to the floor and takes a step away from me. "I think I might go home now."

"Please Gabe, don't go." I beg.

"Look , this is my fault I shouldn't have said anything, but what I was trying to say and only ended up making everyone feel bad is this. Gabe is nothing like Stephen and when I said she was overthinking, I meant that she's too in her head and that she needs to learn to enjoy life. Enjoy just being with someone who enjoys being with *her* as much she enjoys being with *him*. I wasn't trying to imply that what you guys are doing is wrong or too soon." Cat steps away from Joshua and comes to give me a hug. A tight one. "It's not too soon, because let's face it Lex, you left that relationship long before he called it off."

She is one hundred percent right and I know I was ready to walk away from the relationship myself, I was just waiting until after my parents party. Was it because I wanted to have someone there with me, or because I was giving it time to 'get better'.

"You're right. I know you are, and I know you're nothing like him. My ex was a jerk in his behaviour, selfish in every way a human could be, and he used his dad to get himself out of trouble every single time he found any." I look at Gabe, who miraculously hasn't walked out the door and left all this crazy crap behind him. "I'm sorry. I was thinking about him just now and I guess I was comparing the two of you, but not to work out if you were like him or if he was better. He's not, not even close." I take a deep breath. "I was actually telling myself to forget the bullshit. Forget about what others might think and whether it's fast or not and just enjoy us. I like you Gabe and I don't want you to leave. I want you to stay here with me today. In fact any day you want to be here with me, I'm happy to have you." I smile at him and reach out to take his hands in mine, and when he lets me, I've never been happier.

"Yeah?" He asks, and I hate that I made this confident man question what I was thinking and feeling about what happened last night.

"Absolutely. Last night was the best night I've had in years and I want more of them."

"Right then! That's our cue to leave Cat." Joshua places a light kiss on Lexi's cheek and takes Cat's hand in his, leading her towards the front door. "Come on sweetheart, you got what you needed. You had a coffee and you managed to make your sister and her new boyfriend a little uncomfortable, while giving them some shit to talk about. It's been a busy morning for you already and I want to have you to myself for a while."

"Too much information Joshua." I say, even though I'm smiling at him.

Cat drops his hand and gives me a tight hug. She says quietly in my ear, "I'm sorry if I made things awkward, I just want you to realise that Gabe's not like your ex and to enjoy him."

I squeeze my sister tightly right back. "You know you can move out any time you want, right? I mean I love having you here, but you don't have to stay here for *me*."

"I know." She says just above a whisper. I wonder if she's having second thoughts about Joshua, but I've realised that she just doesn't want to leave me alone. So, I grab a hold of her shoulders and push her back so that I can look her directly in the eyes.

"Listen and listen to me good Catherine. I *love* having you here, most of the time, but I think it's time you moved out. You don't need to worry about me, I'm absolutely fine." I smile at her, hoping she can see that I mean what I say.

"OK Lex." She nods in agreement. "I'll move out sooner rather than later."

"Good. Now get out of here so we can all have some fun." I say, making everyone laugh. I walk Cat and Joshua to the door and say, "Maybe I should ask for your key back, then you'd have to move out."

"What?! Do you mean I don't get to keep it for emergencies and –" I don't let her finish.

"Nope. You move out and that key is mine again sis. Now get out of here." I push them out the door and lock it behind them. I know they can still get back in if they really want to, but I want them to understand that I don't want them here right now.

"You know they can get back in if they want, right?" Gabe asks with a laugh.

"Yeah I do but they won't. Well, Joshua won't let Cat come back anyway. He wants her to move out of here and in with him, almost as much as I do." I laugh but there's only a small amount of humour in it.

"Do you really want your sister to move out that badly?" Gabe asks.

"Yes and no." I know my answer confuses him by the scowl that now mars his handsome face. "Let me explain. I love having her here, most of the time. Other times, I would *really* love to have my privacy and quiet time back again, but I also know that she *wants* to move in with Joshua and he wants that too. I know she moved in to make sure I was OK and not alone, but I like my own space. I bought this house so that I would have it and then she invaded my space."

"So, what you're saying is, you don't like people in your space?" He asks.

"Not unless I want them there in it, no." I smile at him. "I like having my sister around, but I wish she wasn't here every day. Been there, done that when we were kids. There are other people I want here a lot more than I do Cat."

"Oh yeah, and who would that be? Lacey?" Slowly we move closer to one another, until we're almost nose to nose.

"Nope. Lacey knows how to make herself at home around here too and it's not that I mind so much, but I like waking up knowing I'm the only one here."

"You want to wake up alone?" He asks me, curiously.

"I used to want to wake up alone. Before this morning that is anyway." I say with a smile.

"Now how do you want to wake up then?" He asks, his voice getting deeper.

"How about with your mouth on my pussy?" I ask, my voice smoky and yet smooth. "Or with my lips wrapped around your cock? Doesn't that sound like the perfect way to wake up in the morning? I can't have that if my little sister is in the house, can I?"

I squeal because the next thing I know I'm hanging upside down over Gabe's shoulder with a perfect view of his magnificent derrière as he walks us back to my bedroom.

"How about we test out how perfect that would be?"

"But we already got out of bed Gabe." I can't help but laugh. I shouldn't be turned on by his Neanderthal behaviour but I am.

"Let's pretend we weren't interrupted, and we can pick up where we left off then, because I want your lips wrapped around my cock." He throws me down onto the bed and I only bounce once, because he drops his body down onto mine, his lips crashing into mine and taking possession of them. He runs his tongue across the seam of my lips, begging for entrance. He nips lightly on my bottom lip, causing me to gasp and that gives him the access he desires to my mouth and our tongues start to twist and battle, until his wins as he plunders in and out of my mouth, fucking my mouth, and making promises of things to come. Namely me and no doubt him as well.

I push on his shoulders, coaxing him to lie on his back and let me take over for a while. I get the feeling he doesn't hand over control very often, but I want to see him relax and enjoy himself for a while, without thinking about me. Slowly, I unbutton his shirt, starting at the collar and working my way down to his waist, where I unbuckle his belt and then make quick work of the button and zip. He lifts his hips, allowing me to strip both his pants and boxers off him. I take just a few seconds to drink him in. He's lying there, on *my* bed, his shirt spread open so that I can see every dip and crevice of his upper body. Naked from the waist down, because he never did get around to putting his socks and shoes back on when he got dressed earlier.

"My word Gabriel Romanetti, do you have any idea how sexy you are right now?" I'm practically drooling all over him and I don't think I can stop. I look up, catching his eyes with mine and they shine with what I can only describe as pride and lust. There might even be a hint of love in there, but I don't want to read too much into one look.

"If it means you look at me like that for the rest of our lives, I will work hard to keep this body just the way you like it, honey."

The rest of our lives. Yeah, I could absolutely live with that, but I don't say a word to him. I don't want to tell him that after one date and a few orgasms that I want forever with him, it's too soon, but I *can* make his eyes roll into the back of his head with ecstasy. With that in mind, I reach out and wrap my hand around his hard cock, working up and down his erection and rubbing my thumb over the head, through the slit and using the pre-cum dripping out it as lubrication for my hand.

"Holy fuck that feels amazing Lexi." He's watching my hand move up and down his cock and I'm watching his face. His hands move to his stomach and he starts rubbing them up and down his chest, slowly. I lean down and take just the head of his erection into my mouth and suck in my cheeks to put pressure on him and his head presses back into the pillow, but his hands stay resting on his chest, I can see his nails digging into his flesh. My hand and my mouth work his cock, up and down, up and down, I find the perfect rhythm that makes him lose all concept of time. My other hand reaches between his legs and starts to play with his balls, and he jumps so high his cock hits the back of my throat without warning. "That's just, fuck Lexi that's out of this world good." If he can still speak then I feel like I'm not doing the job right.

His hands drop off his chest and he fists the sheets, his knuckles white, as I draw my mouth up and down his cock fast a few times, then I take him in slowly a few times and feel his body relax. Then I do it all over again, fast a few times as his body tenses up, and then slowly until I feel his body relax. I don't know how long we go on like that, I'm just enjoying making him fucking crazy, but suddenly he pulls me off his cock and up his body.

"Enough." He growls. "I can't take it anymore. If you keep going at me like that I'm going to come in your mouth, and I don't want to."

"What if I want you to?"

"Fuck! No, not today, I need you Lexi."

"You've got me Gabe." I say, my voice a little rough after having his cock hitting the back of my throat over and over again.

The next thing I know, I'm flat on my back and he's stripping me out of my clothes. There's no finesse, he doesn't seem to have time for that, he's in too much of a hurry and I have to admit, having a man like Gabe want me so passionately does things to my ego. Things that I've never felt before and I know, without a doubt in my mind or my heart, I could fall in love with this man very easily. In fact, I think I'm already half there as it is.

I don't have time to think about the implications of maybe being in love with him, because his lips are making their way up my inner thigh and I gasp, as he wraps them around my clit and sucks. Hard.

Chapter Twenty-two

GABE

I have to move Lexi and her amazing mouth off my cock before I cut our session embarrassingly short, but when she looks at me like I've taken away her favourite toy, I have second thoughts about letting her finish. Those thoughts only last a few seconds though, because my need to be inside her when I come is overwhelming, and no blow job, even one that's the best of my life, will take that away from me. So, instead of letting her have her way, I pull her up my body. She wiggles her hips as they reach my groin and my cock is enveloped by her pussy lips, with my tip pushing against her clit. She rocks her body against me, my need for her intensifying with every bump and grind. The need to touch her everywhere is overpowering. I twist my hand in her hair and pull her lips down to meet mine for a kiss that's so hot I can feel a scorching pulse through my whole body. I flip us over quickly so that I'm on top. I need her out of her clothes, because I don't want anything between us. I rip off my shirt as well, not caring where any of it lands.

"Gabe." My name is nothing more than a moan coming from her lips.

"I know." My own voice a barely audible growl. I need her more than I've needed anything in my life. I feel completely out of control, and yet in complete control of what we're doing, even though the only thing I can think of is her. And me.

I need to feel every inch of her skin under my lips. So, I trail them over her jaw, her throat, to her collarbone and stay there for a minute, sucking. Lexi moans and squirms underneath me, her body moving against mine, causing the best kind of friction. I don't give in to what I know she wants though, it's what I want too but I want to taste her more.

I drag my tongue down between her breasts, a hand on each of them, kneading them and pinching lightly at her nipples. I put my knees between hers and push them apart so that she can't get any friction where she wants it.

"Gabe, please." I know what she's begging for and I'll get there eventually but I'm taking my time. "Now Gabe, please."

"No!" I growl.

"What do you mean, no?" She gasps as I suck a nipple into my mouth and suck, hard. Her eyes squeeze shut, and her hips try to jerk up off of the bed, but they don't get far because my hips push them back down to the mattress. Before she can take a breath, I release one nipple from my mouth and turn my attentions to the other one. My name falls from her lips on a growl and she mumbles fuck, over and over again. Her hands unclench from the bed sheet and they pull at my hair. I'm not sure if she's trying to push me away or pull me in closer, but either way, I move down her body, licking, biting and nibbling along my way.

When I get to her hips, I kiss each of them lightly but it's not enough for her. Her hands, which are still tangled in my hair, try to pull me back up her body so, I grab them and pin them to the bed. Her body stiffens, her first instinct to fight being restrained, but I don't give her enough time to think. I kiss the inside of her thighs and then I wrap my lips around her clit and suck. I suck and then lick, repeating the actions to build her need up as high as I can get it. Her hips are trying to get closer to my mouth, and yet pulling away at the same time.

"Fuck!" Lexi screams, but her voice is hoarse, and her body is taut with tension. I push two fingers into her pussy. "No. No, Gabe I can't. Not again. Too soon." She says she can't, but I can feel her body building up for another release. Her head is rocking from side to side, emphasising her muttered no, no, no.

"Oh yes you can honey." I release her hands and move my body so that I can reach past her to where we threw the box of condoms last night. I've got the packet ripped open, and the condom rolled onto my cock almost before Lexi notices I'm missing. I'm watching her, and I see the minute she starts coming down from the euphoria I had her hovering at. I see when she realises that her hands are free and my body isn't over hers, but she only gets a few seconds to think about what's going on before I'm back between her legs, my knees keeping hers spread wide. "Are you ready Lexi?" I ask but I don't give her time to answer me.

I push at her pussy lips, she's open and ready for me, making it easy to bury my cock deeply into the warmth of her body in one swift movement. When I'm buried deep inside her, I pause for a minute, enjoying being surrounded by her and giving her time to adjust, before I start moving. I pull out and she moans, then I push my hips back into hers, dragging the hardness of my cock over her clit again and again.

Lexi scrapes her fingernails down my back, while wrapping her legs around my hips, pulling me in closer to her body. We're both just about the sensations, the feeling of being together. I can't get enough of her. I can get deep enough. Touch her enough. *Feel* her enough.

Lexi's hands leave my back and move to gently hold my face. The gentleness in her touch is my undoing. When she pulls my lips down to meet hers and gently kisses me, I know I've lost the battle. I can feel her body starting to pulse around me and I'm fighting to hold off my own release so that she has time to reach hers, again. That is, until she pulls her lips from mine, pulling my ear to her lips and I think she's going to bite me or something, but instead she whispers in my ear, "Come for me Gabe." She brings me undone and my hips pound into her uncontrollably as she brings my face back around for our eyes to meet. Her legs tighten their grip around my hips, but her hands are still gently holding onto my face. "Oh fuck Gabe!" That's all I need to hear and as I feel her body shake with release, I feel my own orgasm shatter and then I drop my head to rest in the crook of her neck.

"Lexi." I whisper into her shoulder. I have all these feelings, all these thoughts but I keep them to myself as I feel us both come down from our high. I roll off her body to lie beside her on my back, trying to catch my breath. Beside me, I can hear Lexi breathing heavily and I'm glad to know I'm not the only one that's affected.

I move off the bed, because I need to get rid of the condom and clean myself up a bit and I know if I stay there for too long, I'll fall asleep. So, I walk to the bathroom and do what I need to do. When I get back into her bedroom, Lexi is laying right where I left her and there's a smile on her face that can only be described as bliss. It makes me want to beat my chest with pride knowing that I put that smile there. Instead of going full Neanderthal on my girlfriend, I climb back into bed, slide up next to her and curl my body around hers. We fit together perfectly, as I roll her onto her side and pull her back to my front. She wiggles her butt in my crotch to get comfortable and I growl in her ear.

"I'm not nineteen anymore, I'm a middle aged man Lex, I need a break before we go again." I say with a quiet groan in her ear. I don't hear her laughter, but I feel her body shaking against mine, and one of her hands moves to her mouth to cover any noise that might come out. I run my fingers over her side, tickling her, wanting to hear her light laughter. "You think that's funny do you, Miss Stratton?" I ask, using the arm I tucked under her neck to tickle her stomach.

"No! Stop!" She says with a raspy laugh. ""Gabe, please. Stop. I'm sorry."

I pause my hands. "What are you sorry for?"

"Wiggling around to get comfortable?" She says but it's more of a question than a statement.

"Are you asking me or telling me?" I feel her shoulders shrug under my chin. "Were you questioning my manhood honey?" She squirms around until she's facing me, with her hands resting on my chest. This woman does amazing things to me and I see my future with her.

Her gorgeous dark chocolate brown eyes look straight into mine as she says, "I would *never* call your *manhood* into question Gabriel. It's the best manhood I've ever met, you use it extremely well."

"I can't believe you just said that with a straight face." I laugh.

"I can. I would never call your manhood into question. You're the best man I've ever met." Sighing she continues. "I've known other men Gabe, and my ex, well he wasn't much of man honestly. You're different. You remind me of my dad." I pull back, almost pulling out of her arms, so she tightens her hold on me. "I don't mean that I have a daddy fetish, I mean that he's a good man. He loves my mum and his family. Cat and I are his world and I can see the same values he has in you. I mean, the first night we met you looked after three women you didn't even know, you could have just let us fend for ourselves."

"You mean the night you can't remember?" I chuckle, and her hands pull back from my chest and I think she's going to move away from me, but instead she slaps them both back onto my chest. "That's quite a punch you've got there."

"That wasn't a punch, but it can be mister. My dad also taught me how to fight, and I can pack a mean punch when I want to."

"Your dad taught you how to throw a punch?" I ask, surprised.

"Yeah, he wanted me to be able to land a punch that would knock a guy on his arse if he touched me when I didn't want him to. It came in handy more times than I think he would have hoped and many more than I ever told him about."

I throw my head back and roar out a laugh. I can't imagine being a father of two little girls. Her dads determination that his daughters could defend themselves against boys is admirable. "I can't wait to meet your dad and I hope to be half the father he is one day if we have daughters." I lean down to kiss her forehead and I see the shock on her face.

"You've thought about us having kids?" She asks, her voice a quiet of squeak.

Her questions make me stop to think. Have I thought about us getting married and having a family together? "If you're asking me if I want kids, the answer is yes. If you're asking if I've thought about us having kids together, I guess I'd be lying if I said no considering what I just said, but I don't think I was consciously thinking about it." I see the disappointment on her face. "That being said, now that I've said it out loud, I like it. No, I love the idea of seeing you round with *our* baby and having a mini Alexis running around."

"Really?" I nod, a smile stretching across my face the more I think about it.

"I've always wanted a family Lexi, but I've never envisioned actually *having* kids before, but I can see mini Lexi's running around and me adoring them. I know that any daughters we have would have both of their grandfathers wrapped around their little fingers."

I can't help laughing when I picture my dad and a little girl that looks like Lexi sitting in his lap, smiling up at him. He would adore her and do anything for her. We might be in trouble in the future.

I come out of my daydream and realise Lexi hasn't said anything, she hasn't moved either. "Is everything OK Lexi?"

"Uhuh." She answers, a little too cheery and tries to pull away from me, but I don't let her get too far.

"Too much, too soon?" I ask, holding her tightly and looking her in the eyes, I need to see her response.

"No. Yes." She buries her face her in hands and leans her forehead into my chest. "Maybe. Shit I don't know Gabe. I can't help but wonder if this whole thing is moving too fast. I know I'm insanely attracted to you, and I think you are to me." Does she really question that?

"I am *insanely* attracted to you Lexi and I have been since the first time I saw you. Never, ever doubt my attraction to you honey, but that's not all this is. You know that, right?"

"It's hard not to question what the base of this relationship is Gabe. I mean, we met a while ago but as you've so gallantly pointed out, I don't actually really remember it."

"I didn't mean it like that, I was just teasing you. I didn't mean to offend you, honey." I smile and pull her hands from her face, but she just buries further into my chest, and I didn't think that was possible. If she speaks, I won't be able to understand her mumbles. "Look at me Lexi."

"I know and I'm not offended, the fact is that night is a blur, but it's a blur because I was drinking to forget that my boyfriend just dumped me. At my parents wedding anniversary party. In front of our family and friends. He didn't even care enough to do it beforehand or wait until after. The truth is, I'm not upset about breaking up with him, I don't miss him, and I know I didn't love him. At all. We met that night, after what was supposed to be a heartbreaking break up."

"But you weren't heartbroken. You've told me that before and you said that just now. You're glad that he broke up with you, because you realised that you were together because it was convenient."

"You're right. I wasn't then and I'm not heartbroken now either. In fact, I'm happier than I can ever remember being when I'm with you."

"But?" I can feel the hesitation coming off her in waves.

Barefoot and Dumped!

"But, again, I can't help wondering if we've moved too fast. We had our first date last night and then we slept together. I don't sleep with guys on the first date. Ever." She takes a deep breath, eyes closed tightly for a second until they lock onto mine. "I just can't help myself with you. I feel like I've known you for years. I'm comfortable with you and I love spending time with you. My heart is ruling my brain, and if I'm being honest, it scares the absolute crap out of me, but I can't and don't want to stop."

"The intensity of my feelings for you and how quickly they hit me, scares the crap out of me too Lexi, but I don't want to stop it either. I don't think I could even if I *did* want to and for the record, I don't want to. Ever."

Both of us hold our breaths, this conversation is one we definitely had to have, but she's right, having it so soon kind of feels insane.

"I've fallen in love with you Alexis Stratton." I'm holding her face gently in my hands, looking deep into her eyes. We're naked and sated from amazing sex, but there's more to us than that and I hope she understands that.

"I've fallen in love with you too, Gabriel Romanetti." Her voice husky with emotion as she reaches to take my face in her hands too. Our lips meet in a gentle, loving kiss, but Lexi pulls back before it can go any further.

"I think we need food." She says, as her stomach grumbles noisily and we both laugh.

"Breakfast it is then. Why don't you go have a shower and I'll make us something to eat?" I say.

"We could have a shower together and then make breakfast." She suggests with a smile.

"No, you'll be too distracting, and you need some sustenance before we do anything else today." I wink and smack her butt cheeks to get her moving. What I didn't count on was her squeal and then her pinching my nipple in return. "Keep that up and you'll be punished with more than a smack on the arse honey." I tell her, sitting up and pulling us both off the bed. I swing her over my shoulder, one hand on her very delectable butt, and quickly deposit her in the bathroom. "Shower, now." I point towards the shower.

Chelle Pimblott

"Looks like you're interested in another round, not breakfast." She takes a step towards me and I take two backwards. She's right, my cock is at half-mast after our spanking and nipple pinching, but I want to make her understand that there's more to us than sex, so I walk away, closing the door behind me. "I could have waited a bit longer for breakfast, just so you know." She yells through the door and then I hear the shower start. So, I quickly walk back into the bedroom, pull on my pants and walk to the kitchen to see what I can make us for breakfast.

I decide on eggs, bacon and pancakes, the breakfast of champions and get to work. I catch myself whistling as I mix up the pancake batter and can't help smiling, I can't remember being this happy in a very long time.

I love Lexi Stratton and I'm going to spend every day making her believe that.

Chapter Twenty-three

LEXI

I get in the shower, not because Gabe tells me to, but because I need to clean up. Not to mention, taking a few minutes to stop and think things through always helps me clear my head. Would I have told him he couldn't join me if he had taken me up on my invitation, hell no, but I appreciate having some time alone.

Are we going too fast? Do I care? He loves me and I know I love him. I fell in lust with him the day I bumped into him outside of Berry's Café, and even when I thought he was a weird stalker, I wanted to jump his bones. I wouldn't have, just for the record because I'm not that desperate, but yesterday is when I think I fell in love with him.

His admission about his ex, that beautiful dinner he took me to but mostly, it was the fact that he just wanted to spend time with me and to do that, he came shopping with me. The fact that I was shopping for a dress to wear on our date didn't faze him and then he paid for the damned thing! Which angered me at the time, but I can see now that he was just being generous. Although, I can pay for my own things and I will find a way to pay him back without him realising it.

I turn off the shower and step out, grabbing a towel along the way, I dry myself and then wrap it around my body. I grab a smaller towel and wrap it around my hair. I open the door to walk back to my room and that's when I realise the door wasn't locked, meaning Gabe could have come in any time he liked, but didn't. I can't believe I didn't lock it. I always lock the bathroom door, especially when I'm in the shower, if for no reason other than because it stops my sister or Lacey from walking in without announcing their presence.

When I sit on my bed, I see Gabe's clothes spread over the floor with mine and smile. I could get used to his stuff being mixed up with mine. I laugh at my own ridiculous thoughts, who's moving too fast now? I get dressed, pick up Gabe's clothes and put them on the bed.

I'm about to join Gabe in the kitchen when my phone rattles across the bedside drawers.

Cat: *Don't forget we've got dinner with the parentals tonight*

I had forgotten that we'd promised to have Sunday dinner with our parents, but I know Cat is reminding me because she wants to know if I'll be bringing Gabe.

Lexi: *Thanks for the reminder dear sister*

Cat: *You're welcome, are you coming alone?*

And there it is, the real reason she messaged to remind me that we were due to have dinner with our parents.

Lexi: *See you tonight Kitty Cat*

I reply, walking out of my room and not giving her an answer, while laughing my head off. It'll drive her *insane* not knowing whether I'm bringing Gabe tonight or not. I hear my phone signal that I've got another message and without looking, I'm going to assume it's my sister telling me I'm being mean, but I just laugh again and put my phone in my pocket.

I look up and stop in my tracks. There in my kitchen is Gabriel Romanetti, in just his dress pants from last night and nothing else, cooking pancakes. I know that I should have guessed that's how he was dressed seeing as though I just folded up his clothes and put them on my bed ready for him to put back on after his shower, but the reality of actually seeing him bared chested and moving around my kitchen and making me breakfast, well brunch really, considering we went back to bed after Cat and Joshua left, it's like a dream come true.

"Hi there. I hope you're hungry? I got a little carried away and made enough food for a small army I think." He laughs, a loud, booming kind of laugh and it makes me smile. Stephen never cooked for me, he only went into the kitchen to get himself a beer. Watching Gabe navigate the kitchen with such ease is sexy as hell, so I smile back at him.

Barefoot and Dumped!

"I'm ravenous." I say while laughing with him, only I'm not sure it's only food that I'm needing right now.

"Good. Now sit down, relax and I'll finish cooking, then we can eat." He smiles, and gently nudges me towards the dining table, pulls out a chair and gestures for me to sit down, then pushes my chair in for me. The whole thing brings a huge smile to my face.

"A girl could get used to this you know Mr Romanetti, you're setting a dangerous precedent here." He's back at the stove, flipping his pancakes and he nods.

"Sure, you call it a dangerous precedent, I call it how you should treat the one you love." He glances over his shoulder at me and smiles wide. "I want to cook for you and feed you. Are you going to object?"

"Not even a little bit. They might say that the fastest way to a man's heart is through his stomach, but I believe that to be true of women too. If a man is willing to cook for her, a woman is more than happy to let him do it." I smile sweetly at him. "But you have to clean up after yourself as well, that's the deal."

"You've got a deal honey." He's still smiling as he places a plate piled high with pancakes on the table. The table that I only now notice that he's already set with plates, cutlery and condiments. When I look up from the table, he's bringing over a plate with bacon on it and a big bowl of scrambled eggs as well. I have no idea where he pulled those from, but I'm not asking. I'm too stunned to. "I forgot the butter, I used it to cook the pancakes, just a second." He's gone and back in a second, returning with the tub of butter and happily putting it on the table between us.

"Wow!" Is all I can manage to say.

"Sorry, I know it's a lot of food, I'm kind of used to cooking up a feast for a few people, not just two and I got carried away." He actually blushes, it's damned adorable.

"Maybe we should have asked Cat and Joshua to join us after all?" I laugh, until I look across the table and see the look on Gabe's face. I reach over and take his hand in mine, and I squeeze it. "It looks amazing Gabe, thank you. I just don't know if we can get through this amount of food, but I know I'll have breakfast ready for me for the next couple of days thanks to you." He smiles, but it doesn't reach his eyes and I want to bring him all the happiness he's given me today. "Let's eat."

That's exactly what we do and by the time I've had two servings of pancakes, smothered in butter and maple syrup, a few rashers of bacon and a pile of eggs, I'm too full to move.

"Oh my lord Gabe, that was amazing!" This brings an enormous smile to his kissable lips. "I've never had anyone cook for me before and I can't tell you how much I enjoyed it."

"I'm glad." I stand up and move around to his side of the table. I straddle his lap and lay a kiss on him that's so hot I think my whole body melts. Especially when his hands grip my hips and he starts kissing me back like it's the only thing he wants to do right now. He pulls back way too soon for my liking, "Hold that thought. I need to clean up the last few dishes and then have a shower. Then I was hoping we could spend the afternoon together?"

"That sounds perfect to me but why don't you let me fill the dishwasher while you have a shower." I suggest.

"What happened to me having to clean up my mess? Or are you worried I won't do it the way you do it?" He asks, kissing me lightly.

"Well, you want to have a shower and this way, two things get done at the same time." It's my turn to kiss him.

"Are you sure? There isn't much, just what we used to eat because I cleaned up as I went." I look over his shoulder to see he's right. I hadn't noticed when I first walked in because I was too busy ogling the sexy man standing in my kitchen, but the benches are actually clean.

"Well, you've done more than half of the job, so yes, I'm sure, and even though I *do* have a certain way of filling the dishwasher I'm not precious about allowing someone else to do it." I think for a second and then say, "Although Cat might say differently now that I think about it."

"That's what I thought." Gabe laughs. He lets me go and starts walking towards my front door, where he grabs his keys from the table next the door. I didn't even realise that's where his keys landed last night.

Barefoot and Dumped!

"Are you leaving?" I ask, even I can hear the trepidation in my voice. He won't go anywhere dressed like that, will he? He doesn't even have shoes on!

"I'm just going to my truck to get my change of clothes." He explains.

"Wow! You were pretty confident last night weren't you?" I ask, shocked at the absolute certainty that he had about staying for the night. Which makes me double think everything that's happened, and my doubts settle in again. Before I can even register that he's moved, Gabe is standing in front of me and pulling me into his embrace. One hand wraps around my waist and the other softly holds my head to his chest.

"Lexi, honey, I didn't plan last night. Was I hoping we'd take our relationship to the next level? Yes. I'm not going to lie to you honey, I've wanted you from the first moment I saw you, I already told you that." He places his finger under my chin and lightly pushes it up until our eyes meet. "I've got a duffle bag in my truck with a change of clothes because sometimes I go straight to the gym from work and I can't work out in my suit. Or I go to my dad's after work and I don't want to sit around in my suit there either, but I never assumed that I would be needing it this morning after our date. Am I happy I've got a change of clothes? Yes, because I hate wearing a suit when I don't have to, but I don't have a change of clothes because I planned on staying here last night." Then he drops his lips to mine and kisses me tenderly. "I'll be back in a second." Then he's gone.

He's back in what feels like seconds, because I haven't even had time to move, or think about what he just said.

"So, not because you had last night planned out, but because that bag is always in your truck?" I ask, needing confirmation for the reason he's got a change of clothes.

"Yes. You were almost sitting on top of it the first night we met actually, but you wouldn't remember that because you were asleep the moment your cute rear end hit the seat." He chuckles. I was so stupid that night, and I can't believe my sister and my best friend allowed a stranger to drive us home, even when that stranger was Gabe.

Without another word, Gabe moves off towards the bathroom and I hear the water running before I make a move to go back into the kitchen to finish cleaning up. When I gather up our dishes and start putting them in the dishwasher, I realise that Gabe was telling the truth, he *did* clean as he went, and I don't have much to do.

I sit down in my favourite chair that faces out into the park across the street from my house and stare out at the view without really seeing it. I have to decide whether to take him at his word and believe he wasn't planning on staying here last night or to call it quits now. I want to believe him, and I know that he's nothing like Stephen who used to presume a lot of things while we were together. So, I decide to take a leap of faith and trust him, I really hope that I'm not wrong.

With my decision made, I pull my now silent phone out of my pocket and read the text messages that my sister sent, reminding me that my parents like to know if we're bringing extra people to Sunday dinner. Her last one makes me laugh though, because she tells me I'm rude and ruining her day by not telling her if I'm bringing Gabe or not. I still don't answer her, she can wonder all day for all I care.

I'm answering a text from Lacey when my phone rings. When I look at the screen and see it's my mum I can't help but wonder if Cat called her and mentioned that I might bring someone extra today.

"Hi Mum, how are you?" I answer maybe a little too brightly for a Sunday.

"Good morning sweetheart, I'm really good. How are you?" I relax at the sound of her voice. She always manages to bring me comfort without even trying.

"I'm really good mum, honestly."

"That's good sweetheart, I'm very happy to hear that. You certainly sound much happier than I've heard you in a long while." She says, then pauses like she's waiting for me to tell her something. I'm going to kill my sister when I see her later, she's ratted me out to my parents the shit. "Well, I just wanted to remind you about dinner tonight, just in case you'd forgotten."

"Thanks Mum, but I hadn't forgotten." I tell her.

"Hey Lexi, do you have spare towels anywhere that I can use please?" Gabe calls from the bathroom and I curse myself for forgetting to grab one out for him.

"They're in the cupboard under the sink." I yell back after covering the speaker on my phone with my hand, hoping like hell my mother didn't hear him, but luck is not on my side today.

"Thanks honey." He yells back just in time for my mum to hear him because I removed my hand from the speaker so that I could talk to her.

"Was that a man in your shower sweetheart?" I can *hear* the smile in her voice. "Did you have a date last night? Did he stay *over* last night? Good for you Alexis." Look, I love my mum unconditionally, but I really wish sometimes that our relationship wasn't quite as open as it is.

"Yes mum, that was a man. Yes we went on a date last night and yes, he also stayed over. No you can't have any more details, I'm not sharing them with you." I roll my eyes even though I know she can't see me.

"Don't roll your eyes Alexis, I'm just happy that you're moving on and I'm interested in your life, that's all." She huffs. How did she know I rolled my eyes? Well, apparently I do it often and have done since I was a child. "Is he coming with you tonight, or is it too soon?"

"I don't know mum, I haven't mentioned it. It might be too soon to introduce him to you guys I think." I know we're moving fast but are we moving *that* fast?

"Well, you ask him sweetheart. Any friend of yours is more than welcome at out dinner table and you know we'll have enough food for him if he comes." My parents always have enough food to feed a small army at our family dinners, which means Cat and I always leave with leftovers and eat for almost a week afterwards. "What's his name?"

"His name is Gabe, and I'll ask him when he gets out of the bathroom." I sigh.

"Gabe? Is that short for Gabriel?"

"Yes mum, it is."

"OK then I'll see you tonight. You're going to invite him aren't you Alexis?" I roll my eyes again and let out a quiet groan that I hope like hell she doesn't hear.

"I promise I will ask Gabe if he wants to come tonight, OK? I'll talk to you later."

"Love you sweetheart."

"I love you too," I say, then I disconnect the call and close my eyes, dropping my chin onto my chest. I'm going to kill Cat for getting me into this mess.

"Who was that and where are you asking me to go with you tonight? I'm sorry, I didn't realise you were on the phone when I yelled out from the bathroom just now." Gabe asks from behind me.

"I'm sorry I forgot to get you out a towel." With a shrug of his shoulders the towel is forgotten about again. "That was my mum on the phone. Cat must have spoken to her earlier, after I didn't return her messages. We have a family dinner tonight at my parent's house and you've been invited. You don't have to come, I know it's too soon, but I promised her I would ask."

"I would love to meet your parent's Lexi. That's if you want me to."

"Really?"

"Absolutely honey. I know you still think this whole thing is moving too quickly and maybe it is, but it feels right to me. I'm happier than I have been in ages. If it makes you feel any better, I told my dad about you yesterday and he wants to meet you too."

"Wow! I don't know if it makes me feel *better* about the situation, but it sure does make me happy that you mentioned me to your dad." I smile at him.

"I didn't need to tell him, he actually asked me about you. He said, 'so what's her name?' and when I tried to pass us off as nothing, he told me off. He's the reason I called to see if we could spend the afternoon together. He told me a story about him and my mum, how he almost lost her to another guy, but instead he fought for her. He told me if I wanted to spend time with you, I should just say so and find the time. So, that's what I did."

"He's a smart man your dad."

"He definitely has his moments of brilliance. He'll be happy to hear that it worked out for both of us."

"I'm glad you took his advice too Gabe." It really did work out and I'm grateful that his dad's advice meant we got to spend extra time together. "So, we're doing this? You're going to come to dinner at my parent's house tonight?"

"Yes, I'm going to meet your parent's tonight at Sunday family dinner." He says with a smile that doesn't look nervous at all. How the hell does he do that, because I'm nervous at just the *thought* of meeting his dad. "But I am going to need to go home before we do. I'm going to need a change of clothes."

It's only then do I look him up and down, checking out what he's wearing, and I laugh. "My parents are pretty easy going, but you're right, I don't think you want to meet them for the first time in a pair of ripped up sweatpants with a hole in the crotch. I mean, I like them for the ease of access, but I don't think that's appropriate at the family dinner table."

"Cheeky woman. How about we head over to my place now and I can get changed, then we can decide what to do with the afternoon before we head to your parent's for dinner?"

"Sounds like a plan." I agree. "Just let me message my mum to let her know that yes, I will be bringing an extra person. Not that there won't be enough food for you either way, but it's right thing to do."

I send a message to my mum and she replies, *I look forward to meeting him.*

I send a message to Cat to let her know that I will in fact be bringing an extra person to dinner and my phone dings almost immediately with an incoming text from her.

Cat: *I hope that means you're bringing Gabe and not Lacey.*

Lexi: *Well now that's just plain rude, I thought you loved Lacey?*

Cat: *Like a sister, but I'm really hoping it's Gabe that's coming with you*

Lexi: *Why is this so damned important to you?"*

Cat: *Because he makes you happier than I've ever seen you Lexi and I want that for you*

Lexi: *Love you Cat but I know you ratted me out to mum and you will pay for it*

Cat: *Love you too sis, see you tonight*

It's her turn to dodge giving me an answer this time. I wonder how long it will take her to realise I didn't answer her either?

Gabe walks out of my room with his duffle bag flung over his shoulder and holding his hand out for me to take. "Are you ready to go?"

"Let's get out of here." I say, taking his hand and walking out to his truck.

He's going to meet my parents today! I didn't introduce Stephen to them for months, I guess that should have told me something, hey?

Chapter Twenty-four

GABE

The drive to my place is quiet but not necessarily uncomfortable, although I can feel Lexi thinking from across the truck, so I say, "You know, I don't have to come to dinner tonight. It's OK if it's too much too soon for you."

"What?" She asks as she turns to look at me. "Oh no, Gabe, I *want* you to come to dinner tonight. I do think everything is going fast, but I've decided to just let it happen at whatever pace it happens. I mean, I'm happy and maybe I'm assuming too much, but I think you're pretty happy too. So, let's just let it happen."

Her smile stretches across her face and I can feel mine do the same. "I *am* happy Lexi. Happier than I have been in a very long time." She reaches across the seat and takes my hand in hers and I give it a light squeeze. "So, let's see where this takes us, is that what you're saying?"

"Yup. Let's just go with the flow." She laughs. "I don't think I've ever said that before but there's a first time for everything. It might feel like I just broke up with Stephen, but the truth is, we were apart for much longer than that. So, things aren't moving too fast, they're just moving."

There's the girl I remember from that first night we met. She's clear and decisive, at least until she's had a few drinks anyway.

I pull into the garage under my building and help Lexi out of the truck. We walk in the foyer and Sam, the doorman, says, "Good afternoon Gabriel, how are you today? Miss." And he nods towards Lexi. I know she's never been here before, therefore I introduce them so that Sam knows who she is, and he'll let her in the building in the future, even if I'm not with her.

"Good afternoon Sam, I want you to meet my girlfriend, Alexis Stratton. Can you put her name on my list of pre-approved visitors please? I plan on her spending plenty of time here with me." I say with a smile and Lexi looks at me confused. "I'll explain when we get up to my apartment." I whisper into her hair and she nods.

Shaking his hand, she says, "Nice to meet you Sam, please call me Lexi."

"Nice to meet you too Lexi." His smile is bright and genuine, then he looks back to me. "Of course Gabriel, I shall tell the others and put her name on the approved list." He nods and his smile spreads even further across his face. I know the next time I see him, and I don't have Lexi with me, I'm going to be bombarded with questions about her.

"Thank you, Sam." It's my turn to nod and then I lead Lexi to the elevator. The ride up to my apartment is silent, there isn't enough time to really get in to why I moved into a 'sign in all visitors' and an 'approval list' kind of building.

The doors open and we take a few steps when the door across the hall opens slightly.

"Good afternoon Jessie." I say, looking towards my neighbour. "This is Lexi, you're going to be seeing her around a lot from now on, OK? I promise, she's not going to bring you any trouble." I look at Lexi whose confusion is now palpable. Hell, I have so much I need to explain to her about my living situation. I wonder how she's going to take it all? "Lexi, this is Jessie, my neighbour. There's only the four apartments on each floor and Jessie likes to know who's coming and going." Once again, I lean down and whisper into her ear, "I'll explain when we get inside." Once again, she simply nods her head to acknowledge she's heard me.

Looking towards my neighbour, she says, "Nice to meet you Jessie. I promise I'm not here to cause any trouble or make any noise." She smiles warmly at Jessie. I see Jessie visibly relax and tentatively smile back. I've never seen her react to anyone like that before. She *always* stays pretty stiff and ready to run quickly and far. Even seeing my dad when he visits, makes her nervous and he wouldn't hurt a fly.

"Nice to meet you too Lexi." Then she looks to me and says, "I trust you Gabe." Then she closes and locks the door.

"She seems sweet. Nervous, but sweet." Lexi says as I lead her to my door, unlock it and walk inside.

Closing and locking the door behind us, I turn to Lexi and say, "Look, I know I have a few things to explain but can it wait until after I've gotten changed. Please?"

"Yes, of course."

I walk out of my room after changing into some clean jeans and a button down shirt, to find Lexi curled up in my favourite chair, reading a book she found on the lamp table next to it. She looks up as I enter the room and my heart stutters in my chest. The feeling of her just belonging in my space is overwhelming. "Hey." I say as a greeting, because I don't know what else to say.

"Hey yourself, handsome." She smiles at me and it's a radiantly happy smile.

"Thank you. I want to make a good first impression on your parent's, and those sweatpants would *not* have done the trick." Lexi laughs.

"You'd be surprised actually, but you're right, this is a much better choice." She looks me up and down and it takes all of my strength not to pull her up out of that chair and kiss her until we're both breathless. Instead, I sit down in the chair opposite her, preparing to explain my past and it terrifies me.

I cough, looking down at my shoes and when I look up, Lexi is watching me, waiting. Here goes nothing I think as I launch right into explaining why I live here.

"I guess you have some questions?" I ask, already knowing the answer, but she doesn't ask anything, she just nods her head in agreement waiting for me to speak. "How about I explain it to you and then you can ask anything you want afterwards?" I'm nervous, but she has a right to know what she's getting herself into, right?

"I'm listening Gabe." She says with a small smile.

"Right. So, you know about my ex?"

"Well, I know things ended badly and she used you for your money." Lexi frowns and I can see the thoughts working their way around her head.

"Amongst other things, yes." I sigh, take a deep breath, and tell myself to just pull off the damned bandaid and get on with it. "My ex, she was a real piece of work. She's the reason I live in a building that you can't get into unless you're a tenant or a tenant gives you approval to enter." I take another breath and look out the window behind Lexi, thinking back to where the crazy started. "We broke up almost two years ago, but we were together for less than a year. Somehow she managed to move into my house and have a say in every aspect of my life. To this day I'm not even sure how it all happened but one day it was like I woke up from a nightmare and realised what she'd done. I also came to the realisation after another huge fight over nothing, that I didn't want to be with her anymore. When I asked if she planned on being with me forever and living like that, she said, and I quote, 'You're my first husband. My stepping-stone to getting a better and brighter husband."

"Are you kidding me? She actually *said* that?" Lexi looks at me shocked, her mouth open in surprise.

I laugh but it has no humour in it. "Yeah. Then she said, 'Men like women who have been married before, they like to think they're taking someone else's toy away from them.' So basically, I was her first stop. Her first victim I suppose." Lexi is sitting there blinking furiously, her mouth still open in shock. "I had already decided that I would break up with her before she told me all of this, but when she told me she thought I understood that we were never going to be forever and that I couldn't give her what she wanted, I told her to pack her crap right there and then, and leave. She didn't appreciate being kicked out or broken up with. Apparently it was against the rules in her mind and she took it out on my house. A few weeks after she left, I thought I was good, that she was gone and onto her next stepping-stone so to speak, but then I came home one day after work to find everything in the house trashed, including a few walls and windows." I hear Lexi gasp in shock this time, but I don't look at her, I'm staring out the window remembering the mess I walked into that day. "I'd already put the house on the market because I just wanted to get out of there, it held too many bad memories for me to stay. When I discovered the damage she'd caused I called the police, but they're weren't too sympathetic. In fact, they told me there wasn't too much they could do because I had no concrete evidence it was her and even if they went to talk to her, she could turn it around and accuse me of being abusive. They made the report and said they'd go talk to her, but if she denied doing it, there wasn't anything more they could do about it."

"Holy hell Gabe! That's terrible!" I hear Lexi talk but I'm still too caught up in the memories that I'd thought I'd long since buried. Maybe that's the problem, I buried them, but I hadn't really dealt with them yet.

"I paid a pretty penny for all the repairs to be made quickly and replace the furniture with the bare minimum. I didn't really need any of it. Originally I had been selling the house with all the furniture anyway. I stayed in the house, not really wanting to leave it empty and vulnerable to her breaking in again. Although, the police said there was no evidence of anyone breaking in the first time, so I changed all the locks as well, but even then, I never felt alone when I was home. I had the eerie, creepy feeling that I was being watched somehow and it freaked me out. Weird things happened in the house, things were moved that weren't easily moved. Things went missing and other things appeared. Once all the repairs were made, I locked the place up and moved in with Brent, because I couldn't stay there anymore. I sold the house at a pretty significant loss, but I was happy to just be out of there." I shudder at the memories.

"Gabe." Her voice is soft and full of concern. Hell, is she going to think I'm crazy after all of this? Now that I've started talking about it all, I can't stop.

"I found this apartment building where you have to be a tenant or approved by a tenant to actually get into the place and lucky for me they had someone moving out of one of the apartments. I had to wait a couple of weeks before I could move in and Brent let me stay with him." I close my eyes, remembering how I felt in those weeks after she destroyed my things. I shudder at the memory, because I'm a guy and a built one at that, people think that things like this can't possibly happen to guys like me, but the fact is, unless I need to get physical with a woman to stop her from hurting either herself or me, I won't. I feel the cushion on the chair move slightly and feel her warm touch on my arm. "A couple of weeks after I moved in here and after weeks of hearing nothing at all from her, she tried to get in here, to my apartment. One of the other doormen was charmed by her and he was going to call up to see if I would like my *fiancée* to come on up. She'd somehow convinced him that it had been an oversight that she wasn't allowed up. How I would forget to put my *fiancée* on that kind of list is beyond me, but again luck was on my side, because Sam's shift was just starting. He told her she wasn't allowed in and that if she tried again, he would call the police. Unluckily for her, she *did* try again later that day, after assuming Sam's shift was over. I don't know what Sam does when he's not here, but he's here a hell of a lot. She tried to get passed him by walking in behind a tenant to hide from him. Sam spotted her, held her in their office and called the police. She was charged with stalking and trespassing. That was just over a year ago and I haven't heard anything from her since."

"That's one hell of a story Gabe." I start to move away from her, if she doesn't believe me then whatever it is we're doing stops now.

"It's not a 'story' or wild tale Lexi, it happened." I growl, even as she pushes down on my shoulders and slides around to straddle my lap, resting her head on my chest and holding me tight.

"I didn't mean to suggest that what you told me just now was an untrue story Gabe. What I meant was, she's fucking insane and I'm glad you came out the other side in one piece. I thought Stephen was insane but she's just, she belongs in the looney bin honestly. I can't believe you went through that and I hate that you did." Tilting her head up, she leaves a soft kiss on my jaw and my body relaxes. "I believe what you told me, it's just so freaky that someone behaves like that in real life, you know? I mean I know Lacey and I can be a little hard to handle sometimes, but we'd never destroy someone's property or stalk them.

I don't know what to say, so instead of speaking I wrap my arms around the woman that is quickly becoming my everything and hold her close. A long deep sigh escapes my lips and I realise I'm relieved. Not only to have told Lexi everything, but to have that weight off me.

"Ummm Gabe?" Her voice is hesitant, and I feel my body stiffen with worry again.

"Yes Lexi?"

"Does everyone who lives in this building have stalker problems?" The alarm in her voice would be funny if it didn't seem like a very genuine concern.

"I don't think so, but honestly, I don't know. I don't know many people in the building except for Jessie and I know her because there was an altercation between her and her ex not long after I moved in." Lexi looks up at me and I kiss her forehead lightly. I know she wants to ask me but she's also hesitating, only wanting me to share what I'm willing to. "It's Jessie's story to tell, if she wants to, but what I will tell you is, her ex is a raging arsehole who beat the living daylights out of her daily and she finally managed to escape his hold on her, and she moved in here. Somehow, not long after my ex tried, he got past the guys downstairs and made it up here. I just happened to come home at the right time. Nancy, an older lady that lives in one of the other apartments, had already called downstairs and they were on their way up. The police weren't too far behind them, but he saw me first. I got in between him and Jessie."

"Ohhh Gabe. What happened?" She asks quietly.

"Well, I may not have gotten away without a few bruises and a fat lip, but he looked a lot worse than I did. He got taken away and charged and we haven't seen him since either, but, as you can imagine. Jessie is still pretty jumpy when the elevator arrives up here and new people come into the building."

"Oh my god that poor woman. I'm glad you were here to help, but I wish you hadn't been put in the middle and gotten hurt." She sits back on my knees so that she can see me, and I feel her loss instantly. Gently, she places her hands on my cheeks, looks me in the eyes and says, "You are the best kind of person there is in this world Gabriel Romanetti and I love you with everything I have."

I release the breath I didn't know I was holding, close my eyes for a second until I feel her lips on mine. "I love you too, Alexis Stratton." I say against her lips. "I'm so glad all of that didn't make you run for the door and leave me." I say, giving voice to my fears.

She pulls back slightly, again. "Did you really think that was going to change my mind? None of what you just told me is your fault. You're not to blame for any of it. I'm not going to call you a victim, because I would hate to be called that myself, but you did everything you could to protect yourself and others. That's brave Gabe, and it makes me love you just a little bit more."

"Just a little bit?" I say with a smirk, trying to bring some lightness back into the room.

"Yeah, just a little bit." She says, but she's laughing as well. Then she lays her head back on my chest, tucking her head under my chin in the process and wraps her arms around me tightly. I rest my chin on her head and hold her closely.

I'm not sure how long we sit like that, all I know is it brings me an amazing amount of comfort and peace. I'm so in love with this woman that I don't think I can live without her anymore.

After a while Lexi makes a move to climb off my lap, and I hold onto her hips not wanting to let go of the peace that I'm feeling with her in my arms. "Where do you think you're going beautiful?"

"To the bathroom Gabe, I need to pee." She laughs, and wiggles off my lap when I release her hips. I watch her walk away from me and wonder how the hell I got so lucky. I'm so glad Brent talked me into going out for drinks that night, it's changed my life.

I'm still sitting where Lexi left me when she comes back from the bathroom.

"Hey, are you OK? I know that was a huge emotional dump of information."

"Hey honey, yeah, I'm good, but I was wondering." Hell, I'm not this nervous in the office when I have to fire someone or tell them they've done something wrong, but I want to ask her a question that I'm not sure what her answer might be.

"Hmmm. Yes?"

"I was thinking while you were in the bathroom." I take a breath, "If you'd be willing to go past my dad's this afternoon on the way your parent's house?" Her eyes widen in surprise and her mouth opens, ready to give me her answer, but I stop her by holding up my hand. "Look, I know that it might be a bit too much for one day and I'm not suggesting it so that you're in the hot seat as well. It's just that, I'd really like him to meet you and well, today seems like the day for it." I say with my most charming smile.

"Yes."

"Yes?" I ask, and she nods. "It's that simple?"

"Yes, it's that simple. I want you to meet my parents and I guess it's only fair that I meet your dad. Let me rephrase that. I would *love* to meet your dad, especially if you want me to meet him."

"I want you to meet him." I say, simply.

"Then, I'll meet him today before we go introduce you to *my* parents. Do you need to call him?"

"I should probably give them a heads up, they had something on last night at the house, so they might appreciate the warning."

"They? I thought it was just your dad?"

"Oh it is, but he has a house manager, Maria, who is more a friend than an employee and she mentioned yesterday when I was there that they had people coming over."

"OK, well go ahead and call him then."

Lexi took that suggestion much easier than I thought she would, especially after her worries about us moving too fast, but then again, I think I surprised her when I said yes to meeting her parent's too. Without waiting for her to change her mind, I pull my phone out of my pocket, pull up my dad's name on the screen and tap the call button. After two rings, he answers the phone.

"Hi there son, how are you today?"

"Hi Dad, I'm great, how are you?"

"I'm great Gabriel."

"Good, good. I'm calling to see if you have any plans today? I was thinking of coming by for a visit."

"You want to come over two days in a row? I'm not going to refuse that Gabriel, of course you're always welcome to come home." He pauses for a second and then says, "Is everything OK?"

"Everything's great Dad. I'm actually bringing someone with me, if you're up for it?"

"Do I get to meet the girl you were telling me about yesterday Gabriel?" I can hear the smile in his voice.

"Yes Dad, I'm bringing the girl I told you about yesterday." I smile at Lexi, who is watching me intently. "You were right. I called her yesterday after I left your place and we spent some time together, then we had our first official date last night."

"It's moving pretty fast then Gabriel. Are you sure about this?"

"One hundred percent sure Dad."

"Well, that's fantastic. We'll be expecting you soon and I'm sure Maria will have afternoon tea set up when you get here."

"Thanks Dad. See you soon."

"Looking forward to it Son." I tap the end button and take a deep breath before looking up to see Lexi still watching me. "So, does afternoon tea with my Dad and Maria sound OK to you?"

"Sounds perfect to me, Gabe."

Chapter Twenty-five

LEXI

Listening to everything that Gabe went through with his ex and then to help his neighbour Jessie, I don't know what to say to him. Nothing he told me changed my feelings for him. I loved him before he explained why he chose to live in the building, and I love him even more after he tells me about helping a woman who was effectively a stranger by putting himself in danger. Even though at the same time I want to tell him to never, ever do that again, because I don't want him to get hurt, but knowing both stories now, gives me an insight to the man he is.

I'm not sure how long we sat in that chair after he got it all out, but it was a while and my bladder was ready to explode. When I come out of the bathroom, I stand at the doorway to the living room and just look at Gabe for a few minutes, just taking him in. He's staring blankly out the window and I can only guess that he was reliving the past still. So, he surprises me when he asks if we can go by his dad's place this afternoon before we go to my parents.

I know I surprise him by saying yes so quickly when he asks me, but I didn't say yes because I felt like I had to after he agreed to have dinner with *my* family. No, I said yes without hesitating because he asked me to go. He *wants* to introduce me to his dad and that means something to me. Are we moving quickly? Yes, it's making my head spin a little to be honest but listening to him talk to his dad on the phone and then admit in front of me, that yes, he's bringing the girl he told his dad about the day before, makes my heart expand.

"What time do we have to be there?" I ask when he ends the call.

"We'll need to leave soon because it will take close to an hour to get there." He smiles warmly. "Are you sure about this?"

"Absolutely." I reply, giving him a warm smile of my own. "Why don't we go get a coffee and I'll find a cake or something sweet to take with us." This brings a loud, booming laugh out of him.

"Oh honey, if we take cake or something else sweet, other than you of course, over there, Maria will be *very* offended." He says, reaching for my hand and curling our fingers together, pulling me to my feet, into his side. "We can pick up something to take to your parent's house if that's what you normally would do?"

"I don't want to offend your dad before I've even met him, but I will need to stop at the bakery near my parent's house on our way. If that's OK? I'm not really a baker, or a cook for that matter, so they don't expect too much from me." I look up at Gabe, and see him smirking, trying not to laugh.

"It's not Dad you'd be offending honey, he would find it absolutely delightful but Maria's the one you'll offend. She's the resident baker in the house and the one who will organise afternoon tea. She'll be polite, don't you worry about that, but you don't want to start off on the wrong foot with her. She runs that house with an iron fist. She's loving, caring and compassionate, but she's an absolute hard arse, she's had to be over the years to keep my dad in line."

"Was she running the house when your mum was still here?" I ask quietly, because he rarely talks about his mum. My question causes him to sigh and I wish I'd never asked. It's been a big and emotional day already, I should have left the subject of his mum alone. "I'm sorry, you don't have to answer that."

"Never apologise for wanting to know things about me Lexi. It's just that my mother's death is still a touchy subject. I guess it always will be." He says with a shrug and squeeze of my hand. He grabs his keys and wallet, while I pick up my handbag and then we walk out his door. As he locks it I look up and see Jessie looking through a small gap in her door.

"See you later Jessie, it was nice to meet you." I smile and give her a small wave. She smiles and waves back, then closes her door. I hear the locks and then her fading steps as she walks back into her apartment.

Barefoot and Dumped!

"Wow! You've got a special touch with her, I haven't seen her talk or acknowledge anyone but me since I moved in. Well, that's not completely true, I've seen her talk to old Nancy before, but I've only ever seen her watch Jane and Marcus, the couple in the other apartment, I don't think she's ever spoken to them."

"I don't know what to say, maybe she just needs people to treat her like a normal person? I'm not asking her to step out of her home, I'm just acknowledging her existence and that's all everyone asks, isn't it?"

"Absolutely." Gabe smiles at me and places his hand on my lower back, leading me towards the open doors of the elevator.

I can't help thinking that he thinks I'm doing something special, when in actual fact, I'm treating Jessie just how I would hope that I would be treated if I was in her position. Enough 'normal' has been taken from her, she doesn't need me to treat her like she's a freakshow of some kind. We've all got our issues we're dealing with, it's just that hers have been more or less out of her control and I want her to feel like she has more control over her life. If that means she smiles when I say hello to her, then I'm happy to do it.

"You're incredible, you know that?" Gabe kisses me lightly on the top of my head and moves his hand to my hip, pulling me in close in a tight side hug.

"No I'm not Gabe. I'm human and I treat people as if they're human as well, because we all have our idiosyncrasies and issues that we're dealing with. I'm not going to judge Jessie over a situation that wasn't in her control, I just want her to feel like she has some of that control back. That's all." I explain to him.

He laughs quietly and says, "And that's what makes you special honey." I don't get to reply to him, because the doors open and he's ushering me out of the elevator and into the garage before I can even think of something to say. I get the feeling it wouldn't make too much difference even if I *could* find something to say to him. So, I keep quiet as he leads me to his truck and helps me in and then walks around to get behind the wheel.

"Are you OK, Lexi?"

"Hmmm? Oh yes. Absolutely." I smile at Gabe. One of my favourite things since we've gotten to know each other, is watching this man command his truck. It just suits him.

"I'm sorry if I said something to upset you before." He smiles at me, but it's a small, hesitant smile and I hate that I've made him feel like he's done something wrong. I reach over and take his hand in mine, squeezing it lightly.

"No, you haven't upset me. I just wouldn't have looked at what I did with Jessie the way you did, but you treated her like a human being as well when you went to bat for her with her ex, so maybe we're not so different, hmmm?" I smile, a big toothy grin.

He coughs uncomfortably, "I did what I hope any guy would do, especially if it was my sister in trouble." I've learned something else today about Gabriel Romanetti , he's about as good at taking a compliment as I am, and I can't help smiling a little to myself. "Are you nervous about meeting my dad?" He asks.

"Hell yes." I answer before I can think about what I'm saying, making Gabe crack up. "Eyes on the road funny guy." I say.

"Sorry, I wasn't expecting quite that honest an answer, but I should have known better." His smirk is sexy, but right now I wish I could swipe it off his face without him crashing us into the gutter. "Hey," he says, bringing my hand to his mouth and leaving a kiss on the back, "You're going to be fine. He's going to love you as much as I do, Lexi."

"You make it sound like your dad is going to be so easy. I'm actually feeling OK about meeting him." I answer him.

"Then what's making you so nervous?" He stops and then looks at me, hurt in his eyes, asking before I can answer him, "Are you nervous about me meeting your parents?"

"What!? Oh my god, no! No, Gabe, my parents are going to love you. They never did like Stephen, but you're not him and they'll see that right away. Not to mention Cat's already put her two cents worth in and told them they'll love you." I laugh, because my sister didn't like Stephen either. "You've already met Joshua as well, and he's not easy to impress, but you two got along within seconds."

"Then what are you nervous about?" He asks, confusion all over his handsome face.

"Honestly?" I ask nervously.

"Always." He nods and squeezes my hand again.

"I'm nervous about meeting Maria." I say quietly, hoping that he didn't actually hear my confession, but I know he did because he lets out a loud belly laugh. I try to take my hand from his grip, but he just holds it tighter. "Well, you've made her sound like a hard arse *and* a surrogate mum to you and your sister. I feel like I have to impress her, more than I do your dad at this point."

He brings my hand to his mouth and kisses it softly again as he slows the car down and then brings it to a stop. "She's going to love you Lexi, because I do, and you make me happy." I go to speak, and he holds his hand up to stop me. "She *is* all of those things, that I will admit, and she didn't like my ex. Neither did my dad for the record, but she is going to *love* you because I do. Without a doubt honey, when she sees how happy I am, she'll be more than happy that I found someone perfect for *me*."

"I love you Gabe." I say quietly.

"I love you too Lexi. Now let's get this show on the road shall we?" He drops my hand and gets out of the truck to walk around to help me out, because that's just what he does and that's when I realise he hasn't stopped just anywhere. He's stopped in the driveway of the most amazing mansion I've ever seen in real life. Mind you, this is the first one I've ever seen in the flesh so maybe I'm too easily impressed.

"Wow!"

"Yeah, the house is pretty amazing. My dad restored it and he's done an amazing job of it. It was a pretty special house to grow up in to be honest." He smiles, and I can tell he's remembering the fun times he had here when he was younger.

"It's incredible!" It's all I can manage to say. He's right, it's a gorgeous house but I can't imagine ever living in a place like this or growing up in it either. "It must have been full of amazing adventures when you guys were kids." I knew that Gabe came from money, but I had no idea he was from *this* kind of money and now I'm nervous about meeting his dad as well as Maria.

"Relax Lexi, it's just a house."

"That's not a *house* Gabe, that's a mansion!" The words are out of my mouth before I can think about how that might sound to him. I don't mean for to insult him. I know to him, it *is* just a house. His childhood home, but for me, it's a little confronting.

"Come on, let's go inside. It's a little less intimidating when you're inside it." He chuckles and takes my hand in his, leading me to the front door that's opening, and an older version of Gabe stands at the threshold, grinning like a Cheshire cat.

When we get close enough he draws Gabe into a tight hug. "Good afternoon son."

"Hi Dad." Gabe returns with a smile.

"And this young lady must be Alexis, and the reason I'm seeing my son two days in a row. I must find a way to thank you young lady." He smiles at me and then pulls me into a tight hug of my own.

"Dad let her go. Don't squeeze the life out of her, I like her. A lot, and I want her breathing if that's OK with you?" Gabe chuckles but I can hear the warning in his voice as he pulls me away from his dad and into his side.

"I'm sorry Alexis, I'm just excited to meet you." His dad says. "Come in, come in. I'm sorry, I didn't mean to attack you both before you even got inside."

Gabe steers me past his dad and into the house. My breath catches in my throat again as I take in the interior of the house. It's even more spectacular than the façade and I'm in awe.

"I promise I taught these two men more manners than they're currently showing." A female voice from behind Gabe's dad says. "I'm Maria," she says, reaching her hand out for mine, "And this is Gabe's overexcited father, Vincent."

"Lexi." I say, taking her hand in mine. "Nice to meet you both." I say, smiling at them.

Barefoot and Dumped!

"Nice to meet you Lexi." Maria says, then looks between both of the men and admonishes them. "I know I taught you both better than to not introduce yourselves to guests, honestly." She sounds terse and yet affectionate at the same time.

"I didn't need to introduce myself woman, she knew she was meeting Gabe's father, I figured she would assume that's who I was considering I was welcoming them *and* giving her a hug."

"Except greeting people at the door and inviting them in is usually *my* job Vincent." A male voice says from behind me and I startle. "Sorry Miss Lexi, I didn't mean to startle you, just trying to make a point."

"This *is* still *my* house, right?" Vincent asks.

"Yes, it is but you just live here." The gentleman says laughing gently. "Good afternoon, I'm Edward." He takes my hand gently.

"Good afternoon Edward, I'm Lexi." I smile at him, because he's such a sweet man, he makes me feel at ease instantly.

"It is nice to meet you Lexi, and it's good to see you again Gabe. Even better, we've had two visits this weekend." He says with a smile and a wink. "I'll go check that everything is running on time. Why don't you two lead them to the dining room and take a seat?"

"Now look who's taking on someone else's job?" Maria says, but while there might be a hint of annoyance in her voice, it's mostly filled with an affection between two long term co-workers.

"I can check on things in the kitchen as well as you can Maria. Why don't you have a rest this afternoon? If you choose to visit with Gabe and Lexi, even better." He says with a smirk and leaves before Maria has a chance to say anything.

"Come on Maria, Edward is right. Come and have afternoon tea with us. Please?" Vincent asks, almost pleading with her and sending her the same damned smirk his son gives me when he's trying to be adorable. It works on Maria too.

Maria relaxes and smiles back at Vincent. "Are you OK with me joining you Gabriel?" She asks, swinging her gaze his way.

"Absolutely Maria, you're part of the family." Gabe gives her a smirk of his own, causing Maria to shake her head and laugh.

"Watch out for these Romanetti men, Lexi, they're trouble." Maria says, still laughing, while Vincent places his hand on her lower back, guiding her towards what I assume is the dining room.

"Is there something going on between your dad and Maria?" I whisper in Gabe's ear.

"Funny you should ask, because I've been wondering that myself lately." He whispers back in my ear, with a deep laugh.

"What are you kids whispering about back there? No, don't answer that, I'm not sure I want to know." Vincent laughs.

"Leave them alone Vincent, young love is special and theirs is brand new. They're allowed to be whispering sweet nothings in each other's ears, without the old folks knowing about the details." Maria admonishes him.

"You're absolutely right Maria. No-one wants the gory details of anyone else's sex lives." Vincent says.

"You have to have one first in order to share." Maria jokes.

If I had to guess, I'd say she just hurt Vincent's feelings, but he recovers quickly. "Think I might leave that to the kids, my old hips can't deal with that kind of action these days." He quips back.

"Uhuh." Is Maria's only response.

Now I can't tell if there's sexual tension between them, or whether it's just plain old tension zipping between them. Beside me Gabe is still quietly chuckling and doesn't seem at all bothered by the tension between his dad and house manager, so who am I to judge either of them.

When we reach the dining room, Gabe pulls out a chair for me at the table. It's much smaller than I was expecting considering the size of the house it's in and my surprise must show on my face.

"This is our family dining room, Lexi. We have a much more formal dining room, but we prefer this one when it's just family in the house." Vincent says with a smile.

"You have a beautiful home Mr Romanetti."

"Call me Vincent, please, Lexi. Mr Romanetti is *my* father and I like to think I'm a little more easy going than Gabriel's Grandfather." Everyone but me laughs.

"Vincent it is then." I reply with a smile that I hope isn't too awkward looking.

"My Grandfather was a force to be reckoned with. He built the company from the ground up and did *not* like handing the reigns over to my dad." Gabe explains.

"That's the understatement of the century son." Vincent says with amusement lacing his voice.

"That's true. He was a grumpy bastard that's for sure."

"Gabriel! Language!" Maria admonishes him, causing both men to laugh loudly. "What would your mother say?"

It's quiet for a few beats around the table as they all seem to go back into their memories of Mrs Romanetti. "She would have laughed and agreed with me." Gabe smirks at Maria and she nods her agreement, even though it seems to pain her to agree with him. Gabe turns to me and explains, "He gave her a hard time before she married dad. He didn't think she was good enough to join our family. He was all about appearance and pedigree."

"They ended up with a very fragile truce when I told the old man that he could either be happy that I was marrying the love of my life or I could cut him out of our lives and he'd never see his grandchildren and not have anyone in the family to take over the business when he retired." Vincent smiles at the memory, because obviously he won that particular fight. "Being an only child can have its advantages at times. Anyway, the need for the family name to be carried on and the business to stay within the family, made his choice for him, but he never really forgave Rosanna for *my* ultimatum. Even the arrival Gabriel and then his sister, Susanna, never really healed the rift." He shakes his head in disbelief. "They died within a few years of each other and I can't help wondering if they're still giving each other grief, wherever it is they are."

"I like to think they're still keeping each other on their toes, wherever they are. Although, I'm sure my grandfather isn't in the same place as mum, she was an angel." Gabe says with certainty and a glint in his eyes, causing his dad to let out a loud, honest laugh. "He certainly enjoyed controlling as much as he could, even in retirement and old age."

"You're right there son, on both accounts." Vincent replies with a vigorous nod, when he's caught his breath. Gabe and his dad enjoy another round of laughter and I look over to see Maria sitting there quietly, studying her hands like she's never seen them before. I'm about to ask if she's OK when Vincent coughs and gently pats her hands, but he quickly removes his hand when Gabe notices the gesture. "Enough about the past, I'm sure Lexi doesn't want to hear all the gory details." His smile doesn't reach his eyes when they meet mine.

"I'm always happy to learn something new about Gabe, but maybe if we save them it will give me the excuse to return for another visit."

"Oh sweetheart, you never need an excuse to visit me. With or without my son, you're always welcome."

"Thank you Vincent." I smile at him and he returns my smile warmly.

Then, with what has to be the most perfect and practised timing ever, Edward chooses that moment to come into the dining room with a tray laden with the makings of coffee or tea in every combination you could possibly dream of wanting. Close behind him there's another member of staff with a tray of the most amazing looking sweets and pastries.

After everyone gets their drink of choice, the tray of goodies is passed around.

"I don't know which one to choose, they all look so amazingly delicious." I exclaim, not really meaning to say it out loud, but I'm glad I did when I see Maria's face light up. "Gabe told me you were an excellent cook and baker, but he truly under sold your abilities Maria."

Maria blushes at my remark, waves her hand in my direction and says, "Oh hush you, you haven't even tasted one yet."

"I don't think I need to, because if they taste anywhere near as good as they look, I'll be visiting the house often just for baked goods."

"Have a slice of the chocolate cake." I look at Gabe, silently asking how he can make me choose. "Trust me honey, you'll love the cake *and* the frosting, add in some fresh whipped cream and you are going to be in *heaven*."

I feel the smile spread across my face. "I trust you Gabe." Without taking another second to think, I take a slice of the chocolate cake that Edward is offering and then a spoonful of the cream on the tray as well.

"Enjoy." Edward smiles and then leaves the room, hustling the other staff member out of the room with him.

I scoop some cream onto my spoon and then some cake and bring the loaded spoon to my mouth. I look up to see Gabe watching me, as I put the spoon in my mouth. As soon as the deliciousness hits my tongue, my eyes close and I let out a quiet moan of pleasure.

"Don't forget you've got an audience, honey." Gabe whispers in my ear, his voice deep and laced with humour.

My eyes spring open and I look across the table at Maria. "You *made* this?" I ask, both surprised *and* impressed.

"Yes." Is her simple answer.

"From scratch? Like no mixes, packet or otherwise?" I ask before I can stop myself and I hear both Gabe and Vincent laughing.

Maria sits up a little straighter, her head raised and replies, "Yes, there are no boxes or packet mixes in my kitchen, Lexi. Everything is made from scratch. Unless of course this one decides that he wants to make his own food." She says, jabbing a thumb in Vincent's direction, making him laugh even louder.

"It's true, dad has crappy taste in food and Maria has been trying to change it for years, but nothing seems to work." Gabe holds my hand under the table. "Does it Maria?"

"No, he still makes mac and cheese from the box, or eats store bought cookies and cakes."

"I love *your* food Maria, but sometimes a man just has to eat some junk, you know?" Maria shrugs her shoulder and looks away from Vincent. "But nothing ever compares to your baking and we both know it."

"Then I don't understand why you need that other junk." Maria mumbles.

"Because sometimes a man, a person, just has a craving for crappy, pre-packaged food." She shakes her head but seems to accept his explanation and forgives him. I get the feeling that it's a common argument between the two of them. I can feel Gabe's body shaking slightly with laughter, so I think it's almost a gentle ribbing from his dad as well.

"I can't cook anything, so I admire you and I am thoroughly enjoying every morsel Maria. This is better than anything I've ever bought from any bakery. You can tell you put a lot of love and effort into everything you make." I smile at her, genuinely beside myself with enjoyment.

"Even the cake we had last night?" Gabe asks with a knowing smile.

"Yes, even better than the cake from last night. Maria's baking beats everything and if I could buy a cake from her, I'd take it to my parents tonight instead of the bakery one I plan on getting." I say, and poke my tongue out at him, completely forgetting where I am.

"She's absolutely delightful Gabriel. You make sure to hold on tight to Lexi, because you won't find better than her. She's going to keep you on your toes my boy and that's exactly what you need in a partner." Vincent tells Gabe.

"I'm not letting her go anywhere dad, she's staying with me." Gabe tells his dad, but never takes his eyes off me and I can feel the blush spreading across my cheeks.

"I don't plan on going anywhere Gabe." I say, leaning in and planting a kiss on his lips.

"Isn't young love grand." Vincent says, but he's just background noise, because I'm lost in Gabe as he kisses me back.

Chapter Twenty-six

GABE

"So, its official, my dad loves you." I tell Lexi as we drive to her parent's house for dinner.

"How do you know?"

"Well, for one, he had a smile on his face the entire time we were there and for two, when he pulled me into that man hug, that I can tell you never really happens, he told me." I say, lifting a finger off the steering wheel with each point I make. "Not to mention the bear hug he gave you as we were leaving as well. He's never done that before either. Don't get me wrong, he hugs my sister and he's an affectionate dad, but I haven't seen him like that when I've bought a girlfriend home before." Lexi blushes again, and I find it more adorable than I should. She's such a confident woman and yet she can't take a damned compliment when she gets one. "It's true honey."

"I was just wondering what made *you* think he liked me, that's all." She says.

"What did he say to you while you were trapped in that bear hug?" Knowing he said *something* and wanting to know what it was. "I saw his lips moving and he gave me a look that told me he was up to mischief." I say with amusement. "I know my dad pretty well."

She nods her head an acknowledgment but doesn't reply right away. "You really want to know what your dad said to me?" I nod my head yes in answer, because now I'm suddenly a little nervous about what he said to her. "He told me that he's never seen you happier than you were tonight and that your ex was a piece of work and he's happy that you've found someone normal, sweet and kind. He laughed when I whispered back that he didn't know me very well yet and he should reserve his judgement. He told me he was pretty sure his assessment was right, then he hugged me tighter." I don't say anything, but only because I have no idea what to say to that. That conversation captures exactly what I love about the two most important people in my life right now and knowing that they saw that in each other brings a lump to my throat that I don't know I could talk around even if I wanted to. "You wanted to know what was said." She says with a shrug of her shoulder, looking out the window, and I realise she's taken my silence as something it isn't.

"I'm just." I croak out, so I cough to clear my throat so that I can speak. "I'm glad you had that conversation with my dad and I'm even happier that you told me what you both said." I look towards her and then back to the road ahead. "He's right you know?"

"About what?" She asks, finally looking at me.

"You *do* make me happy. *Really* happy Lexi." I admit.

"Cool." She says looking pretty indifferent to my admission.

"Cool?" I repeat, raising an eyebrow in question.

"Yeah, cool." She repeats, as her lips curl up in a delighted smile that sends my pulse racing. "*Very* cool, because you make me *very* happy too, Gabriel Romanetti. Happier than I could have ever imagined." That smile of hers spreads across her face and there's a sexy twinkle in her eye that makes me want to kiss her until her toes curl and she can't breathe, but I can't do that because we're on our way to have dinner at her parent's house. How would it look if I showed up to their home with their daughter looking like I ravaged her in the backseat of my truck? My cock likes the image those thoughts conjure up in my mind and he stands to attention.

"Are you OK Gabe?"

"Ahhh yup. I'm good." I croak out.

"Good, because my parent's house is the next driveway." She informs me the amusement clear in her voice.

Barefoot and Dumped!

I pull into their driveway and turn the truck off. Suddenly, the front door flies open and Cat comes racing towards us, heading towards her sister on the other side of the car, thank god!

"You're here!" She squeals and moves to hug Lexi.

"Step back Catherine, if you ruin this cake in any way I *will* become an only child very quickly." Lexi says, her voice allowing no argument. She's so harsh Cat actually takes a step back from her, and I no longer need a few minutes for my body to calm down from my earlier dirty thoughts.

"Geeez Lexi, no cake is *that* good!"

"This is not just any cake, Catherine and it's not good. Oh no, this is the most delectable cake you've ever had in your life. The lady who baked it is a goddess and you will never say anything bad about her or her baked goods, do you hear me little sister?" While Cat got a talking to about Maria's baked goods, I get out of the truck and walk around to Lexi and Cat to take said cake out of Lexi's hands so that she can jump out and join us.

When Lexi hands the cake over to me to hold while she grabs her bag and a few things, Cat complains, "So, you'll let *Gabriel* hold your cake but not *me*? I see how it is now. I get it." She scowls and folds her arms over her chest in a typical scorned child move and I can't help laughing at her behaviour.

"*Yes*, Gabe can hold the cake. You want to know why?" Before Cat can answer her, Lexi keeps going, because obviously she didn't really want an answer. "He knows the value of cake and in particular *this* cake because it was baked by his dads cook, and it is the *best* thing I have ever tasted."

"The best ever hey?" I mumble, causing Cat to laugh and Lexi to roll her eyes at me.

"Lexibear, you're here and you bought my favourite dessert." I look up to a man about my dad's age coming out the front door to hug his daughter. I'm glad it's not just my dad who can't let us *in* the house before saying hello. "And this must be your new fella. Nice to meet you Gabriel, I'm Jonathon, Lexi and Cat's dad." He reaches out and shakes my hand.

"Please, call me Gabe, Mr Stratton." I say, as he lets go of my hand.

"Jonathon, please. We don't stand on ceremony around here, Gabe." He replies with a friendly smile.

"Jonathon it is then." I agree, returning his smile and he eyes the cake that's still in my hands. "I can see where Lexi gets her love of chocolate cake from." He starts to respond but a voice calls out from the front doorway.

"Jonathon, let them in the front door before you steal the cake from the poor lads hands." She fondly admonishes her husband, ushering him inside the house, following behind him.

I follow their lead into the kitchen and ask, "Where shall I put the cake Mrs Stratton?"

"Ohhh call me Julia, Gabe. As for the cake, you better give it to me so that Jonathon and Lexi can't get to it until after dinner."

"Are you sure they can last that long?" I ask Julia, without cracking a smile and my eyebrows drawn down into a frown of concern.

"If we feed them dinner at the right time, and manage to distract them in the meantime, we might just succeed." Julia answers me with a serious look.

"So should we get them working on something to distract them then, what do you say?" With a nod and a grimace on my face.

"You're right. They can set the table for me, what a wonderful idea Gabe." Julia smiles at me, her eyes gleaming with amusement and her mouth twists from holding back her laughter.

"Well, I guess you get along with my mum pretty nicely." Lexi says, sarcasm lacing her words and I know if I look back at her mum, I'll crack up.

"To think I was ready to really like this one Lexibear. After all the good things Cat and Joshua have told me about him and this." He says waving his hand between his wife and myself. "*This* is what I get instead. I get a man willing to mock my love of chocolate cake with my *wife*." I'm about to apologise to the man, cause hello, he's the father of the woman I love, and I don't want him to hate me, when Lexi finally speaks up.

Barefoot and Dumped!

"Oh Dad, let's face it, they're right. If we were left with that cake in front of us there wouldn't be any left and Mum would be yelling at us because we ate it all and because we didn't want the dinner she's cooked."

I laugh and say, "You make that sound like the two of you have done it before." When I look around the room, no-one else is laughing.

"Ummm that's because we have Gabe." Lexi rolls her eyes, telling me without words that I'm an idiot for *not* knowing that.

"Really?" I look between Lexi and her dad for confirmation and they both nod their heads. "I knew you loved chocolate cake, but not *that* much!"

"They've done it more than once Gabe, and trust me, no-one wants to see it happen again. Ever." Cat says, a shiver running down her body like the memory scares her.

"OK, well, let's move on then shall we? That's not something I want to relive." Joshua pipes up, while standing up from the stool he's been sitting on at the bench and coming over to shake my hand. "Good to see you again Gabe."

"Good to see you again too Joshua." I say, taking his hand in mine and shaking it.

"So, now that's all done, are you going to tell me all about meeting Mr Romanetti?" Cat asks Lexi, bouncing on her feet in front of us. "I bet the house is *amazing*!"

"The house is *amazing* Cat. It feels like a home." I tell her. Lexi pats me on the chest as if to say, 'Let me handle this.'

"It's a gorgeous home and you would love it Kitty Cat, *but* do you know what's even better than the size of grandeur of the house?" Cat shakes her head, enthralled. "The best part is that Vincent, Gabe's dad, has renovated the whole house, interior and exterior and it feels like a home that's lived in. Not to mention, Vincent is *very* welcoming, *and* he has the most amazing cook living there and *she* made the cake we bought over tonight and it's better than anything I've ever tasted before."

"Alright Catherine, leave your sister and Gabe alone, so that we can set the table and eat whatever it is that your mum has cooking."

"Great idea Joshua, then we're closer to having the cake that my oldest daughter is describing as the best she's ever tasted." Jonathan says with a smile that looks almost dreamy.

"Oh yes, it's a real hardship to have to eat a roast dinner that you didn't have to lift a finger to prepare, cook or serve up, isn't it Jonathon?" Julia says, her voice full of sarcasm. "It's a real shame that you have to have a roast *before* you can get to the cake."

Jonathon moves faster than I was expecting and he's beside his wife in a flash, pulling her into his arms.

"You know I love you Sweetie." He nuzzles her neck and whispers something in her ear that makes her blush and I know without a doubt in my mind that I don't want to know what he just said to her, but I can't help laughing when I look over to see the disgusted looks on their daughters faces.

"Guys cut it out."

"Your parents are sickening."

The girls say over one another causing everyone else in the room to laugh loudly and the girls grimace again. I pull Lexi in close and whisper in her ear, "You should be glad both of your parents are still here and still obviously in love." She looks into my eyes, as I pull her tighter into my arms.

"You're right but I would be neglecting my duties as a child *not* to be grossed out by their loved up behaviour." She says, before kissing me and then resting her head on my chest.

"Alright lovebirds, let's get dinner on the table before everyone ends up making out in separate rooms." Joshua says to the room and then walks up to Cat and pulls her in for a quick, but passionate kiss as well. I guess he didn't want to be outdone.

Everyone gets to work and in no time, the table is set, the meat is carved, and dinner is served up and on the table. There's teasing and laughter. Talking and arguing with more laughing. Everyone gets asked about their week, even me, and everyone listens attentively and offers advice if appropriate, but it's never done in a condescending way and I love it. The conversation flows and I'm comfortable telling them about my day, my week or maybe even my year, but when the subject of my parents comes up I clam right up, letting Lexi answer for me.

"As you know, I met Vincent, Gabe's dad earlier today and he's a wonderful and kind man." Lexi takes my hand in hers and squeezes it to reassure me and then continues. "His mum, Rosanna, passed away a few years ago."

"Ohh Gabe, I'm so sorry." Julia says and reaches over to squeeze the hand I have resting on the table. This is why I hate talking about what happened to my mum, people apologise for something that isn't their fault and they feel sorry for me.

"Thank you Julia, but I used to spend a lot of time with my mum before she died and even though I wish she was still here, that won't bring her back and I have my memories." Then there's an uneasy silence, the first of the night and I feel the heaviness of that on *my* shoulders. I'm the reason for the darker mood at the table, that is, until Lexi comes to my rescue once again. I can't help but wonder if she understands just how much I love her.

"It must be time to attack that luscious cake about now, don't you think dad?" She asks her dad.

"Abso-freaking-lutely Lexibear, I can't *wait* to get into a slice of that lusciousness." Jonathon says, while stacking up all the empty plates, and just like that, the dinner dishes are cleaned up and the cake, along with plates are set out on the table.

"You cut it." Lexi says to her dad while holding the knife out for him to take.

"No, I think you should do it Lexibear." He says to her shaking his head.

"No, I think you should have the pleasure, I've already seen a beauty almost exactly like this one today." Lexi tells her dad.

"You mean you had *cake* without your dear old dad?" Jonathon asks, hand on heart and looking horrified.

"You knew it would happen when I moved out of the house Dad. You shouldn't be so shocked after all this time, honestly." Lexi rolls her eyes at her dad, while her mum sits there shaking her head and laughing at their exchange.

"Does this happen with every cake?" I ask.

"Every god damn time." Joshua answers me, his voice full of annoyance. "Give me that damned knife Alexis, I want cake and I want some tonight and some of us have to be up early for work tomorrow." He says while taking the knife from Lexi's hand, much to *her* annoyance. "Your girl doesn't like giving up the control of making the cuts into a cake, you should know this about her before things get too serious."

"That's a good thing to me, I never cut cakes evenly, so if Lexi wants to take over those duties I'm more than OK with it." I tell him with a smile.

"You're a perfect match then." Joshua grumbles as he slices into the chocolate cake that Maria sent us away with earlier today, a gigantic smile spread across her face after Lexi asked if she had one she could bring to her parent's tonight.

Cake is dished out and coffees are made, all the while the conversation is flowing but no-one talks over anyone else. I almost don't want to leave, I feel so comfortable and welcome in Lexi's parents' home.

Joshua starts the movement to leave though, by taking Cat's hand and saying, "Come on sweetheart, it's time to get going."

"We should get going too. I know you hate it when we leave at the same time mum, but we do all have work tomorrow and it's been a big day for Gabe and myself. It's not often that you meet *both* sets of parents in one day you know! Most people take that one set of parentals at a time, but not us, nope. We decided to kill both birds with one stone and knocked you all off today." Lexi says to her mum and I know she's trying to take some of the heat off me, again. So, again, I pull her in tightly to my side when we stand up.

I don't feel too bad about leaving all together, we all helped clean up the dishes and we've left the kitchen as clean as it was when we got here. Which means Julia and Jonathon can either relax in front of the TV together for a while or just head to bed.

"Good night Julia, Jonathon. It was lovely to meet you both and dinner was amazing, thank you." I say as I lean into kiss Julia on the cheek.

"You are welcome any time Gabe, with or without our daughter as company." Julia says, with a wink and a smile as she hugs me tightly.

Barefoot and Dumped!

"Well, he's welcome any time if he brings a cake like the one they bought today." Jonathon says, then he grabs me in a manly bear hug and says in my ear, 'Look after my girl. She looks tough and she is, but everyone needs looking after every now and then."

"I promise Jonathon" I say in *his* ear.

We break apart and Jonathon says, "You're a good man Gabe and my daughter is lucky to have you, but just remember you're luckier to have her and we'll get along just fine."

"That's the same speech you gave me old man when I first met you. You need some new material Jonathon, I'm disappointed."

"Why you cheeky-" I don't get to hear what Jonathon calls Joshua because Lexi drags me out of the room.

"Come on, let's get out of here before those two start on one of their 'fights', otherwise we'll be here for another hour and as much as I love my family, it really *has* been a *long* day and I'm ready for it to be over."

"OK, let's get you home then."

"Goodnight crazy family, love you." Lexi yells out as we head for the door.

"Ummm goodnight everyone." I yell out.

There's a chorus of goodnights and then we're at the front door before Julia speaks.

"Good night you two. Drive safely and let me know when you're home please Lexi."

"Yes mum, I promise." Lexi rolls her eyes, again, but I can see that she actually likes that her mum wants to make sure she's safe.

"It was nice to meet you Gabe. Hopefully you're a permanent fixture at Sunday night dinners." She smiles at me, then wraps me in her arms and I feel the warmth of a mother's love.

"Thank you, it was nice to meet you too. I hope to become a very permanent fixture in Lexi's life and therefore a regular at Sunday night dinners too." I say smiling warmly back at Lexi's mum.

"Come on, stop sucking up to my mum before we get dragged back inside to settle some stupid argument between my father and stupid soon to be brother in law. Come on let's move." Lexi pulls on my arm, dragging me towards my truck.

"She's right, you should leave now while you can, they'll be a while now that they've started." She laughs. She watches us until we get into the truck and pull out of the driveway, waving the whole time. There's a tightening in my chest because I know, without a doubt, that Julia Stratton and Rosanna Romanetti would have gotten along like a house on fire if things had been different.

Chapter Twenty-seven

LEXI

"Are you OK Gabe?" I ask quietly. "They weren't too much were they?" He's very quiet and kind of brooding and I haven't seen this side of him yet. He reaches over the centre of the car, taking my hand in his and squeezing it tightly.

"No, your family are amazing Lexi, I had a great time." He says with a smile that doesn't quite reach is eyes. It's a similar look he had on his face when he told me the whole story about his ex and Jessie.

"Are you sure? I'm only asking because you don't *look* OK. You look like you've swallowed something that isn't very appetising."

"I swear Lexi, honey, I'm fine. I had a really great night." He takes a deep breath. "Your parents are amazing, and I already knew Cat and Joshua, sort of anyway. It's just that having your mum give me such a warm and welcoming hug, it made me think, that's all."

He speaks the last sentence so quietly I almost miss it and my heart breaks for him. "You were thinking about your mum?" He nods yes and I watch as his Adams apple bobs as he swallows. I squeeze his hand, then bring it to *my* lips to lay kisses along his knuckles.

"I just know your mum and mine would have gotten along like a house on fire and well, it just made me miss her a little extra tonight." He coughs around his emotions and I want him to know that he's allowed to miss his mum.

"You're allowed to miss her Gabe."

"I know and I do every day and while I'm really happy for my dad if there *is* something going on between him and Maria, she's not my mum." He shrugs a shoulder, as he says, "But getting affection off *your* mum just reminded me of *my* mum and I realised how much I think they would have gotten along, and I missed her more than most days."

"Ohh Gabe."

"That look right there, is why I didn't want to say anything. I don't need or want your sympathy Lexi. My mum's gone, and yes I miss her but there are people out there a lot worse off than me. A hell of a lot worse off than me and I still have my dad, and my sister. We're still a family, we're just a smaller version of what we had."

"I know but that doesn't mean you're not allowed to miss her Gabe." I tell him sincerely.

"I know, but." He hesitates so I finish his thought for him.

"But you're a man and you think you shouldn't miss your mum so much." He nods again. "Would you tell me the same thing or your sister? Or your dad for that matter? That the way they're feeling or missing their mother and wife, that they're wrong?"

"Well no, because they're you're feelings and you're allowed to have them."

"Exactly. Never try to hide your feelings from me Gabe, please. This relationship will only work if we're honest and by that I mean with your emotions and feelings as well as all that other stuff." I kiss the back of his hand again. "What if we have kids, would you tell your son that his feelings don't count because he's a boy and he's supposed to be tough and strong?" It's not until I register the shock on his face, that I realise what I just said. "Oh shit I didn't mean *our* kids. I meant, ahhh fuck it! I just meant when *you* have kids, is that what you would want your son *or* daughter to believe?" Could I be any more ridiculous right now? I'm making more of an idiot of myself by explaining my slip of the tongue than I could have by just leaving it be.

"You want to have kids with me Alexis?" Gabe asks me, his voice a mix of gravel and smoke. Gawd damn it, it's sexy as hell and I feel it's vibration in my clit.

"Well, now I didn't say that per se. I just meant that." I don't get to finish because Gabe cuts me off.

"That's not what I asked, Alexis. Do *you* want to have kids with me? Have you thought about us having a family in the future?" Gawd, that voice! "Well? Yes or no?"

I close my eyes and try to release my hand from his, but his grip gets tighter. "Yes." I say and it's so damned quiet I'm not even sure how he could have possibly heard my answer.

"Yes? You want to grow my babies in your belly?"

"Yes."

"You've thought about us having a family. Together? Is that something you want?"

How many times and how many different ways is he going to ask me the same fucking question? I snap my head up and stare directly into his eyes before answering, "Yes damn it! I've thought about having your children. Having mini Gabriel Romanetti's running around with silky black hair and the most amazing brown eyes I've ever seen. I want that and if that's all too soon for you, well stiff because you asked, and I told you. We promised to always be truthful, so there it is." In my rush to get everything out, I didn't realise that Gabe had pulled into my driveway and turned off the car. I didn't even know we'd been travelling for that long to be honest.

Before I know it, he's out of the truck, opening my door to help me out of the truck, and we're at my front door.

"Keys Lexi." I look at him blankly. "Where. Are. Your. Keys. Lexi?" He says the words slowly but forcefully and suddenly my brain kicks into gear.

Reaching into my handbag, I pull out my keys and hold them up in the air like I just won a damned trophy. Gabe growls and takes them from me and opens my front door, pushing me inside as he does. I hear the door slam shut. All I can see is Gabe and then his lips are on mine in a bruising kiss. I drop my bag to the floor and reach up to hold on tight to his biceps to keep me steady.

Gabe breaks the kiss and my lips chase his, until my eyes open to try to see where he went. He's looking at me, there's a storm in his eyes and I *think* it's lust and desire but I'm not sure.

"I want that." He takes a deep shuddering breath. "I want that too Lexi. I want kids with you. I want to marry you. I want the white picket fence. I want it all honey." He says breathlessly, looking deep into my soul. I know I want all that too, but it feels too much. "Not right now. Not tomorrow or next week but I need you to know that's the end game baby."

"Honestly?" I ask, my own voice a little hoarse.

"A hundred percent yes. A thousand percent yes." He closes his eyes for a few seconds and takes a deep breath, again. "I want us to spend time together, to get to know one another and learn everything about each other, but yes, in time I want it all with you and I've never wanted that with anyone else. Ever. You're it for me Alexis Stratton, you have to know that."

My heart swells to the point where I think it might explode. I could never love this man more than I do right now, I'm sure of it.

"Me too. I want it all eventually as well, because you're it for me, Gabriel Romanetti." I kiss his lips because I can and wrap my arms around his neck. "I love you Gabe."

"I love you too Lexi." Then his lips are on mine again and we're kissing. Exploring each other's mouth and tongues and it's the sweetest and hottest kiss all at the same time.

I hear a door slam, but I don't think anything of it until the front door opens and my sister and her fiancé walk in the door. Again!

"They're at it again Catherine." Joshua points out the obvious as he walks past us and into the kitchen grabbing himself a glass of water. "This is why you need to move in with me, that way we can *all* have our privacy."

"Leave them alone Joshua! They're enjoying their young love. It's fresh and it's new and all exciting still." She laughs as Joshua walks up to her and pulls her into his body.

Barefoot and Dumped!

"We're still exciting too baby." He says and then slams his lips on to hers. That's my little sister and I really don't want to watch her making out anymore. Fiancé or not, I don't need the images.

"OK, OK we stopped, you can too." I whine at them.

"I don't think I can stop now." Joshua murmurs on Cat's lips. "You sure you want to stay here tonight?"

Cat giggles and pushes him away. "Yes I do, I have a few things I want to get done before the big move next weekend."

"Fine." Joshua says, and even though he's trying to look grumpy, he's got a smirk on his face because he knows this time next week, he'll have Cat living in their house with him. "I'm leaving now then, before I don't want to leave at all."

"You can stay you know." Cat says, running a finger down the front of his shirt.

"No." He says, grabbing her wrist to stop any further movement. "We made a deal and I'm sticking to it." Cat growls and Joshua kisses her on the forehead. "Goodnight baby, see you tomorrow."

"Bye." She mumbles as he walks out the door.

"I'm going to go too Lexi." Gabe says, sounding for all the world like he doesn't want to go anywhere.

"You don't have to leave." I say, but I'm not going to touch him, because that's too tempting, for both of us. I can see it in his eyes, he's pleading with me not to touch him so that he has the strength to leave.

"I do. I kind of promised to help Brent deal with getting an unwanted house guest out tonight and I forgot all about it. He just messaged me to see where I am. I'm sorry honey." He says and he looks so sad that I can't be mad at him.

"You made a promise to a friend, you have to go help him. I'll see you tomorrow?"

"Definitely. I'll message you to let you know I'm home, but you don't have to answer me, you'll probably be asleep before we're done." He kisses me hard on the lips and I know he's struggling to leave, so I push him away. "Don't forget to let your mum know you got home safely. I don't want her to think I can't look after you." He winks at me, says goodnight to Cat and then he's gone. Locking the door behind him.

"You're in love with him." It's a statement, not a question.

"I am Cat. Do you think it's too soon?" I ask, still a little unsure of how fast things are moving and needing to hear my sisters thoughts on the matter.

"Not if you both know that it's right. No." Cat says, hugging me tightly. "And if you want my opinion, for what it's worth, I think the two of you are perfect together. He loves you too."

"I know." I say, I can feel the dreamy, goofy grin on my face, but I don't want it to go away. Being with Gabe makes me happy. Life in general is pretty awesome right now. What could go wrong? It's nice to know that my sister approves of the love of my life as well.

"Text mum. I call shotgun on using the bathroom first." Cat calls out as she closes the bathroom door behind her, and I hear the lock slide into place.

Damn it! Why did I get a house with only one bathroom? That's right, I wasn't expecting a roommate to be living here indefinitely, but I've loved having her here despite the bathroom issue.

I smile as I send mum a message.

Lexi: *We're both home safe and the boys have gone home too. Love Lexi*

Julia: *Thank you sweetie, that makes me happy. We approve by the way. 100%. Love you too*

I don't think my heart could be any fuller right now. Gabe loves me and wants a future together. My sister is moving out of my house and she loves Gabe and I together. My parents love me, and they love Gabe as well. Life is pretty perfect right now.

When the lights flick off and on I don't think anything about it, even when Cat screams out from the bathroom, asking what the hell is going on. I don't answer her because it was just the lights playing up and I don't think anything of it.

Barefoot and Dumped!

Until a few minutes later when it happens again. There's an almighty crash and a scream from the bathroom. I run over there but I can't get in, she locked the damned door!

"Cat, are you OK?" I yell at the door.

"What the fuck are you doing out there? Why are you playing with the lights and the water? I slipped and hit my elbow!" She screams at me through the door.

"I'm not Cat, I swear. I don't know what's going on, I'll go out and have a look at the fuses." I start to move away when she yells through the door again.

"No! If it's not you doing this, then just wait a second for me to rinse my hair. Fuck!" she squeals. "The hot water came back on for a minute now it's cold again. Please wait for me Lexi?"

"Yeah sure. Hurry up." I say. Then the lights flicker again, only this time they stay off. Fuck. "Hurry up Cat!" What the hell is going on?

"I'm coming!" She yells back at me.

I use the torch on my phone to make my way to the kitchen and start looking for the torch that I know is in here somewhere. Hopefully, the junk drawer. "Bingo!" There's two of them in there. The next thing is, I hope they have batteries, working ones at that. I haven't needed a torch in forever.

I click the button on one and it lights up. "Woohoo!" I yell out.

"What are you so happy about?" Cat asks from behind me, scaring the shit out of me.

"Geezus Cat, what the hell?" I ask her, *after* I jump *and* squeal in fright. "I found torches and this one actually works."

"I can't believe I scared you. You're so hopeless Lexi!" She shakes her head and in the shadows from the light of the torch, I can see her disappointment. "You were expecting me out here, especially after you yelled at me to hurry up and you knew I was in the house."

"Yes to all of those things and yet, here we are. It's dark and I was concentrating on getting us some working torches, not listening to see if you were walking up behind me." I kind of whisper yell at her.

"You'd never survive in a horror movie big sis. I think you'd be the first one to die and that's probably because you'd die of fright or a heart attack." She shakes her head again and takes the other torch out of my hand, presses the on button, shining the light in my face.

"You'd be the first one killed because I'd push you in front of the murderer." I say testily.

"Well, isn't that just lovely? I'll remember to tell our parent's that you'd be willing to sacrifice *me* for *your* life. Seems fair I guess."

"There isn't a murderer, so it doesn't matter Cat." I can hear the frustration and irritation in my own voice and take a few deep breaths to calm down, because what I said is right. This isn't a horror movie, and this *isn't* how we die.

"I'm going to message Joshua and see if his power is out." Cat says, pulling her phone out of her pocket.

"Good idea. I'll message Gabe, he doesn't live that far away, you'd think his would be out too if ours is." As I reach for my phone on the bench, I see a dark shadow move across the window in the kitchen. "Oh my god!" I whisper yell to Cat. "Did you see that?"

"What? I didn't see a thing. What are you talking about?"

"I swear to god I just saw a dark shadow walk past the window." I whisper as I move closer to my sister. My *kid* sister!

"No you didn't. I'm sure it's nothing Lexi." She says, swallowing loudly. "I'm sorry for talking about horror movies. I know they freak you out and well, this is the perfect scenario and -."

"Just shut up Catherine!" She motions zipping her lips and throwing away the key. Something we've done with each other since we were little girls and it comforts me enough that I let out a small giggle and I relax. That is until she lets out a muffled squeal, as she jumps in fright a second later.

"Don't look now," She says out of the corner of her mouth. "But I think you were right and someone's out there."

My phone starts ringing, scaring the crap out of both of us and I fumble to hurriedly answer it, especially when I see Gabe's name on the screen.

Barefoot and Dumped!

Just as I answer, Cat's phone chimes with an incoming message, no doubt from Joshua trying to find out what's going on.

"Gabe." I whisper into the phone.

"Why are you whispering Lexi?" He asks, sounding amused.

"We think there's someone outside and they cut our power." I whisper.

"What!?" His voice booms through the phone and I swear anyone within a half mile radius could hear him, including the dogs.

"Shhhh they might hear you!" I whisper yell. "Is your power out?"

"I don't know I'm not at home, I'm at Brent's remember?" He reminds me.

"Oh, yeah right. Sorry, I didn't think. Cat freaked me out talking about horror movies and I was hoping your power was out as well. It would have made me feel better, but I forgot you didn't go straight home from here." I say quietly into the phone.

I see the shadow move across the windows in both the living room and the kitchen. Cat must see it too, because we both let out a quiet squeal and cling to each other.

"Lexi?" I can hear the concern in Gabe's question.

"I definitely think there's someone here." I whisper into my phone.

"Uhuh." Cat says in my ear.

"Hang up now Alexis and call the police. I'm on my way honey, I'll be there in a few minutes." I hear his truck roar to life and kick up some gravel as I hang up the phone. I start to dial the police when we hear smashing glass and we both let out a very loud, bloodcurdling scream.

When the operator answers, I tell her in a hushed voice exactly what's happening, and she tells me that the police are on their way. We stay on the line with her, quietly telling her what's going on, but it's suddenly very quiet. That is until we hear this strange whining noise and there's a loud thump on the side of the house somewhere.

In the distance we can hear the wail of police sirens, but whoever is outside doesn't seem to think they're for them because the strange noise continues. So does the thumping noise and they're both getting closer to us.

I reach behind me to the knife block on the bench and pull out the first knife my hand wraps around. Pushing Cat behind me, I look at the window just as the shadow appears there again. The sirens are getting louder, but whoever this is doesn't leave.

"Come on mother fucker! You want something from me? Why don't you come on in and try and take it! I've got a knife and I'm not afraid to fucking use it!" I scream at the top of my lungs. I don't know what comes over me, but I just want this over with, I can't stand the suspense anymore.

"For the love god, what do you think you're doing?" Cat whisper yells in my ear. "You never invite the killer *inside*." She says.

"And how many times have you been in this kind of situation Cat? Hmmmm?" I whisper yell right back at her, and when she doesn't answer me, I continue. "That's right, none. Whatever they want, they can fucking have it Cat. My heart can't deal with the suspense of not knowing what's going to happen."

A loud bang at the door makes us both jump and scream loudly, again.

"Police! Please open up." Comes a deep voice from the other side of the door. While a quieter, softer feminine voice says, "You idiot!"

We walk to the door, still stuck to each other like Siamese twins, and look out the window beside it.

"We've got the culprits in custody ma'am, but I need you to open the door so that we can come in and talk to you." The male officer says.

"Ladies, we really need to come in and talk to you. I know you've had a real scare tonight, but we need to come inside please." The female voice says, as her face then appears next to the male officers at the small window.

I nod and try to open the door, only to realise that Cat and I have become so entwined together that I can't actually move. "Cat, you have to let me go for a second so I can let in the officers."

Barefoot and Dumped!

"How do we know they're really the police though Lexi?" She whisper yells, and I'm pretty sure the officers can hear her.

"Because of all the police cars and red and blue flashing lights?" I say, trying not to sound too sarcastic because I completely understand how freaked out she is right now.

"Right. Yup, OK, valid point." She says as she nods to reinforce her agreement, as she untangles our limbs so I can open the door. "Of course."

"Good evening ladies, I'm Officer Robinsen and this is my partner, Officer Cameran." The female officer introduces herself and her partner.

"I'm sorry for the loud bang on the door and scaring you more, I slipped, and my boot slammed into your door. No harm to the door, but I'm still sorry for adding to the stress of your night ladies." He offers in apology.

I can't speak just yet, so I just nod my head.

"Can we come in and talk to you please ladies?" Officer Robinsen asks. "We need you to tell us what happened here tonight."

"Umm yes, of course. Come in." Cat and I say, together.

"Have you got someone we can call to come and stay with you tonight?" Officer Robinsen asks.

I nod, "Yes, my boyfriend is on his way." I say while nodding. "I called him before I called you, because he lives close by and I wanted to check if he had power, because if he did then it was just a power outage, but while I was talking to him, I saw a shadow move across the window in the kitchen and he told me to hang up and call you."

"Smart man." Officer Cameran says with a small smile.

There's a commotion outside and I feel Cat stiffen next to me.

"Lexi!" There's more scuffling and then I hear Gabe ask, "Is she OK? I'm her boyfriend I just want to know that she's OK. Lexi and her sister Cat were both home, I need to know that they're alright. Please." He begs the officer outside.

"Gabe!" I yell out, then turn to Officer Robinsen and say, "That's him, that's my boyfriend."

"Let him in." She yells out to the officer at the door, just as we hear another voice.

"Catherine! Sweetheart, are you OK?" There's a second of silence and then Joshua says, "Gabe what the fuck? Are they OK?"

"I don't know man, they were just about to let me go inside when you got here."

"That's my fiancé." Cat says quietly to the officers.

"OK, let them in Joey." The Officer at the door nods once and the guys come barrelling in the door straight to us.

Gabe heads right for me, sits down next to me on the couch and pulls me into his lap, while Joshua does the same thing to Cat.

"It's OK honey, I'm here now and I won't let anything happen to you." He whispers into the top of my head, to the officers he says, "Do you know who did this? Did you find them?"

"Yes, they're in handcuffs and in the back of a patrol car as we speak. We just need a few details from the girls, and then we can be on our way." Officer Cameran says.

For the next twenty minutes we go over and over the details of what happened tonight, and I feel Gabe's arms tighten around me with every explanation and detail.

"Thank you ladies, and gents, for your patience. We've got everything we need to charge this guy and hopefully, put him away for a while. You try to enjoy the rest of your night." Officer Cameran says with a small smile.

"I would suggest you cover up the broken window tonight and get it replaced first thing in the morning." Officer Robinsen says. "We checked your electricity and water. They were just flicking the switches, there was no actual damage to anything, so everything should be working properly now."

"Thank you Officer, we'll get that sorted right away." Gabe says, while Joshua holds my sister close, murmuring in her ear.

"Good. We'll be in contact if we need anything else." They both nod and leave the house, closing the door behind them. Then there's just silence. No more noise and flashing lights, just the four of us sitting quietly.

It's then that I realise there's someone else in my house. "Who the fuck is that, Gabe?" I ask, looking at a guy sitting on a stool at my kitchen bench, his back towards us, either giving us all some privacy or hiding from us.

"Oh shit, sorry. That's Brent, my best friend." He turns around with a smile on his face as he says hello and it all feels like the next few minutes happen in slow motion as his mouth turns into a circle and the surprise registers on his face. His next words make me understand his shock.

"Holy shit! You're Stevie's Alexis!" Brent says, surprise lacing his voice. Gabe scowls in confusion, and for just a second, he's not the only one who's confused. Then it hits me!

"You're Kyle's brother! The other house mate?" Holy shit is right. How the hell did I not put all those clues together? "Of all the guys in the world, Gabe had to be *your* friend." I say, not disguising the disgust in my voice.

Chapter Twenty-eight

<u>GABE</u>

"How the hell didn't I put two and two together before now." Brent mumbles, shaking his head in disbelief. "How the fuck did I miss that the night at the bar?"

"The same way I did I suppose?" Lexi says, her shock now laced with questions.

"*You* were too busy eyeballing Gabe here to notice anything or anyone else, but how the fuck did *I* miss it? I was there the first night and I recognised Lacey the night at the bar when you two reconnected. I never did actually *see* your face when you sat down with Gabe that night, because you had your back to me and then Lacey joined me at the bar for a drink. We sent you guys over some food and then left. I'd met Sophie that first night and even though Lacey is a *very* attractive woman I wasn't interested. We went our separate ways that night."

"You're right!" Lexi exclaims. "Until today, I couldn't have told anyone what Gabe's best friend looked like. We've managed to dodge each other. Until now. Holy crap!"

"You mean this is-" Cat asks but doesn't get to finish because I need some answers myself, and now.

"What the hell are you two talking about. Who is whose roommate?" I break into the conversation, cutting Cat off. "What's going on Lexi?" I ask, my gaze swinging between my friend and my girlfriend, looking for an answer. "What do you mean when you say she's Stevie's Alexis, Brent?"

"Brent is Stephen's roommate." Lexi says.

"You mean your ex?" I ask to make sure I've got this right.

"Stevie *is* Stephen, Gabe." Brent says, amazed. "And he's not my *roommate* Alexis, he's *my* house guest that has more than outstayed his welcome."

Through the stunned silence, Brent's phone starts ringing, and he steps away to answer it. While the four of us are left just standing there, looking at each other in stunned silence. Until Brent yells into the phone, "WHAT?! It was YOU?" Making all of us jump in surprise. "FUCK! No, Kyle, you can wait. I'll be there when I get there." He yells into the phone. "Why? You've got the balls to fucking ask me why? I'll tell you why, because I'm at Lexi's trying to clear up the fucking mess you and that dickhead created." He hangs up the phone and hangs his head, his chin resting on his chest for a few seconds before looking up and meeting my eyes.

"What happened? Is Kyle OK?" I ask, worried because he's like a brother to me.

"No, he's an idiot." He replies to me, looking uncomfortable, before looking at Lexi. "Lexi I'm *so* sorry, I didn't know what they were doing. If I'd known I would have stopped them, please believe me."

"They did this?" She asks, her voice barely above a hoarse whisper, and Brent nods.

"I'll pay for the repairs. Anything you need." Brent tells her.

"Hang on, back it up a second please? Are you saying that Stevie, your brother's best mate that I was helping you throw out of your house tonight," I look at Brent. "Is your ex Stephen?" I ask Lexi.

"Yes." Lexi and Brent answer me at the same time and I'm struggling to come to grips with this revelation when I realise another one.

"And, are *you* saying that Kyle and Stephen did this." I ask Brent, looking around Lexi's house, and spreading my arms wide to indicate the fucking mess in it.

"Yes." Brent says simply. I guess he knows there's nothing else that *can* be said.

"How do you know for sure?" Lexi asks him quietly.

"Because that was Kyle on the phone asking me to come bail him out at the police station." He answers, closing his eyes for a few seconds. "As you heard, I told him he can fucking wait. I'm in no hurry to pick his stupid arse up."

The reality of what Brent has said and what he and Lexi have suddenly put together hits me and I can't contain my anger any longer. "I'll fucking *kill* him."

"Now hold on Gabe, he didn't really mean any harm. He didn't know what Stephen had planned and if he did, he wouldn't have been here." I don't let Brent finish, I can't. I feel for him, because honestly his brother isn't a bad guy, he's just got shit taste in friends and is easily led.

"No harm?" I growl at him. "NO FUCKING HARM!! Are you fucking kidding me Brent?" I can't help roaring at him. "When he saw what was going on, he should have left. He *should* have called you and told you what Stephen was doing or called the fucking police himself."

"I know Gabe, but you know Kyle, he wouldn't hurt a fly and he certainly wouldn't knowingly hurt a woman." Brent defends his brother, but I notice he didn't defend Stephen. "Stephen is a first class jerk and I was trying to get him out of our lives tonight, you know that. Neither of us made the connection between him and Lexi. I'm truly sorry for that Lexi, if I'd known, well I don't know what I would have done, but I would have tried something."

"And yet he went along with the idiots stupid plan and look! Look at what happened because of their stupidity Brent. You were standing next to me when Lexi called because she was fucking terrified that someone was going to break in. Have you *noticed* the damage done to *her fucking home*? We're going to have board up a couple of windows and make sure the place is secure so that no one *else* can get in and do any *more* damage while we get everything fixed." I take a deep breath. "Did you not notice that Lexi *and* her sister were fucking terrified tonight? They could have been seriously hurt because of their idiotic behaviour and yet here you stand, in front of *all* of us saying, 'well they didn't *mean* any harm so it's OK.' No, Brent it's not fucking OK."

"Go and get Kyle, but I don't want to see him or Stephen any time soon." I tell him.

"Stephen won't be a problem, he's out of my house as of tonight just like I planned and if Kyle wants to keep hanging around with the douchebag after what happened here tonight, he's on his own too."

"You shouldn't walk away from family Brent." Lexi says quietly, reaching her hand out and resting it on Brent's shoulder.

"After everything they've done to you tonight, you're telling him it's OK?" I ask her, not able to hide my surprise.

"No, that's not what I'm saying Gabe, but family means something, and I believe that Kyle was stupid, but it was Stephen that did this. He was the mastermind and yes, Kyle was stupid to go along with it, but hopefully he learns a lesson from this." Lexi drops her hand from Brent's shoulder and comes back to almost bury herself in my body and I pull her in tight. The need to protect her is overwhelming tonight.

"I can't believe you can be so forgiving Lexi."

"I can." Cat pipes up from beside me, Joshua's arms wrapped around her. "Don't get me wrong, I'm as mad as hell at the *both* of them, but you forget, we've known Stephen for a long while and he's a manipulative bastard. Getting Kyle to do something like this wouldn't have been hard for him."

"Go bail out your brother Brent and take him home. Get him to explain to you what the hell happened tonight and why they did it. After that, I don't really want to talk to him, and I'll be throwing the book at Stephen if I can."

"Daddy likes to get him out of any trouble he gets in to, Kyle isn't that lucky, and he's always left behind. Maybe this time he'll decide enough is enough." Brent says and walks out the door without another word to any of us. He doesn't even *look* at me as he walks by.

"I can't believe him." My rage not really fading, I can still see red.

"He's looking out for his brother and you've told me before, that Kyle is a good kid and you couldn't understand what he saw in 'Stevie'. Well, at a guess, it's excitement and the balls to do whatever you want. Cat's right, Stephen knows how to manipulate any situation, so I feel for Kyle, if he truly is the good guy that you think he is." Lexi says, wrapping her arms around my waist and moulding her body to mine. "But, I want to thank you for backing Cat and myself up tonight, I truly appreciate it."

I don't say a word, I'm not sure I can. She's being so understanding and forgiving. Instead I wrap my hand around the back of her neck and pull her in for a kiss.

"What they did was stupid and wrong. We knew they were up to something, and we were trying to stop whatever it was by kicking him out of Brent's house. Knowing what we know now that it was you that he planned on hurting, it tears me up inside Lexi." I murmur against the top of her head quietly, my voice deep with emotion. "I wish we'd gotten here sooner. I wish I hadn't left you alone." I regret leaving her to go to Brent's.

"You're not the only one Gabe." Joshua mumbles. "I left the girls here alone too you know."

"You didn't know Gabe. None of us knew, how could we?" Lexi asks, looking at all of us in turn. "I mean sure, maybe I could have predicted Stephen's behaviour and the fact that he would recruit someone to help him, but I didn't. He's been gone for weeks and I thought that he'd moved on. Obviously, he was just biding his time so that getting back at me for *him* breaking things off with *me* would be more effective. What's done is done." She says looking at both Joshua and myself, trying to reassure us, but I doubt it makes either of us feel any better. "Why don't we take a window each and clean up the mess, cover them up and then just relax for a while."

We split off in couples and start the clean-up. Lexi sweeps up the broken glass and I tape cardboard to the frame. I step back, looking at my handy work and feel my anger flare up all over again. Lexi comes up behind me and wraps her arms around my waist, resting her head on the back of my shoulder.

"Don't Gabe. I know you're mad and you're wishing that you'd connected the dots sooner, but honestly, he's just an inconsiderate, spoilt brat, who thinks everyone else will bend to his will." She kisses my shoulder leaving me wanting more, her touch always does.

I turn her around and wrap my arms around her. I never want to let her go. Maybe if I can keep her wrapped up in my arms like this, I can keep her safe, forever. It's not realistic but a man dares to hope, can't he? What's wrong with wanting the one you love safe?

"It's over Gabe." I'm not as sure as Lexi but I don't voice my concerns, she's been through enough tonight already.

"Well kids, Catherine's exhausted and I would like to get her to bed. Are we all staying here or is someone leaving for the night?" Joshua asks, breaking our quiet moment and now I understand why Lexi wants her sister to move out of her house.

"Someone has to stay here for the night, because those windows, while covered aren't secure, anyone could get in." I confirm.

"You guys can all go home and yes that includes you Cat. We both know your home isn't here, and it hasn't been for a very long time. Go home, to your home, with Joshy boy." Lexi smiles and reaches out to ruffle Joshua's hair.

"Hey, don't do that and don't call me that, you know I hate it." He grumbles.

"I do know that and it's why I say it. Come on, there's been enough seriousness for one night. You two kids get going, Gabe won't be far behind you and I'll be safely tucked up in bed." Joshua's mouth opens but I'm the one who speaks.

"Umm there is *no* way in hell you're staying here alone tonight. If you stay, I stay and that's that. There is no room for arguing with me woman." I tell her, holding her tighter so she can't get away from me.

"OK, we're going to get out of here then, if that's OK Lexi? I mean, if *you're* OK?" Cat stumbles over her words and I've not heard her do that before.

Lexi pushes out of my arms and I let her go. She wraps her sister in her arms and whispers in her ear, making Cat giggle and nod. "OK." She whispers.

"Goodnight Cat." She says kissing her sister on the cheek.

"Goodnight Joshy boy. Look after my sister and thank you for coming tonight when she needed you."

"I will be here whenever either of you need me, I hope you know that. We're family Lexi." Joshua replies, kissing my girl on the cheek. He reaches out and shakes my free hand, the other one has already pulled

Lexi back tightly into my side. "Thanks for helping the girls out tonight Gabe."

"I will always help out my girl, and yours. We're family." He nods his agreement and approval at me, and I nod back.

"Get out of here you two." Lexi hustles them to the front door and almost pushes them out.

"Anyone would think you want to be alone with your man, Alexis." Joshua smirks at me and I growl, because he might be Lexi's soon to be brother in law, but that doesn't mean he gets to talk to her like that. My growl just makes him laugh as he tugs Cat in closer to his side. Then, they both say goodnight and disappear into his car and drive away.

Stepping back, I watch Lexi close and lock the door, then make sure that it's locked. She's more rattled than she wants anyone to believe. I place my hands on her shoulders and rub lightly, trying to get her to relax. "It's OK honey, he isn't coming back tonight and if he does, he'll have me to deal with and I'm not sure how much would be left for the police to arrest again."

"I don't want you to do that Gabe. He's not worth it."

"No, he's not, but you are Lexi. I love you and I won't let anything happen to you." I promise her.

"You can't be around all the time Gabe, but I really appreciate the sentiment." She kisses me and then leaves her lips resting lightly on mine when she says, "I love you too Gabriel." She has no idea what she does to me when she says my name like that. Or maybe she does, because she stretches up on her toes and whispers in my ear, "Let's go have a shower. I need to wash this day off." She takes my hand in hers and leads me to the bathroom. "No interruptions tonight, it's just us in the house. Isn't it nice?"

I don't get the chance to respond, because she takes what feels like seconds to strip herself of her clothes and then starts on mine. It feels like they just evaporate but I know that's not true. I'm just so mesmerised with Lexi that time doesn't seem to be relevant.

I feel the shower turn on and realise that Lexi's lead me to the shower stall and closed the door behind us.

I'm distracted by her amazing hands travelling all over my body. Over my biceps and shoulders, her nails scraping down my back and then her hands working over my pecs and abs. Every now and then, she scrapes her nails along my skin and my body is in sensory overload. When her hands touch my pecs again, she pinches my nipples and I groan. The pain is sharp, but it eases quickly when she sucks each of them into her mouth to gently suck on them. I've never had a woman do that to me before and I fucking love it. "Again." I moan, burying my hands in her now wet hair. Then I'm lost to the sensation of her pinching one nipple, only to draw it into her hot, wet mouth and soothe the stab of pain, but then she pinches my other nipple, and I suck in a breath of pain mixed with definite pleasure. The song is right, there *is* a fine line between them. "Lexi." Her name comes out on a husky breath that I don't even recognise as my own voice.

"Hmmmm, do you like that, Gabriel?" There she goes saying my name like that again and my cock twitches, bouncing off her stomach. "I'll take that as a yes." I can feel her satisfied smile on the skin of my chest. I don't answer her, I have no words, it's just a garbled noise that comes out of my mouth. A cross between words I can't speak and a moan of absolute pleasure. My hands unwind from her hair as her body pulls away from mine. My eyes spring open to see what she's doing, and I'm greeted with the most erotic sight I have *ever* seen. Lexi on her knees, as she wraps her lips around the head of my cock and sucks.

"Fuck me!"

Lexi drags her mouth off my cock, resting her lips on the tip. "That's the plan Gabriel, in case you hadn't picked up on that." She giggles and I don't have time to answer her as she swallows my cock down to the base and my head falls back against the shower wall, my eyes close because I can't think long enough to keep them open. My hands, still twisted in her hair, are running around her scalp, massaging, pulling gently on her hair, as I give in and enjoy the sensation. Her warm, wet mouth dragging up and down my cock. Her tongue, swirling around the head and swiping through the slit, makes my knees buckle.

"Fuck Lexi! I can't. I won't last long. If you. Fuck! Keep. Doing. That." I can't string an entire sentence together. I can't think.

She doesn't respond, doesn't say a fucking word. She just keeps dragging her mouth up and down my cock, sucking, and that tongue doesn't seem to stop circling around the ridge at the tip of my cock. I feel my balls start to draw up my body, getting tighter and I know I'm about to blow but I can't stop myself.

Her hand massages my balls and that's it, I'm done. When I catch my breath, I look down at Lexi, who's still squatting at my hips. The smile on her face squeezes my heart and she's got my balls and my cock in her hands, but her breasts are covered in my release.

"Fuck!"

I hook my hands under her arms and haul her up my body, and I kiss her. I kiss her with everything I have left in me and while I didn't think that I had much left, apparently I do, because I take her mouth like it contains my last breath.

When we break apart to take a breath, she's smiling wide again. "Proud of yourself there?" I ask, returning her smile. How could I not be? That was the best blowjob of my life.

"I've never done that before." She explains and my heart skips a beat.

"You've never given a blowjob before? If that's the case, you're one quick study honey."

She laughs and says, "Oh no I've done that before. I've just never really taken the lead like that before or played with a guy's nipples or run my hands all over his body before. I didn't know if you'd like it." She says it almost bashfully, after everything she just made me feel, there's no way I'm going to let her feel even slightly embarrassed or ashamed.

"I loved it Lexi. You can touch me anywhere and anyhow you like. Hands, tongues, lips, teeth, I don't mind, as long as it's you." A sweet blush colours her cheeks. "I mean it honey, whatever you want to do, or try, you just have to ask. I'm up for anything once." I wink at her to alleviate some of the tension and I'm exceptionally happy when it works.

I drop to my knees and I hear her gasp in shock.

"What are you doing Gabe?"

"Paybacks a bitch baby. Or is it?" I hesitate for a second and then say, "I think I need a new turn of phrase, that's not quite right. How about, 'paybacks a pleasure'?" I smile up at her, my hands resting on her thighs. "Yeah, I like that one. Paybacks a pleasure honey. Now hold on tight."

I bite her thigh gently and she squeals, but my plan works, because she spreads her legs, giving me access to her pussy.

Chapter Twenty-nine

LEXI

I'm about to protest and tell Gabe he doesn't have to do a thing, when he drops to his knees, his hands resting on my thighs and looking up at me through his freaking eyelashes, he says, "Paybacks a pleasure honey, now hold on tight."

I put my hands on top of his head with every intention of pushing him away but then he bites my thighs with just enough pressure to cause a sharp pain. Then he soothes it straight away with his tongue.

A moan escapes my lips, making Gabe growl against my thigh. I feel it vibrate up my leg and it hits my clit with a bang that I wasn't expecting, and my knees go weak. Gabe was obviously expecting it because he's bracing my body with his hands firmly grabbing my butt cheeks to hold me up and I'm grateful for the support because I can't think of anything else but what I'm feeling when he runs his tongue over my clit. When he hums against my skin, my entire body reacts and I'm so wound up, I'm shaking.

"I'm going to take care of you honey, always. Come for me Lexi." He pushes two fingers into my pussy and his lips latch onto my clit, sucking me until I scream.

"Fuck! Gabe. Yes!" I'm not even sure my words are anything more than mumbled pleasure but I'm also beyond caring.

When he adds a third finger, the hand that was still clutching my butt, wraps around my waist and pulls my body in even closer to his mouth and I'm lost.

"So wet. You taste so good Lexi." My hands are scratching at his scalp and pulling his hair. I'm not sure if I'm trying to pull his head away from my pussy because it's so sensitive and I'm so turned on, or whether I want more. Of everything. Of this man, his tongue, his fingers and that voice that is deep and rumbling with arousal.

My hips push into his face and then pull back again, over and over again, riding his face and his fingers to find my release. "Oh Gabe. I'm. I'm going. Yes right. There." I take a deep, shuddering breath and then I'm flying. My eyes are closed, my head flung back and resting on the tiled wall. Gabe's tongue is licking at my release, his hands holding onto my waist as my orgasm makes my body convulse and I have no control over keeping myself upright.

"I love watching you cum and I love licking you clean." Gabe grins as he stands up, leaving sweet kisses up my body as he does. Then his lips are on mine, kissing me deeply and I can taste myself on his lips and tongue. It's so damned erotic that I can feel my body wake up again.

I'm so caught up in my own body and feelings, I don't notice that Gabe's turned off the shower and walked us to the towels, until he's wrapping one around me. He reaches out behind me, for a towel for himself and starts to dry his hair. Neither of us has said a word, but we're watching every move the other makes as we dry our bodies. I watch as Gabe rubs a pale blue fluffy towel over his hair, his shoulders, down his chest missing his cock and going straight to his legs. It's like watching a reverse striptease, and it makes my mouth water again.

It's especially arousing to watch the desire light up on Gabe's face as he watches me rubbing my pale blue towel all over my body. I towel dry my hair, then rub the towel over my shoulders, down my arms, over my stomach and my legs, bending over to reach them.

"I think you missed a spot." Gabe says his voice husky with lust.

"Oh yeah? Where would that be?" I ask, my voice just as raspy.

"Turn around and dry those sexy ankles of yours again." He says, all demanding and hot, without cracking a smile.

I smile at him, and slowly turn around. Taking my time, I dry my back and my butt cheeks, as I oh so slowly lower my body until I'm bent over, reaching for my toes, while spreading my legs. To help with my balance of course, not to give Gabe the show he's hoping for. Nope. It's all for balance baby.

Then all of a sudden I don't need balance as my feet are swept up off the floor and my body is twisted and flung over Gabe's shoulder. One minute I was standing on my own two feet and the next I was upside down with the perfect view of his butt. His *naked* butt and what a view it is. It's so good I can't help slapping him and he stops walking.

"Did you just slap my arse, Lexi?" He asks me, in disbelief.

I can't help giggling, which makes it a little difficult to answer but I manage to in between gasping for breath. "You better believe I did, Gabriel." I say, knowing what me saying his name like that does to him, as I squeeze his cheeks. I wish I could see if his cock twitches but alas, I'm looking at his rear, not that I'm complaining too loudly about that. "You want to go all Neanderthal and swing me over your shoulder, hanging me upside down and allowing my hands easy access to that delicious derrière, you better believe I'm gonna touch it. It's a thing of beauty, love."

"My arse is a thing of beauty?" He repeats, sounding surprised.

"Absolutely Gabriel. All that working out and running you do, it's definitely paying off." I squeeze his cheeks again to make my point.

"Huh." Is his response, making me giggle all over again. He starts to walk to my bedroom again and I rest my hands on his cheeks. You know, to keep my balance, not to feel the muscles stretch and flex under my hands. Nope.

A smile spreads across my face and I'm so distracted by his butt that I don't notice or even think about how long the trip is between the bathroom and my bedroom. Before I know what's happening, I'm sailing over his shoulder, through the air and landing on my back, on the bed. I bounce once because his body covers mine, preventing me from bouncing up again. A small squeak is expelled from my body on a breath, then his lips are on mine in a scorching kiss.

He pulls back suddenly, looking me deep in the eyes, "My derrière, as you so politely named it, it's *not* beautiful. It can be chunky, manly or muscly but never beautiful." He kisses my chin, moving along my jaw and sucking my ear lobe into his mouth, distracting me from being able to reply. "*You* on the other hand, *you* are beautiful. You are gorgeous and delectable and edible, and I will spend the rest of my life tasting every millimetre of you."

"Oh Gabe." I say on a moan as he works his way along my jaw to my other ear, sucking on that one too. "I will enjoy every second of it, on one condition." I say, moving my head to the side to give him easier access to my throat.

"Hmmm and what's that beautiful?" He murmurs against my skin.

"I get to do the same to you." His lips move down my throat and he rests his chin between my breasts.

"I'm counting on it honey." He says, and then trails kisses over each breast, but never taking my nipples into his mouth and they're begging for it. I'm begging for it. Arching my back and pushing them up into his face. Ignoring them, he moves on, pressing kisses over my ribs, down to my stomach. He doesn't touch my pussy and for that I'm almost grateful, he already worked her over pretty well not so long ago. Then he kisses down my leg, to my ankle, then he swaps to the other ankle and makes his way back up my leg, until he's back between my thighs, looking up at me over my trimmed pubic hair, with a smile.

"That must make it my turn then." I say, even though his kisses have made my body feel like jelly. He makes his way back up my body, kissing me when he's within reach of my mouth. I push on the front of his shoulder, pushing him off me but sideways, hoping he gets the hint that I want him on his back. Thankfully, he does, and he lies back with a huge grin on his face. "Hands behind your head, you don't get to touch."

"What?" He says, his eyebrows raised in disbelief. "No honey, I want to touch you."

"You can, when I say so, just not right now." I tell him. "Hands. Behind. Your. Head. Or I'll tie them up."

"Fuck." He growls out, but he raises his hands and places them behind his head, just before he lies back. He looks like he's just laying back and relaxing, but I can see the tension making his muscles tight already and I love it.

"Good. Now, don't move." I demand and while he quirks an eyebrow, he doesn't move a muscle.

He looks so damned handsome and sexy laid out for me like this and I take a minute to drink him in. His cock twitches as my gaze lands on it and I smile, remembering my mouth wrapped around it, sucking and licking. I can see the precum glistening on the tip and I'm glad to know, I'm not the only one aroused beyond belief right now.

I straddle his legs, and run my hands up and down his thighs, never touching his groin but enjoying watching him twitch every time I get close. Leaning over so that my breasts land on either side of his cock, I continue rubbing my hands up and down and over his abs and chest. As I move my arms up and down his body, it makes my breasts rub up and down his cock, every now and then, squeezing my breasts to tighten around him, making him groan, but he doesn't move his hands from behind his head.

I move my body up his, and straddle his cock, rubbing my pussy along it from base to tip. "You feel so good." I tell him.

"I'll feel even better inside your pussy." He grounds out between clenched teeth. "I'm not going to last very long if you keep doing that, beautiful."

"Really? But you just came, shouldn't it take you some time to recover?" I smile sweetly at him.

"Yeah, it *should* but you get me so worked up that I could go again right the fuck now." He hisses. I can see the sweat building on his forehead from concentrating on not doing exactly what his body wants him to. Relax and release the tension. I decide to relieve us both from our misery and shift my hips slightly, causing the tip of his cock to rest between the lips of my pussy. "Fuck. You're so warm and so ready for me, let me in please Lexi."

I can't resist his pleading words or the look on his face, so I slide my pussy slowly down the length of his hard cock. When I'm fully seated, I take in a shuddering breath. "Damn you feel so fucking good Gabe." I stretch up and kiss him like it's the last thing I'll ever do on this earth.

When we break apart, gasping for breath, Gabe asks, "Can I touch you now please, honey?"

"Absolutely." I answer him, smiling.

"You were just waiting for me to ask for permission, weren't you?" He smirks.

I don't answer him, instead I sit up, resting my hands on his pecs and start moving my hips, rubbing my clit and my pussy in all the right places. Gabe's hands rise up and start massaging my breasts and I moan because together, everything feels amazing. Beyond amazing and I'm lost to the sensations once again.

My hips move faster, and Gabe's hands move down to my hips, holding me where he needs me, his hips bouncing off the bed to meet mine. I can't hold back any longer. "Gabe." Is all I manage to say before I fall into oblivion and collapse onto his chest. I feel his roar of release rumbling in his chest, more than actually hear it because I think I blew out my eardrums just now.

Gabe wraps his arms around me and gently kisses the top of my head. I feel cherished and loved in this moment and I lie there until I feel both of our breathing come back to normal, then I climb off his body and fling myself onto my bed. I sigh in contentment.

I get up and go to the bathroom to clean up and that's when I realise we didn't use a condom. Holy fuck, I've never forgotten to use one before and I never, ever thought I would.

I walk back into the bedroom to see Gabe sitting on the edge of the bed, his head in his hands. Looks like he's realised what we did, or didn't do actually, as well. He looks up at me as I approach the bed, his eyes telling me everything I need to know before he even speaks, "Fuck Lexi, I'm so sorry. I got so carried away I forgot to put on a condom. Please forgive me honey?" *He's* begging *me* for forgiveness?

"There's nothing to forgive Gabe, it takes two to tango baby, and we're *both* responsible for protection, but just so you know, that's the first time I've ever had sex without one and I'm clean."

"Me too, for both." He pulls my body into his, burying his head in my stomach and holding me tightly. I run my hands through his hair and then down to his shoulders, where I try to massage the tension away.

"I'm on the pill, so we should be OK." I say, my voice shakier than I expected.

"What if we're not?" Gabe asks.

"Then we deal with it, one way or another." I tell him. I feel him nod against my stomach. "Nothing we can do about it tonight though and I can't say I regret what we just did for a second. I love you Gabe."

"I love you too, Lexi." He says, falling back onto the bed and taking me with him. He somehow manages to move us around so that we're lying on the pillows at the head of the bed and pulls the covers up over us. There's a noise outside and Gabe says, "Please tell me that's not your sister at the door?" Making me laugh.

"No, that's the neighbours in the yard." I roll over, pushing my butt back into his groin and snuggling into his warm embrace. "That being said, remind me to get the key off her tomorrow would you?"

He chuckles behind me. "You got it, now get some sleep, it's been a long day."

"It sure was an interesting one, wasn't it?" I ask him. He murmurs something that sounds like 'uhuh', into my hair and pulls me in tighter. I move away from him to turn off the light, but he growls and tightens his grip. "I need to turn off the light Gabe, I promise I won't go far."

"OK." He mumbles and loosens his grip on me just enough that I can turn off the light, but as soon as I lie back down, I'm drawn back into his body. I feel safe. Protected in his arms and it's just what I needed tonight after Stephen and his stupidity.

I still can't believe I didn't put two and two together and realise the connection between Stevie and Stephen, but it's done now and hopefully, his dad won't bail him out so quickly this time.

I don't want Stephen and his rotten behaviour to be the last thing I think about before I go to sleep, so I snuggle in closer to Gabe. I turn my head enough so that I can *just* reach his lips and kiss him. "I love you Gabriel Romanetti, more than you know."

"I love you too, Alexis Stratton. More than you will ever know." I gasp in shock, I thought he was already asleep and even though I would have told him I loved him at any time, I'm still surprised he answered me. "Now, get some sleep. We've got some more work to do in the morning to get repairs made."

"Goodnight Gabe."

"Goodnight Lexi."

I feel his body relax behind me, and the fact that he's lightly snoring, is the giveaway that he's actually asleep this time and I can't help smiling to myself. I'm happier than I have been in years, even with the stupid events of earlier tonight.

This man that I love, loves me back. Everything else is just icing on the cake.

Chapter Thirty

GABE

I know I should be more worried about the fact that we didn't use a condom and perhaps the worry should stop me from sleeping, but it doesn't. Lexi's right, whatever happens we'll deal with it, together. I would love to see her round with my baby, I just hadn't planned on that happening just yet. What I do know, is that I plan on building a life with Lexi, so kids now or later, it makes no difference to me, because I'm not going anywhere.

Waking up this morning with Lexi in my arms is the best feeling. I don't know if we slept like this all night, I doubt it because we went to sleep spooning. This morning I'm lying on my back, one hand behind my head and the other wrapped around Lexi's waist, and Lexi is snuggled into my side, her head on my chest, an arm slung over my waist and a leg thrown over mine.

It's cosy. It's comfortable and I don't want to move but we have a lot to get done today thanks to her idiot ex and Kyle.

I'm lying here, taking her in. She's so peaceful and after the night she had I want to let her keep sleeping, but there's an almighty crash from the front of the house like the front door has just been busted in by the police conducting a damn raid. Before I can react more than sitting up in the bed, which in effect wakes Lexi up and makes her sit upright as well, there's a voice screaming in the other room and getting closer to the bedroom.

"ALEXIS JOY STRATTON! WHAT THE HELL? WHY THE FUCK DIDN'T YOU CALL ME LAST NIGHT AND TELL ME WHAT THAT DOUCHECANOE HAD DONE? WAKE UP BITCH AND EXPLAIN YOURSELF TO ME!" Then in a blur of dark hair and black clothes, Lacey is standing next to the bed with her hands on her hips and her eyes as round as saucers.

"Geezus Lacey, what the fuck?!" Lexi says, still half asleep.

"Cover up your boobs Lexi, we're best friends but we're not *that* close!" Lacey says, but she doesn't cover her eyes, mainly because she's actually staring at *my* chest not Lexi's. "I can see why you were still curled up in here, with your man. That's where I'd choose to be too. Instead I took the morning off work to come and make sure you're OK." She stands there ogling me while Lexi pulls the sheet up over her chest.

"Good morning Lacey. Would you mind giving us a few minutes to put some clothes on, please?" I ask, trying to catch her eye but not succeeding. Instead I reach down and make sure the family jewels are covered so she doesn't get an eye full of those too! "Lacey." I say, snapping my fingers. "My eyes are up here." Her head flicks up and at least she has the decency to blush as her eyes connect to mine.

"I'm not going to apologise for looking." She says, shrugging her shoulders. "You're a fine specimen of a male Gabriel, but I would never, ever touch. I wouldn't do that to Lexi. Ever."

"Nice to know and just so we're on the same page, I'm not looking, and I wouldn't touch either. I love Lexi, she's the only one for me." I feel like I need to explain myself, just because she did, but I don't hesitate when I tell her to leave the room again. "Now, can you wait out in the kitchen while we get dressed please? A cup of coffee would be very much appreciated too." I say, smiling at her.

"Right. You've got it." She turns on her heels and walks back out the door, hopefully to make coffee. I'm more worried about Lexi, she hasn't moved.

"I really have to get my house keys off people, this is getting fucking ridiculous!" She says without looking at me and shaking her head. When her shoulders start shaking, I think she's crying, so I moved to take her into my arms but when I reach her, I realise she's actually laughing. "I have to laugh, after everything that's happened in the last 24 hours, I *have* to laugh and get my keys back."

I pull her back to my front and wrap my arms around her shaking body. "At least you have people who love you and care about you. You gave them the keys for a reason." I chuckle in her ear. "Come on beautiful, let's put on some clothes and go out to see Lacey, before she comes back in here to talk to you."

"Ohh gawd, she ogled you, didn't she?" I nod my head, not really comfortable admitting it out loud. Lexi puts her head in her hands and laughs some more. "I need new friends. I'm sorry Gabe."

"Hey." I say, pulling her hands gently from her face and crouching down in front of her. I found my pants on her side of the bed and pulled them on, but they're not done up yet. "It's OK. She didn't see anything she wouldn't see at the beach, the rest is for your eyes only. I promise you that." I say, laughing because really, what else is there to do? "Come on. Put on some clothes before she comes looking for you again." I pull her up and put her on her feet. I know what I'd rather being doing with her this morning, but I understand that Lacey was worried about her and needs to see her friend.

I pull on my t-shirt and do up my jeans. "I'm going out there, I'll see you out there honey." She nods and moves to find some clothes to put on, still shaking her head in disbelief.

I walk into the kitchen to find Lacey leaning against the bench, one ankle crossed over the other, the coffee machine making noises indicating it's brewing up some morning goodness.

"Good morning Gabriel." She says with a smirk.

"Good morning Lacey." I return, reaching up to the cupboard for mugs.

"Did that arse face really do this?" She asks, her voice low so that Lexi can't hear her from the other room.

"He did." I nod my head because if I say much more, I'm going to get angry and I don't want Lexi to see my anger, she needs support.

"And the cops got him?" I nod again. "And that idiot friend of his?" I close my eyes, thinking about Kyle being a part of this really hurts. I nod my head to answer her, again. "And they're *both* being charged?" She asks, raising an eyebrow in question at me. I guess she knows about Kyle and Brent then.

"As far as I know, yes, they're both being charged. With what, I'm not quite sure of yet, we haven't spoken to the police this morning. We just woke up when someone barged in the front door and scared the crap out of us both."

"You know, I don't know if I can trust my best friend in your care dude. I mean it's not like you moved quickly to defend her from an intruder." Is she fucking serious right now?

"Are you serious?" I ask her, in amazement. "Did you want me to come running out here with my tackle swinging and use that as my only weapon?"

"Well, it would have been a sight and you've painted it pretty well, but no, I guess that wouldn't have worked out too well for anyone, especially our girl if you lost your *tackle*." She says, then starts laughing hysterically, to the point where she's bent over trying to catch her breath. I can't help laughing along with her.

Lexi chooses that moment to walk into the kitchen. "What's so funny?" She asks, innocently when Lacey takes in a deep breath. Lacey looks at me and then laughs hysterically again. I shake my head at the woman, wondering how the hell she gets anything done.

"Lacey and I were just discussing how I *should* have defended you when she came busting in the house just now." I tell her, trying to keep the discussion clean and quiet, but no such luck when Lacey's involved.

"He didn't want to, shall we say, put his manhood in danger by coming out naked to defend you." She says with a straight face and shaking her head. "He thought that having his tackle swinging around might not be ideal."

"Geezus Lacey!" Lexi shakes her head as she buries her face in her hands. "You didn't say that to him, did you?" She mumbles into her hands.

"No, I didn't, he did." Lacey answers and points her finger at me.

Lexi looks through her fingers at me and says, "You didn't, did you?"

"I just asked if that was how she wanted me to fight off an intruder this morning and if she thought that was the best use of my *tackle*." I tell her, trying not to laugh myself.

Barefoot and Dumped!

"Of all the things to worry about this morning, you two are talking about my boyfriend's dick, seriously?" She shakes her head some more, but all I heard was her call me her boyfriend and I can feel the grin spreading across my face. "What's that grin for? I'm seriously wondering about you right now. Her I can understand," She jabs her thumb in Lacey's direction, "But *you*? You I expected more from honestly."

"You called me your boyfriend." I say, still grinning like a fool and stalking over to take her into my arms.

"Isn't that what you are, Gabe?" She asks me, and I don't like the uncertainty in her voice.

"Oh honey, I plan on being much more than that, but for now, yes, I'm your boyfriend." I say before dropping my lips to hers and making her believe me.

"Alright kids, you can have that discussion later. Preferably when I'm not around and I don't have to watch your displays of arousal right in front of me." Lacey tells us.

"I love you Lexi, and I am definitely your boyfriend." I say quietly against her lips just before I take a reluctant step away from her. If I don't, Lacey may get the show she missed out on earlier, but I do take her hand in mine and don't let go.

"Lexi." Lacey snaps her fingers in front of her friends face, trying to get her attention. My confession and my kiss have left her a little dazed. "Alexis Joy Stratton!"

"Yes Lacey May Edwards, what can I do for you?" Lexi answers Lacey with a sigh.

"You can tell me what the hell happened here last night and *why* I had to hear it from your sister, quite by accident I might add, and not you. Why didn't you call me yourself? I mean I understand that you've got this hunk of a man to protect you now, but I'm still your best friend and I want to know when shit happens." The hurt in her voice kills me.

"I'm sorry Lacey." Lexi drops my hand and throws her arms around her best friend. "I honestly didn't mean to upset you. It's just that Gabe and I spent the day together and I knew he was at Brent's to help him to get his houseguest to move out, so I called him." She huffs out a kind of laugh crossed with a sigh. "You'll never guess who Brent's houseguest is."

"Who?" Lacey asks, looking completely confused.

"Stephen." Lexi says the amazement still in her voice and on her face.

"Stephen? You mean your ex, Stephen? The douchebag?" Lacey asks, looking just as shocked as we all were last night when we worked it all out.

"Yeah. The douchebag's best friend Kyle?" She asks Lacey, who nods for her to continue. "Yeah he's Brent's little brother."

"No fucking way? How the hell did we not figure this out earlier? I mean, last night wasn't the first either of us met or spoke to Brent. How did we miss this?"

"Well, I didn't see Brent the night that Gabe and I met again, he was already at the bar with you and *you* hadn't met him when I was with Stephen because I rarely hung out there and you refused to go with me if I did. I have to be honest, I barely remembered Brent myself, I didn't look around when I was there. It wasn't until he said, 'you're Stevie's ex' that I realised who he was." Lexi shakes her head, still not believing any of us, especially her, didn't put it all together sooner.

"Unbelievable!" Lacey says, shaking her head too. "And he did this? They did this? Whatever this is because I only heard second hand what happened here last night from Cat."

"Well, it started with flickering lights and Cat blaming me for messing around." Lexi says and then launches into the whole sordid story of what dumb and dumber did last night.

I don't want to hear it again, so I quietly turn on some music on my phone and start to make us all some breakfast. I move around the kitchen pulling together some bacon, eggs and a few slices of toast, answering when Lexi asks me something, but mostly keeping myself busy cooking and cleaning up behind myself.

As Lexi finishes up with all the details I dish up three plates of food.

"Wow Lexi, you caught a good man here. He cooks, cleans up behind himself and his tool seems to be in fine working order."

Barefoot and Dumped!

"Shut up Lacey, leave the man be. Thank him for breakfast and enjoy your food." Lexi scowls at her friend but has a smile on her face. I'm not sure how the hell she pulls that off, but she does, and she looks adorable doing it.

"Thank you for making breakfast Gabe." Lacey says, leaning over to kiss my cheek.

"You're welcome Lacey. I'd say anytime but I don't actually mean it. Enjoy." I tell her with a wink.

"Thanks for looking out for my girl as well. I'm glad she had you to rely on." Lacey says quietly.

"You're welcome, but you never have to thank me for that, I'm always going to be here for Lexi whenever she needs me." I get up, kiss Lacey on the cheek, returning the favour from earlier. I clear up the dishes and give Lexi a kiss. "I'm going to go have a shower and let you girls talk amongst yourselves for a little while. Let me know if you need anything."

"You don't have to leave us alone Gabe." Lacey starts to say but I cut her off.

"I know I don't *need* to Lacey, but I want to. You girls can talk about whatever you need to without my ears around. I have a sister remember, I know girls like to talk things out with their friends." I give Lexi another, slightly longer kiss. "Maybe you can tell her all about my tackle." I wink at Lexi and she tries to smack me on the arse, but I jump out of the way and laugh my way to the bathroom.

I'm feeling pretty light this morning. I woke up with the love of my life in my arms, she nor Cat were hurt last night and it's nice to know that my girl has a friend that cares so much about her that she comes into the house demanding to know if she's OK. I just wish Brent and Kyle weren't caught up in this whole mess.

I don't know what I'm going to do about that situation. Could there ever be an excuse that Kyle can give me that will make me forgive what he let that idiot do last night? I'm not sure there is, but I don't want to lose Brent's friendship over this either.

I stand there under the steam after washing myself just thinking when I feel a cool breeze across the back of my shoulders and realise the door was opened and closed.

"Hey honey, I'll be out of your way in a minute, I just want to soak my muscles." I tell her.

"How did you know it was me?" Lexi asks.

"Well, the only other one in the house when I came in here was Lacey and I'm going to assume that you wouldn't have given her permission to come in here and sample the goods." I haven't turned around, I've got my head resting against the wall, with the steamy water beating down on my shoulders.

"You really should lock that door you know. All kinds of lunatics come walking in that door at all kinds of weird times." She jokes.

"But, if I'd locked it, then you wouldn't be standing in here now would you?" I ask as she runs her hands over my shoulders and down my back, massaging my muscles as she goes.

"That's true. I wouldn't have the perfect view of your delectable derrière if you'd locked the door." She says seriously, but I can hear laughter in her voice.

"Delectable hey?" I ask, as I turn around, grab her by the waist and pull her naked, wet body in tightly against mine. Then I slam my mouth down onto hers and kiss her until neither of us have any breath left in us and I feel her knees buckle. Before she can catch her bearings, I slap her on her derrière and walk out of the shower. "Enjoy your shower honey." I say, while taking a towel off the rail and drying myself with it, then I wrap it around my waist. The truth is, you never know who's going to be in the house and I don't want another half-naked encounter this morning. Unless it's with Lexi and we're both completely naked.

"What? No! You're supposed to stay in here with me." Lexi says as I open the door to leave.

"No honey, you're supposed to shower so we can both call into work and let them know we're not coming in. Then we need to start getting these repairs done, and if we shower together, the only thing getting done is each other. You know it and I know it, so I'm going to get dressed and you can get clean." I grabbed the clothes off the floor that I took off to get in the shower and leave her to it.

I left my phone on her dresser and once I get dressed I check it for messages. There's a couple from Cat, one from Joshua and at least twenty or more from Brent. I don't know what to say to him, so I check Cat's and then Joshua's.

Cat: *I hope you looked after my sister last night*

Cat: *Shit! I didn't mean like that! Although I'm sure you did*

Cat: *forgive me? we had a traumatic night*

I can't help laughing at Cat's messages. She says something dirty but usually it's quite innocent and she starts trying to correct herself and then it turns into something hysterical. I have to stop laughing so I can send her a message back.

Gabe: *Yes Catherine, I looked after you sister last night. In every way. I* put a winky face at the end just for the hell of it.

Still chuckling I open Joshua's message.

Joshua: *Gabe, thanks again for last night. We'll be over shortly to help sort out the repairs.*

I look at the time the message was sent and realise that they could be here any minute. I send back a message that tells him I'll see him soon, then I take a deep breath. I know I have to read Brent's texts and deal with them, but I don't know if I actually want to. I click on Brent's name and about a dozen unread messages are sitting there. I start at the one timestamped last night and read them all.

All of them are similar in content. He's sorry that it all happened. If he'd known what they had planned he would have stopped it from happening. Kyle's sorry that he had anything to do with it, but he swears he was trying to get the douchebag to stop and just leave. Nothing new from what he already said last night, but it's the last one he sent, while we were having breakfast with Lacey that kills me.

Brent: *Gabe, please answer me. Kyle would like to talk to Lexi, if you will let him. He wants to apologise to her personally and you. He knows what he did was wrong, he wants to try and make it right.*

I rub a hand over my face. I don't know what to think. What to say to him or what to believe.

"What's the matter babe? What are you worrying about? Is your dad OK? Is Maria OK? Is your sister OK?" All of Lexi's questions come out in a rush. She was terrorised last night and she's worried about my family and their wellbeing. She hasn't even met Susanna yet.

"Everyone is fine honey." I answer her once she stops talking and I smile at her.

"You're smiling but it's not a real one. So what's going on? Gabe we promised, no secrets." She looks at my phone in my hand. I don't know if she can see the messages or who their from, but she's right, I'm not hiding them from her.

"Your sister and Joshua will be here shortly to help with the repairs." I tell her.

"That's nice of them but it's hardly necessary, we just need to call the glazier and wait for him to come and repair the windows."

"True, but they're already on their way and I would bet they'll be here any minute because Joshua sent the message before I got in the shower." I close my eyes and take a breath, before I look at her again and say, "I've also got a few messages from Brent."

"Oh." She says and that's about the response I was expecting. "What did he say?"

"He wants to meet up today. Kyle wants to talk to you. Apparently he feels really bad about what happened here last night, and he wants to explain. To talk to you or something." I say, shrugging my shoulders. As much as I love Kyle and think of him like a younger brother, I'm still mad about what happened here last night and I'm not sure I'm ready to talk to him.

"He said he wanted to talk to me?" Lexi asks.

"Yes he did but I want you to know that you don't have to see him at all, ever if you don't want to." I pull her in, to stand between my knees, so I can pull her in close to me.

"I want to see him." I go to speak but she places her finger on my lips. "I understand you don't want me to or will say I don't have to, but I know all that. Will you be right beside me when I talk to him?"

"Absolutely." I don't hesitate answering.

"Alright then, I'll talk to him, but not here. I don't want him here any time soon. Maybe we can go to their house? I don't have any attachment to it, and I won't be going back any time soon."

"Fair enough. I'll text him back to let him know we'll be over sometime today." That's what I'm doing when Cat and Joshua walk in the door.

When we explain what's going on, Cat loses it.

"I don't understand why you're taking her there Gabe. Why did you even ask her if she wants to go?"

"I didn't. I told her what was in the messages, Lexi is the one who said she wanted to talk to him, but he isn't welcome here, so we're going there." I say, defending myself.

"Don't blame Gabe, Cat. He's only doing what I asked him to, on so many different levels. I need to do this, I want some answers." Lexi explains to her sister.

"The explanation is simple. An absolute arsehole, led the stupid fool around by the nose and then tried to scare the shit out of both of us last night." I'm not going to argue with her assessment, it's pretty accurate but I'm also not telling Lexi she can't go. I'll go with her this way, if I said no I wouldn't take her, I have a feeling she'd go anyway.

"That's true Cat, but I just want to talk to the kid. OK? Not Stephen, I couldn't care less why he did it or how he's feeling. I just want to see Kyle for a few minutes."

Before Cat can protest any further, Joshua speaks up. "Why don't you guys go now and get it over and done with? We can stay here and wait for the new glass for the windows."

"Thank you Joshua, that would be great." Lexi says and kisses him on the cheek. "If that's OK with you Gabe? To go now I mean."

"Fine by me. The sooner we get it over with the better."

"See, Gabe doesn't want you to go either." Cat grumbles at her sister.

"No, he doesn't but he also understands that this is something I need to do and he's supporting me." Lexi walks over to her sister, pulls her in for a full blown bear hug and leaves a big sloppy kiss on her cheek.

"Ewwww that's gross Lexi!" Cat says, wiping the slobber off her cheek, while Lexi laughs at her.

"I'll see you when we get back, OK?" Without giving Cat another chance to voice her disapproval, Lexi takes my hand, grabs her handbag and puts her phone in her pocket, all while dragging me outside to my truck. I can hear Cat and Joshua in the distant background.

"I don't think she should go see him, I have a bad feeling about this." Cat says.

"Nothing bad is going to happen to her Cat. Gabe's with her and he won't let anything bad go down. Trust me on this."

"Yeah, I know you're right, but it still worries me." Cat says.

I can't help but smile at Joshua's comment and Cat's reply. I'm happy to know that they both think that about me in such a short time. It warms my heart.

Lexi doesn't wait for me to open the door and help her into the truck, she's already sitting in her seat before I can think about it. So, I slide in behind the wheel, crank over the engine and without a word, we're heading on over to Brent's house.

The drive is quiet. I imagine Lexi's thinking about the questions she wants to ask to get the answers she needs. I'm thinking about trying to not land myself in jail for beating the shit out of the kid for what they did.

I won't do it because I don't want to think about leaving Lexi alone, but Kyle better watch what he says today, otherwise he could be in for a world of pain.

Chapter Thirty-one

<u>LEXI</u>

I don't know what to expect when we walk into Brent's house. I never felt comfortable there but that had more to do with Stephen never really trying to make me feel welcome, I realise that now.

Gabe knocks on the door and when Brent opens it, the look of surprise on his face tells me a couple of things. One, Gabe didn't tell him we were on our way, so they didn't get any warning and two, Gabe doesn't usually knock, because Brent has a go at him.

"Why are you knocking on the door man? You never have to knock, you know that."

"I didn't know if we would be welcome, so I thought I would be polite." Gabe says stiffly and I appreciate the fact that he added me into that thought. Not that *he* wouldn't be welcomed, but that we came as a couple.

Brent has the decency to cough and look uncomfortable. "Yeah, well, you're always welcome and so are you Lexi." He says, looking at me with hope in his eyes.

"Thank you Brent, but let's see how this goes first shall we?" He nods his head and steps back from the door to wave us inside.

It feels really strange to be here and not be with Stephen. It's like I've stepped into another world that looks and feels familiar but is strange all at the same time.

"Hi Lexi. Hi Gabe." I look towards the voice to find Kyle standing next to the couch looking nervous as all hell. I don't know if he's nervous to talk to me or Gabe. I think he's more scared of Gabe than he is worried about me.

"Kyle." Gabe says, his voice clipped and filled with anger.

"Hi Kyle, how are you doing?" I ask him, and I feel Gabe's body stiffen next to me. I know he's wondering why I'm talking to Kyle like that, but I'm honestly concerned about him.

"I'm OK." He answers me with a small smile, until Gabe growls beside me.

"Hi Gabe, nice to see you again." A woman who I assume is Brent's girlfriend says as she walks into the room.

"Hi Sophie, I'd like to say it's nice to see you, but I wouldn't want to lie to you." Gabe grumbles until I elbow him in the side. "Sorry honey. Sophie, this is my girlfriend, Lexi. Honey, this is Sophie, Brent's girlfriend."

"It's nice to meet you Lexi." She says, extending her hand for me to shake. "I just wish it could have been under better circumstances. "

"Don't we all." Brent mutters loudly.

"I just want to tell you, Lexi, how sorry I am about everything that happened last night. I had no idea what he had planned, and I wish that I never went along with him." Kyle pipes up.

"Then why *did* you go along with him, Kyle? You know better than that. You *know* he's a moron." Gabe says, and I can feel his rage being barely held in. His body is almost vibrating beside me.

"I went to make sure he didn't do anything stupid. I didn't want him to hurt Lexi, I was pretty sure he wouldn't get physical, because when it comes down to it, he's a pathetic loser who's more talk than action, but I didn't want to chance it. I like Lexi, I always have, and I could never understand what you saw in him." He says to me almost shyly. "Then I saw the two of you together the other day and I knew I had to do something. I knew that Brent was getting ready to kick him out of the house and I figured I could use that to my advantage to get him out of my life as well."

"When did you see us together Kyle?" I ask him. It has nothing to do with anything, I'm just curious.

"At the shopping centre."

"You were with him then, weren't you?"

"Yes."

"He saw Gabe and I together, that's when he decided he wanted revenge, isn't it?" Kyle doesn't speak for a few seconds.

"Tell her the truth Kyle, please." Brent begs his brother.

"Yes. He said that if he couldn't have you he would make it so that Gabe sure wouldn't want you."

"Why didn't you tell one of us Kyle? For fucks sake dude, we could have done something. We could have helped you out." Brent tells him.

"I heard you talking to Gabe on the phone and I knew they were going to be out all day and I thought if I could get Stevie to go there when no-one was there, there wouldn't be any trouble. I swear, I didn't know he planned on scaring you or breaking the windows. I tried to talk him out of it, but he just wouldn't stop." Kyle says.

"Why didn't you call one of us when you were there last night Kyle? Two women, two fucking people, alone in a house where the lights go out and the windows start getting broken. What did you think was going to happen?" Gabe asks, he's barely holding in his rage. "He did all of that because Lexi moved on?"

"Yes. He thought it was too soon, even though he didn't love her. He never had." Kyle seems to realise what he's said then looks to me and says, "I'm sorry Lexi."

"It's alright Kyle, the non-feelings were quite mutual." I say with a small smile.

"He did this because of me didn't he?" Gabe asks, his anger impossibly rising.

"Gabe, baby, calm down. He's not worth it." I say to him, trying to calm him down.

"I can't believe you're dating *her*, but I guess if you want my hand me downs you can have her." We all turn, surprised by the unexpected voice. Standing in the doorway is Stephen, his gaze moving from Gabe to me. "I always knew you were a whore, but you've stooped low, even for you Stratton."

Before I can say anything to insult him back and tell him he has a tiny dick that never satisfied me, he's on the ground, holding his face in his hands.

"You stay away from Lexi, do you hear me? In fact, you stay away from all of us, you piece of shit. If I see you anywhere near Lexi, I will make your life a painful living hell." Gabe says to Stephen, standing above him.

"Did you hear that Kyle? Gabe threatened me, you can be my witness." The little weasel screeches, as blood starts to drip from his nose.

"No, I can't moron. I can't believe it's taken me this long to see it, but you were never my friend. You're just a boy who thinks he's tough. Don't contact me again, lose my number and forget I ever existed."

"What?! You're going to lose a decade of friendship over a chick? One that you'll never fuck even though she likes to give it out freely?" The jerk squeaks as Gabe makes a move towards him again, until I put my hand on his arm to stop him.

"Don't bother Gabe, he's not worth it." I say. I don't want him to get into trouble over this idiot.

"You can come pick up your stuff tomorrow, I'll have it all packed up by then." Brent tells him.

"What? Where the fuck am I supposed to go tonight? You're kicking me out of my house?" I can't believe I ever thought I loved this man, he's disgusting. His sense of entitlement is unbelievable.

"I don't care Stevie, and it's *not* your house. It's *my house*, I just let you live here for a while and now you've been evicted. Hand over the keys, now."

"I thought we were brothers man. I thought we were friends and now you're all dumping me over a stupid chick?"

Brent takes a step towards Stephen, and he flinches shrinking back. "You're not my brother, you never were. I let you stay in my house so that I could keep an eye on what you were getting my brother involved in. You are nothing to me."

"Come on Brent, he's not worth it." Sophie says quietly, pulling him away before he does something stupid.

"Two o'clock tomorrow, come get your stuff. If you're not here at exactly 2pm, I'm putting it all out the front with a sign that says, 'free to good home,' and it will be first in, first served." Brent warns him.

"You can't do that! That's my stuff, it's illegal." Stephen screams at Brent.

"Push me little man. I'll tell anyone who asks what you did and that you owe me rent, then we'll talk about what's illegal." Brent says to him.

"My dad will come after you, he'll come after *all* of you, mark my words losers." He screams at us.

"Keys, now." Brent says, holding out his hand. Stephen takes them off his key chain and hands them over in a huff. "Your dad won't do anything to us *Stevie*. How do I know that, you might be wondering. I know because he's already told me that he's tired of bailing you out and this time, he's letting you live with the consequences. Now get out, you're not welcome here."

Gabe and Brent stand on either side of him and march him to the door, open it and toss him out onto the street.

"This isn't the last you'll hear from me." Stephen screams at them.

"Is that a threat Stevie, because I think you're in enough trouble without adding that to your charges." Brent sneers.

"You can't prove a fucking thing you idiot."

"Actually, we can." Sophie tells him and holds up her phone. "I've recorded the whole thing, so feel free to claim whatever you like." She smiles sweetly at him and then the guys slam the door in his face.

"With any luck, that's the last we see of Stephen Phoenix in a long time, if not forever." Gabe says, as I watch his body relax right in front of me.

"Thank you." I say as I launch myself at Gabe, wrapping my arms around his waist and resting my cheek on his chest. "You guys too, thank you, Brent, Sophie and Kyle."

"What are you thanking us for honey?" Gabe asks me, his lips resting at my temple.

"For having my back." I feel him take a deep breath, and I know what he's about to say. "Stop Gabe. Whether you want to believe it or not, Kyle actually *did* have my back. He was trying to do what he thought was for the best and I can thank him for that."

"Thank you for being so kind and forgiving Lexi. I know what we did was wrong, even though I didn't physically smash your windows or turn off your power, I knew it was wrong. These guys are right." He says looking between his brother and Gabe. "I should have told one of them, if not both of them, because I was completely out of my depth. I just." He stops for a second and closes his eye, when he reopens them, he says, "I just wanted to prove that I wasn't the little kid they think I still am. Instead, I proved how much of a moron I am." He drops his head, not looking anyone in the eye.

I pull out of Gabe's embrace and walk over to Kyle, taking him into my arms. "You're not stupid, or an idiot or anything else you want to call yourself. If you're those things then so am I. I'm the one who dated him." I smile and pull back from our embrace to look him in the eyes. "I agree with you, you know? I have no idea what I saw in that guy, or what took me so long to realise it, but I had decided a while ago that I needed out of the relationship. I was just waiting for my parent's party to be over so that I could walk away cleanly. I was just too busy with other things to bother doing it beforehand."

"He knew that too. That's why he dumped you, barefoot on the beach at your parent's anniversary party. He had to get in first. There was no way he was going to let *you* dump his sorry arse." Kyle shakes his head. "His loss is Gabe's gain and honestly, I think you're perfect for each other. He's a great guy Lexi, you couldn't get any better and you deserve a guy who will treat you right."

"You do realise that you just put both myself and Sophie down with that little speech of yours, right? I mean, I'm *not* a good guy and Sophie can do better?" I'm trying to work out whether Brent is genuinely offended or not when Gabe punches him on the shoulder. "Ouch man! I told you to stop doing that. I don't want Sophie to see you hurt me like that!."

"I didn't hurt you, *man* but I can if you'd like me too." Gabe growls at Brent.

"Take your man beast out of here Lexi before he does some permanent damage to himself trying to, but not succeeding, in being better than me." Brent grumbles.

"You're an idiot with an ego the size of a fucking elephant." Gabe ribs Brent. "How about we *all* go out together for dinner tonight?"

Just like that, the two guys are joking and ribbing each other like only old friends can, with Kyle getting in on the action as well.

"Absolutely." The three of them say together and I can see that Brent is relieved that this shit is all over.

"Thank you Gabe." Kyle says.

"Well, we have to head back to Lexi's, but we'll see you all later tonight, right?" Gabe says, and I feel bad that he hasn't acknowledged Kyle. Brent nods and Gabe then turns to Kyle and says, "You've got a lot to make up for dude, but you're welcome to come to dinner too."

We head back to my place and have lunch with Cat and Joshua.

The windows have been repaired, meaning all the remnants of last night's events are gone.

My parents have been placated after a very anxious phone call with them after lunch. They're glad the guys came over and helped but my Dad was still furious. Surprisingly, it was Gabe who talked him down from finding Stephen and killing him!

Then Cat and Joshua go home, after I ask her for her key. She hands it over with a grin before walking out the door. Finally, Gabe and I are alone for a little while to just relax on the couch before we head out for dinner.

After a few beers, some delicious food and lots of laughter, I feel like we're all back on even ground. It might take Gabe a little while to fully trust Kyle again, but he's definitely back with the two guys he considers brothers. Stephen hasn't been mentioned and that's the way it's going to stay. He's in the past and we don't need to be reminded of him tonight, or any other night.

I've decided to give Cat's old key to Gabe tonight when we're home, alone. Yeah, home. Maybe it's the beers talking, or maybe it's the trauma, I don't know. I'm hoping he can let go of his baggage from his ex and he can move into my house. I don't think I could live in an apartment after being in my house, but I can't help wondering if he can give up the security he has there.

I know that I've been slightly distracted while we've been out with his friends, but I think they're all giving me a break because of everything that's happened. Little do they know I'm actually feeling nervous about asking Gabe to move in with me, but your heart wants, what it wants, and you just *know* when it's right.

We say good night to everyone and we're just about to leave when Kyle comes up and stops us. He looks so lost, and when he asks me if I can ever forgive him, I tell him that I already have. Stephen has this way about him, I'm not sure if the people he sucks in ever really like him, but for some reason they get pulled in by him. What I *do* know is that I am one hundred percent certain Stephen Phoenix is a terrible human being. I don't even remember saying yes to going on a date with him or agreeing to be his girlfriend, and I've been thinking really hard about it for a couple of days too. It just all happened, and I accepted it. Crazy I know, but that's how it was.

I've been lost in my own thoughts and I don't realise that we've pulled up in my driveway until Gabe asks me if I'm OK.

"Hmmmm? Oh yes, I'm fine, just thinking."

"About?" He asks and I can see the concern on his face.

"Can we go inside to talk, please?" I ask him without giving him a chance to answer before I'm out of his truck and at my front door.

We get inside and I put my handbag and everything else, except the key down. The weight of the key, and the expectations that come with it, feel really heavy in my hand.

"Is everything OK Lexi? You're starting to worry me, honey." He says, stepping in front of me and taking me by the shoulders, effectively stopping the pacing that I wasn't aware I was doing.

"Everything is fine. I hope." I continue on fast, not giving him a chance to respond. He looks so confused. "What I'm trying to say is. I got all the

Barefoot and Dumped!

keys back. You know off Cat and Lacey earlier today while they were all here at various points and well, I want you to have one."

"You want me to have to a key to your house? So that I can come and go whenever, even when you're not here?" He asks, and I'm not sure what the tone in his voice means. Is he shocked? Is he happy? Is it too soon and he thinks I'm insane?

"Well, I imagine you'd like a key to the house you're going to be living in, you know, so that you have the freedom to come and go as you please, whether I'm home or not." I say with a hesitant smile.

"Are you asking me to move in with you? To live *here*, with *you*?" That is definitely shock and surprise in his voice now. I did it all wrong, I made the move too soon, but I can't take it back now and if I've made him run a million miles to get away from me, then so be it. It wasn't meant to be after all.

"Yes." I keep my answer simple, but he doesn't say anything else. He's just standing there, in the middle of my living room, looking like a new statue I just bought. "I know it's probably too soon, and I know you love your apartment and the building because of all the security, but I'm sorry. I just don't think I can live in an apartment building indefinitely after living in my own house for so long."

"No." He says his voice a raspy sound.

"No?" I ask confused. I really did screw this whole thing up. He doesn't want to move in together and I read our entire relationship wrong. That's what I get for jumping feet first into this relationship. We've been together weeks, if that and I knew it was too soon, but I thought he was feeling the same way. "Oh OK. No worries, I'll just. I don't know what I'll do actually but maybe you should leave, I want to be alone. It's been a big, a huge weekend and I need some space."

"No." Geezus, now he won't *leave*! What the hell is going on here? "No, I won't leave. I want to stay. I want to stay here, with you and my key to the house. Shit! I meant yes! Yes I'll move in here with you, as soon as you want me to. I mean no, it's not too soon. When you know, you know, right?"

"So yes you'll move in here with me?" I ask because after all that, I need the clarification.

"Yes, I definitely will. We'll help Cat move out and I'll move in honey." He smiles broadly at me.

"What about your rent and your notice?" I ask.

"Don't worry about that, I'll sort it out in the morning. It won't be an issue." He says scooping me up in his arms and spinning around. "I'm moving in with the love of my life and I can't wait."

I laugh uncontrollably as he continues to spin us around until he gets too dizzy and falls down onto the couch, taking me with him. "So you're OK with living here?"

"Absolutely." He says, giving me a lip smacking kiss. "Hell Lexi, I thought you were trying to find a way to break up with me. I mean after the crazy shit that's happened in the last twenty four hours and working out that I knew Stephen as well and how him trying to get his revenge only to screw it all up, again. I really thought you were going to tell me that you couldn't do this anymore, that there's too much insanity. Instead you asked me to move in with you."

"I don't want to live without you Gabe, so I don't think I was going to break up with you." I laugh, kissing all over his handsome face.

"I don't want to live without you either Lexi."

Then he's pushed us both up off the couch and he's leading us towards my bedroom, *our* bedroom. "What are we doing Gabe?"

"We're celebrating Lexi." His smile is so big it almost splits his face in two, and I'm pretty sure the smile on my face matches his. "We're celebrating life and being together." He answers me.

Who am I to argue with the man? So we celebrate. We celebrate all night and take another day off work to celebrate for a little bit longer. It's a beautiful celebration everything a girl could want, and more.

I love Gabriel Romanetti with all my heart, and I couldn't be happier.

Epilogue

GABE

Moving out of my apartment and into Lexi's house felt something akin to freedom. It probably seems strange to most people. I'm going from living on my own to living with someone else, that would normally equate to less freedom to some, but I've gone from living in a very secure building to a house without a doorman.

Speaking of doormen, saying goodbye to Sam wasn't the easiest thing I've ever done. Who would have thought I'd have such an emotional attachment to the guy, but I did. He saved me from a situation I didn't even know was happening and for that I'll be forever grateful.

It was even harder to tell Jessie that I was moving out, because while I could tell she was happy for me, I also saw the panic in her eyes. I hope that some of her fears were relieved when I told her that Kyle was taking over my apartment for the time being. He needs to distance himself from Stephen who started harassing him the day after Brent kicked him out of his house. What better way to do that than to be living in a secured apartment building?

Moving into the house and moving Cat out in one weekend was a challenge. It was hectic, but we did it. Catherine and Joshua are now happily living in their home together and enjoying married life.

A couple of months later, one Sunday at Lexi's parent's house for family dinner, I pulled her dad aside and asked him if he would have an issue with me asking his daughter to marry me. The man pulled me into a warm bear hug and welcomed me to the family.

"You don't think it's too soon?" I asked him, curious and I have to admit, a little cautious about the timing myself, but Jonathon didn't hesitate with his answer.

"No son, when you know, you know. Right?" He said to me, and I couldn't help smiling at him. "A lot of people said it was too soon when I asked Julia to marry me, including my own father, but look at us now. Two beautiful daughters, two amazing son in laws and thirty years of marriage later. I wouldn't change it for the world."

"I'm not sure when I'm going to ask Lexi, I just wanted your blessing to ask her." I told him.

"You have it Gabe, for whenever you decide to ask her." Jonathon said with a huge smile and a slap of my shoulder, just as Lexi walked in the room.

"What are you two up to?" She asked.

"Secret men's business young lady, never you mind." He answered her without even blinking.

"Come on Dad, seriously? Secret men's business?" Lexi scoffs and wraps her arms around me while snuggling into my side. "You don't have to tell me but don't pull that one! We were all wondering where you'd gotten too, it's dessert time and it's unlike you to disappear before you've had dessert."

I looked up at Jonathon in panic, because she was absolutely right, I'd mistimed this entire conversation, but once again Jonathon didn't miss a beat.

"I know, but after thirty years of marriage, I'm also very certain your mother would keep some aside for me because she loves me." He winks at his daughter as he walks passed us and heads to the kitchen, where his wife and dessert are. The man is a legend.

"So, what were you and my dad really talking about Gabriel?" Lexi asked me, knowing exactly what saying my name like that does to me, but I refuse to give in.

"Secret men's business." I tell her, pulling her in closer to me so that she can't smack me on the chest or in the stomach as is her habit. "Let's go get dessert." I know the way to my woman's heart, through sweet treats.

Barefoot and Dumped!

"Whatever, don't tell me then, see if I care." She mumbled but allowed me to lead her back into the kitchen where dessert and the rest of her family were.

About a month later, I took Lexi out for the day and that was when I asked her to marry me. It was the most amazing day of my life. Brent asked me beforehand while he was helping me with a few details, if I was nervous and my answer was a definite no. The gods honest truth was, I wasn't nervous at all. Was I one hundred percent sure she would say yes to my proposal, not really, but I knew I wanted her to be my wife and I wanted to be her husband. Forever.

The moment she said yes, with tears of happiness in her eyes, was the best of my life that is, until the day she told me about *her* little surprise.

~~~~~

<u>LEXI</u>

Gabe took me to the beach one night after dinner at the restaurant where we had our first date. That night feels like it was a lifetime ago, not only six months. I had no clue what was coming or how he'd managed to plan a thing, but one minute we were walking along in the light of the sunset, hand in hand and enjoying the quiet. The next, Gabe had stopped walking and while I was enjoying the colours of the night sky, he dropped to one knee and tugged on my hand to get my attention.

I remember turning around to see what he wanted, only to find the man of my dreams on one knee, holding my left hand in his and the other hand holding up a blue velvet box.

"Alexis Joy Stratton, will you make me the happiest man on earth and be my wife?"

I didn't hesitate for a second, but I also couldn't speak. I just kind of squeaked and nodded my head a million times.

"Lexi, honey I need you to answer me." Gabe said in a very strained voice. Did he really think there was a chance that I would say no?

"Yes!" I finally croaked out and all the emotions I had managed to keep under control before I spoke, came tumbling out. Tears streaking my cheeks.
~~~~~

"I hope they're happy tears honey?" He said, as he slid the ring onto my finger.

"Yes! Yes! Yes! And hell yes!" I answered him as I jumped up and flung my arms around his neck.

"And here I was wondering if you'd agree to be my wife or tell me to fuck off because it was too soon." Gabe chuckled into my hair.

"It's not too soon Gabe." I said and then pulled back to look at his face. "It's not too soon is it? If you thought it was too soon, why the hell did you ask me?" Just like that I'm the one panicking.

"I wouldn't have asked if I wasn't ready Lexi, but I thought maybe you'd think it was too soon."

"When you know, you know." Then I kissed him. I kissed my soon to be husband until neither of us could breathe.

"Let's go home and celebrate." Gabe said, and that's exactly what we did. After I called my parent's, my sister and of course, Lacey. Gabe called his dad and sister to share the good news as well.

We celebrated all night and almost all the next morning. We could have had more, but our families came over to celebrate with us and take us out for lunch. Lacey volunteered to come to the house first so that, 'no-one saw anything they didn't want to see', and we were able to look our families in the eyes forever. That's my best friend, always taking one for the team. Fortunately, or unfortunately depending on your view I suppose, she didn't interrupt anything except us relaxing on the couch. It's our secret that we were getting hot and heavy before she knocked on the door and put paid to that session.

While we were out to lunch, the main question was when were we going to set the date. I hadn't had a chance to think that far ahead and the only thing we'd agreed on at that point was that we didn't want to wait very long at all.

So, a few months later Vincent paid for both of our families and close friends to go to Hawaii for our wedding. My parents tried to protest but Vincent wouldn't hear it. So, instead they insisted on paying for all of my wedding needs and my sisters.

Barefoot and Dumped!

My mum came shopping with me to find the perfect dress and I knew when I found the right one. I didn't want anything too long or flowing because we were going to be on the beach. Instead I found this gorgeous knee length, lace over satin dress, that flared out at my hips to a semi full skirt. I fell in love the minute I put it on.

Walking out to show my mum, Cat and Lacey, it just felt perfect. When my mum cried and couldn't speak. The two girls couldn't say anything except, 'oh my god that's perfect!' I knew I'd found the dress for me. I chose not to wear shoes, but I found these gorgeous crystals that hook around your toe, up your foot and around your ankle to look like sandals but they're really just very pretty jewellery for your feet. I know Gabe will be barefoot, so I'm not worried at all. We got to have a week in Hawaii for our honeymoon once everyone else went home. It was bliss.

It was the best day of my life, until about two months later.

Staring out the kitchen window in our new home that we bought just after we got home from Hawaii, I'm trying to decide how to give Gabe my news. I know he's going to be happy, but I want to tell him the right way. I hear him walk into the kitchen behind me and so, I tell him exactly how I'm feeling.

"You know what babe? I've never been happier about being left while barefoot on the sand at my parent's anniversary party than I am right now." I say smiling broadly.

"When are you going to be barefoot in a whole new way for *me*, Mrs Romanetti?" Gabe asks as he wraps his arms around me from behind and I snuggle into his embrace.

"Sooner than you think, Mr Romanetti." I say with a smirk. Two can play this game.

He grabs my shoulders, spins me around and holds me at a distance so that he can look in my eyes, to see the expression on my face.

"Are you serious?" He asks, eyes darting across my face.

"Yes." I answer him and I can't hide my smile any longer as it spreads across my face.

"When? How?" He asks all at once.

"Well if you need me to explain how then perhaps I'm wrong." I say, somehow with a straight face. "As for when, I'm thinking about eight weeks ago in -" I don't get to finish because his lips crash onto mine in a kiss that takes my breath away.

Gabe breaks the kiss and rests his forehead on mine. "Really? While we were in Hawaii?"

I shrug my shoulders. "The timing fits, so I think so, yeah." I answer him.

"When can we find out the sex?"

"You want to know?" I ask, surprised.

"You don't?" I mean, if you don't want to know, we don't have to find out but yeah, I want to know if we're having a Princess or Prince. How about an Hawaiian name as a reminder? I like Alani for a girl and Keanu for a boy. What do you think?"

"I love them." I say. "And which would you prefer?" I ask him, because I'm curious as to which way he'll go. I can't believe he had names ready to go!

"I want a Princess with chocolate brown eyes and brown hair with blonde streaks, who looks just like the most beautiful woman on the planet." He answers, kissing me on the forehead, nose and then my lips.

"You say the sweetest things." I say as he hums his agreement on my neck. "You don't want an Hawaiian Prince to carry on the name?"

He pulls back and looks me dead in the eye. "Any daughter of mine will be strong enough to carry on the name, without the help of any idiotic male."

And that right there, is why I fell in love with Gabriel Louis Romanetti. He's the best man I know. Besides my dad that is, and I know, without a doubt, he's going to make the best father as well.

Barefoot and Dumped!

*****Birth Announcement *****

Alexis & Gabriel Romanetti

Would like to welcome their daughter

Alani Rosanna Romanetti

Who entered the world safely on

Saturday, 26th September 2019.

Mother and baby doing very well.

Father was heard yelling,

"This girl is going to rule the fucking world!"

****

Barefoot and Dumped!
Other books by Chelle Pimblott:

SNEAKY LOVE SERIES

Sneaky – Book 1
Sneaking Around – Book 2
No More Sneaking Around – Book 3

BUILT FOR LOVE

Built to Last – Book .1.
Built for Trouble – Book .2.

STANDALONE

Barefoot and ... Dumped!

COMING SOON!

THE DRAKE FAMILY SERIES
Vineyard – Book .1.
Winery – Book .2.
Brewery – Book .3.

STANDALONE

Never Again!

Chelle Pimblott

FIND CHELLE PIMBLOTT HERE:

https://www.goodreads.com/author/show/17494691.Chelle_Pimblott

http://facebook.com/chelle.pimblott

https://www.amazon.com/Chelle-Pimblott/e/B07M71H7T2/ref=sr_ntt_srch_lnk_3?qid=1548928985&sr=8-3